THE ITALIAN WINE MAKER'S GRANDSON

DEDICATED TO

DAVID SLABBY AND MARGO Ungari

To my wife if she did not take me on an adventure I would not have met Margo and David

Without their generosity I would never been able to write this book.

Special honor to Gayle Moody that edited and made revisions over a ten year period to help me to this book.

Thanks to Michael White the artist, for the cover

Contents

Introduction

Everyone loves a mystery. I have loved them since I saw my first classic mystery movie on a cold rainy night when I was a child of seven. TV was still new to us then. What fun!

Right after we had moved from the Cutting Blvd. housing projects in Richmond to the nicer area of East Oakland, I became friends with Albie Burger. Albie lived two doors away and he had a TV and a phone. My mom said they were rich. We got the TV almost a year after we moved in, but we didn't get a phone for almost three more years.

Most days after we walked the two blocks home from school, Albie would invite me to his house to watch "Howdy Doody." His mom was so nice; she would fix us snacks. His dad, Big Al, had recently opened the first 'fast food' hamburger eatery in San Jose called Burger's Burgers. It is still there, run by his youngest son, Paulie. It was recently featured on a segment of the "Today in the Bay" TV show. Every once in awhile Big Al would bring home a burger for Albie and one for me.
They were cold, but still a treat for us. Once we got our own TV, my mom insisted that I quit mooching off the Burger family. I missed the snacks, so I kept complaining, and she finally gave in to allowing me to go there on Mondays and Fridays. I had to promise to be a good Catholic and not eat meat on Fridays. I was faithful to that until I was 12 years old.

So the night of my first mystery, we had only had a TV for a month and it was still exciting to me. We already had our favorites: "I Married Joan" with Jim Backus, "Studio One", "Friday Night Fights" (sponsored by Gillette Blue Blades), and "Show of Shows" with Sid Caesar and Mel Brooks.

And I also had my favorite daytime shows. I would run home from St. Elizabeth's Catholic school to watch "Flash Gordon" and flush my mind of the horrors inflicted on me by Sister Moremean (her real name was Maureen, but my dad gave her this appropriate nickname). Flash Gordon was exciting. It took place in the distant future, in outer space, with rocket ships and monsters. Every half hour would end in a cliffhanger, with Flash seconds away from certain death. The fact that these shows were made in the early '40s with cardboard spaceships and monsters that looked like they were made out of crepe paper by fourth graders totally escaped me back then. "Jungle Jim," followed with the same cliffhanger endings. I liked it because the hero had the same name as mine.

Next came "Beanie and Cecil." Cecil was a seasick sea serpent made out of a sock with two buttons for eyes. Finally, the crown jewel of the afternoon TV experience: What time is it? "It's Howdy Doody time." How many of you remember this trivia? Howdy's friend was Dilly Dally, his cousins were Double Doody and Heavy Doody.

While my mom and I waited for my dad to get home, I sensed that this night had just the right atmosphere for a mystery. The driveway light showed rain and a thick fog as I peered out the window on 'dad watch'. And, then, something slowly emerged through the fog; our '49 Chevy with my dad behind the wheel. After he parked, he ran in so fast he was almost completely dry. He gave quick hugs, grabbed a beer and a 'church key' to open it, and plopped down on the four-passenger couch between my mom and me, just as the movie started. It was the classic black- and-white, "Laura". I will never forget the atmosphere of that cold night, the thick fog, the falling rain and a great story with a lot of twists and turns that cemented my love for mysteries.

About two dozen movies and a year later, I discovered my own mystery to investigate. It involved an old man living on my grandparents' property and two photos of little boys. One was the old man's blond son and the other was a dark-haired, dark-skinned four-year-old in a military uniform on the wall near my grandparents' portrait. Who were these boys? No one wanted to tell me, so I began to explore.

The years of my search were filled with the people who visited my grandparents' home, the place I called "Big Pink," and many wonderful Italian meals prepared by my Nona. The old man might talk about the blond boy in the picture when he was drunk, but whenever I asked about the boy in the portrait on the wall, it would disappear for awhile, like the topic was off-limits. And, one time, a family friend started talking about someone killing a family member and everyone shut him up, but not before I heard, "It would be terrible if little Jimmie found out about his family." What terrible thing were they discussing? I needed to find out.

So, join me on a journey to Rutherford in the heart of the Napa Valley where my old-world Italian grandparents settled in 1925, and where I spent my first two-plus years and most weekends until the place was sold in 1974. I was too young to appreciate the full tranquility of being surrounded by grapevines in the shadow of the mountain range far behind us, but now I will take you on an unforgettable journey through visions of beauty so all-consuming that one could get lost, cradled in this quiet peaceful valley.

And I will tell you a story. It is a true story, even though some parts may seem outrageous; some characters may be so big, and so absurd that they will seem to have they jumped off the pages of an Italian version of Cannery Row. And, yet, they are all real characters in my kingdom. Come and solve the mystery with me.

Chapter 1
A Tour of Heaven

"When I was young, it seemed that life was so wonderful, a miracle, oh, it was beautiful, magical." Roger Hodgson

When you experience something as a child, the beauty and intrigue of it leave a burning memory that is hard to communicate. It is a feeling, a mood, and sometimes euphoria. As I remember the Rutherford of my youth in the Napa Valley, I have this same difficulty. (My desire is to paint in your mind the images of this stunning location.) The beauty of the Napa Valley is breath-taking and ever-changing, just like sets on the stage of a play, with each season presenting a new backdrop for the next dramatic act. I was blessed to have these as the scenarios for my childhood and young adulthood.

I remember harvest in Fall, as being the most dramatic time. There is incredible beauty in the Valley when the grapes are on the vines, their strands of purple, green or yellow fruit full in their ripeness; it looks as if someone ran a paintbrush along the middle of the vines. These natural colors mix in with the green and multi-colored leaves of each grapevine with each skinny vine reaching out to its neighbor, linking together, across wires, making a beautiful quilt covering for acres and acres. The land is mostly flat, but then, in some places, it is rolling with the small hills, which the vines cover. In many cases, these quilts go all the way to the mountains. The mountains add the accent colors of brown dry grass and green trees that look like fresh broccoli. Then, peeking out from among the trees, there are stone castles and houses. Those old houses actually blend in and add to the vision, in most cases in an attractive way. In recent times, there are others, newer structures that don't peek out. They shout out, 'Here I am, notice me.' This causes one to wonder, "What were they thinking and how did that ugly monstrosity ever get approval to visually pollute the beauty of the Valley?"

Then, the fruit changes color; the leaves change color; they grow until they reach their peak and then they begin to disappear. What is left are empty vines with the trunks growing thicker and starting to gray a little in color.

There are also times when a low ground fog settles between the vines; adding an almost heavenly, spiritual touch. It also works like an acoustic blanket, holding sounds down so they fall dead soon after they leave their point of origin. The fog brings a quiet and peace to those that are out early, like I often used to be, sitting on the back patio, under the fig trees, with the scent of wood burning in a stove in the kitchen. On those mornings, I would relax with a cup of hot cocoa or, when I was older, a cup of coffee. I liked looking up at the mountain, with the vineyards in the foreground. Any stress was forgotten for at least a few moments. All was right with the world.

When the mustard blossoms, in Spring, the result is like a new artistic painting hung for view. Take down the green, brown and red leaves with purple and green grapes, and put up the new rendition with bright yellow flowers with green leaves. Mix in the bare brown and gray wood vines and grape stakes. Finally, to add drama, notice the long skinny offshoot vines, sticking up out of the fog, long and thin, looking like many spider legs or some beast out of a Sci-Fi movie.

The seasons change the beauty, beauty you can get lost in. The changes of so many different colors, textures and sensations are awesome and inspiring. It becomes a place of peace and calm, a place of healing and even rebirth as it was for several people in my stories after experiencing various horrors.

In more recent years, there have been some new additions to the Valley like those new houses I mentioned earlier, huge and gargantuan, built too close to the road or towering tall on the top of mountains, too out of place to those wanting to see nature, not architecture. Another developing change is due, I guess, to the extreme cost and dwindling availability of an acre of vineyard. For decades now, people have had to go higher and higher up off the valley floor. Now the mountains, instead of just having brown dry grass and trees, are also covered with vineyards. Most of these are relatively new, and the baby vines are scrawny and almost sickly, not as full as the vines on the valley floor. So, rather than a quilt that covers the mountains, it looks like sprouts of yarn are preparing to become that beautiful quilt someday.

To me, though, most of today's vineyards, even the mature ones, look 'thin' compared to the vineyards that I grew up with. My Nono's vines were not grown up onto wire as they are now, and the old vine trunks were about the size of an adolescent crabapple tree trunk. Looking back as I remember them, I think they grew together as one big mass, the vines extending across, down, up, next-door and everywhere. I used to play a game where I would run full speed ahead into these intertwined vines and try to break through them, too stupid to understand the damage I was doing. But I never did that in my Nono's vineyard; I just did it to the Morriseli's behind our house. Well, there may have been a few times that I ran through Nono's. These old trunks were thick, gray, twisted sculptures, ugly but interesting. Now, the new technique is not only 'neater and cleaner' looking; it is much more productive as far as the crop and is much easier to tend to, and absolutely easier to pick. What you see is what you get; it's right there in plain sight. Back when I was picking grapes, it was like hacking through a jungle with a machete getting to the fruit the old way.

The new vineyards on the hills have, in some cases, a 'landscaped' look, being peppered with sizeable rock formations, too large or too costly to remove. I guess the developers had to factor in the cost of blasting out the rocks, fines from the county and how much anger and hatred would be elicited from neighbors, especially those down the hill from them. It used to be that natural growth, rocks, and earth were removed when you planted a new vineyard, and a lot of soil, maybe even half your new vineyard, would wash down onto your neighbor's land. And those neighbors were probably longtime Valley residents, familiar with the "flood season." But, no matter. Even with more vineyards, new houses, and wineries, the Valley is an awesome sight.

Of course, there are still old buildings that have not changed for a hundred years or more. The little wood-beamed Catholic Church on Niebaum Lane in Rutherford, with its old, hard, wooden pews, stained glass windows, and its small cozy feel make it an experience I recommend. Then, there is the old two-room green and white schoolhouse with "1888" on its bell tower, the year it was built, not the address, on the corner of Niebaum Lane and Hwy 29. This is the school where my mom attended 1st through 6th grade. And the front main building of BV Winery still looks the same. When the vines are growing up the walls it is quite a romantic sight. There are a number of the old wineries that are still at least partially in their original buildings.

My story is set in this wonderful Valley. The story is true, even though some parts may seem outrageous. Some of the characters will seem to be too big, so overboard and absurd that they might have jumped off the pages of an Italian version of Tortilla Flat. We could call it "Polenta Valley." These were real people that I grew up with in the '40s, '50s, '60s, and '70s in the heart of the Napa Valley on 2.4 acres of vineyard with a house, bunkhouse for eight, a barn and a dilapidated and decaying, haunted slaughterhouse, all owned by my grandparents.

They and their friends were Old-Country Italians who came to the U.S.A. from the same area of Gerola in northern Italy. The different families arrived over a six-year span sometime around 1910. They first set foot on American soil on the East Coast, but most came to California, ending up in San Francisco, Oakley and the Napa Valley or points north. Wherever they settled, they brought their culture and customs, and they formed their own new "Little Italy" communities. They came for a new life and were filled with optimism about the future. It seemed that every possibility they could dream of was attainable. It was a good time to come to America. There were so many new inventions that weren't available in Gerola, like automobiles on roads all across the nation and telephones in people's homes.

Those who settled in the city of San Francisco discovered a new and exciting life. There were so many new things available, so much to see and do, all within walking distance. None of them had ever lived in a city. Some of their home villages didn't even have a tavern, so for a while, they were like kids in a candy store. Those who chose to live in cities missed the peace, beauty, and tranquility that they had grown up in. They were eager to visit their friends outside of the cities where the terrain reminded them of their homeland. They came for a weekend, a week, or even longer, the city-dwellers made the trip to my grandparents' place in Rutherford.

Five of these main families had grown up together. Some were part of the New Americans group that had gathered in my Nono's family store in Gerola, Italy, once a week to plan their move to the United States. As they got together, they decided who would go first and how that person would pave the way for the next, as they each paid it forward, so to speak. They were determined that one day, they would all be Americans, and they developed a bond as strong as family that would last a lifetime. In fact, many of them would have stronger relationships with these transplanted friends than with the family they left back in Italy.

My grandparents made a return trip to Gerola in the '50s to see family they had left behind forty years earlier. Sadly, some family members had passed away. They didn't enjoy the trip as much as they expected because Gerola seemed primitive after the comforts of the U.S.A. It just wasn't how they remembered it. My Nona hated all the walking on the steep bumpy, dusty roads. But my Nono enjoyed it because he always enjoyed a party; well, at least drinking and eating with old friends and family.

My grandparents, Salvatore and Rosi Curtoni, first settled at a ranch in Lodi. Nono came in 1910 and Nona arrived a year later. He tended the vineyards and Nona was the cook for the cowboys and ranch hands. After a time, they moved to Rutherford, but there was a certain amount of secrecy in the family about it. I was a curious child and I wanted to know everything about everybody, but my family didn't like answering my questions about their past. I was told, "It's not your business." So, my way of getting answers was to act like a detective. When we got our new TV, my parents would watch old mystery movies and I became intrigued with mysteries. I became a "super sleuth" sneaking around and listening, just like the detectives on TV. There were always some old friends at Rutherford who liked to tell stories about the past and, especially as the evening moved closer to the next morning and many glasses of wine had been consumed, the stories became more personal and soul-wrenching.

I was able to piece together fragments of my grandparents' past. I knew they moved away from Lodi suddenly after an event of unparalleled horror and tragedy struck. I didn't know what that terrible event was that so devastated them, but I was determined to find out. I knew they had fled to San Francisco to stay with their friends, the Tonella's, where they began the impossible task of trying to heal. They decided it was time to move out of the city. They wanted to move to Rutherford where they had a friend, Joe. He had been the ranch manager at Lodi before 'retiring' to Rutherford and he encouraged them to move close to where he and his family lived. The year was 1925, and there was a third Curtoni, my mother, who had been born five years earlier.

A month before the move, they went hunting for a new home. They knew the general area they wanted to move to, close to Joe. He picked them up in his machina (pronounced mock-ee-na, meaning machine). This is how all Italians referred to automobiles. He met them at the little rental house on Elizabeth Street in San Francisco which had survived the 1906 earthquake. They had driven for quite a while on their way to the Napa Valley when suddenly my Nono said, "Stop! This right here is where I want my family to live, in this peaceful valley. This is the most beautiful view I have seen so far in all of America." He was in luck. There was a house for sale in that very area, and, as a bonus, Joe lived within walking distance. The property for sale included an old ramshackle dump of a house and outbuildings in an equal state of disrepair.

When Nona saw this, she protested, "Holy Mother! What a horrible place. Oh, Sally, my dear Sal, no. Let's keep looking."

But my Nono had a different vision. "This will be our new home. We will tear down this old house and build a big new one. Look around you, Rosi. Turn in a circle in every direction. You see nothing but beauty. This is a place to be reborn, a place to forget what happened to us."

"I will do anything to erase what happened to us at Lodi," She replied. "I know you still love me and want only the best for me, even though I still don't think I deserve it."

She would repeat variations of that same theme over the years, and every time Sal would say, "You will always be deserving of all my love."

My Nono and Nona lived in the bunkhouse while they demolished the old house and completed the new one. Once completed, it was unique in the Valley. It's exterior was pink stucco. In the '50s, my dad gave the house and property its name, Big Pink, and it was referred to as Big Pink ever after. It became the stage where many life events played out and turned out to be not only a place for healing and redemption for the Curtonis but for countless friends, too. It was like a vortex or black hole where everything negative was sucked in and devoured and everything good and positive moved in to fill the void.

Many broken people came over the years and many were healed. It seemed that everyone who came brought the ingredients that helped someone else in need. Big Pink became a place of joy and happiness, where great food, wine, and other alcoholic beverages were consumed in huge quantities, stories were told, love was given and love was received. Those that had much shared with those who were in need. It was a place abundant in everything that was important in life, and, as a bonus, it was a beautiful, calming environment.

In 1945, I was born in St. Helena, and more or less grew up at Big Pink with dozens of characters, lots of wild and crazy people. The bunkhouse slept eight people and there were two extra bedrooms in the big house which slept four more. And, there was a double bed and hammock outside that slept three more. All in all, there were sleeping accommodations for fifteen guests. Someone was always flopping there, and they were always welcome. It was almost as if Big Pink were a cruise ship where guests enjoyed an all-expenses-paid cruise, minus the ship and water. Indeed, they got an all-you-could-eat-and-drink feast!

My Nana was a legendary cook, and she loved to share her creations with friends and family. She catered dinners for the wine royalty of the Valley, the owners of BV, Krug, and Inglenook, and she sold her pastas to Pometta Deli in Oakville. She never referred to a recipe and never measured; she just did it all on instinct. She did have a scale in her kitchen, but it was just used to confirm that she got the poundage that she paid for. She loved to go back to the butcher at Keller's Meats in St. Helena and shove the package of meat in his face and demand that he reweigh it and correct the meat deficit. As much as she gave Fritz Keller a bad time, she liked him. During World War II, many in the Valley boycotted his store because he was German. Somebody even threw rocks through his front window, twice. My Nona was loyal to him and more or less insisted all her friends be the same.

My Nona didn't take crap from anyone. She was a formidable person. Husky and sturdy, she ran Big Pink like a resort and winery, which in essence is what she owned. She was never bested by any woman or man. Strong-willed and intelligent, she had an organized mind; she thought out solutions for any and all problems and planned out ways to reach her goals. She was a woman who did not show very much emotion and was usually stoic. However, she was loving, kind and affectionate to me. She liked to have me help her make her raviolis; I got to use the little tool with the metal wheel to cut them apart. I also helped make gnocchi, even though I hated to eat gnocchi. I plucked the feathers off the headless chickens and helped burn off the pin feathers on the stove's flame. After awhile getting used to it, I didn't mind doing this gross task; I just hated watching my Nona grab one of the chickens I had fed hours before from the yard pen. She would wring its neck, slit its throat, and then tie it upside down from a rope hanging from the fig tree. The ground under that tree had a big permanently rust-colored stain. I found it sickening when she first tied up a headless chicken. It was still jerking around, with blood splashing all around.

I never understood why my Nona often seemed unhappy or like something was bothering her. She would get a look of distraction or concentration like she did when she would read me a story. I should say she didn't really read to me because she couldn't read English.

Instead, she would look at the illustrations in the books and make up a story that she would tell me in a mix of Italian and English. I saw old photos of her clowning around, acting like she was guzzling a whole bottle of wine, romping with my Nono's pipe in her mouth and his hat on her head. What happened to that slim, fit, energetic lady who loved to dance, sing, and bring her joy to every gathering? I learned the answer eventually, but not until I was 17 years old, and ever since then, I wished I could forget that answer. It has been 45 years since I solved the mystery, but it still haunts me.

I was fascinated by the parade of adults that drifted through Big Pink. Even though they had lived in the U.S.A. for over thirty years, most of them still spoke Italian or a mixed blend of Italy-English. I was able to understand Italian and their blended language, so when they switched to Italian to tell a joke, unbeknownst to them, I still understood what they were saying even if I didn't comprehend it. All these characters had nicknames, but not the kind that was given to the Mafia, like Johnny 11-Fingers or Joe Banjo-Knuckles. The people who lingered at Big Pink were given nicknames by my dad, who had to make a joke out of everyone's name. I guess I inherited that gift, for better or for worse and put it to good use in high school. But my nicknames usually were based on a person's appearance, like Twisted or The Dog. The names my dad made up were usually a distortion of their real Italian name. Chez-a-rae became Che-zer and Lena became Hyena. No one ever used these nicknames to their face, of course. Every once in awhile, because my dad used these names when he talked to my mom and me, I would slip up and call Mr. Cy-o-ka, Mr. Coyote, or Domingo by the name Flamingo.

Even as a child, I loved the dramas that unfolded on the performance stage that was Big Pink. Like the one with their friend Louie, Skinny Lou-we-gee. He was about 5'2" and was always bent over so that his body looked like a human letter "C". He weighed about 80 pounds and was bald unless you counted the 12 hairs greased and combed from the back of his head to his forehead. He was always shiny, glistening with sweat, the blood veins in his arms and on his forehead bulged out as if they were trying to flee all the stress in his

17

body. His eyeballs would have been fleeing, too, bulging out of their sockets as they did.

Lou-we-gee had plenty of reasons to be stressed. He was the third husband of Lena Hyena. The first two had died under mysterious circumstances. Both had been rich and left her with lots and lots of money. Lou-we-gee was also rich and he felt like he had a target on his back. Why he married her, I'll never know. He was never happy and always had something to gripe about, rubbing his head and face as he complained. He always grumbled in Italian, muttering in a quiet voice and someone would yell, "Shud upa you mouth, Louie!" The longer he rattled on, the faster he muttered, until it sounded like a record at the wrong speed. He was one of the few guests that didn't gorge themselves on food. So it was truly hilarious when he began rubbing his sunken tummy, whining, "Oh, my gut! I think I've been poisoned."

Lena Hyena had been married to him for several years. She was a large woman, and looked like an opera singer, except she had very tiny feet always garbed in very expensive high heel shoes, and small delicate hands that were blindingly shiny with a multitude of diamond rings that went nicely with her diamond earrings and necklaces. She dressed like she was an opera Diva. She could afford it; she had killed off two husbands. Well, at least she outlived them; no one ever proved that she killed them, and certainly, no one even joked about it to her.

Hyena was very vocal and usually dominated the conversations with her booming voice and string of profanities. She was well-liked because she was rich, but really, because she was funny and fun. She was a lady, but she was one of the guys, too. She was one of only two women at Big Pink that played the card game, Pedro; the other woman was my Nona. Even though she was not really an opera singer, Hyena did have a good singing voice. I didn't understand some of her songs, but they were punctuated with a lot of hand gestures that were easy to follow due to the flash from her rings. I figured the songs were dirty because the other women guests would turn red or get flustered and the men would give a nasty laugh. She loved life and she loved men, and that brings up the other reason for Lou-we-gee to be stressed.

You see, their boarder, Che-zer, was having an affair with Hyena. I knew this, even though I was a child. Che-zer was everything that Lou-we-gee wasn't. He was an "Italian Stallion" with a good build that he liked to show off by wearing short sleeve shirts unbuttoned down to his navel or t- shirts now known as "wife-beaters." He was tanned and had countless gold chains gleaming on his chest hairs, which I saw him combining more than once. His always-present cigar was tucked in the corner of his mouth and he had a constant smirk like he was thinking of a dirty joke that only he knew. Yes, he had a dashing, daring swashbuckler look about him and all the women found him handsome, even if he was a flirt. Che-zer had a big gold watch on his right wrist and a total of six rings, all of which were gifts from Hyena. Everyone joked that they were for "services rendered." Yes, every minute of Che-zer's life seemed to be a party. He loved to barbecue and drink bourbon and often did both at the same time. The ladies were drawn to his charisma, but the men were also drawn to his bold, brassy zest for life. Maybe they were just a bit jealous, too. My dad once noted, "I would be happy all the time, too, if I lived room-and-board free and had a lady buying me expensive gifts for being her stud." I asked, "Isn't a stud a horse?"

These are only a few of the cast of characters I want to introduce you to. I hope that by the end of this tale, you will wish, as I do, that it was possible to go back to Big Pink for even one night, out on that back patio on a warm summer night listening to one outlandish story after another. You could hear the ping-tick of the night bugs hitting the tin shades on the two lights that hung from the trees overhead and the sound of cards being slapped down, followed by some Italian words that were along the lines of "Take that and choke on it." In the background you would hear the old songs on the static-accented radio and once in awhile, the crazy drunken rooster doing his early wake-up yodel. To add to the experience, we would enjoy the scent of pipe tobacco, brandy, garlic, wine and other less pleasant but familiar odors, and savor food, drink, and desserts in abundance. Those were the days, my friend.

19

Chapter 2
A Friendly Home in a Vineyard

It was Friday, just after 5 PM. I was sitting on the top step of our hard, cold, downright uncomfortable cement front porch with my dog, Ladybug, a brown and white Springer Spaniel. When she was a pup and wasn't 'potty trained,' my dad called her a Sprinkler Spaniel, because she was wetting all over the house. I had been waiting impatiently for a half-hour for my dad to get home from work so we could make the one-hour journey up to Rutherford.

While I waited for my dad, I did what Nona Zirkelbach had taught me to do when afraid or nervous or waiting a long time: pray. Finally, by my fourth prayer, my dad drove up. When he got out of his car, Ladybug and I ran over to him and welcomed him home with a hug and face licking. You can guess who gave him what. I told him we were ready to go: Big Pink was calling us. I knew Lady had the same thoughts I did of running free and wild up in the wine country and going to the lake swimming. Ladybug loved swimming, fetching sticks thrown far out across the water.

Having just arrived home from his job driving a bus for eight hours, Dad was not quite ready to go; he needed a beer and a sandwich. As he was eating, I paced back and forth through the house, bouncing a rubber ball and chanting over and over, "Can we go now, can we go now, can we go now?" trying to be as irritating as possible so he would be encouraged to hurry. He didn't, and it just made him grouchy. I really wanted to go before it got totally dark. I didn't like the trip up when it was pitch dark. It was strange and a little scary. In fact, I absolutely hated and dreaded it.

When I was younger, it took me a bit of time before I understood that the trip up there followed the same route at night as it did when we went up during the daylight hours. It was just that when we drove up at night, there was very little to see and it seemed to take twice as long. After we drove past Vallejo, the rest of the trip to Rutherford was mostly dark, because back in the '50s, there were almost no businesses to illuminate the path, no streetlights and very few cars.

So for most of the trip, all we could see was the road and white lines illuminated by two weak headlights a short distance in front of the car. On several trips, as various animals ran across the road, our headlights alerted us to the fact there was a living obstacle in our way. My mom would scream out, "Oh, my God, Bob! Stop the car!" as if he would just keep driving and hit it if she didn't screech out her silence-shattering warning. Many of the animals were cats crossing the road, and when my mom saw them, she would warn them in a sweet high-pitched voice, "Look out little Mitzy," as if they could hear her. Mitzy was her name for all cats, so whenever my dad saw a smashed cat on the road, he would say in a really sappy voice, "Oh look a Meat-C." Old road kill, that was smashed flat and dried out was called a Sail Cat, because if you peeled it off the road, you could throw it and it would sail, like a yet-to-be-marketed Frisbee.

There were only a few things on the night trip to break the monotony. I always expected to see the few regulars because they were my clues to how close we were to my Nono and Nona's. One of the first milestones was the Carquinez Bridge. That was identified by the strong exhaust smell that blew into the car as my dad rolled down the window to give the toll-taker a dime. Then, just as sure as he would pay the toll, he would say,"Don't take any wooden nickels." And I would wonder each time, 'I have NEVER ever seen a wooden nickel. I don't get it.'

The next night sight with lights would be the old truck stop cafe that is still there. I didn't know its real name because my dad would always announce, "Here is the Greasy Spoon café." After that, came the old, very old, broken down Yountville Inn. I still have a clear memory of what it was like; I just don't know how close my memory is to reality. I remember it on the corner of Hwy 29 and the road to the cemetery. The cemetery is still there. It has some very old tombstones, including the grave of George Yount, who, as we know, had Yountville named after him.

What I remember most about the Yountville Inn was its front porch extending across the entire front of the old decrepit inn. The boards looked worn and warped; the porch had more ups and downs than a roller coaster track. There seemed to be a persistent fog of smoke enveloping everyone out on the porch. The ever-present dim orange lighting always revealed more than a dozen old men. Some were staggering around; some were sitting on a variety of old broken-down chairs and some were standing, leaning on the porch posts. They were always smoking, chewing and spitting, and drinking, usually out of pint bottles. Those who weren't missing body parts were missing something even harder to live without, their soul. My dad called them drunks and they always seemed to be. Once my dad stopped there to run in and use the bathroom. He parked out front and close to the old guys. Their staring at my mom and me scared the wits out of me.

Many of these guys walked down from the nearby Veterans Home, where vets from WWI and WWII lived. Over the years, several guys had been hit in the road in front of the inn as they were staggering across the street to their home. To me, they seemed very old and ghastly. When I compared them to all the old Paisanos that hung out at Big Pink, none of our friends looked as old or worn out as those poor souls who had left their glory years on the battlefield in a far-off country. At my young age, I was not able to appreciate the sacrifice they made for their country. I just saw some creepy, strange remnants of humanity that I wanted to get far away from.

I think that the teachings about Hell I had as a Catholic school student caused me to think that the Yountville Inn was what Hell is like. The waiting room to hell was my second-grade classroom at St Elizabeth's Catholic school, where my teacher wasn't really a nun but a fallen angel in disguise and each day was a nightmare of physical abuses. But the Yountville Inn had to be the actual Hell. The orange-glow-hell-light, the brown mist-smoke shrouding the old, old men whose bodies showcased physical deterioration: missing teeth, blind eyes and missing body parts, and stranded on this old bumpy rotting wood porch, all of them looking forlorn and rejected. The Inn is long gone, and I suppose some of these old men are now in the real Hell, while some have gone to a hero's welcome in Heaven. Even now, almost 60 years after it was demolished, I still imagine it being there. During daytime, it seems there is a little orange-brown twister dust cloud always present there.

Going north after the Inn on the left side of Hwy 29, there was the friendly redwood sign illuminated by two spotlights. It was painted with a bunch of purple grapes and had white lettering welcoming us to Napa Valley. Shortly after we passed that sign, we had to slow down so we wouldn't miss the little dirt driveway that took us right to the loquat tree where we always parked the car.

In winter, no one would be outside to greet us, so we would head inside. There were several dozen cement steps leading us up from the car, through the mud porch, delivering us to the warm, bright, happy kitchen. The wood-burning stove would ...yes...have wood burning in it. My Nono would be smoking his pipe; this added a pleasant aroma welcoming us to the comfort of being there at our second home with my grandparents. They were two people who always gave me love; sometimes, it seemed, more than my parents. My grandparents never gave me a swat or scolded me.

On this visit, it was a warm June night when we arrived at Big Pink. I expected my grandparents would be outside waiting to greet us. They had good ears and could always hear cars driving over the gravel, making rice crispy sounds under our tires, "Snap-Crackle-Pop." Our car's headlights would flash on my Nono and Nona, like a spotlight, illuminating them both. I knew I could always count on them to be there for me, to welcome me with a hug and kisses. What I didn't know was, that by this time next year, only one of them would be illuminated in our headlights, the other shockingly deceased by several months. But for this summer I was going to enjoy time with both of them.

I anticipated my Nono's big smile; he was always so happy to see us and always greeted us with a warm smile and a wave. It took me almost a year to get used to his perfect teeth after he got dentures. I had been so used to seeing my Nono with his crooked, dirty teeth, that his new Cheshire Cat smile, glaringly white, scared me. He smiled a lot, laughed a lot, and was happy most all of the time. He loved life. My Nono was the perfect example of sensibly following the saying "Live each day as if it were your last."

Nono loved people, food, and wine and always surrounded himself with an abundance of all those. I loved seeing him in these settings, "working the room or the crowd." He would often invite a bunch of friends over for dinner and just as often, he would encourage them to stay the night.

After all, they certainly shouldn't be driving home, or even walking home, in the condition they were usually in by evening's end, somewhere around 1 AM. He would also give an extended invitation to the ones from out of town to stay for the weekend, although they probably would have stayed, on their own, without an invite.

In summer, there were always so many people there. Most were regulars, but there was always someone new, too. Guests would bring friends and these new friends would become regulars, and then, they would bring new friends. They were all unique; each had some quirk that I picked up on. Then, I would classify them, like Chezerana (my dad nicknamed her Chest-arena for reasons that were obvious); she was The Eater since she was constantly eating food. If no food was being served, she would go through the refrigerator or the cooler cabinet. If that wasn't bad enough, she didn't use a fork or knife. She would grab a salami, hunk of cheese, or loaf of bread and just chew off some. Seeing her eat spaghetti was a stomach-churning experience. My Nona would yell at her in Italian, saying in essence "Hey.....what the hell! What the hell! Where were you born..." Chest-arena would respond with, "Basta basta, don't be a tempasta!" Then she would just move to a new location, maybe out by the fruit trees or the vines to grab some not-yet-ripe grapes. She usually wore an apron that looked like a Jackson Pollock painting of food splatter. In her apron pockets she carried crackers, dried figs and apricots; she said they were a "good complement" to other snack foods that were offered, "Because Rosi never serves enough of anything." She also carried cigarettes, stick matches, and nickels in her pockets which she offered to me, my cousins, or neighbor children so we would perform for her by dancing, singing a song, or doing a trick. She even offered two nickels to anyone brave enough to kiss her. Some of the guests joked that "Kissing her would be like eating a whole meal."

The interesting thing to me was that my grandparents welcomed her back. My Nono said, "Once someone is your friend, they are friends for life. Everybody has problems or things about them that we may not like, but because they are friends, we overlook those faults." So I learned to look at those gross things or quirks as things that endeared those people to me. It was hard for me to pick favorites, but there were a few I didn't like because they were mean. My Nono did make an exception to his "friends for life" rule. He gave two men the boot because they had been mean to me and rude to my Nona.

I loved to hear the stories those friends told about their experiences coming from various parts of Italy, to whatever part of California they were currently living in. They were stories of the wild and rugged days of old San Francisco, Monterey, Napa, and Lodi. I knew that in the beginning, my Nono had worked as a cowboy; his spurs still hung on the junk wall in the barn along with gopher traps, two rusty swords and dozens of other rusty, dusty items, most decades old. After awhile, he began taking care of the grape vines rather than the cows. This became his specialty, and the rest of his walking days he took care of someone's vineyard or crops. My Nona enjoyed taking care of the ranch hands at Lodi, cooking and doing laundry for them, and she would also pick up stuff that the ranch hands requested on her trips to town to purchase food goods. She called them her "Bambinos."

Of the San Francisco friends, six of them worked at a place called Royal Tallow in the City. They made soap there; at least I knew when they came to Big Pink, they made these ugly, crude, deformed, hunks of soap that smelled revolting when they were making it. The soap worked almost as well as the red Lifebuoy bar soap that my parents liked and it was a lot cheaper, almost free. From the few times I had soap put in my mouth for saying something improper, I knew the homemade soap didn't taste as hair-curling bad as the red Lifebuoy. Soap in the mouth was one of many stupid forms of punishment that was on the verge of being abuse. I was surprised when, in the movie Christmas Story, the mom used the same soap as my mom.

When these people were not making soap, they did what everyone liked to do up there, playing cards while telling embellished stories. They were always smoking pipes or harsh-smelling and even worse-tasting hard Italian cigars. I learned how horrible the cigars tasted when I snuck two of them, and a friend and I smoked them when we were 12-years-old. Actually, we only made it through three puffs. It took a pack of Lifesaver lime candies to rid our mouths of that burned rubbish taste. I was sure our lungs had been scorched for life.

The guests were sure to take a mid-afternoon nap on the hammock between the two fig trees or on a bed under the shade of the wisteria that provided them an interesting canopy of green and purple with strange pods hanging on long thin green vines. Some had no outside choices left and had to sleep on a bed in the hot bunkhouse.

Everyone was always in festive spirits, enjoying everything Big Pink offered them as if it were one big party.

I loved and looked forward to a long list of things:
• The taste and smell of countless foods and drinks.
• Hearing the voices of family, friends, and friends that were like family.
• Listening to the scratchy, faint background music of Enrico Caruso, Mario Lanza and other Italian favorites playing on the old record player.
• The feel of many different textures: smooth grapes, the rough dry skin of salami, the hugs of friends, greasy kisses and whisker burns.
• The pleasant aroma of the variety of flowers around Big Pink, and even
• The unpleasant smell of the chicken coop which had been there as long as I could remember.

During all these get-togethers, my Nona was always the perfect hostess. She worked hard preparing and serving three meals a day, while my Nono played cards, drank homemade wine and Brandy Manhattans, told stories, laughed and enjoyed every minute of the day with his friends.
When he had too much to drink, his stories and jokes started out slowly but got louder and faster and higher pitched as he went along.

He would switch from Italian to English, then back to Italian and so forth. His face would get a little red and he would pound his fist on the table to punctuate key points until the climax of his story when he and everyone around him collapsed in a laugh riot.

All the fun these friends had together fascinated me. Most of them totally enjoyed their lives and the world around them. I became a student of people, interactions, conversations, relationships, love, friendships, loyalty and support to each other, seeing what made them happy, and even how the quietest of the group contributed to the social environment. It was rare that there was a heated argument. There were disagreements where one might yell, "Stupido." And another would be a reply like "Bastardo". No one insulted anyone's mother, the Italian mother being almost sacred. And there were no fisticuffs.

I became the social animal that I am as a result of my many sit-ins with my Nono, Nona and their friends. The seeds were planted back then for my passion to bring friends together to enjoy each other, music, meals, spirits, and lots and lots of stories.

On this June night, I knew the smile I would see on my Nono's face for the same reason I had an ear-to-ear grin. We were both happy about all the adventures we would be enjoying over the next few days. I knew that he would need me to help him with all his weekly tasks. He was my pal, my buddy; he was the only grandpa I had and he was always one of my favorite people in the world.

All of these things completed the Big Pink experience.

Chapter 3
Another Weekend; Another Trip

After an hour of travel, we were finally there. We would soon make the left turn off Highway 29 onto the dusty dirt driveway that would deliver us to Big Pink. It was a bumpy ride, this driveway, and the dust we kicked up smelled like there must be something rotten in those clouds of dirt.

Once in awhile, Nono would cover the driveway with gravel, but it wouldn't last long. It would kick up after hitting the undercarriage of the car making noise like popcorn on a tin pan lid and then ricochet out from under the car into the vineyard. If you looked at newer tires with plenty of tread left, you could see many of the pretty-colored rocks.

To distract myself from thinking about what might have died and decomposed into that stinky dust, I rolled up my window and held my nose. I would count how many potholes we hit, "kathunk kathunka," as we bounced over each one. With each one we hit, my dad would let fly his semi- angry tirade: "&%%% ^ this $^^&*&& mother-fletching *$%^%% excuse for a road!" The cuss words might change, but his closing was always the same: "There goes my alignment." Looking back now, I suppose if it had really bothered him, he would have gone out with a shovel and filled the holes with dirt. But, no, he just got his blood boiling on every trip down the driveway.

It was all an act to get attention. He did like to be dramatic and pretend he was outraged about various trivial things. It was his idea of humor. To be honest, he was funny as hell. He always had me in tears of laughter. Of course, my mom almost never thought it was funny and she would turn to me: "Jimmie, shut up with that stupid horse laugh of yours!" I would quickly be silent, but my dad and I would look at each other, smile, look at my mom and burst out with belly laughs.

That dusty-dirt driveway was just long enough to cover the car with enough dust to write your name on the trunk. This was the thing that really pissed my dad off, and it wasn't drama or funny. He was really distressed because he loved and cherished his '49 two-door turquoise Chevy. He washed it several times a week, waxed it once a week and detailed it once a month. He always carried a rag and Windex so he could be prepared for any speck of dirt or something really horrific like a bug splattering his guts all over the hood. His obsessive-compulsive actions to protect his car sometimes backfired, like the time he parked under the loquat tree so his car would be covered and thus protected from the sun. We all laughed hysterically at his expense when half a dozen loquats splattered on his car, along with the droppings of the flock of birds that roosted there.

Dad never let us eat in the car, either. One time at the beach, we were eating our meal outside on the trunk when a brisk breeze blew our paper plates over and smeared food all over his clean car. We figured he got what he deserved for making us eat in out in the cold.

On this night, the trip down the driveway was no different, as we bounced about, kicking up the stinky dust. Dad completed his tirade before the driveway changed to gravel deep enough to be noisy. I could hear the grinding metal of the car twisting as it hit the potholes and became airborne. Of course, the crunching gravel was a perfect doorbell to notify my grandparents they had company.

Just moments earlier, I had been filled with apprehension, fear, and anxiety over the possibility that my grandparents might have been harmed since we had been there last. But, no. There were Nono and Nona, greeting us as usual. Although we were arriving at Big Pink in the dark of night, we were greeted with contrasting brightness. The patio was ablaze from the patio lights, two hanging tin 'pool table' lamps, and additional light from two new spotlights mounted above the back door to the house. They beamed down on the guests who would be there for the whole weekend with us. That brightness was enhanced by the light and warmth of everyone's smiles.

The light reflected off Nono's large mother-of-pearl belt buckle. It was made from an abalone shell he brought back from a camping vacation at Jenner by the Sea, a favorite getaway for his old friends. His belt buckle had a big "SC" in the center, the initials for Salvatore

Curtoni. The letters were set from stones that looked like diamonds. It was very snazzy.

There was something interesting about his first name. "Salvitori" is how I saw it spelled on some of his mail, but most times he would spell it "Salvatore." When I finally asked him, he said something that didn't make sense to me. "Jimmie, it depends on who I am dealing with. If I want them to think I am Sicilian and possibly Black Hand (which is what people now refer to as Mafia), then I spell it with the 'i' at the end and in the middle. "Salvatore" is a gentleman from Northern Italy." Interestingly, I only heard this story after we saw a movie about Al Capone and the mob at the tiny movie house in St. Helena. I never knew Nono to lie, but he did like to tell tall tales. In hindsight, I think it was just a matter of people spelling his name wrong on the mail, but his answer was more fun.

Sometimes he just signed his name, SC, and, sometimes, if friends were feeling extra close, friendly and casual (in other words, plastered-off-their-ass drunk), they would call him ESSEY. He didn't mind that from close friends, but from the general public, he preferred the more respectful Salvatore. In 1955, Nono replaced a rotting wooden porch walkway around the bunkhouses with a new cement one. As congratulations to himself for a hard job well done, he put his initials in the wet cement: "S.C. 1955. This virtually meaningless gesture would have a major impact on the future of these 2.4 acres that were Big Pink, on who would purchase the property and how this old homestead would become part of my life again.

On this night, when I got out of the car, I ran over to Nona and she swept me up in her arms as if I weighed no more than one of the chickens. She passed me off to Nono and I asked him why he was wearing his fancy dress-up belt. I could see that he was not in the fancy clothes he usually wore the belt with. Instead, he was wearing his gray work pants and matching shirt. This, along with his khaki pants and shirt, was his work "uniform." He worked all around the farm every day except Sunday and never wanted to get his good clothes dirty. But, you know, I don't remember him being dirty hardly ever, even though he was always working hard.

His cleanliness and personal grooming were greatly appreciated by me. Most of the Italian male family members and friends could have benefited from following his example. All the "old Italians" insisted on a hello kiss on the lips from me. Even today the kiss on the lips, even male to male, is tradition among the old Italians. The problem was that they often had wine or whiskey breath, and because they didn't always shave daily, I got whisker burns (which I called whisky burns) from their stubbly, rough faces. Mostly, they smelled of stale cigar smoke, cheese, salami, and sardines, along with just plain old B.O. They would call to me: "Jimmie, come-a gimme a kiss," and I wanted to say, "First take a bath, put on clean clothes, shave and brush your teeth, then I'll give you a kiss." But, I never did. I would just shuffle over with my arms down to show them I wasn't going to hug them and give them the obligatory kiss.

Nono, though, always looked good, especially when he went to town. When he went to San Francisco to visit his sister-in-law's family and other friends, he always dressed up in a three- piece suit and fancy shirt with French cuffs and the cuff links with SC on them. He even dressed up when he went to downtown St. Helena to Keller's Meats, Steve's Hardware, the feed store or Bank of America. To top off his Dapper Dan look, he wore a very nice Borsalino hat, which I still have. He carried the look well; he looked like a real dude, in the old definition of the word.

I enjoyed going to town with him. I could see that everyone seemed to know him and they showed him an attitude of respect. He was addressed differently by friends in town. Most called him Mr. Curtoni, but Guidie, the owner of St. Helena Olive Oil company called him Salvatore, and Ray, who owned the bar on Main Street where Nono stopped for a Brandy Manhattan on every trip to town, just called him, "Hey Curtoni!" A few even called him Sal.

I respected Nono deeply, too. He was always dependable, honest and trustworthy to me. He was a man who took pride in everything he did and he was always there for everyone who needed help of any kind, whether it was working in their vineyards or slaughtering a lamb. I believe he could do just about anything, except drive a car.

At least, I never saw a task he couldn't do. He had a muscular body, sturdy legs, a solid chest and big hands. He was strong but gentle.

Nono included me in almost everything he did. I even watched him shave with his straight razor. I got to lather the brush up on a bar like soap and watch him brush it on his face. It made me nervous to see the very sharp, gleaming, threatening-looking dangerous razor on his face or neck, so when he offered to let me shave him, I said, "No thank you, Nono." He shaved slowly, carefully, and I never once saw him knick or cut himself. I couldn't say the same for my dad. When I was a very little child and watched dad shave, I thought the object was to cut yourself, because he seemed to be bleeding every time he shaved. I remember they both used Gillette Blue Blades because they sponsored the Friday Night Fights on TV that my mom and I had to suffer through every Friday.

Nono would put on his brown "uniform" when we went hunting for rabbits, birds or wild pigeons. We used a .22 rifle, though once we used the Colt pistol he had bought when he was a night watchman at BV Winery. But neither one of us could hit a rabbit the size of an elephant, let alone a small one. After I was twelve, I got to use the Colt for target practice behind the slaughterhouse by the garden. I killed a lot of crab apples, tomatoes, and even a penny. When we did catch a rabbit, Nona would put it in gravy (sauce) to go over the polenta she made in a big copper pot on the old wood-burning Wedgewood stove. Her polenta was great, but I wasn't always excited about the meats that were thrown into the sauce.

My Nono's real passion was his wine making, the whole process, from vines to the bottle. He enjoyed being out in his vineyard daily unless it was raining, and sometimes, even then, he would put on a raincoat, rubber boots and a plastic cover for his hat and go out in the mud. He would do pruning, trimming, cutting, experimenting, picking and tasting. I went with him on many days.

I would use a little knife with a curved blade, somewhat like a small scythe, to cut grape bunches off, or clippers to cut off the unwanted vines, the ones he called suckers. When I worked beside him, I felt like one of the guys, one of his buddies. He was patient, loving and kind to me; and, always, he was a good teacher. He always told me that it was so hard for him to do all that work by himself when I wasn't there to help. It was a great feeling to be depended on, to contribute and feel of value.

Nono would also include me in some steps of the winemaking process, most of which I have forgotten. The clearest memory I have had something to do with burning a sulfur stick in the barrel hole. I remember a huge wood barrel in the lower half of the slaughterhouse; it extended all the way to the ceiling. This is where the juice went after crushing to wait and age until it became wine. This changed over the years. The big barrel vanished and wood grape crates went in its place.

In the wine cellar below the house, there were wood racks about three feet up from the cellar floor. The racks needed because the cellar flooded every winter. There were usually two wine barrels full of homemade wine on these racks. Nono would fill gallon jugs from these. Then, up on a table on the mud porch, he had regular-sized wine bottles and a funnel so he could keep these bottles filled without having to down again to the wine cellar. Not that the cellar was that far down. It was just that the stairway was like walking across the Grand Canyon on a tightrope made of one strand of dental floss. As to how good his wine was, I can't say. From the time I was six until I was twelve, they always added 7-Up to my wine.

I do remember the harvest. My Nono's grapes were picked by Nono, Nona, mom, dad and me, plus Scarpaché, usually called Paché, and Joe. Joe was the one who had hired Nono to work at the ranch he managed in Lodi, California, a job that enabled him to come to America, and later to bring his fiancée over. Joe got her a job at the same ranch. If Nono needed more help, all he had to do was go to the Oaken Bucket Bar, buy a round of drinks and ask, "Who will help me pick my grapes?" Then, he'd buy another round for the volunteers and have his second drink with them.

Picking was a fun experience. I liked to work next to Paché. He was very funny, though not intentionally, and was always screwing something up. I would laugh at him. Once we were at a party for the workers of BV Winery and he was sitting at a table that had a large candle burning. He thought it would look nice on his own outside table, so he put it in his pants pocket with the flame still burning. Soon it was burning a hole in his pants and his leg, too.

I remember "Pickin' Day" as fun, but it was also hard work for me. The old vines had so many leaves and branches and stems that it was like fighting an octopus to find the grapes. Cutting the grape bunches off the vines using that small knife was a struggle for my small weak hands. I needed to grip the grape bunches so hard that sometimes I ended up with a handful of grape juice and pulp. I had to cut away some leaves and stems so I could even see the grape bunches. It reminded me of those movies where the macho man hacks his way through the jungle underbrush with a machete. I left a deep green trail of debris behind me on the ground; there was a lot of foliage twining and creeping on those old vines.

I was also very slow. Paché picked a whole row in the time it took me to do one crate. The crates themselves were a chore; they were wood, big and heavy. The wood was stained with decades of grape juice. There were different names painted on the ends in big letters: DECHENZI WINERY, BV VINEYARDS, KRUG, INGLENOOK and others.

In addition to his vineyard, Nono worked daily in his much-loved vegetable and fruit garden. He would put on his work "uniform" and a hat, he always wore when he was outside, at least until the sun went down. Hats suited him; they were him. He had a variety of seasonal work hats, but in spite of that precaution, he still got skin cancer. Nono cared for and primped the crops, spraying bug killer from an old hand-pump sprayer. At different times of the year, he would plant new crops. The reward for his efforts was picking the vegetables for dinner and the fruit for dessert or breakfast. What he liked best was watering, which he did by setting up the hose and relaxing on a wooden grape crate smoking his pipe and reading his Italian newspaper while the water ran for about twenty minutes. He had devised a series of ditches and hose holders so the whole process was hands-free.

I often ran up to my bedroom, grabbed a few Little Golden Books and ran down, asking my Nono to scoot over. Then I would sit by him reading "The Saggy Baggy Elephant, "The Poky Little Puppy," or some other book that I had already read dozens of times. He would fold his paper over so he could hold and read it with one hand, putting his other arm around me and snuggling me closer to him. Sometimes he would give me a kiss on top of my head and say, "Jimmie, I a-love you so a- much."

It was so quiet and peaceful, with the only sound being the burbling of the water and the kathunk sound of Nono when he banged his pipe on the grape crates to dump the old tobacco ashes out. There was one sound I didn't like, though, and it was the BZZZZ of the huge black bumblebees as they made fly-bys around my head. If getting stung by a regular bee was like getting a shot, I was sure a sting from one of those black bombers would be like having a nail pounded into your arm. Nono loved his garden so much, he told me, "Heaven must look just like this garden; it's so beautiful."

Chapter 4
Nona and the Ghoul

On that warm June night, as we were driving up the driveway I saw Nona in our headlights, standing with her arm around my Nono's waist. She wore a dirty apron over her red and green tomato-print house dress and her white, fluffy hair was going in every direction. The light that came from behind made her hair glow, giving the appearance of a halo. Saint Rosi.

Nono and Nona didn't move to come to us; they waited, almost as if coming too close to the macchina (car) would suck them in and grind them up. Nona had her stern "let's get down to business" expression on as if she were saying something like, "Okay, you're here; now, get out of the maledetto macchina (damn car)." So much for Saint Rosi. She didn't smile very often. She was the opposite of my Nono in this, as well as in many other ways. He was a good balancing act for her negatives.

But she was the same as Nono in her love for me. After all, I was the only grandchild, and a boy. They had always wanted a son, but after my mom was born, they did not have any more children, so I was the next best thing.

Nona was a very serious person, and her rare smiles were usually directed at me, which made me feel special. My heart always soared when she or anyone else smiled because of me. When someone's face and eyes and mouth lit up in a genuine smile, now that was something to make me feel valuable. I remember all her smiles.

I remember her proud smile as I worked by her side, helping her make gnocchi by smashing my thumb down on each little ball after she rolled it in the flour that covered her "ravioli table." She would wipe the perspiration off her forehead with the back of her left hand, leaving a puff of flour on her forehead. She would sweat a lot when she worked, so she had a very white forehead, matching the color of her hair.

I remember her happy smile when I would run upstairs in the middle of the day to see if I could help her with anything. She would always have something for me to do, even if she made it up on the spot. I would always get heaps of praise and a dozen crushing hugs for whatever I did.

Mostly she would ask me to do something simple, like getting wood from the bin on the mud porch and putting it in the wood-burning Wedgewood stove. The bin contained a mix of old grapevine, twisted trunks, and scrap wood as well as regular firewood. Sometimes I would get to measure scoops of coffee out of the 25-pound Hills Bros. Coffee can into the pot for the next day's morning coffee. I can still see in my mind's eye, that huge red can with a picture of some old guy with something like a turban on his head, wearing a robe and walking while he drank his cup of coffee.

I especially enjoyed doing the test tasting of her biscotti. She called them "wine cookies" because they were so hard you couldn't eat them unless you dipped them into wine, or, in my case, wine and 7-Up. It didn't work as well to dip them in coffee because the hot coffee dissolved the cookies and you ended up with a cup of sludge. Sometimes, after she killed a chicken . Feathers flew all over the house and landed on me. Yuck! If that wasn't disgusting enough, she took it over to the stove and burned the pin feathers off. It took me a week to get that revolting smell out of my nostrils and head. After awhile, I got used to it.

I also remember her big, "have a great day" greeting smile each morning when my nose directed me from my bed at the end of the long dark hallway into the bright sunny kitchen where bacon was frying and coffee was percolating in the dented tin pot. If I hadn't brought the wood in the day before, my Nono would get the wood from the bin to start up the wood-burning griddle. The burning wood heated the kitchen, as well as the coffee pot. I liked watching the coffee pop into the little glass top, the liquid turning darker with each perk. The very first coffee I ever had came from that coffee pot.t was about 90% milk and doctored with five spoonfuls of sugar. The frying eggs were the freshest you could ask for and they were cooked in the huge, ancient cast iron fry pan which was black and seasoned to perfection by thousands of eggs and many pigs' worth of bacon. I rarely ate bacon or eggs, but the aroma of Nona's kitchen was a great way to wake up. Her kitchen was always such a happy place in the morning, brimming with the promise of a great day for each of us.

Early morning was the time for my grandparents to spoil me until my parents woke up. I am blessed to have a mind that transports me back to some of the wonderful events of my past. I can feel all those contented emotions and my senses are revived. I'm back at Big Pink in that big kitchen with sunlight streaming through the three large windows intermingling with the overhead lights making the room bright and cheerful. And just thinking about that kitchen makes my mouth water for Nona's homemade raviolis and delicious gravy (sauce).

At bedtime, Nona would sometimes read me a story based on the illustrations in the book. She would show me the illustrations to help me follow the story. Nona always would seem to look smarter when she had her half-lens reading glasses on. They sat at the end of her nose and made her look like Ben Franklin.

On that June night, when I saw my Nona there, looking so serious, I wanted to change her sour face to a smiling one. I was anxious to get out of our two-door Chevy on a mission to give and get love. My mom opened her door, but before she could get out to fold down the seat for me, I squeezed out of the back seat and ran directly to Nona. Just before I slam-crashed into her, she bent down, swooped me up and gave me a king-sized hug, and then, a kiss, smack on the lips, sharing the flavor of garlic, wine, and anchovies.

I always felt safe and secure in Nona's big strong arms. It was as if she could carry me around forever and never be tired. She would protect me from any threat, which she did when I was being attacked by a huge hog, two different roosters and the neighbors' mean, wrist-biting dog. She even stood up for me against a too-strict mom. When my Nona was around, my mom was a child again, obeying the commands of her mother.

Mom once told me, "Your Nona was real strict with me when I was growing up." But I never saw it directed toward me. Mom told me a story of when she was about three years old and threw a temper tantrum. Nona calmly walked over to the table, picked up a glass of cold water, walked back to my mom and threw the water into mom's face. I asked, "Did it work?" She replied a bit embarrassed, "Yes, it did." I said, "You're lucky she didn't add ice cubes in her water."

There was a Ghoul

Nona might have protected me from my mom, but I sometimes doubted that she could protect me from the Ghoul in the slaughterhouse. Oh, yes. I knew about this ghoul and what he looked like because my dad had brought me a sack full of comic books he found on his bus. Only these weren't comical. They were something like "Tales from the Crypt," and they were frightening, but I couldn't stop reading them. I read about the Ghoul that came through a hidden door in a man's closet and killed everyone in the house.

The Ghoul was big and green; he had clumps of hair scattered around on his deformed naked body and he was rotting, just like our slaughterhouse. There were decayed hunks of ghoul-flesh falling off him. Shortly after I read about him, this ghoul began coming after me, escaping through a secret door in the ancient, decrepit slaughterhouse. I could hear his footsteps on the gravel driveway. At night, he walked right under my window on his way to the front door, and from there, he would head for my bedroom. A couple of times, I heard the door to the mud porch open, its rusty springs squeaking, and then, the "kathump thump" as the door slammed shut, bounced back and shut again. When I heard the footsteps on the kitchen floor, my hair stood on end and I broke into a cold sweat, screaming, "Nona, he's here!"

Nona quickly came into my room, picked me up and carried me into the kitchen, turning on all the lights to show me that there was nothing spooky there. After this happened a second time, my mom threatened me: "The next time you scream out like that, I will do something that will be worse than anything that Slaughterhouse

Ghoul could do to you!" That was when I knew it was real. My mom even called it by name, acknowledging its existence.

I tried to feel confident that if the Ghoul got his teeth into me, I would scream in pain, and Nona would get extra strength to come and save me. She could fight off anything, man or beast, as far as I knew. She was definitely known as a person you didn't want to mess with. People only made that mistake once and then she gave them Rosi's Old Italian evil one-eye squint and her voice would boom out in a stream of stern words in Italian: "Merd tasta, pisciare cervello!" as she made a motion with her left hand, the same one she made when she was wringing a chicken's neck.

That did it for most people, except the Clan, that inner circle of best, long-time friends and frequent visitors. They would tease her, drink with her and joke with her, but she hardly ever laughed unless she had consumed a lot of wine. I remember seeing Cheezer slapping her hefty bottom on several occasions and laughing with his half-open mouth full of food, his gold teeth showing. But then, I would hear him choking after she punched him hard in the chest. Nona didn't put up with it, but he could slap another plump bottom, that of his lover Hyena, who just happened to be married to skinny, nervous and sweaty Louwege. I always remembered that Hyena was huge, the largest lady I knew. Years later, when I saw of photo of my Nona with Hyena, I discovered they were both the same size. Strange how memory works; we don't usually see the faults in family members we love.

Nona was a strong and sturdy woman, not fat, just solid, with thick ankles bulging over heavy- duty, thick-soled shoes. At least that's how I saw her. She did the same work around Big Pink as my Nono, chopping wood, planting, and gardening. People often said, "If Salvatore didn't have Rosi, he couldn't make it. He wouldn't know how to take care of himself and the vineyard. Hell, he couldn't even take care of those ratty-looking chickens." He proved them wrong years later.

My Nona's hair style reminded me of one I had seen in my school's history books, that of George Washington. She wore no makeup or other decoration, but sometimes she wore a scarf on her head. I'm sure there's a name for the way she wore it, but I don't know it. I called it "old washerwoman style." I strongly disliked it and, when she wore it, it put me in a crabby mood because she no longer looked like my Nona.

Every Sunday, Nona would dress up and sit at the kitchen table, sipping coffee until she heard the bell ringing at the top of the little Catholic Church on Niebaum Lane. Then she would put on her dress coat with the fur collar. That fur looked to me like a dead cat that had been smashed on the highway and in some way fashioned into a collar. Her "dead animal" costume was completed with a hat that looked a bit like two pigeons had smashed into each other and somehow found their way to the hat after being run over. I hated these dead animal clothes almost as much as I hated the washerwoman scarf. But, people said it "looked good on her."

So, all suited up, she walked through the Villa's vineyards and continued through Degia's vineyards to the one and only Mass of the week. She sat on the hard, dark wooden pews for an hour and said her rosary. Her mind might wander looking at the Bible scenes on the stained glass windows and then she might try to think up a new recipe. She had to keep her mind busy because the Mass was in Latin and she couldn't understand it, although every once in awhile she heard a word that sounded like Italian. Many times she fell asleep even when she tried to focus on the priest's words. Then, she would snore until Mrs. Tachonci, her regular pew mate, nudged her awake. That was embarrassing.

Except for Sundays, Nona wore an old "house dress," just like her sister, my Zia. In fact, just about every old Italian woman wore the same style of plain dress, with the only difference being the faded pattern in the material they chose. My Nona's always had some variation of a rose pattern. I thought that was because her name was Rosalie Acquistapace Curtoni, shortened to Rosi by her friends. Over her house dress, she usually wore an apron with pockets. I could typically find a pocket knife in those pockets. It had many uses, peeling an orange, cutting up an apple, slicing off a piece of her rock hard homemade salami or a piece of cheese. It was even used for slitting the chicken's necks.

There was excitement crackling in the air the night we arrived. I could see just beyond Nono and Nona that there was company, and the party was already going full-speed ahead. Everyone was gathered on the patio which was about the size of a one-car garage. It was painted a faded red color, maybe to match the pink stucco of the house. It was this stucco that gave the house its nickname: Big Pink. Over the patio were two of the biggest fig trees I had ever seen. The trees were rumored to be about 75-years-old. The old friends were sitting at the big table. It was topped with a thick sheet of linoleum, making it durable enough to withstand the thousands of meals, countless gallons of wine and Brandy Manhattans consumed and spilled on it.

After Nono set me down, I ran over to the table to greet Curddy, Lou-we-ge, Hyena, Cheezer and Pistol Pete. I was able to get a brief greeting from everyone before I heard my mom's sing-song, "Beeeeedddd tiiiimeeee!" As Mom escorted me upstairs to bed, I was happy knowing that I would have lots of time visiting with all of them over the next few days.
Because there were so many guests, my bedroom at the end of the house was occupied, so I had to sleep on a cot in my parents' bedroom, the middle bedroom. I liked my room better because if there were people still down on the patio and my bedroom window was open, I could hear their friendly voices. It made me feel safe and reassured because I knew no beasts or creatures could get to me.

The Ghost

On this night, after I said my prayers, I was wide awake and not sleepy. As I lay there, I sensed something strange. As the seconds past, I looked at the closed bedroom door when, suddenly, someone or something passed right through it. It had a human shape the size of a man and I had the feeling that it was male. I couldn't see any features, but it appeared to be covered in something like dripping brown tar or shaggy fur.

This "thing" didn't seem to see me or sense me, but that didn't matter. I was frozen in terror and could not move. My scalp tingled and I broke into a cold sweat, while my stomach felt like I had been gut-punched. I could not see it well in the broken moonlight; the huge crepe myrtle trees outside created shadow zones and when the ghost moved into one of these zones, I couldn't tell if he was coming to get me. My whole body began to tremble. Then it stepped into the light and I could see its face looking in my direction. I think I stopped breathing, and my body froze, becoming motionless like ice.

The ghost moved to the nightstand on the other side of the bed, my dad's side. I decided it didn't know I was there, so the idea of screaming for help was a big, "NO!" As the apparition kept walking to the head of the bed, a beam of moonlight gave backlight to him, and I could see a perfect silhouette. But it still seemed out of focus. Then something it did made me unintentionally jump up and back on my little cot. Now I was wedged in the corner of the room as far away from it as I could get. The only other alternative was running out of the room and I was afraid I wouldn't make it if I tried. The ghost bent down like it was going to get under the bed, and then, it was gone.

I don't know how long it was before my parents came in, but I didn't move the whole time. I hadn't stopped staring at the spot I last saw , so I croaked out as best I could with my now-dry throat, "I think a rat ran under your bed." As my dad knelt down, I spit out prayers like casings from a machine gun. When he returned to his feet, he brushed off his pants, saying, "No rat.
Nothing but dust." So I didn't say a word to them about what I had seen. In fact, I never told anyone about it until I was in my 60s. I nearly forgot about it for most of my adult life. Frankly, the only people I have told, had the reaction I expected: "It was just a dream; sometimes dreams can seem so real." "Your imagination got the best of you." I don't share it much anymore so people won't think of me as a "nutcase."

Needless to say, I didn't sleep that night. The morning after the ghost, I was especially in need of comfort and feeling protected. I was in the best place for that. My grandparents always gave me comfort, love, and strength to move on and conquer my problems. The cure for almost any traumatic event, pain, injury or heartbreak, was for me to sit on my Nona's lap with her plump arms wrapped around me. She would give me a warm hug that said, "You are safe now. I will keep bad things from harming you and I won't let go until you are smiling." Her lap was soft and comfy and her words soft, too, a few in English and some in Italian. While she reassured me, I would drink hot "chacolata." Altogether, this "magic elixir" would bring about healing.

I can still clearly see where this comforting took place in one of the eight chairs around the large kitchen table. These chairs were painted the same seafoam green as the kitchen and patio table. It was a color used a lot around the house. Nona's chair was at one corner of the table closest to the stove. In my memory, I am sitting on my Nona's lap, feeling the warmth of her hug, the comfort of her ample lap, and I can smell the flour on her hands from the buns she just made. I hear the crinkling rustle of stiff paper as my Nono pages through his Italian newspaper, La' Italia,
the one he walks a half mile through the vineyard to the post office to get. I hear my Nono striking a Diamond brand match on the metal sculptured ashtray, and the sucking, puffing sounds as he gets his pipe going. I can smell the wood smoke mixed with the smell of sulfur from the match and the sweet pipe smell, and feel the heat from the old grape vines burning in the stove. I can still taste the sweet coffee my Nona doctored up for me.

Chapter 5
Introducing Curddy

Of all the old Italians at Big Pink, my favorite was my buddy
Curddy. He was my first adult friend that was not a relative. What I
mean by 'friend' is that he actually did things with me. We played
games that he taught me; he took me on hikes or down to the creek
to wade in the water, and even let me go with him to help do his
chores,. I asked him several times, "How do you know all these
things that are fun for a kid?" He gave me two different answers; one
was that he had a son once. When I asked him where his son was, his
answer was that the boy was in Italy, but that is all he would tell me.
His second answer to my question was that he used to work and live
at a job location that had four little boys and one girl. These children
always wanted to play with him. I was strangely jealous, even
though it was in the past. I thought he was my buddy and I wondered
if he liked them more than me. He would never say any more about
those children.

I don't remember when I first met Curddy. It seemed like I always
knew him, so I guess I was an infant when we met. He was always
around Big Pink because he lived in a room of the bunkhouse. He
was a hero to me because he was always there for me when I needed
something that required a big person's help, especially when I was
afraid of the Ghoul from the slaughterhouse or the black widow
spiders in the barn and wine cellar or anything else that scared me.
He didn't look like a typical hero, but he had the heart of a
Superhero.

Curddy was a stout and sturdy man, shorter than my Nono; maybe
he was about 5'8". He had a big belly that protruded far beyond his
belt. He had a round head, like a pumpkin, with ruddy cheeks and a
'gin blossom' nose from too many years of drinking. At night time, I
knew he drank a lot of wine and a drink called Brandy Manhattans,
and he would end up drunk at the end of the evening. He would
shuffle his feet through the gravel that covered the driveway on his
way to his small, lonely bedroom. I overheard my mom once talking

to my Nona saying, "I know he has gone through hell several times over, but he is killing himself by always drinking and being drunk."

Nona said, "Everyone deals with tragedy in different ways; no matter what anyone says to him, he can never forgive himself, so he drinks to help himself forget."

At the time I didn't have a clue what they were talking about, but I figured it didn't affect me, although my mom did tell Curddy, "You can take Jimmy with you on walks or as he calls them 'adventures,' as long as you are sober, but never take him if you are drunk. He loves you; don't let him down."

I sometimes called him Roly Poly because of his big, soft round belly and basketball head. Sometimes I would run at him and ram the top of my head into his tummy. My mom heard me call him Roly Poly and saw me ram my head into him. I got a royal scolding and felt so bad that I had unknowingly been mean to my friend, Curddy. I cried and felt terrible that I might have hurt his feelings or his tummy. I told him over and over, "I'm sorry, I'm sorry," but he responded in his gravelly voice, "You didn't hurt me at all. I love you. It's all ok; don't cry my friend." Then, he pulled me to him and gave me a hug and a sandpapery kiss on my cheek.
Curddy always seemed in need of a shave and shower. And he was forever in need of a nose hair trimming. Those brown hairs shot out of his nose, looking to me just like the tobacco that my Nono shoved in his pipe to smoke. Actually, I thought it was tobacco sticking out of his nose and I kept waiting to light it up. Stupid and gross, I know, but I was only a little kid. Curddy never wore a hat, either, not even when his bare scalp turned to pink, then bright pink and on to red over the summer, after too much time in the sun. He was mostly bald, although a few brown strands were combed over from the right side of his head to the left. I thought he went to the same barber as Lou-we-g.

Curddy always wore fragrance of tobacco mingled with a kind of musky body odor, like the inside of a well-used baseball mitt. It wasn't unpleasant, more like comforting and familiar. Sometimes when he was all cleaned up he smelled strongly of Lifebuoy soap. I hated that soap even though it was a cool looking red color. It had a harsh unpleasant odor that stung my nostrils. I much preferred Curddy with an aroma of musk and tobacco scent.

Curddy could have also been better acquainted with the washing machine. He wore the same 'uniform' each day: brown flannel-like pants with a full menu of food stains covering the front of them. There were also countless cigarette burns on the pants. This was a result of rolling his own cigarettes when he was drunk. They would be rolled too loosely and fall apart, dropping the glowing tip on to his pants, burning through the fabric and sizzling a wound into his leg or thigh. There were dozens of sewn-on patches going from the cuffs up to the beltline, some of them not even brown. But brown was the color on the tummy part of his shirt, even though the shirt had once been white with black pinstripes. It now looked like he rubbed up against a bale of wet tobacco leaves. Every shirt he wore looked the same.

Curddy wore work boots that were once black, now faded to gray. The right boot had a slice through the toe part of it; he told me it was from when he dropped the butcher knife as he was preparing to chop the head off a chicken. The old blood stain around the knife hole bore out that story, confirming that he had pulled the knife out of his boot and his toe. When I asked him, "Why don't you wash the blood off of your shoe?" He answered, "It is there to remind me to be more careful."

Even though he was big and strong, and had first-baseman's-glove-size hands, he was gentle, a gentle giant. One of the most notable aspects about him was his arms, or more specifically, the scars on his arms. The scars started on his hands and ran all the way up until they disappeared under his shirtsleeves. When we went to the creek to swim and he took his shirt off, I saw that the scars covered his stomach, chest, and throat. I often noticed when we were out together somewhere that people stared at his arms. Some of them had a kind of wide-eyed, grimacing expression. But I never found the scars to be repulsive or gross; they were just a part of him that I accepted, like his big blue veined, raw meatball nose. It made me mad when people stared at him, and I would bug my eyes out and

47

stare back at them. I never asked how he got the scars, well except for one time. I asked my mom about them and she said, "He did something very brave and that was the price he paid. The scars on his arms and chest and the scars on his heart, that's what he was left with."

To me, Curddy was always a hero, and he never had to sacrifice any body parts for me. To me, the scars looked like a mountain lion had shredded him; it looked like there would have been a lot of pain on the day that he earned all those scars. There was a partial tattoo on his left forearm, a heart split in half by scars, so that it looked like a broken heart. There were letters on the heart, too, but too much of it was gone for me to see what those letters used to say. It would be a decade before the mysteries of his scars and what happened to his son, were solved for me.

Curddy lived in the last bunk room of the bunkhouse. That room would become my second bedroom in Rutherford. When I was a teen, I would steal wine from the wine cellar, and my buddies and I would spend the night out getting drunk and, usually, sick. The bunkhouse was comprised of four rooms together; inside each room there were two beds, a dresser, a closet and a bed pan/pot. Curddy was the last of the eight boarders that used to live in the bunkhouse. They were vineyard workers, friends; some lived there for years, some for months. They got three hot meals of the best Italian food in the Valley for what started in the '30s at $1 a day room and board, and went up to $50 a month in the early '50s. But then, my Nona decided it was too much work and gave everybody their walking papers, everybody except Curddy. When I asked Nona why she let Curddy stay, she answered, "He is one of Nono's best friends and we owe him a big favor." I asked what that favor was and she just said, "Something that we could never pay him back for." I asked where Curddy and Nono met, she said, "Now, that is a good story; they met on the ship coming over; have him tell you some time." It was a good story indeed.

Curddy really had nothing. He owned no car, no house or property, no belongings except a few clothes and a nice pocket watch that had a piece of twine tied to it and fastened to his belt. The twine looked just like the ones used to tie up the grapevines. He would tug on this twine to pull out his watch dozens of times a day. I think it was more to look at the photographs on its inside lid than to find out the time. When you have no place to go and nothing to do when you get there, what difference does it make to know what time it is? For a long time I didn't know what the photographs were of but one day he told me they were of his wife and son. I did find some old photos of him when he was younger; he was very good looking. He had his shirt off and he didn't have scars or a big tummy, he looked like a muscle man, like Tarzan. What had happened to him, I wondered?

Chapter 6
Adventures at Big Pink

On foggy days at Big Pink, I loved to play outside. It was a whole new world. Some days, the fog would be lying low, concealing the grapevines or mustard and everything else near the ground. Then, it would start rising until only the top of the mountain was covered and, above that, there was blue sky. When the fog was heavy, that big wall of fluffiness invited me to jump off the porch into its feather-pillow softness. But deep whiteout fog was the most fun.

Sometimes I ran backward through the fog to see how I left a wake of clearer air behind me. I felt like the master of the fog. I could make it open, like Moses and the Red Sea. As the fog curled and swirled around me, I could enter the opaque mist and pretend I was on another planet, weird and spooky and, somehow, other-dimensional. I could explore new territories in the fog because nothing looked the same as it was on clear days. It was an alternate universe and everything was clean, fresh, soft and comforting. The fog wrapped around me like a cold, damp blanket.

But it was the danger of the fog that made it the most fun. I never knew exactly what was concealed just inches beyond my vision. I liked to play the daredevil, running full speed, blindly into the murkiness. I might find the trunk of one of the fig trees, the wall of the barn, or the two- story stone and cement fishpond. Running into one of them would end up in a lot of pain or even bleeding. But, it could be the hammock or grapevines, or something soft, like Curddy's belly. I admit I modified this behavior after tripping on the old car tire around the base of the loquat tree and smashing my forehead on the way down. After that, I started using a six-foot-long branch as a "blind man's cane," swinging it left to right as I walked around the property. I called it fog cutting.

On this day, though, I wasn't doing much "fog cutting." It was really cold, and I was soon huffing and puffing out my very own mist, my personal fog machine. I trotted over to the pigeon coop, opened the latch and went in. Only two pigeons were home; the others were flying around the valley. I had my very own pigeon, Homer. He was a unique rust color, one of a kind, and I loved that little bird, not yet fully grown. He would sit in my hands, sometimes rubbing his head on my chest and making his cooing sounds. I fantasized they were words that only I could understand. Afterward, I would tell Curddy or Nona my stories of what Homer told me. I gave him a kiss on the head and put him back in his comfortable nest.

"I'll be back tomorrow, Homer!"

As I prepared to leave the coop, I heard the buzzing of a bee and saw him circling my head. Fortunately, my Nono had taught me to stand still if a bee came around so he wouldn't sting me. I still learned the hard way by swatting at one and getting stung. So, today, I stayed still and followed the bee with my eyes as he flew away through the chicken wire walls. He flew low over the dirt service road right behind our house, a "dirt highway" for tractors and other farm machinery. After he crossed the road, he flew higher and into a hole on the wall of the ominous structure I preferred not to look at. But, there it was, right in front of me, looking sinister. I called it ….

The Monster

The Monster was a good name, considering how my relationship with it created a distressing feeling that still haunts me when my mind wanders back to those days. Those feelings reminded me of the dread I felt because of its evil presence lurking in the back of my brain. I never wanted to look directly at it, but I could feel its pus-dripping Cyclops eye glaring at me. It was probably just hundred-year-old honey oozing from a ragged hole in the building, but you couldn't prove it by me. That image is the one you know is there, but intuition tells you, "Don't look; if you do, the horror will be with you forever."

The Monster was a huge, menacing shed big enough to store four busses, a whale, four T-Rexes, or about 1001 Zombies. Its "skin" was the darkest wood I had ever seen, almost black, like staring into the depth of the universe. Its "body" had chunks torn out of it. And, on the side wall, facing the neighbor's house, I saw skulls. They were skulls of a variety of deceased creatures, LIKE some kind of cow, bird, or rat, something with a long snout; the larger one could have been some kind of beast like a bear or ape. Lastly, there was something that looked like a human skull, only it wasn't like the ones I had seen on TV. It had a flat crown and longer jaw. That one was dark, kind of a chewed-tobacco brown, like the stuff my Zio would aim at his spittoon. My fear was that, regardless of what color they were, these skulls might fly off the wall and grab my neck in their menacing, evil-smiling jaws.

On the other Monster wall nearest our house, there were chains hanging from large (some were huge) railroad spikes pounded deep into the walls. At the end of the chains were hooks with something reddish-brown on them. Was it blood? I could hear a faint sound, too, like a quiet siren's song trying to lure me closer. The entire structure was just evil like it had risen from the deep part of hell and could think of terrible, inhuman acts to carry out on those that got too close.

I didn't really have kids my age to play with when I spent time at Big Pink. My parents would ask "Where are you going?" and I would answer something like, "To be with my playmate, The Attic" or "My playmate, the Slaughterhouse". I kind of did that to make a point. I wanted to bring my friends up there to play and go on adventures with! It could be pretty boring. Soon I did bring friends up on almost every visit.

There were some pretty unsettling places I explored; the attic and the slaughterhouse were two. There was also the far back corner of the wine cellar, and even the living room and dining room held their mysteries. And, now, The Monster joined them. But only one place at Big Pink was haunted, the place where I saw the real live, dead ghost, my parents' bedroom.

The fog had cleared away by now and the warm sun beat down on me in the chicken coop. A pigeon suddenly fluttered its wings behind me and I screamed and jumped, my heart pounding. I turned and opened the latch with shaking hands, flung the door open and fled, leaving The Monster behind me in a cloud of dust.

After that day, I saw The Monster many times. I noticed new things over the years. On the back side, different birds had made nests in some of the holes, holes punched into the walls by some beast or giant. At times, The Monster appeared different and I would stare at it for a long time trying to figure it out. Several times, I took my .22 rifle out and shot at it, shooting the bees, the skulls or any part of it that seemed strange. But the very unnerving thing about The Monster is no one else appears to know it existed. My mother, years later, said, "I don't know what you're talking about; there was nothing behind us but grapevines. And other long-time valley residents with whom I had lunch, questioned, "Shed? What shed? There was no shed back there." I have even looked through the old photos hoping to find The Monster in the background.

I pretty much decided that I would ignore it. It didn't move and its basic appearance didn't change. If it wasn't alive, it couldn't come get me. My Nona Zirkelbach, who was always there to listen and encourage me, told me: "What you think about rules your mind. If you are afraid of something, it is in your mind; it is not real. Just pray, and Jesus will protect you. Think good thoughts; even in bad situations, look for something good. There is always something good, and, even if it is small, you can make it big in your mind so it becomes bigger than whatever is bothering you." Armed with this advice from my very wise grandma who loved God and people every day, I headed out on my adventures for the day.

Stolen Fruit

One beautiful morning, the sky was my favorite color of deep blue, like the glass jar that Vicks came in. (I loved the jar, but hated having Vicks on my chest at night). I began with the idea of eating one of each fruit that was ripe, and my mind began to consider all the tasty fruits on our property. But the first one that came to mind was on someone else's property. I hadn't met him yet, but my parents called him Cliff-C, and we had been eating his plums for years.

I walked through our gate and out to the service road behind the house. I looked right and left, and listened, hoping a truck or tractor was coming so I could hitch a ride. I liked to run out and stand in the middle of the road when I heard vehicles coming. If the driver was a grouch, he would swerve around me without even looking me in the eyes. Then he would yell something like, "Get the hell out of the road, you squirt." But some of the drivers were nice and would slow down or stop and talk to me. I would ask where they were headed and, if it was somewhere I had never been, I would try to hitch a ride. I loved going to new areas to explore, but the bad part was I would have to walk back home. My parents had rules for hitching rides, of course: "Do not go past Manley Lane or Niebaum Lane or past the plum orchard."

It took me twenty minutes walking down the service road, through the vineyards, to get to the plum orchard. When I got there, I took a folded up paper bag out of my back pocket and set it on the ground, open. Then I started picking plums and dropping them in the bag. While I picked with my right hand, I held one in my left and nibbled it. I didn't know it, but a man had quietly walked up behind me.

"Hey, big fellow, are the plums sweet? Well, even if they aren't, you can't complain when you get them free.
His voice boomed out loud and fast and startled me so much that I jumped up so high that I stumbled. I recovered and was able to land on my feet. I was shaking a bit and it felt like bats were flying around in my belly, but I bravely turned to find out who it was that went with the voice. The man had a friendly look to his face. He was wearing Levis pants and a Levi jacket over a blue work shirt that looked like it was Levi, too. In my frightened, high-pitched voice, I told him,

"My parents told me to come back here and steal your plums." I felt no guilt in selling them out.

He replied, "I have known for years that your family has been stealing my plums. It's all right; I've been stealing your grapes, too. But you should be careful around here; there are some places that are dangerous for a lad like you."

I just shrugged my shoulders and raised my hands, palm up:
"Perché?"

"Big fella, I'm not Italian. Say it in English."

I nodded and answered, "Okay, sorry. I asked 'why?' Why are some places dangerous? Where?"

He sat on the stump of a former plum tree and motioned me to sit on the ground next to him. He talked slowly, his words filled with kindness. He told me all about his ranch, the swimming and fishing pond that needed someone to use it, his horses that wanted someone to ride them. He offered me a job to do all that. He said,

"You don't remember, but I met you before. I am a friend of your Nono's. I even gave you rides on my tractor. Let's go. I'll show you my ranch and introduce you to my two sons and daughter.
They are teenagers, but you will like them. Then, I'll give you a ride home on Jesse James, my horse."

I went off with him to his ranch. In that day and age, there were no stranger-danger fears. All the adults I knew were nice and no living human had harmed me. It was fun meeting new people.

Well, there was the time when Chest-arena, known as the Eater, grabbed my right hand and put it in her mouth. I guess she thought it was one of the pig knuckles she loved to gnaw on. But Cheezer was next to her and saved me by throwing his glass of wine in her face. That was pretty funny, too, because his fingers were so slippery from all the greasy salami, canned sardines and pieces of blue cheese he had been eating that the glass flew out of his hand and smacked her in the nose. She dropped my hand and started wiping off her face with her hand; then she licked her hand over and over like a cat would.

Yes, I was still innocent and trusting when it came to people. It was fun meeting new people like Cliff-C. I liked his pond and asked if I could fish in it. But he told me there were no fish, just frogs.
Meeting Powder Burns

The next day, I was ready to discover something new. I came out the back door and looked at the apple tree behind our house, full of ripe apples. It was so tempting, but the tree was only a skull's throw from

The Monster. I worked up the courage to go pick a few apples in spite of my mom's warnings about what would happen if I ate one.

She told me, "Those are bad apples; if you eat them, you will get sick to your stomach and they will have to cut open your belly and dig out the apples with a shovel." Just a bit of exaggeration there. Of course, I didn't believe her, but I still had stomach cramps every time I thought about it.

Finally, I challenged her, "Why can't I eat those apples? Is it like the apple tree in the Garden of Eden? Did God tell you we shouldn't eat the fruit of the tree or whatever the Bible says?"

"No, Mister Wiseacre." She replied. "Those are crab apples."

I didn't know what crab apples were, but I knew what a crab was. I looked at her and said, "Yes, captain, sir!" I saluted her and skipped out the door, double-skipping across the pink patio, through the gate, across the dirt and straight to the apple tree, and climbed up to the very tip-top.

I picked the biggest apple I could find. It was a reddish pink; maybe that's why they called them crab apples because they were almost the same color as the crab shells my Nona had smashed the night before to get at the sweet crab meat. She had tossed the crab in a huge pot with her secret tomato sauce, along with prawns, white fish, scallops, clams and mussels still in the shell. It was the best cioppino ever, but, sadly, my mom never got the recipe, so it died with my Nona.

Suddenly, the thoughts of the unwelcome Monster intruded into my memories of Nona's wonderful meals. I climbed down the tree quickly, keeping my back to the shed, but keeping it in the corner of my eye to make sure it wasn't coming after me. Then, I heard a whistling sound and looked up to see a pretty little bird singing from a high branch of the tree. After the bird-song, an unfamiliar voice asked,

"Hey, Johnny Appleseed, what are you lookin' for up there?"

My knees buckled in fright. Someone had sneaked up behind me again. Was it something from inside the Monster coming to get me? I turned quickly and said, "My name is Jimmy…. Jim, not Johnny Applesauce. Salvatore Curtoni is my Nono, my grandfather. Where did you come from; where do you live?"

"I can't answer all your questions standing here baking in the sun! Why don't we sit down and relax? You look all wound up like a cheap alarm clock."

He turned and started walking toward the Monster.

"No!" I yelled. "I am not going in that rat trap."

He gave me a big brown-toothed smiled and said, "You can trust me. I am the father of three boys close to your age. I'm a Yankee Doodle Dandy; I'm a cowboy and a retired gunslinger." Later I found out he had lied; he didn't have any children.

With that, he drew out a gun from the holster I hadn't noticed he was wearing and spun it around doing tricks. He tossed it up and caught it behind his back; then, he shot an apple out of the tree. I was awestruck. He was as good as Hop-Along Cassidy on TV.

He winked and smiled; then he said,"My name's Powder Burns, at your service, my lad. If'n you are wondering why I talk funny, it's because you're used to everyone up here talkin' eyetalian. I'm a tough hombré from the best state in the USA. Texas"

Right then and there I knew that he would make a great playmate and we could go on all kinds of adventures together.

Chapter 7
A Cowpoke Named Powder Burns

I just had to say something about the guy's ridiculous name, so I laughed: "Powder Burns?" Is that a nickname? I know all about nicknames. My dad gives one to everyone he knows or meets. Did you meet my dad? Did he give you that funny name? What is the name you were given when you were born?"

He looked at me and replied, "Hold your horses, Buffalo Bill. We ain't playin' 20 questions."

He grabbed one of his holsters with one hand and his belt with the other hand and pulled it all up higher on his waist. Then, he put his right thumb to block his right nostril and blew a mass out of his left nostril and did the same to clear out his right. I gagged. "Yuck. That is sickening."

He ignored my comments and answered an earlier question. "My momma and daddy named me Powder. It could have been worse. They could have given me my Uncle's name, 'Ass'."

I had to ask, "People called him 'Ass…Burns'? That sounds like the pills my Nona takes when she has malda tasta, a headache."

He shook his head slowly. "No. Everyone called him by his real first name…. 'Your'. His middle name is 'Ass'."

I didn't get it, so he smiled and said, "He was called 'Your Ass Burns'."

I thought, yep, that's dumber than his name. I almost asked his dad's name and thought, forget it. Instead, I asked, "Is Powder like baby powder? Is that what you're named after?"

He squinted, and in an imitation of Burt Lancaster in the pirate movie I had seen the night before at the tiny movie house on Main Street, he said, "You scallywag! Not baby powder; gunpowder!!" I am dangerous to every man jack who gives me a hard time. I am explosive! Get it? Like gunpowder: KABOOM!"

I responded with a line I'd heard my dad use when my mom said, "I ate so much I feel like I'm going to explode." So I said to Powder, "It's just gas; pass it and you won't be so explosive."

He squinted, spat on the ground and snorted: "You sidewinder. You're a'funnin' me again. No one makes fun of my name and lives to talk about it. I might just string you up in that there apple tree." And with that, he took a rope off his belt, made a lasso and tossed it. Before I understood what was happening, the lasso had gone over my head and was tightening on my arms. He quickly gave the rope a few twitches and I was free.

He spat again and drawled, "O and K; okay, cowpoke. Let's mosey over there and get us a cold beer."

I jumped backwards beyond his reach or lassoing distance. I didn't trust him yet. Taking another look at the Monster shed, I shook my head violently and shakily squeaked, "No. I won't go in there! If that's where you live, you should change your first name to Soul, because the nuns taught us that if you live with evil, then your Soul burns in hell. That place is evil!"

He laughed and responded, "You are a funny little boy, clever. Your mind works fast as a jackrabbit with his ass on fire. Those were great comebacks about my name and my brother's."

So, Powder waved me over toward him and pointed behind himself again and made the offer: "Let's go over here and sit down and then you can tell me your life story. That should take about 4-and- 1/2 minutes. Then for the next hour, I'll tell you mine. I gar-in-damn-tee-you it will be the best story anyone ever told you. Because I am the most root-toot-tootinest cowboy you'll ever meet."

"But," I objected, "I told you. I don't want to go in the Monster shed today."

"Not in there, for the love of Roy Rogers. Not in there! Are you kidding? No one or nothing is livin' in there. Don't be a horse's fanny. I live there in a real house." He pointed to the house next door.

I challenged him again. "You don't live there. Flea Bag and Flamingo live there." (Their real names were Fleta and Domingo, but my dad had christened them with those nicknames.) Powder nodded and said, "Yep, I do little pardner."

I still didn't get it. "You live with them?"

He used his left thumb to push his cowboy hat back further on his head, revealing curly, sandy- blond hair and motioned, "Come here." He squatted down and pulled a knife out of its holster on his belt. He used it to draw a rectangle in the dirt and divided it down the middle. He wrote Dom on the top section and said, "This is where Domingo and Fleta live." He then stabbed the name 'Dude' on the bottom half, saying, "This is where the King of the Cowboys, me, lives." You see, it is like two separate houses stacked on top of each other.

First off, I got to thinking he was a phony, fake, pretend cowboy. But I really didn't care; I loved the show he was putting on. What he could have said in simpler terms was that Flamingo was living on the top story and he lived downstairs.

Then he said, in a strong determined voice, "You can trust me. I will never harm you or let anyone else harm you. I have a feeling we are going to become best friends. Let me explain who in the Sam Hill I am."

I jumped on that. "Wait! Who is Sam Hill?!?!"

He stared at me with one eye closed and the other eye squinted, like a scientist looking through a microscope at an alien life form. Then, he shook it off and made a sound, "Ya ya ya ya, brrrrrrrr." He looked at me and said, "Excuse me. I have to do that to kick start my brain after it freezes at the nerve of some people that make more sassy remarks than I do."

I stared at him, sizing him up. His skin was deep brown and leather-like. He had some wrinkles around his eyes that I later found out were from his squinting when he talked about or listened to anything that was emotional. His face was an amusement park of features. His eyes were deep blue and stood out in their dark, crinkly frame. His nose was a bit twisted, like someone with a bat had tried to hit a home run with it. There was a scar across the bridge of it that showed eight stitch marks, making it look like he had a caterpillar crawling across his nose. His big droopy blond mustache covered his thin upper lip and the corners of his mouth. His lower lip stuck out so his mouth looked like a carp's mouth. His chin had a crease down its center and his large ears stuck out as if they were there to keep his hat up. When you throw all those features together, I saw a face that was friendly, tough, worldly and honest. He often had an expression like he was thinking of a PRIVATE joke, and he always looked like he was enjoying life. His body was fit and trim, with hands that looked almost too large to get his trigger finger into the finger guard.

Finally, I broke the silence. "Let's go over to my place. We can sit on the patio." He nodded his shaggy head vigorously. "I'm for it, Tonto. We can get the hell out of Death Valley here and sit in the shade of the fig trees."

As he started walking off to Big Pink's patio, I followed, and we sat at the big table under the fig trees. Just then, the back door opened and my dad trotted down the stairs with my Nono following. Dad said, "Oh. I see you met Powder Burns. I told him all about you and the adventures you go on with Curddy. He said he would like to take you fishing at a secret pond one day. Sounds fun, huh, Jim?" I just nodded.

Then Nono said, "Oh, Jimmie. You met our new neighbor. It's..... something.... burning....?" My dad looked around and sniffed, saying, "I can't smell something burning." "No," said Nono. "No. I mean his name. Something burning.... Oh, yes. It's Powder burning."

Powder groaned. "I need a beer. Make that three beers! I'm parched from all these scorching jokes about my name." I was amused as I watched my Nono, dad and Powder talk and laugh while drinking their beers and wine with brandy chasers. I was happy to be with them.

There was something about Powder Burns that I really liked. He had a very pleasant voice and talked slowly with patience and kindness in his tone. I thought about some of the radio shows I listened to, like Gunsmoke, and decided he sounded like Marshal Dillon, someone you could trust with your life. And this guy was also funny. I could just stand there and watch him for hours, like Milton Berle on TV. I was happy he was at Big Pink.

Now I wanted my dad to become friends with him because Powder Burns was the funniest man I knew, other than my dad. I wanted to see how funny things would be if I got them together on a fishing trip, or, better yet, at the shooting range. We could bring all of our guns; Powder could bring his, and we could trade off. I was a great shot for a kid. My dad set up a target range in our backyard in Pleasant Hill. He made a "deer" cut out of tin beer cans, then mounted it on straightened wire coat hangers. When you hit the deer, it would spin on the wire. We also had paper bullseye targets we mounted right on the wood basket-weave fence. The only gun allowed at this Zirkelbach Shooting Range was a BB rifle. Sixty-plus years later, you can still see hundreds of BB holes in the wood and some even still have BBs in them. But I was also good with our .22 semi-automatic rifle with a scope. Oh, how I loved to shoot that rifle!

As Powder prepared to leave, he thanked my dad for the beers and I said goodbye. "Can I come over and visit you tomorrow? He smiled and winked, responding, "Yes indeed, Tex."

"Hold it," said my dad. "I have a question. You knew Curddy from before he came to Rutherford. Tell me about him. How did he get those horrible scars? And, what happened to his wife and son? Why is he an alcoholic? Is he drowning his past? And, is it true he killed five men in Italy?"

"Whoa!" Powder turned slowly. "I understand your curiosity, but you can't pry answers outta me like clams with a crowbar. See, he's kind of a partner and I think his secrets should stay with him."

And with that, he tipped the front of his hat and said, "Adios!"

Next I knew, he'd had to go back home to help his dad with something and I didn't see him for a long time. I was mad that he didn't tell me he was going away.

Months Later on Another Cold Morning at Big Pink

I walked down the back stairs carefully, balancing the hot cup of coffee in my hand. I had spilled hot coffee on myself before and it burned like what I figured hell would feel like. The cup was white and very thick. My dad had pocketed six of them when he was in the Navy. He said they were so thick and heavy because they were able to keep the coffee hot on the top deck of an aircraft carrier in the middle of the ocean in the middle of winter in the middle of a war. But the heaviness of the cup made it even harder for my skinny wrists to hold it level.

Sometimes, Curddy would come up and drink his coffee with all of us, but there were other times when he was too far down in the dumps to move that far. This was one of those days. As my feet crunched across the gravel driveway, I looked over at him as I approached. He was sitting on an obviously uncomfortable chair made out of grapevines on the wooden walkway that ran in front of the bunkhouses. His head hung down staring at the warped boards of the porch. The sun was just hitting the roof of the bunkhouse, causing the damp shingles to steam, just like the coffee cup. In a minute the sun would shine on Curddy and he would perk up….. a little. I stood in front of him, but he didn't sense my presence yet. I just looked at him, waiting and thinking.

I felt sorry for my buddy Curddy because he didn't have his own house. In fact, his one lonely sad room in the bunkhouse was smaller than half of my bedroom at Big Pink. He had no, kitchen or living room, only an 8x10 room with a dresser, small closet and two beds.

There was a bathroom at the end of the bunkhouse that he shared with guests. Even though I was just a kid, I knew it would be a sad life to have no possessions, no family, absolutely nothing. Once, when I told him that, he responded, "I am not lonely; I have you, your Nona and Nono. That is more love than a lot of people have." Still, he was a man of many mysteries. He didn't like to talk about his past and he hated answering questions.

I noticed that the steam off the coffee was less than the steam off the roof and I could tell that Curddy's coffee was getting cold, so I kicked my feet in the gravel to get his attention. He looked up and took a few seconds to focus. "Good morning, Jimmy," he said. "Thanks for the coffee. Let's go to my room while I drink it."

While I was in his room, I walked around and checked things out. There wasn't a lot to see. Suddenly, I noticed something shiny hanging at the back of his closet. I reached out to move his pants aside to see what it was, but I wasn't fast enough. When my fingers were only inches away from the target, he grabbed my wrist, gently, but with enough strength to stop my arm from moving any closer to my goal. With a tone of voice that sounded regretful and ashamed, he said, "I would rather that you didn't touch that...... Well, now. Let's go outside and play cribbage."

And so we did. It would be two more months until I got my hands on that shiny item at the back of his closet, and when I did, I was shocked.

Asking Questions

In 1952, I was 7 years old, and I loved helping my Nona make raviolis. We were in the kitchen, and it was a bright sunny, happy day. The familiar smells of wood smoke from the stove blended nicely with the mouth-watering aroma of her spicy tomato sauce, or "gravy". She went to the cooler cabinet every few minutes to select herbs and spices, and then returned to add them to her big gravy pot, stirring and tasting, adding more until she got it just right. The cooler cabinet was right above the wine cellar, open at the bottom, so cool air could come up from the cellar and keep the cheese, salami, sausages and vegetables fresh. There was chicken wire at the bottom of the cabinet to keep the rats from sneaking up to eat our cheese.

Every time Nona opened the cooler cabinet, a rainbow of rich scents would drift through the kitchen. There was a familiar mix of aromas: different cheeses, garlic, onions, and sausage mingled with the smell of wine and the musky odor of the cellar. It reminded me of fun times in that kitchen on rainy winter nights with friends and family. I can still feel the love and comfort of being with her and enjoying the "perfume" she created with her cooking.

Working with Nona gave me a great opportunity to talk with her and ask questions. I thought maybe this would be the time I could ask about Curddy, and then I might even slip into questions about why she didn't laugh. I began, "Nona, why is Curddy sad most of the time? He never really seems happy. I know he has fun when he's doing things with me, but other times, he is a mope. Did something bad happen to him? How did he get all those scars? It looks like someone dumped him in a vat of acid and then ran over him with a tank. Is there any skin on his body that doesn't have scars? Is that why he's so sad?"

She answered in an unfriendly tone, "That is none of our business. It's his secret for however long he wants to keep it."

"But," I continued, "What makes him happy?"

She thought for a few moments. "He likes to get together with the Old Dagos to eat and drink and watch everyone party."

"But," I replied, "He is quiet; he doesn't joke or tell stories like everyone else does. He only talks if someone asks him questions." Why do you let him live here for free? Why did he tell me his wife and son are dead, but he told Joe he sends them money? Where did you and Nono meet him: I heard two different things."

She didn't respond, so I thought she was thinking of an answer. While I waited, I continued to think more about Curddy. Why were there so many lies about him? He was never jolly, even though he did enjoy some things in life. No one ever thought of him as happy.

It was like pieces of his mind and emotions were held captive in some distant past, another time and place. He was really nice, friendly, and pleasant, and he never complained. In really big group settings, he was especially withdrawn, even more than when he was with his Old Italian friends. He generally blended into the background, a silent observer, drifting in and out of awareness of what was going on around him, usually with a hangdog countenance. Curddy didn't like getting into arguments; he didn't much care if he won or lost at cards. In fact thinking of him as competitive is as difficult as seeing him performing brain surgery. And he never ever bragged about himself. As I tried to sort of these things in my mind, I decided to make one more try with Nona.

"I'm worried for Curddy, Nona. If I knew what made him sad, maybe I could cheer him up. When I'm sad, you always want to know why, and, then, you try to think of things to cheer me up. I want to do that for Curddy."

She stopped what she was doing, looked at me, shook her head and breathed heavily. "Tempasta! Stop pestering me! Go ask him. I didn't know him when he got those scars or anything else that's wrong with him. I didn't know him back them." Just another one of many lies.

That was the end of that round of inquiries.

Chapter 8
The Happiest Place on Earth

It was a beautiful day with bright blue sky. As Curddy drank the coffee I'd just brought him, I sat and watched him, waiting for him to finish so we could go an adventure together. Now, I was remembering the many rumors I had heard about Curddy. On many a warm summer night, guests would gossip about him after he went to bed drunk. They said he used to be a gangster in Italy; that his wife and child were murdered. That he had killed half a dozen men as revenge. He was supposed to have been in bar room fights beating up as many as five men at once and laughing while he did it. I found all of it hard to imagine. I never saw that side of him; I didn't want to believe it. It was hard for me to think of him as young and tough, fit and healthy and without scars. Yes, he had mysteries that hung over him like the cloud of stinky smoke from the cigarettes and cigars that were always hanging out of the corner of his mouth. Like a lot of Italians, he could hang them there and smoke without ever touching them.

The guests that came to Big Pink were all Italians, with the exception of a very few who were nicknamed according to their country of origin, like Ole "the Swede", or "the Turk." They all knew how to enjoy life, but if they weren't enjoying it, Big Pink was a safe haven where sad, stressed, depressed and broken people could come to be healed. It was the "happiest place on earth," at least until Disneyland came along.
It was a "law" that anyone who came to Big Pink had to stop at the foot of the driveway before they crossed the railroad tracks and leave all their stress, problems, worries and any other negative thoughts right there on the road beside the tracks. They had to dump it all. No 'downers' could venture across the tracks. There were a few times that people arrived grumpy or stressed and they had to be sent back up the driveway. They were required to go back across the tracks and weren't allowed to return until they had dumped their load. They were usually escorted by Nono because he was always in a good mood. One of his goals in life was to make sure that his guests

always had fun. In most cases, by the time they got all the way to the tracks, they were already in a good mood and had nothing to dump. That was the effect Nono had on everyone.

The favorite place to gather and celebrate life in the summer was at the back patio, which was furnished with a couch, a coffee table and two chairs made from grape vines. Most importantly, there was a large table with benches. In the winter the gatherings moved to the warm kitchen with its welcoming table and wood-burning stove. Everything happened in these two places: feasts and fun, tears and arguments; friendships became bonds of brotherhood, and love and romance bloomed there.

Big Pink had everything my grandparents could have possibly wanted. All Italian couples back then wanted a son. It was a huge deal. The strange thing is that if all Italians wanted sons, and they didn't want their sons to marry anyone but an Italian girl, where would all the Italian girls come from? My Nono and Nona didn't have a son, but their daughter had given them a grandson, the boy child they had always wanted.

To me, Nono and Nona were rich. Their list of wants could have been written on the cork of my Nono's wine bottle. Their Thanksgiving list would have required a roll of butcher paper like the kind used to wrap up cheese purchases at the St. Helena Olive Oil Company. They owned everything free and clear, the big (pink) house and over 2 acres of vineyard,. They had large supplies of food and drink from the slaughterhouse where my Nono made his own wine. The wine cellar stored many barrels of that wine, and there was a closet in the cool part of the cellar filled with Mason jars of fruit, jam, pigs' knuckles and ears, and vegetables that Nona canned every year, plus the sausages and salami she made. I watched her make that sausage one day in the cellar and helped grind up the meats. When I asked, "What is that tube-like thing you're stuffing the meat into?," she responded in Italian, "The inside of an animal's ass." I ran out of the cellar and never ate her sausage again.

My grandparents had countless chickens to eat, fresh eggs, dozens of pigeons would become squab. My Nono had a huge vegetable

68

garden. And there were many fruit trees: peach, apricot, apple, plum, and white and purple fig. Needless to say, there were grapes, lots of purple ones, some green. My very favorites were the Muscat grapes, but there were very few of those. There were also two olive trees, so my Nona could put up her olives each year. These olive trees were rumored to be 50 years old in the early 1950s. My Nona made her own pork chops, raviolis and pasta. They had enough food and drink to last a dozen people a year.

When guests came, they would always come loaded with food items. The best of everything always came with the San Francisco friends and relatives: they would bring beef steaks, veal, cold cuts, cheeses, breads, pickled mushrooms and peppers. No one ever got thirsty, they brought Pabst Blue Ribbon beer and bourbon in bottles that looked like crystal and reflected light and colors like Mrs. Manni's many diamonds. Someone always brought a gallon jug of Brandy Manhattans and, for after dinner, there were wine cookies, biscotti, sweet wines and sweets of all kinds.

In addition to all that, someone usually brought a burlap bag of coffee beans. There were letters stenciled on the bag, but they didn't make words that I knew. I could understand words spoken in Italian, but I couldn't read them. The beans were to go in the old hand grinder to make the strong coffee that was much needed in the morning to get everyone's engines started after a night of big eating and drinking and hard living. I liked grinding the beans; it was fun and they smelled, oh, so good. And Nono always said this fresh ground coffee was lots better than the coffee I would get out of the huge Folgers can.

There was hardly anything that my grandparents needed to purchase from the market. Still I would look forward to Monday afternoon. That was "going-to-market" day. I was excited because, if I went, I would get a comic book or two. My favorites were Plastic Man and Scrooge McDuck. If it was a hot day, I could get an ice cream and Nehi orange soda. I would walk to the store, usually with Nono, because Nona had "bad ankles" and long walks were painful. She only made the trip when there was some special ingredient needed for her gourmet feast and she didn't trust Nono to get the right thing. Nona didn't ever use a cookbook; nothing was written down. Each ingredient for everything she cooked was catalogued in her head and it was always just right.

The few items that had to be bought at the store didn't cost much. There was no water bill because their water came from their own well. The only other bills were gas and electricity and two deliveries of heating oil each year. Their income came from my Nono's disability Social Security and money he earned as a part-time night watchman at BV winery, plus what came from the sale of the grapes he didn't use to make his own wine. In addition, Nona was paid for catering winery banquets and selling her pasta to the deli in Oakville. So, with so few expenses and a good income, they were set. I thought they lived in Paradise! It was a good life filled with abundance, and they loved to share it with all their many friends!

Time with Curddy

It was at the patio where I heard most of the stories about Curddy. My Nono told me the version that Curddy had given him on the ship when they were coming to America. I didn't know for over a decade that, even though my Nono told and retold this story, he never really believed it. Because Curddy felt it important enough to lie to my Nono, his only friend in America back then, Nono would respect Curddy's need to set a false history for himself. Curddy never would answer my questions about his past, but just before he died, Curddy told me one truth. He promised me that when I became an adult the whole story would be revealed: "When you are a man, you will be able to understand better why I did what I did."

The Curddy I knew was a good guy and did everything right by me. We did a lot of fun things together. When we went on hikes, Curddy would tell me stories that he made up as we walked, and the protagonist was always a boy named Jimmy. I liked holding his hand when we walked up the mountains and back down. Even though his hands were covered with scars that looked like he had fought a wildcat, holding them gave me a feeling of safety and reassurance. At that young age, I had a deep fear that wild animals living in the mountains would attack me. Every night, I feared that bears and other wild animals were going to come over the mountain behind Big Pink, climb in the window and eat me, so I was really afraid to take hikes up the mountain. In an effort to heal my fear, Curddy started by leading me up the mountain just a little way, and each day we would go further. My fear was greatly reduced by the fact that Curddy took along Nono's double- barreled sawed off shotgun and extra shells. I had to wonder if he thought we were going to attacked by so many animals that he would need all those shells. We never quite made it to the top of the mountain, but I remember reaching the three-fourths point.

In addition to the personalized stories he made up, Curddy and I talked a lot about whatever was on our minds. When we took rest stops, we would drink from my army canteen which was covered by army-green canvas. My dad said it came from World War II. If I soaked the canvas cover in water the evaporation would keep the water in the canteen cool. During those rest stops, the conversation took a more personal tone. I told Curddy about my fears and the things I didn't understand, anything that was bothering me. He was a good listener, patient and reassuring. It was so much easier to talk to him than with my dad. My dad often answered my questions with sarcastic or humorous zingers; it was always about getting a laugh for my dad. With Curddy, all questions were fair game, except personal questions about his past. I quit asking after I saw how upset he got when he tried to tell me he didn't want to talk about it.

I could tell Curddy anything and never feel embarrassed. He always had something to say that took away my fears and cheered me up. I thought he was very perceptive and wise. I knew in the depths of my heart that he was a good man, and I considered him a hero, along with my dad and Nono.

I needed several heroes at night. One might not be enough to protect me from everything that was lurking in the dark, licking its lips and drooling in anticipation of eating me. I had just discovered in the Tales from the Crypt comics that there were meaner, more vicious things wandering around the world than wild animals. They were unlike anything I had ever seen; things from outer space, things that

I never thought existed. They were capable of murder. Yes, I hated going to bed at Big Pink because there was a zoo full of wild animals and monsters waiting in line to climb up a ladder into my bedroom and it was pitch black, as if someone had covered my eyes with tar.

When I told Curddy about my fears, he told me he would keep his door open. Then he would hear anything that walked by toward my window. Because his doorway was straight across from my bedroom, I figured he could cover it. That helped. Each night before I got in bed, I would go to my open window, look down to see his open door and yell, "Goodnight, my good friend!" He would yell back, "Good night, my dear boy!"

We did more than just hike. Curddy taught me card games. We would sit out on the patio under the two huge fig trees playing Cribbage or Rummy with a deck of Bee playing cards that looked like it was decades old. The cards were brown with dirt and the two jokers filled in for the lost 2 of hearts and the 4 of clubs. Someone had written those identifiers on the cards with a fountain pen. With all the creases, bent corners, dirt and seasoning they were a much more comforting deck to use than a new stiff one. Curddy tried to teach me Pedro, a card game that the old Italians played nightly, but I never did understand it.

The Monster Shed

The next morning, sunlight streamed in the three kitchen windows over the sink and made the cream-colored paint glow a happy sunflower color. As I ate my cornflakes, I listened to Nono and Nona talking about the Madoni's house fire and murder. Nardi and Leoni Madoni were found stabbed to death 100 feet from the smoldering ashes and debris of their mansion, far behind Big Pink, almost at the foot of the mountain. The sheriff had not found any clues as to who the murderer might be, but everyone thought it could be the same person that made off with a dozen of Pettoni's chickens and killed his cats. I loved mysteries so, rather than being scared, I listened intently. If my parents had been in the room, they would have shushed them. As I listened, I savored my rock hard wine cookie as I dunked it in my cup of diluted coffee. The almond and butter flavor of the cookie mixed with the coffee and cream was yummy. But, my grandparents changed subjects and began discussing the menu for their party on Saturday and I lost interest. I drank the rest of my too-sweet coffee and ate the last few bites of my now-soggy cornflakes and took the bowl and heavy coffee mug to the sink.

As I ran out the door into the bright sunshine, I said, "Bye, bye, Nono, Nona! I'm going to visit Powder Burns. See you later." And I was gone before they had a chance to reply or give me any restrictions on where I could go or what I could do. I jumped down the cement stair two at a time and came down on the patio running.

On this morning, it was warm enough to wear just my swim trunks and some cowboy gear. The sky was pale blue with wisps of smoky clouds. In keeping with my theme for the day, one cloud looked like a cowboy hat; one looked like a horse and another was a big fat cow. At that point in my life, Roy Rogers was my hero and I loved everything cowboy. I had on my cowboy hat and was wearing my double holsters, just like Powder's, hanging low over my swim trunks. Like Powder, I had the guns with the handles facing forward so I could draw the right side gun with my left hand and my left-side gun with my right, crisscross, just like I saw Powder Burns do. Well, my guns were only toys that fired caps; Powder's guns fired real bullets and he was a very good shot. Every time I thought he was a phony, a guy imitating a TV cowboy, he would pull off some cowboy talent like shooting or lassoing.

I ran quickly past the pigeon coop and had to put on my brakes, kicking up dust, when I saw Powder next to the crab apple tree staring at the Monster Shed. I backtracked, walked through the back gate and over to him. Without looking at me, he asked, "Why do you call that sewer of a shed the "Monster Shed?"

"Because it scares me as much as a big monster would." I answered. "What is it? Who owns it? Why do they have all those skulls on the wall?"
He reached into his shirt pocket and brought out a white cloth bag of tobacco and some yellow cigarette papers and quickly rolled a nice size cigarette. He fished around in the watch pocket of his Levis,

pulled out a stick match, struck it on his whiskers and lit it. I scoffed: "That was a fake, a trick. You didn't really light that on your cheek. If you did, you would have burned your whiskers!"

Powder ignored my comment and answered my earlier question. "I don't know who owns it or anything else about it. It really is a mystery. I think it's dangerous and you should stay away from it. I mean it! But I do know something about the strange-looking brown skull. I hung it up there as a joke, kind of. It was given to me by one of my teachers ages ago. He said someone in Africa had sent it to him. He thought it was made by putting together some animal skulls with a human skull; that's why it's so weird looking. Well, either that, or it was from a real monster. The teacher thought it was cursed because he had numerous tragedies, illness and crimes committed against him after he got. it So, he gave it to me and then I started having horrible things happen to me. I nailed it up on that wall and I've had good luck ever since."

He criss crossed his hands and drew both pistols, firing off two shots at the tree, but this time no apples fell to the ground. "Hey, Powder," I remarked, "My dad told me to be careful about what is behind the targets when I was practicing with our .22 rifle because a bullet can travel for a mile.
.22 longs can travel even farther. Aren't you worried that one of your bullets will go as far as the Stacks farm and shoot Granny Stacks in the eye?" But Powder replied, "It isn't a big deal to fire shots into the air. Everyone in the Valley is shooting at something." Looking back I realize that true gun safety hadn't made it to the Valley yet. But, after I commented to him, Powder took off his gun belt and told me he was heading into town. "Can't take my guns to town. Etzio the Police Chief already warned me about that."

Now that he was gone, I decided it was time to explore the Monster Shed, especially since Powder had warned me not to. I ran around it until I found a door. It had rollers at the top, just like the door to the slaughterhouse. It made me wonder if the Monster Shed was used for slaughtering too. I acted like a bold cowboy, grabbing the door handle with both hands. It was rusty and felt rough and flaky in my hand. I yanked hard and the door opened less than a foot, but it was enough room for me to squeeze in. The wooden door was rough and I got a few splinters in my butt and hands. Once inside, I blinked my eyes a few times, adjusting to the dimmer light. When I looked around, I could tell I was only in half of the shed. The half I was in was about as big as a four-car garage. There was a big hole in the roof where the light shone through, and the only other light came from the door opening.

The floor was damp dirt, almost mud, and there were countless mold patches here and there on the floor and walls. I saw an old calendar on the back of the door from 1932. Against the right wall there were soot marks and, under that, charcoal and partially burned pieces of wood. Next to the fire pit, there was a pile of bones to small to be anything but a bird or mouse. There were also some that I recognized to be chicken bones. Actually, there were a lot of bones, like someone had been eating in there. There was also an old tub with a lot of maroon stains, probably rust, but my brain was telling me blood. And there was a pile of rotting wood.

The smell in there was disgusting and I used my cowboy bandana to pull up over my nose. The wall looked shiny and I was curious, so I put my hand on it. Immediately I yanked it away; the walls were slimy, gross! I wiped my hands off so hard, I thought I might wear a hole in my swimsuit. In the back corner there was a big pile about six feet across and three feet high. When I walked over to it, I saw that it was a pile of wet, moldy and rotting old magazines. I saw something in one that scared me. The nuns had told me that it was a sin for boys to look at photographs of naked women, so I sensed them looking over my shoulder as I stared.

Suddenly, there was a scraping sound and I jumped. I thought it was my dad and he would know that I had been looking at the naked ladies. But as I quickly turned around, I screamed loud and long. I was looking at a monster of some kind. I froze in place, my legs planted in the dirt floor. The monster was human in shape, but very short. It was wearing dirty rags and its face was almost completely covered with hair. Its huge eyes stared at me, not moving. Its mouth was open in a snarl, showing lots of ragged teeth. I screamed again and managed to move my legs, running for the door. I tried to push

75

and it wouldn't budge. I had forgotten that it slid open. I slammed into it head first and tried to squeeze out the opening. But I got stuck. With my face outside the door and my body trapped inside, I couldn't see what the monster was doing. I kept on screaming, and then I smelled it. The stench was so revolting, I almost puked. It must be coming closer.

Chapter 9
Rescued

There I was, stuck halfway out of the door to the Monster Shed. The worst part was that I was still halfway inside and in there was some kind of monstrous creature very close. I could smell it; I could sense it closing in on me. I screamed, "HELP!" in fear for my life.

All I could think of was the Madoni family, murdered and their house burned down and killed Joe's two white cats. I remembered that Nono had told me, "Anyone that can murder two people and those cats has to be a beast!" Maybe it was the beast in the shed behind me. Terrified, I assessed my situation. My skin felt like it was crawling, retreating from the anticipated touch of the beast.
My throat and mouth were dry as dust from the screaming and I think every bit of fluid in my body was in my bladder, seconds away from exiting my body. My eyes wouldn't cry, but my body was crying silently and I started feeling light-headed. My scalp tingled, my legs shook and I was getting weaker and weaker as I struggled to get away.

I closed my eyes and tried to think of being somewhere else. Anywhere else. If only Curddy had gone on this exploration with me. He almost always had his shotgun with him. After all, my dad told me, "He acts like he's a Mafia bodyguard; maybe the Mafia is actually after him!" That always struck me as odd. If they thought the Mafia was after Curddy, why did they let me hang around with him? I returned to my current predicament, my real-life terror, and put my last bit of energy into a useless croaking scream. I closed my eyes tight.

Suddenly, I felt a strong hand on my shoulder and one around my waist and with a strong pull I was out of the doorway, FREE! I was still panting, sobbing tearlessly and gasping for breath. Then I opened my eyes and saw Powder Burns. At first, I thought I was just imagining him, but he was really there, rescuing me. The next thing I remember, Powder was carrying me into his house. He sat me down at his kitchen table, opened a bottle of Pepsi and offered it to me. I yanked it from his hand and guzzled it, while he put his arm around me and began telling me funny stories.

Finally, I started laughing. But then I remembered. The hideous image reared up in my mind, and I realized that Powder didn't know about the horrible thing in the shed.

As I recounted what had happened, carefully describing the terrible beast in the shed, Powder listened, still hugging me close to him. Finally, I settled down, almost to normal, and he said, "Wait here, a minute! I'm going to do a little target practice. He took his holster with two guns off the peg next to the door and walked out of the kitchen.

My mind was flashing on the images of what I had seen in the Monster Shed only moments ago. The pile of bones, the bathtub and its dried blood and that gross sticky stuff on the walls. Remembering that I had touched the sticky gunk, I ran to the sink and washed my hands with the harsh Lava soap. I scrubbed several times just to be sure it was all off. But then I couldn't find a towel, so I had to dry my hands on my cowboy neck scarf. The putrid stench of the monster hung in my nostrils and I ran to the bathroom to grab some toilet paper. Blowing my nose didn't help though. That odor wouldn't go away.

Still nervous, I walked around the kitchen opening drawers. Finally, I found a big knife, like the Bowie knife I had seen in a movie. I lifted it out of the drawer; it was heavy. Then I moved to the back door and opened it. If Powder needed back up, I was ready.

Then I heard three shots.

I don't know how long I waited, but the next thing I knew, I could hear Powder singing "Deep in the heart of Tex-as…" As I looked out the doorway, I soon saw him, smiling and giving me a thumbs up. I ran to him and gave him a huge hug, both in thanks and also for my need to feel safe and protected when he hugged me back.

I couldn't stop the questions that were burning a hole in my bravado: "Did you shoot it? Did you, did you? Did it hurt you? Is it dead so it can't get to me?"

"Never fear when Powder Burns is in the neighborhood! I will protect you from animals, criminals, monsters and even the Ghoul from the Slaughterhouse. You are my pard'ner; a guy never lets his pard'ner down."

I was chomping at the bit: "What were those shots? Did you get it? What was it? Were you scared?"

He put his hand on my back and gently pushed me back into the chair I'd been sitting in earlier. He handed me what was left of my bottle of Pepsi.
"I'm going to down a few snorts of whiskey and, then, I'll tell you what happened."

He took a pint of Old Grand-Dad and a shot glass out of the cabinet over the sink, opened the bottle and gulped down a healthy dose. Then he walked to the sink, turned on the water and filled the shot glass and swallowed his water chaser. Finally, he burped, smiled, winked, cleared his throat and began:

"I walked carefully out to the shed, looking from side to side to make sure the creature was not trying to ambush me. I also looked up in the trees. You can never be too careful, especially when dealing with strange creatures. You never know if they can jump up high on to a roof top or a tree."

"I didn't see anything strange, except for Patzo's three-legged cat eating a crab apple. Now that was strange. I ain't never seen a cat eatin' a crab apple before. Now, I had a mangy ol' dog that liked cucumbers if you put salt on 'em...."

I yelled out: "I don't care about a dog eating crabs or a cat eating straw or even a rat that can fly!!! Did you shoot it?!?!

He took a few steps back, almost as if he was bracing for a punch to his chin.

"My, my! Are we a little bossy today? You shouldn't interrupt someone when they're talking. Well, I suppose you can do it all you want; just don't do it to Powder Burns, the legendary gun man from the Old West. And, by the way…. that would be me."

"I'm sorry. I'm just still afraid of that thing I saw in there." I countered.

He smiled, ruffled my hair, patted my head and replied, "Okay. No sweat. So, after looking high and low, and I do mean low, I kicked the dirt around to make sure there were no varmints that burrowed in the dirt and were hiding in there."

"Then, I got to that doorway you were stuck in. Because I didn't know what I was up against, I fired three shots through the door. Next I yanked that door as hard as I could. It squeaked and groaned as it opened about three feet more. I pulled out my second gun, cocked the hammers back on both guns with my trigger fingers ready and ran in, ducking low. My eyes scanned the whole room in seconds. My eyesight is as sharp as radar, you know."

No one nor nothing alive was in that shed. Well, unless you count the mold. I walked over to the mound of rotting paper and kicked it around to make sure nothin' was under there. But there wasn't. I even checked all the way up to the rafters. Whatever you saw wasn't there; it was gone with the wind. "Gone with the Wind," get it."
I responded rudely, "No. I don't get it." But I really did. I just didn't want to encourage him to come up with any more jokes or side stories. My dad referred to Powder's stories as "BS" and I knew that "B" was for bull. At that age, I didn't know what the "S" was for, but I figured it wasn't good.

Powder finally got to the point. "No, you little sidewinder. There was nothing alive in there, just as I told you. I did scout around and saw footprints in the mushy dirt in there. It looked like something or someone had been eating a lot of little creatures, and maybe a few chickens. Or maybe they were collecting bones for a hobby. Now, it is possible that whatever creature you saw was responsible for cats and stealing chickens. And it might even have been the one that murdered the neighbors."

He shook his head and went on: " It was not smart for you to go in that shed alone. I told you that just before I left for town. Do you remember me telling you that?"

I hung my head and slowly nodded. Then he continued, "If I didn't remember that I had left my wallet in the bathroom and returned to get it, I wouldn't have been back for an hour. With you stuck in that door for that long, your goose could have been cooked, just like whatever meat used to be on those bones in there, cooked and eaten."

'Course, I doubt the creature would have cooked you. He'd a probably just chomped on you raw. Pard'ner, I'm not being mean or trying to scare you. I care about you and I don't want anything bad to happen to you. You have to start using your noggin' so you don't do something stupid that could kill you or something worse. And, yes, there are things worse than death."

I gave a nervous laugh, "Yes, eating my mom's stew is worse than death. Sitting in church every Sunday and listening to a hundred-year-old priest talk in some weird language that I don't understand, or…."

"Okay, now stop." He interrupted. "Now you're joking around. But I'm serious. There is someone up here in our peaceful valley, killing animals and people, and you need to stay at Big Pink, unless you have someone with you. Your dad told me about when Curddy would take you on adventures. He always had your Nono's shotgun with him because you were always afraid that wild animals would attack you."

"You need to know, now, that there really is something around here that could hurt you. Whatever you saw is gone. I don't think it'll return to the shed. I'm sure it heard the gunshots and fled and know if he comes back, I'll blow him to pieces."

On that day, in Powder Burns' kitchen, I knew I was safe.

81

The Real Powder Burns

When I told my friends at school about my new neighbor at Rutherford, the incredible Powder Burns, I got the same response as I did later as an adult when I told stories about my adventures with that old cowboy. "Be honest; he is a made up person. There is no Powder Burns, nor was there ever one. I didn't blame them.

I wondered from the moment I met him what the real story was. He acted like the cowboys and gunslingers in the movies; he was too much like some of the cowboys on the TV shows we watched, and we watched almost every single one. I loved those heroes on horseback that could shoot, quick draw, rope and beat up every bad guy. So when this guy shows up acting like the hero of my dreams, I thought it was a prank my dad came up with.

My dad was the king of pranks; he loved a good laugh and he provided many funny situations for a laugh for himself and often for others. Something like this guy was right in his wheelhouse. So when this 'cowboy' with his six-shooter came up behind me in the vineyard to shoot an apple out of the tree above my head, well, at first it scared the hell out of me. Those old revolvers were loud. After I recovered, I thought, 'this can't be real.' And, when he told me his name was Powder Burns, I accused him of making up a fake name. "Did my dad give you that name; he loves making up funny names?" Besides what kind of maniac would shoot a gun at an apple in a tree in a vineyard with houses nearby!?!?

I continued to be suspicious when I heard him talking to my dad or my Nono. He didn't use the same terms he used with me, like "Hey, Hombre! You're looking at a root-tootin' quickest draw in all of the West." He didn't have the same pronounced accent. But on the other hand, he was good at everything a real cowboy did on TV. He was a great shot and could set beer cans on the top of a fence and shoot them all off, even shooting with both guns at the same time.

One summer about a month after he moved in next door, he asked me if I wanted to go horseback riding with him. I said "Heck no. I won't ever ride a horse again. The last time I was on a horse, I ended up face first in a stream picking gravel out of my face." But, I figured if he asked me to go riding, he must be able to ride a horse. He was good at everything a cowboy was supposed to be good at except lassoing, not so good at that. He tried to lasso me a couple times and couldn't even get the rope over my head. He gave up trying.

So who was he really, what was the truth about him?

A few years later I found out Powder Burns was born Robert Burns. It wasn't until he was nine that he earned the nickname Powder. He was born in Paint Rock, Texas, around 1920. Paint Rock would remain one of the ten worst towns to live in all of Texas. He had a rough childhood growing up on a chicken farm; along with the chickens his raised pigs. The family made money from selling eggs and the chickens, which young Robert had to kill, gut, remove all the feathers from and walk into town to sell them to the small store, where he also sold the eggs. He was lucky he didn't have to slaughter the pigs. A family several farms away had a slaughterhouse. One of the sons from there would come by when the pigs were 'ripe' (That was the term his dad Kenton used to refer to pigs old enough to be butchered) and toss them in the back of the truck and hand Kenton cash. It was an ugly landscape, an even uglier town, tough and harsh with a lot of mean people around.

Robert's mom loved poetry, probably to add some beauty to her life. So she named her youngest son Robert after the poet. He loved reading, not poetry but 'dime novels.' There were some museums in Texas, none close to Paint Rock, but Robert's older brother Val drove him on a few field trips so Robert could see the Alamo and other historic places. Robert couldn't get enough of the 'Old West'.

Then when he was seventeen he saw his first Wild West Show. Annie Oakley and Wild Bill were 'permanently retired,' but this show was in essence the same as their show had been. He decided he had to be apart of that scene, so his brother took him behind the scenes, something
he might not had the backbone to do on his own. Val didn't approach any of the performers; instead, he went up to the guys feeding the

horses and asked if there were any job openings. The response was "No".

Then Val tried a different approach. "My brother loves this lifestyle and the Wild West. He would love to travel with this show and learn from some of these experts. He is a good hard worker and he'd work for you for free. You wouldn't need to pay him; just let him hang around the cast and learn how to ride, how to shoot, how to rope, the whole ball of wax. He has experience working on a farm, but he doesn't have experience with horses. He's a quick learner, though, and shoveling horse dookie is the same as shoveling pig dookie. It won't cost you anything but food."

When they got back to the sad excuse for a farm in the sad excuse of a town, Val told Robert, "Let me do the talking." He told their parents that Robert got a job and he would be leaving home. "It is a rare chance for him to get out of this hell hole and learn a career." They gave in.

It took years for Robert to be good at shooting, riding, quick draw, and all of it, except the roping stuff. He finally was in the shows, got paid, and was living the life. Then, after twenty years with the show, it went broke and everyone was out of jobs. Robert had a friend in the show who had a cousin in the Napa Valley who owned two houses in Rutherford, California. The houses were one on top of the other. The cousin was looking for someone to move into the upstairs house, take care of the property, fix up anything the downstairs renters needed, basically do anything that the property needed, including taking care of the vineyard and fruit orchard. For that he could live there free. He had a lot of money saved up so he was set.

When he came to Rutherford, he continued the role he had played for almost two decades. By then he had been this cowboy persona for longer than the person he was for the first almost eighteen years. So yes, he was the real thing.

"How did he get the name Powder?" Well, when he was new to the Wild West show he was constantly pestering all the cast to teach him to shoot and ride and soon they started yelling......"Take a powder; get the hell out of here!" And that's how he became Powder Burns.

Back at Curddy's Room

I didn't like to spend much time in Curddy's room. It was small and smelled bad. It was also dirty and everything in it was beat up. Each mattress had a man-sized indentation that looked a bit like a fabric fox hole, except the enemy in this room wasn't men with guns, but the kind with 8 legs.

Eight legs, a shiny black body and a designer red hourglass on its tummy. Black Widows! They were everywhere at Big Pink. They terrified me and I could find them in every direction, including directions not invented yet.

There was also an old dresser in the room with an oval mirror on top, just in case you wanted to watch yourself sleep. There were spots on the mirror where the silver was peeling off. The dresser used to have three drawers, but the one on the bottom was missing. That was fine for Curddy. One drawer fit all his belongs and still left room for a piglet to take a nap. There was the free-standing closet, just big enough for his 3 pairs of pants, 2 shirts and his threadbare jacket.

The room was papered with buttermilk-colored wallpaper with some kind of pattern, maybe purple grapes, although in my mind it could have been instructions on how to skin an animal. When it got hot in the summer, the odor of rotting paper and old glue added to the stench created by the mattresses. The paper eventually began to peel off the walls in large scallops. There was a single light bulb hanging from the ceiling on a fabric covered cord. It was clear glass and it was cool to look at; you could see the little workings of the bulb, a coil in the middle that started to glow when you turned it on. The glow would grow brighter over the next few seconds until it reached its glaring maximum brightness. It gave me a headache if I looked at it too long. I imagined it was a light like what they shone in people's faces to get them to confess, the way they showed it in the movies.

The view from the front window was blocked by the dresser, preventing the morning sunshine from entering in to cheer up the dismal room. But, the window in the back filtered in the afternoon sun and had a view of paradise: vineyards and a lush mountain range behind the bunkhouse. It was such an inviting view I sometimes felt I could be sucked right out the window and float over the vineyard to the mountains beyond.

Seeking the Mystery Photo

I was still curious about what was in Curddy's closet, so I looked for a time when I could get back there. It was November of 1953. On this morning, I trotted down the back stairs of the big house on my way to mischief when I saw Curddy sleeping in the hammock hanging between the two fig trees. That was as good as a written invitation for me to explore his room.

I inched my way across the gravel driveway being very careful not to make a sound that might wake up Curddy. I could hear every pebble of gravel grinding together under my shoes making noise that sounded as loud as an avalanche to me. Every once in awhile I would step on a dry leaf from the loquat tree and it would emit a crackling sound as loud as a forest fire. The trip across that ocean of gravel must have taken at least as long as it took Christopher Columbus to get to America.

The next test was treading the old boardwalk that ran in front of the bunkhouse. The boards were over seventy years old and every time someone walked on them they squeaked and groaned and moaned as if they were begging to be put out of their misery. It was quite an ordeal and I felt that I was making as much noise as Fred Astaire tap dancing on stage.

Finally I grabbed the handle of the screen door to pull it open. It let out a loud squeal. I thought maybe it should be called a scream door. But Curddy didn't move or lose his rhythm of snores.

Once inside, I inspected the dresser drawers. I found a white ivory plastic comb filled with hair and dirt, some worn-out under shorts and t-shirts and a letter that was torn and tattered. It looked like he must have read it hundreds of times. The envelope was postmarked 'Italy' and looked like it was written by a lady's hand. It said....

I don't know what it said. It was in Italian. So I put everything back, closed the drawer and turned slowly to my right. I had saved the best for last. I waited a few seconds, enjoying the building suspense. There was an electric fear buzzing around my head. I was only inches from my goal.

When I couldn't stand it any more, I reached out, just like I had weeks earlier, only this time there was no one to stop me. When I moved the clothes aside, I saw a photograph hanging on the back of the closet. It was old and faded, and had a brown tone to it. The picture was in a cheap wood frame and the glass covering the wrinkled, torn and tattered photo held it together. Otherwise, it would have been like so many loose puzzle pieces.

But, when I looked at it closely, I froze. I was confused… something was wrong with this picture, and what was wrong was who was in it. This photograph was of the same child I had seen in another photo. It was the same little boy in the mystery photo that sat on the fireplace mantel in the big house. It was the boy no one would identify for me. I had been haunted by it for several years.

Curddy's photo showed the boy at about 4 years old. He was smiling; on his head was a hat like Donald Duck wore. He was sitting on a fancy chair and was wearing a foreign looking Navy shirt. It looked like a studio photo.

I knew the photo in the big house was the same boy. He had different clothes and was more dressed up, and he looked a bit older. That one was in an oval silver frame. I wanted to know who that boy was and why did Nono and Nona have his photo up there when there wasn't a single photo of my mom up anywhere? But no one would give me a straight answer. When I asked my mom, she was dismissive, saying, "He was the son of a friend." Nono smiled, patted me on my knee and said, "He is a cousin in Italy."
Once, when my dad was out washing the car I interrupted his car radio music and asked, "Dad, who is that little boy in the photograph on the fireplace mantel?" His sponge did a kind of stutter skip across the car hood. He lost his rhythm, stopped, caught the beat and started

his metronome sponge movement again. Without looking at me, he said, in a fake Italian accent, "Itza ya Nono's brodder as a bambino."

Somehow I knew none of them were telling me the truth. I didn't think it was any relative. He didn't look like Nono. He didn't look like any family member! He had a really big nose and Shirley Temple blond curls trickling from under his hat. When I told my mom I wanted blond hair, she responded in a tone that told me my request was outrageous, "Ha! Your hair isn't going to turn blond. No one in the family has blond hair or blue eyes!"

I knew the boy in Curddy's closet was not Curddy's son. I had seen the photo of his son several times. So, why did Curddy have this same boy 'living' at the back of his closet? It was a mystery.

I put the photo back on the nail at the back of Curddy's closet and turned to sneak out, and there was Curddy, standing on the boardwalk, looking at me through the rusted screen door. His stare bore into my soul.

Chapter 10
Discovered

When it was too cold or wet to go play outside, I liked to play in the big, bright, warm kitchen where my parents and grandparents would hang out on those dreary days. Nono would alternate between smoking Toscanelli cigars or loading his pipe with Granger tobacco. Dad didn't smoke; well, except for what we now know is second-hand smoke. They would play cribbage or rummy and than after a few games of cards, they would both read. Dad enjoyed paperback novels while Nono preferred the Italia newspaper, the St. Helena Star or old letters from one of his many brothers. Dad would drink beer, while Nono chose wine.

Mom and Nona were usually cooking, eating or just sitting at the big kitchen table drinking coffee, wine or brandy to warm them up inside. They would talk in Italian using lots of hand gestures and drama in their voices, but they never skipped a beat in whatever they were doing whether it was cooking, eating or drinking. Their tasks were on autopilot; their gab-fest took a lot of thought.
So, when I played, if I made too much noise, my mom would say, "Go into the dining room to play. I can't hear myself think with you playing in here."
I hated playing alone in the dining room. That little boy with the strange clothes and the even stranger haunting smile taunted me with all his unanswered questions from his position above the fireplace mantel. And now I had found a different picture of the same boy in Curddy's closet.

I was transfixed, staring at that picture in Curddy's room. I didn't consider that while I was invading Curddy's bedroom and his privacy, he was silently witnessing the whole thing. He was probably sorting out what he was seeing and matching it with all his prior thoughts of the person he thought I was, as well as his feeling toward me. In seconds, my relationship with Curddy would change.

I don't know how long I had stared at the photo when I noticed a presence behind me. I quickly turned to see Curddy glaring at me. I froze; I didn't breathe and my eyes opened wide. Time moved as if someone had put molasses in the gears of a clock, and my heart was pounding so loud I could hear it. In the distance there was the sound of someone pounding grape stakes into the ground in some distant vineyard. That kathunk-kathunk sound kept time with my heart beat, almost like an executioner's countdown. I could also hear Curddy's loud, heavy breathing. His wheezing made him sound like a bull ready to charge, building up steam to blow up.

The screen in the door was at least 50 years old and was rusty, clogged with dust and full of holes. There was a ray of light coming through the back window. It beamed through the biggest hole and reflected off Curddy's left eye, giving the impression of an all-seeing, all-knowing supernatural eye. It was creepy. And there we were, staring at each other, unmoving. I was standing on one side of the screen door and Curddy was on the other. The rusty screen gave his face kind of a cinnamon-brown complexion. But something was missing….. his smile.

The problem was that we were on the wrong sides of the door. I was in his room where I didn't belong and he was on the porch looking at a bad boy who was sneaking around his personal belongings. I felt an icy cold chill over my whole body and the hair on my arms stood up as I got goose bumps. Suddenly, I had to pee really bad. My brain circled around in my skull like water going down the drain. Yes, down the drain, just like my relationship with my best buddy was about to. I saw his face twitch, just once and he squinted his power-vision left eye. But I couldn't utter a word; my voice box was embedded in a block of ice.

Curddy's mouth twitched; I flinched and then, like a fool, I ducked. I could see his face move slightly around his mouth, and then it creaked open. Without emotion, he spoke: "Your mom and dad are looking for you. They're ready to go home."

He opened the door for me to come out of his room. On the way to the door, I noticed, tacked on the wall above the mirror, my color drawing of 'Curddy the Hog Slayer.' I thought of what he had said: "I will keep it forever. It will be proof of our bond of friendship and my promise to protect you." I remembered that day when he had saved me from the huge charging hog. I suppose right now, he probably felt like blowing his nose in my drawing.

I exited out the door and down the two steps like a Slinky, low and spineless. I headed for our car that was parked under the loquat tree at the end of the driveway. He walked up behind me and yanked the photo out of my hand without speaking. I didn't even realize I still had it. I skipped a step and kept going, not looking back. My parents got in the car, and everyone said goodbyes, and no one seemed to notice that mine was without enthusiasm. I looked out the open car window at Curddy, sad that he didn't even walk us to the car. Was he mad? Was he hurt? Would he ever forgive me? Did he still love me?

What is sin?

It was my fault, totally, not just for ruining the day, but possibly my relationship with a beloved friend. I should have known it would end badly, but that day, I wasn't really thinking wisely. I was a child on a mission and all I could think of was my goal. That mission caused me to trespass where I didn't belong. I knew better. The nuns told us about the things that were sins. They daily impressed upon us that we were sinners and our souls were impure, tarnished, dirty; that we had to be purified, have First Communion, go to Confession, earn God's blessing. That was all I understood at that time. They made me afraid because they constantly told me how bad I was.
Outside of my Catholic schools and churches, the world was a great, happy, loving place. But I both hated and feared these houses and schools of the Lord, and if I hated them, how much more horrible could Hell be?

But now I was learning the difference between all those "sins" and the very personal accountability I had for violating a person's trust. All the way home from Big Pink my mind beat me up. I was sure Curddy was mad at me. He must think I was a sneak thief; he would never trust me again. He would never want anything to do with me and we would never go on another walk together ever again. Maybe, if I had been more mature, I would have understand that even though I thought all these things, it might not be what Curddy was thinking.

But, when I got home with my three best friends, Albie, Jerry and Kathleen, I put the whole "caught by Curddy" incident on the back burner. Once I got back to school the burner died out totally.

I think it was a sin to think about anything other than God when you were in the first or second grade classroom at a Catholic school. I think if any parents had spent a day or two in the classrooms and seen how there children were treated, there would have been a lot of dead nuns and no kids at the school. Pain was a daily occurrence, caused by ears or hair being pulled. There was pain from pinching the children's skin under their arms or neck and twisting, and pain from a ruler across the palms, knuckles, legs or knees, and once, for me, there was pain from a slap across the face.

There was also embarrassment. If we had to pee other than at recess time, we were out of luck. I don't remember how many times some of us sat in a puddle of piss on our desk chair, or when we would have to stand in the corner until pee ran down our legs to make a puddle for everyone to see. Then, we had to wipe it up ourselves. If we wanted to get out of our wet clothes, we would have to go to the coat room at the back of the class, strip naked and wait for the nun to come back to give us a robe we could wear until our clothes dried. Sometimes both boys and girls were naked back in that coat room. Now that had to be a sin.

After awhile, though, the embarrassment level dropped because most of us had had it happen to us. We shared an understanding and a kind of compassion for one another. But we feared the nuns. We feared the 'fathers' and were told that we were supposed to respect them. I remember that when we saw a priest, we were to lower our heads and say, "Good day, Father." We were all taught to fear a stern and vengeful God. Almost everything we did was a sin and we would be punished for it either in this life or after we were dead, or maybe both. There was no escape.

Alive we would be punished and escaping to death we would still be punished. I think there were as many children abused by nuns as there were boys molested by priests. But that's all I'm going to say about that.

Returning to Big Pink

Ten days after I slinked out of Curddy's room like an embarrassed rat deserting a sinking ship, my parents and I drove back up to Big Pink. It was a hot day, but an easy drive. Once we got to Vallejo, I started anticipating getting an ice cold Coke from the Oakville grocery. My parents gave me an allowance that I saved up to buy toys, fishing gear and model airplanes. They would also give me their pennies and I would use them on baseball cards, candy or sodas. Both of my pockets were bulging with pennies and I dug out two handfuls. Once we got to the store I didn't want to waste any time getting the money out of my tight jeans.

Mom asked, "What do you want to do this weekend?"

That was easy. "I want to go swimming at the dam. I want to hike up the mountain with Curddy. And I want to help Nono in his garden."

"Well," Mom replied, "If Curddy is busy, what do you want to do with your dad?"

Now that was a strange thing for her to say, and I said, "Curddy is never too busy to do things with me, and Dad is always too busy to do things with me." Right after I said it I thought, 'Oh, no. That sounded bad. Now Dad is going to be pissed off.' But he didn't say anything. So I asked in a cheerful voice, "What are you going to get when we get to the Oakville store?"

After several moments of silence, Dad spoke: "We're not going to stop."

I was surprised. "I got my pennies together just for this. I need a Coke, bad!"

"No," Dad responded quickly. "No. We're not stopping. You don't need a Coke from the store. When we get to your Nona's you can get a 7-Up there."
I snapped back, "I hate 7-Up! I want a Coke!"

And Dad said, in his Clark Gable voice, "Frankly, my dear son, I don't give a damn…. Oh, sorry. I shouldn't use that word…. that word 'frankly.' Really, my son, I don't give a $&*%!"

93

At which Mom responded, "Bob….. Language!"

I was going to turn red in the face and throw the twenty pennies I had been clutching tightly in my white-knuckled fists all over the back seat. I had been so happy thinking about stopping at the store and fishing that ice cold coke out of the cooler. But before I had time to erupt, we were making the left turn to the dusty driveway to Big Pink. I snapped out of it. I would have been embarrassed if anyone other than my parents had seen me acting like a mad Tasmanian devil.

Resigned to the fact that I wasn't getting a Coke and that throwing ten fits wouldn't get me anything, I dropped the pennies on the floor of the car.

As soon as we drove over the railroad track, we were on our family's property. Even if I was blindfolded, I could tell when we crossed those tracks. Rain and water from an overflowing ditch ate away the soil so that the tracks were about four inches above the road and our old cars rusty springs screamed out as we 'kathunked' over the tracks.

As soon as we were on the property I was struck with the memory of the last time I saw Curddy. The guilt and fear set in as I remembered me sneaking into his room and getting caught. I started squirming, expecting the worst.

We drove slowly, grapevines on both sides of us, walls of green, with vines bulging like they were pregnant and past their delivery date with lots of purple fruit surrounded by yellow, brown and red-orange leaves and decorated with a blackbird here and there. Then, on our right, I saw Nono's flower garden. I loved this garden because it had dozens of flowers that I never saw anywhere else. They were blue, red, orange, yellow, white, and pink; there were tiny purple flowers and big orange flowers with big purple leaves. The flower garden also had a few statues here and there, but my favorite was the lizard, made by one of the boarders that lived in the bunkhouse during the Depression. He was a blacksmith that worked at the Beaulieu mansion for the de Latours. To help pay part of his room and board and make a little extra money, he made fireplace andirons, ashtrays, decorative sculptures, etc. for Nona and the neighbors.

He also brought home stories of Mme. de Latour, Georges or their children Richard and Hélène. She would eventually travel to France, marry royalty, and return to Napa Valley as a celebrity. The de Latours had a house in San Francisco and were a part of "high society" there. Their mansion in Rutherford was a getaway for them. Hélène's husband was the Marquis Henri de Pins. After their move to Rutherford, there was a constant flow of famous people coming to spend time in the beauty and peace of the Valley. The locals were thrilled to see Winston Churchill, Clark Gable and many other rich and famous people.

I tried to think about these things and how good I always felt when I was in the garden to distract my mind from the apprehension of being confronted by Curddy. It was easy to think those good thoughts. I loved to walk out to this garden in the heat of the day. It was cooler under the two huge trees that were covered with pink flowers, color-coordinated to match the house. Nona and I would walk out to the garden in the afternoon with bread scraps from lunch and some stale crackers to feed the fish in the small pond. There were a dozen fish, huge goldfish, some orange, one white and one with spots. I named each one and they were like my buddies. In the peace of the garden with the comfort and love of my Nona by my side, the garden was a good place to be.

Straight ahead, at the end of the driveway, sat the barn. The barn door was open, but there wasn't a car or 'mach-key-na' in it. That is because no one that lived at Big Pink back then drove, so no car. Depending on his mood, my dad would drive into the barn to park. This day, he ignored the waiting barn and instead turned right. As he did, I looked to my left. There, to the right of the barn, was the bunkhouse and something on the porch made me drop my jaw. A shivering chill went down my back and I blinked several times, saying a quick prayer. What was I seeing? I was stunned, confused and bewildered. Something was wrong with this picture.

1970. Dr. UMME PSYCHOLOGIST

Chapter 11
The Mysteries of the Attic

Sometimes we search our past to solve mysteries; sometimes we regret finding an answer." Vincenzo Edwardo

The counselor, Dr. Umme, didn't waste any time. As soon as I sat down in his office, he fired a question at me, punctuated with a bit of spit that landed on his lap to join food stains sprinkled all over his pants.

"What is the most disturbing memory of your childhood?"

I answered quickly because I didn't have to sort through or weigh different events. One stood out clearly; so I told him. It felt like I was choking on the details, but I told it raw and rough, not pulling any punches. I had never before told anyone the story of that one night that had destroyed so many lives.

After I answered his question, he just stared at me for what seemed like almost the whole 50 minutes of his one-hour session. I was waiting for him to respond, to tell me something that conveyed to me that he understood how this incident haunted me. I wanted him to tell me how to purge my mind of these troubling images. But he just sat there with his elbow on his knee and his chin in the palm of his hand, just like the famous statue, The Thinker. I might have renamed his particular rendition of the statue The Stinker, just because of his poor personal hygiene and dirty, sloppy attire.
I thought perhaps he wasn't responding because of the horrifying nature of what I had just told him. He continued to stare at me, his stare and silence causing me to fidget. I looked around his small, dark, dismal office. There was nothing on the walls, no art, no framed certificates, just baby-poop-yellow-brown painted walls. His desk had a four-foot pyramid of folders, books, a pizza box and a KFC box. The blinds were closed, and the only light was from an overhead bare bulb that appeared to be around 40 watts. The room seemed like a "brown hole" capable of sucking joy out of everyone that sat in that uncomfortable guest's chair. The chair was fastened to

the floor. I suspected that was so you couldn't move it. Dr. Umme didn't want anyone moving into his space. Or maybe he was afraid a client would break the chair over his head after discovering he had paid all that money so the dear doctor could sit and stare at him, mute.

The only sound in that tomb was the doctor clicking his pen, 'click' click' click.' I felt like saying, "If you click that pen one more time I will shove it up your…. nose." or "You should see a therapist about your uncontrollable nervous habits. And, by the way, what's up with this chair being bolted down?" Here I was in a room where people who entered were hoping to be uplifted and repaired. Instead, it was depressing and boring just like Doc's name. Umme. On top of that, this doctor was actually inducing anxiety!

Finally, he moved. He stood up, took off his suit jacket and threw it on his desk, causing an avalanche of folders. The coat, along with everything else, ended up on the floor. But he acted like he meant for that to happen. I thought, 'This guy is a freaking nut case.' I vowed to myself that I would never come again.

The purpose of this session was to rid me of the five re-occurring nightmares that had me losing sleep for the past year. They were so terrible that they ended with me screaming out loud and sitting up in bed covered with sweat. They started right after my divorce, but they didn't have anything to do with my divorce as far as I could tell. Now, it looked like I wouldn't be getting any relief from these nightmares after all.

I looked at the distance between me and the door, trying to judge the chances of me making a break for it and running out of that crypt. Dr. Umme made no move to pick up his folders or jacket. Instead, he sat back down, loosened his ugly brown tie that matched his drab, downer office, and straightened to sit stiff and tall on his chair. I was still determined not to speak again until he responded to my story, so I stared back at him, noticing his beard which he had probably grown in an attempt to look like Freud. Instead, it made him look like an anemic Abe Lincoln.

With his arms settled on the arms of his chair, he now looked like another famous statue, the one of Abe in his Memorial in D.C.

97

Dr. Umme cleared his throat with a noise that sounded like a kazoo. I thought he was finally going to ask me a follow-up question to clarify the event I had just described. I was wrong. Instead of commenting on my answer to his first question, he asked another question, a very simple one. "How was your childhood?" Some people might have answered easily with "good" or "bad," but for me, it was complicated to answer simply. As I thought about the easy answer, "good," several images flashed through my mind, images of events at Big Pink that came to me looking like a losing poker hand of five bad cards. My whole thought process jammed and ground to a halt. I could have answered, "My childhood was fantastic, couldn't have been better," and it would have been the truth, with a few caveats. But those images prevented it.

I suppose we all have things in our past that haunt us, things we wish we could forget. Some of them are terrible events that can crush us if we dwell on them, the loss of a loved one or a pet, or a divorce. Sometimes things in our past resurface and bring us abundant joy; but just as quickly, others can bring nightmares. I had a few of those. The one I had just told Dr. U was one of them and it had earned me the staring contest.

When I finally replied to his second question, I said, "Some of the happiest moments of my childhood took place at my grandparents' n Rutherford, in Napa Valley. Big Pink was the name we gave to the big pink stucco home, vineyard and four other buildings. But some mysterious, troubling and scary times happened there, too."

I began with the parties that ran past midnight when everyone came together on the patio. There were five "gangs" of Old Italians that joined us there under the lights hanging from the old fig trees. The San Francisco Gang included those who had come from the same area of Italy and others they had met in the "Little Italy" area of San Francisco. There was also a Lodi Gang and a Sonoma Gang. But the best of all of them was the Napa Valley Gang. These Italians had all come to America between 1910 and some as late as 1925. They formed new communities and become a tight-knit group. Because the Napa Valley group had settled in an area that most reminded the Italians of their home country, all the others came to visit the Napa Valley group, often and for days. The bunkhouse was always full in the summer with a mix of Gang members. It was a seven- day-a-week party and they all loved me and I loved them. I was special because I belonged to Nono and Nona, the "son" (grandson) they had always wanted. In the light that illuminated the patio area with all these "Dagos", I felt warm, safe and happy. They could have killed any monster with their breath. The later the party went on, the less dark hours for me to be alone in my bedroom.

Beyond the patio, it was pitch black and I felt cold and frightened. I was especially terrified in my bedroom, for I imagined monsters, ghosts and ghouls from the slaughterhouse, barn, and attic would be coming after me. So during the daylight hours, I tried to explore those areas and prove to myself that the spooky places didn't hold anything that could harm me. In addition to knowing that nothing evil was hiding around Big Pink, there were a couple of mysteries I wanted to solve, like how did Curddy get his scars and who was the boy in the picture? And, so, I told Dr. Umme about the mysterious and scary places at Big Pink, the ones that were most inviting and strangely, to me, addictively fun. Even though they scared me, the Crypt comics drew me toward them, like steel to a magnet, even though they gave me the frights. For reasons I never understood, that's how I was drawn to the creepy places at Big Pink. The scariest one was The Slaughterhouse; just the name says it all. The second scariest was the attic above the barn.

The adventure to the attic was scary before I even got there because I had to enter the barn en route. The barn was mustard yellow with a rusted tin roof. It was the depth and width of a four- car garage, but it had never had more than one car in it at a time. The first bay was where my dad parked the car when it was raining. The two middle bays were mounded with junk that my Nono found in ditches along Hwy 29, in local vineyards or salvaged from friends who were throwing stuff out. The stack was at least ten feet high and covered with dust so thick that it looked as if someone had purposely dumped dirt on it. It was a messy jumble of strange, unidentifiable items from another world, occupied by spiders whose webs indicated they might be the size of cows. I never explored this pile directly, but I saw shadows of an old crank record player, chairs with two legs and lots of rotting cardboard boxes. The pile reeked of mold and dust, a perfume I called El Limburger Musk. My mom used to say it couldn't smell that bad unless it contained the rotting bodies of dead animals. My dad, making his usual joke about something serious, commented that Pig Bristles Maroni might be sleeping underneath the junk. But my mom objected, "Oh, Bob. He doesn't smell that bad." There was also something in that pile that was tall and shaped like a person. It reminded me of Nona's friend Fache Cavalo or "Horse Face" as my dad called her.

Whatever it was, it scared the hell out of me, and I always passed quickly, afraid that this thing wasn't creeping toward me.

I entered the barn through the fourth bay which had a huge door on rollers that was always open. I passed the huge workbench built out of two enormous planks 6" thick and 20' long. It was beat to hell, with chunks of it missing as if someone or some thing had taken a hammer to it. Half a

century earlier, when the slaughterhouse was slaughtering animals and selling their meat, the bulls were penned nearby. It seemed as if some of them had danced around on the workbench and left their hoof prints behind along with a variety of stains. There was an open can of kerosene by the door and the odor mingled with the oily smell of the workbench where my dad and Nono oiled things. The only light came through the open doorway and the one 2'x4' filthy window. All the cobwebs that covered it let in a gauzy glow that highlighted a Rutherford-green wall cabinet, the only other furniture in the barn. The cabinet was always locked and I vowed to pick the lock some day and find out what was so special that it had to be locked up.

Finally, adding to the barn's dreary charm, was the wall above the workbench where Nono put the hangable junk. It was covered top to bottom, right to left with rusty, dusty stuff: mole traps, bear traps, ax heads, cracked leather strips, whips, rusty chains and cowbells, spurs, rolls of wire and other things that looked sinister. If something could hang, it was on that wall. If it was too large to hang, it was tossed into the junk pile in the middle bays. I saw Nono add stuff to the wall, but I never saw him use any of it. Eventually, when Nono sold the place, everything in there would be thrown out to the dump where it all belonged.

Actually, the only thing that was saved from the junk in the barn was the "sharpening stone." This was a big stone wheel about three feet in diameter mounted on a sawhorse with a foot pedal. It was the only uncontaminated thing in the barn, the one thing I actually saw Nono use. I watched him sit on the sawhorse and pedal, getting the clean white stone spinning as he pedaled faster.

When it was really sailing, he would hold anything that needed sharpening, a kitchen knife or ax head for example, against it. He had mounted an empty olive oil can with a hole in it four inches above the wheel which dripped water on the stone to cool it. I loved it when my Nono would let me sit and pedal it. His strong hands would guide my small hands to sharpen various instruments. I loved being in the barn with Nono, my dad, or my big strong buddy Curddy. Otherwise, the barn was just a means of getting to the attic. Which is where I was headed on this day.

There was only one way up to or down from the attic, a shaky ladder with slippery rungs. The top end of the ladder went through an always-open trap door. When I started to climb, the ladder bounced and slid back and forth. My feet would slip every few rungs, but I hung on. I hated that my head was the first thing through the trap door hole. That meant I could only look straight ahead when I got to the top. If there was something horrible and monstrous waiting to jump me or rip my head off, it would be easy for it to be out of my sight. Once, I tried to twist around quickly to see, but I lost my balance and fell. I tried to grab the ladder on my way down but was unsuccessful. I fell flat on my back on the dirt floor. Fortunately, the dirt was soft and deep. I was knocked out, but Doctor Wood, the Doc that delivered me and over a thousand babies in the Valley in his 101 years, said, "Nothing broken. He has a hard head, but he shouldn't hit it again too soon."

Once up in the attic, it was dark and creepy. The only light came through the small trap door and a 6-inch square window at the far end. When there is enough light, your eyes can see any dangers around you and your mind will give you options, if needed, to move to safety. But, in the dark, your mind takes over the job of your eyes and it can sometimes create monsters without finding a way to safety.

If the spiders in the barn were the size of cows, the ones in the attic had to be bigger. There were hundreds of them and their webs held corpses of hollow bugs with their life's blood sucked out of them. I not only hated spiders, I was stark-raving terrified of them, no matter how small they were. If I got too close to a spider and suddenly noticed it, I jumped, my mind moving me faster and further than my legs could carry me. It gave new meaning to being "scared out of my skin." I knew many of the webs in the attic had spiders in them, alive and waiting for food or a small child to get too close and become trapped in their net. My parents had introduced me to these dangerous shiny black monsters, turning them over to show me the red hourglass on their bellies. My dad kept telling me that if one of these Black Widows were to bite me, I would drop dead on the spot. Entering the attic had already raised my level of fear.

Now I began to paw through some of the boxes, most of them containing a lot of nothing. But in the fourth box, I found something. As soon as I opened the box, I felt a chill. My body shook and my mind flashed with scary thoughts. I couldn't move. I was holding something that felt evil, only I had no clue what it was. I wanted to find a big person to help me understand what it was and keep me safe. I knew that my dad, Nono, and Curddy had all gone to the feed store and I began to panic. Was something following me as I exited the attic, or was I holding the danger?

Then I saw Greasy Lips Lipitti sitting at the patio table, drinking whiskey and playing solitaire. He and Pistol Pete were part of Petaluma gang, the old Italians who had settled in Petaluma. So, I walked over to Greasy Lips, noticing that he had on his maroon shirt buttoned to his neck. Over that, he had a gray shirt, and the way his chest and stomach bulged out, he looked like a robin red-breast. He almost always had a cloth napkin tucked into the top of his shirt. His pants were Levi's that were too small and ready to pop buttons because he ate and ate. I jumped up on the bench next to him and gave him a hug; he gave me a greasy kiss on both cheeks. I loved Greasy
and he was always nice to me. My mom said, "He wants to have children of his own; he loves them so much."

I anxiously whispered in his ear, "Do you know what these things are?"

He took a look and said, "It's a Ouija board."

"What does it do?" I asked.

The tone of his response told me he was fearful, "People use it to talk to dead loved ones." I was totally mystified. Why would anyone want to do that? "Who uses it?" I asked.
He inhaled deeply and said, "It is your Nona's."
Now I was really getting scared. "Why does she want to talk to dead people?"

He paused, guzzling some whiskey straight from the bottle, some of it dribbling down his chin. He began, "She wants....."

But, just then, Pistol Pete came rushing down the stairs of the main house. "Shut your greasy mouth, Lipitti!" He interrupted. "Jimmy, Lippitti drinks too much, as you can see. He makes stuff up. No one can talk to the dead. That's a game.... give it to me." He yanked the two pieces out of my hands.

"I'm going to ask my Nona about it!" I said, angrily.

"Don't do that!" He cautioned.

So when my dad, Nono, and Curddy came home, I ran to Curddy for a comforting hug and explained about the strange board I found and how Pistol Pete was mean to me and took it from me. I was surprised when he said, "That board is not yours. Your Nona found it in the cooler room of the slaughterhouse, so it is hers. It is not a game or toy. And it is NOT for children to use. I'll explain it to you when you are older."

If my Nona was using that strange board to talk to dead people, why? And who was she talking to? Did all families have so many secrets and mysteries or just Italians? Or was it just my family?

Curddy continued to promise things that he would tell me when I was older, and I eventually did find out some of it from him after he died.

Chapter 12
The Séance

Doctor Umme interrupted me, "What do you mean, Curddy gave you answers after his death? Are you telling me you saw his ghost? You expect me to believe you saw a ghost?"

I groaned out slowly "Yes, I saw a ghost."

He asked, "Did you see the ghosts with help from the Ouija Board?"

As I began to answer, Dr. Umme interrupted me again. "Think of each of your re-occurring nightmares as movies. What would the titles be?"

I had been surprised earlier when Dr. Umme said he had time and we could extend our session. But it turned out to be a very short extension from my perspective because he kept interrupting before I was finished answering his questions. Then he said that the time was up, and he suggested that I should try to figure out why some of the events that took place in my childhood still haunt me as an adult. He also advised, "You should also sort out what those recurring nightmares are really about."

As much as I thought he was a worthless, clueless con-man of a therapist, what he suggested about investigating the nightmares and childhood trauma rang true to me. Nevertheless, I had an issue with paying him for a 50-minute hour when he spent most of the time staring at me in silence. Then there was his pen-clicking, toe-tapping and kazoo throat clearing to disturb me even more. I first thought he was clearing his throat to prepare to talk. No such luck. Most of the time he sat there as if his lips were super-glued shut. In the end, his contribution to the session was several questions and a few sentences which could be summarized as a suggestion to figure it out myself.

I did inquire, "Do many people appreciate this "mime style" of counseling? You ask me questions that I am paying you to answer, for you to tell me why I have these dreams and how I can get rid of them and for you to tell me how to flush my mind of that major family disaster and the other incidents of distress." His response was to sit unmoving and silent, staring at me and clicking his pen. With that, I left his office for the first and last time. All the way home, I thought about those nightmares and what might have caused them.

When I got home, I parked in my garage, turned off the engine and silenced the radio. Quiet followed, except for the "tick, tick, tick" from the cooling engine. Sitting there, thinking, I decided that I would go outside and sit in my peaceful backyard. It was a great place to contemplate life, liberty and the pursuit of happiness, a good place to meditate. I began to feel good, positive, even a bit excited to start doing my own psychotherapy. As I began to sing, "All Right Now," I opened the car door a bit too exuberantly and it smashed into a shelf, knocking loose a can of motor oil which landed, "Koonk" on my head, and elicited some wretched outburst of pain.

Continuing the mood-ruining set of circumstances, as I staggered to the front door rubbing my head, I noticed the newspaper in the planter, soaking wet. I began to lose my focus. I twisted the paper to drain the water back into the planter where it belonged and took out the sports section so I could check on the A's and threw the rest of the paper in the garbage, as I did each day. But then, I discovered that the Oakland A's had won the night before and were four games ahead of Kansas. I was in a good mood again, forgetting the bump on my head and refocusing on the new project I was going to work on.

I walked into the front room and picked out an extra long cigar from the humidor, one that would last an hour. I took off the cellophane, put the cigar up to my nose and took a sniff of the rich smelling, aromatic tobacco. Good fresh cigars have a scent as enticing as fresh ground coffee, only I wouldn't want to smoke coffee or brew tobacco. I clipped off the end of the cigar and then lit it with a wood stick match, and took a rewarding puff. Nice. Then I uncorked a very good bottle of 1965 Beaulieu Rutherford Cabernet.

I loved Beaulieu, aka BV, wine. It also helped that I was able to get a 50% discount on all BV wines because both my mom and Nono used to work there in the early '40s. Nono shared the job as horticulturist with three other men at the mansion owned by the De Latours, the founders of BV. He also worked in their vineyard keeping the vines healthy. Then, after World War II he worked weekends as a night watchman at the winery, Colt pistol, big flashlight and all. That Colt became a source of enjoyment for me in my teen years. My mom's job at BV varied. She worked on bottling and wherever else she was needed in the winery. Mom had many interesting stories about working there and all the cavorting that went on amongst the huge floor to ceiling wine barrels. That is until all the young men left working in the winery for working in the war. Their absence caused the winery to lose its spirit of fun and created a dark cloud hanging over everyone as they began to hear reports that some of these young men would never return to work here or anywhere else.

When I was an adult, and I went to the BV tasting room to buy a case of wine, my mom would ask for her employee discount, and they would ask when she worked there. When she told them the years she was there, everyone asked: "Did you work with the legendary winemaker Andrè Tchelistcheff?" She would smile as if she knew some private joke about him and say, "Oh yes he was everywhere in the winery. He was a big shot legend alright."

So with my bottle of wine that came with a history, I grabbed a big bowl wine glass, my cigar, and an ashtray and I walked outside to sit in a lounge chair in my lush tropical-themed backyard. My favorite attraction at Disneyland was the Jungle Cruise and I loved that jungle environment. If they had a jungle in the "Happiest Place on Earth," I decided my backyard could have one too, minus the fake animals, of course. It was a great place to escape from the realities of the world and relax.
Sitting on the deck overlooking the fish pond, listening to the sound of the waterfall and watching the golden Koi swim around and around was refreshing, almost hypnotic.

After enjoying two glasses of wine, I was able to clear my mind of all the static of the day, including the falling oil can and wet newspaper. Now I was ready to start picking apart the nightmares that most likely were based on distorted versions of incidents from my past. I started making a mental priority list for future in-depth analyzing. Soon I had my game plan; I would take each of the unwarranted, troubling incidents from my childhood, and see if they had become intertwined in my nightmares. Then I would use logic to debunk, first, the incidents and then, the nightmares. Sitting there, enjoying the soothing environment, my sense of taste having a festival with my cigar and wine, I was starting to think that I really could deflate these bogus fears. While the incidents that created my phobia of black widow spiders were actually unjustifiable, my child's mind had made them something more, much more dangerous than they really were. I had endured several years of being close to black widow spiders and had once frozen in fear watching one crawl across the back of my hand, up my bare arm and onto my shirt sleeve, where I flicked it off using a baseball card (the card was Ted Williams). Yet, despite all those exposures and not one bite. Finally, in third grade, we learned about spiders and I found out that I would not, in fact, drop dead if a black widow bit me. My dad had terrified me with lies about them, but now it should be an easy fear/nightmare to erase.

I decided that the power to cleanse my mind of all these 'dis-eases' was not going to come from a doctor, but from within me. I became convinced that my mind, my mental strength was more powerful than the 'fairy stories' that lingered in the back of my mind. Some were frightening things that felt insurmountably terrifying at the time, but in reality, I had survived and it was all okay. I had to think over the nightmares and dismiss each part of them one by one.

The Nightmare

The nightmare begins with me locked in the living/dining room at Big Pink. I hated that room in real life for real reasons. No light entered the room from the windows which were covered with heavy dark green drapes and only a bit of dim lighting came from a small overhead light with four fake-flame light bulbs. The atmosphere was creepy. There was an absence of any vibrant color; everything was either dark green or brown and lifeless. The word 'dismal' makes it seem more cheerful than it was. The only furnishings in the room were a round wood table with eight hard chairs with even harder cushions and a couch that felt like it was cast iron. It was always cold in that room. While the room had a fireplace, which could have warmed up the mood and temperature of the room, it was never used due to my mom's and Nona's pathological fear of indoor fires of any kind.

I never understood how no one in my family could feel that there was something wrong in there. The doors to the dining room were always closed, which told me that at least one person felt there was something in there that they didn't want getting out. The room was almost never used; everything took place in the kitchen in rainy weather or on the patio for everything else. So this dining area was only used for special holiday dinners, and, often, something bad would happen.

One Thanksgiving we ate in there and invited Aquesto. He got drunk and started an argument with our guest Paché; he ended it by throwing a glass of wine in his face. Then he staggered out the back door and fell down the stairs, breaking his arm and splitting his forehead. He was left with a big crescent-shaped scar for the rest of his life. Not that he had a pretty face before the dinner.

One Easter, my Nona almost choked to death on a piece of lamb. Another Easter, Paché noticed during dinner that his zipper was down. Looking around to make sure no one saw him doing it, he zipped up, but he also unknowingly zipped the tablecloth, too. When he got up to go to the bathroom, he pulled the tablecloth and everyone's dinner off the table onto the floor. At another dinner, everyone got food poisoning. And those were only a few of the bad experiences in that room. It was almost like it was haunted. The room was newly built around 1928, so whatever gave this room its bad vibes happened in the prior 25 years or so.

There were three doors leading out of the room. One went out to the front porch, but no one ever used it. After all, the kitchen was the heart of Big Pink and the back patio was its soul. The back porch door went from the kitchen to the patio and that's the door everyone used.

The door opened to the long hallway that went past each of the three bedrooms and ended at the one and only bathroom. I hated this hall, too. There was only a 40-watt overhead light in the middle of the hall, which left each end of the hall dark. In addition, every step you took caused the floorboards to give a groan like an old man in pain, and the cold hardened linoleum crackled like breaking bones. I sprinted down this passageway as though I was racing through purgatory.

The third door went to the bright happy, warm kitchen where family was always waiting to greet anyone that entered.

In the dream, I am locked in that room. There is no light, not even a candle, only a bit of half- moon light coming through a broken window that someone has ripped the drape from. I am almost frantic, trying to claw my way through the door; it is hard for me to breath. I feel like I am drowning in air that has become thick, brown and syrupy. It continues to thicken, making it harder for me to walk or even move. Then, I sense something moving close to me. I am afraid to turn my head and look, but I can feel hot breath on my cheek. I smell death. Then I hear a deep throaty growl. I start to scream and am soon crying for my Nona to save me, but I realize she is dead. Then I call for my mom, but there is no response. I hear voices behind me and turn around. There at the table are my Nona, Curddy, and an old nun, my second-grade teacher from my Catholic school days, who is also dead.

In my dream, I know these three people are dead, but I also know that my Nona and Curddy loved me, so I struggle to walk over to them. I am terrified and find it hard to move through the thick air. When I finally make it to the table, I try to ask them for their help to escape the room, but they don't hear me. They are chanting, eyes closed; their hands are on a Ouija board. I know it's a séance and they are trying to talk to someone dead, but who?

Then people who look like zombies come falling down the chimney into the fireplace. There is a fire going, and as each zombie walks out of the fireplace, it's flaming. The zombies stagger toward me and I open my mouth to scream, but nothing comes out.

That's when I wake up screaming, drenched in sweat, and I can't get back to sleep the rest of the night.

It's now obvious to me that my nightmare came from my contact with the Ouija board, beginning with the day I found it. That's where I will start tomorrow, with that day.....

1953

After Pistol Pete yanked the Ouija board out of my hand, I was angry. I ran out into the vineyard and sat down under a grapevine and threw a tantrum. I tore grapes and leaves off the vines and threw them up in the air which, looking back on it now, was pretty stupid. Some of the smashed grapes landed on my head, "SPLAT." That pissed me off even more. Then, as if to add insult to injury, a crow landed on top of a raggedy, gray grape stake and made a "Caww caw" noise at me. I thought the crow was laughing at me, so I grabbed a dirt clod and threw it at him. I missed the crow and sent the clod flying way above my black-feathered tormentor. Then I heard a shout and someone yelling in Italian. When I stood up and looked in the direction of the yelling, I saw Greasy Lips brushing dirt out of his thin, gray hair. I hurriedly ducked back under the vines, trying to hide, and I waited. As I heard another crow land on the top of a vine, I looked up. But I didn't see the crow because my eyes suddenly focused on the spider web right above my face and, in that web, the biggest spider I had ever seen. I let out a scream and sprinted out of the vineyard and up the stairs into the kitchen and into the arms of my Nona. She must have heard my siren scream because she was waiting, with arms open.

Shortly after that, my dad, Nono, and Curddy got home, and I ran straight to the person I thought would be most likely to help me get that board back, Curddy. I was surprised and hurt when he said that he couldn't help me. I had thought that I could always depend on Curddy for what I wanted. Now I wanted to play with that board and Curddy wouldn't help me. If it made the adults so out of sorts, there must be something fun about it.

That strange board I had found in the crumbling cardboard box in the attic puzzled me. Obviously, since the adults were acting so strangely, it held some kind of magical power. I hadn't gotten a real good look at it because of the weird vibes I had felt when I held it. It had seemed to tingle, and that scared me and thrilled me at the same time. But when I had tried to find an adult to explain it all to me, Pistol Pete butted in and took it away. I tried to remember everything I could about the board and the other wood piece that went with it. I knew there were letters and numbers on the stained, yellowed-with-age paper that was glued to a stiff board. One of its corners was peeling up, it was so old. I also remembered strange symbols on it. I wanted to look at it again; I had to find out where it was and what it was.

Sometimes when my grandparents or my mom gave me the run-around, I could get answers from my dad, especially if he didn't know that they didn't want me to know something. So, off I went to find him. As I skipped across the powdery dirt under the fig trees, it sent up dusty smoke signals that, in my mind, spelled out, "Help me." I found my dad in the pigeon coop, talking to his feathered friends. He was a big lover of animals and critters and had about a dozen pigeons in a variety of colors. I had only one, my Homer, so named because he was a homing pigeon just like his coop mates.

The coop had been built around the same time as the slaughterhouse, around 1894. The wood on both of them had the same appearance, gray and weather-beaten, with just a hint of whitewash left. The pigeon coop was about 8' x 11' and its outer frame held chicken wire. Inside, by the front door of the coop, was a cement fountain. The fountain was built in 1936 by the same man that made the garden fishpond for my Nona's birthday. The wild birds loved to frolic in the 2 or 3 inches of water in the top tier of the fishpond, just as the pigeons did in that coop fountain. There were 14 little partitioned nests where the pigeons slept when they were not splashing in the fountain, eating seed out of the V-shaped trough, or otherwise occupied. There was a pigeon exit; it was a screen trap door that my dad opened in the morning so they could do what birds want to do, fly over the beauties of nature. Once they were all out, he would close the trap. There was another 'trap door' that had stiff wires that hung down and could be pushed in so the pigeons could come back home, as was their nature to do every early evening; but they could not exit that way. My duties were to put some seeds in the trough each morning, dried peas, seeds and other things that bird-brained creatures liked. Then, I turned the knob to add water to the birdbath fountain.

When I got to the coop door that day, I looked through the screen to make sure no pigeons were close to the door waiting to fly out after their curfew. I turned the wood latch, opened the door and slid inside. A couple of my favorite pigeons landed on my shoulders to greet me and I greeted them with a handful of seed from my right jean pocket. It tickled when they quickly pecked with their beaks; they did it over and over because they only got a few seeds per peck. If you watch pigeons walk, their heads usually dip down and quickly back up, over and over. Even when they are not eating, they're just in the habit of dipping their heads.

I confessed, "Dad, I found something funny in the attic. It was… I think it is called a Wee Gee board. What does it do?"

"You shouldn't be playing with that!" He exclaimed. "The nuns and priests would think that is a sin."

"Come on, Dad. Why is it a sin?"

"I didn't say it was a sin. I said the nuns and priests would think it was a sin, just like they think it's a sin if you eat meat on Friday. My mom, your Nona Zirkelbach, raised us as Catholics. Your Nono and Nona are Catholic, and so is your mom. Your mom wanted you in Catholic school. Okay, so we're all Catholic. Not that I agree with all their rules. I don't believe that children are born with a heart full of sin and if you don't have First Communion you are destined for hell. I looked through the Bible to find where it says if you have a hot dog on Friday, it is a sin and you have to go to confession. Where does it say in the Bible that we have to pray to Mary? Don't get me started! If I keep going, I might get so mad that I will walk through the vineyard to your Nona's little church and punch Father Petrochelli in the nose."

113

"DAD!" I screamed. "Please. I don't want to talk about nuns! It makes me want to walk back into St. Elizabeth's and take the 3' long poker out of Sister Fuser's hand and whip her with it, to see how she would like it."

"Bob, what are you telling him?" My mom said. My dad and I both jumped because we hadn't noticed her sneak up on us.
Dad replied, "I'm not telling him anything he doesn't already know. He found your mom's Ouija Board and wanted to know what it does and why she had it. Pistol Pete took it away from him, so he asked Curddy to get it back before he asked me. Well, Curddy told him no, so he comes to me. I told him that the church would consider it a sin."

Now I got Mom's famous stern, I'm-not-happy-with-you look. "Jim, go upstairs and wash up; we have to head home soon." I did as I was told. I walked to the bathroom, passing Nona with my head lowered out of embarrassment for taking her Ouija board.

Soon, we were ready to leave. Nono picked me up and gave me a big hug and kiss on the lips. Nono handed me over to Nona and she gave me a crushing hug, causing me to go "Ooooffff."

We got in the car and started up the driveway to Hwy 29. As I looked out the back window, I knew I would see Nono with his left arm around Nona's ample waist, waving with his right hand and Nona, waving with her left. This was the same exact scene every time we left.

That comforting scene should have settled me down after the troubling incident with the Ouija board. Instead, through the dust clouds our tires kicked up, I caught a glimpse of someone or something standing in the doorway of the barn. My first thought was that it was a bear; it seemed to be brown and shaggy. I jumped and let out an involuntary shout, "Ahhhh!" My mom demanded: "What's the matter now!? Why are you yelling?"

I responded, "There was something scary in the barn. I think I saw it! A bear."

My mom calmly responded, "Jim, we have talked about this before. There are no bears around here. There are none in Oakland and there were none in Richmond. It is all in your imagination."

I remember when my fear of bears had started about three years earlier., We were living in the housing projects in Richmond, California. My dad bought me a Little Golden Record to add to my collection entitled "Bear Comes to Town." The records went with the Little Golden Books, with titles like "The Saggy Baggy Elephant" "Little Red Riding Hood," etc. I loved all the books and the records, except "Bear Comes to Town." The bear had a scary, deep growling voice and it frightened me so badly that I would actually hide under the covers. For years afterward, I was afraid a bear was going to rip me apart. Now, when I was sure I had seen a bear in the barn, my mom thought I was just scared because of that record.

But, that night I could not sleep and the rest of the week was rough too. I kept worrying that the bear had killed my grandparents. They didn't have a phone, so I couldn't call to check on them. That week I did a lot of praying and apologizing to God, in hopes that He would take care of them.

On the following Friday, we headed back to Big Pink, but I had conflicting emotions. I was anxious to find out if my grandparents were alive, but I was also afraid of the bear, or whatever it was, and I dreaded our return visit. What if it wasn't a bear, but something even scarier?

That was the state I was in as we bumped down the driveway. I decided to close my eyes and cover my face with my hands. I didn't want to see the empty driveway with my grandparents missing because they had been the bear's dinner. I was so sure when we left the last time I saw a bear or worse yet a monster in the barn behind my grandparents.

When I heard my mom screech, I almost pissed my pants. I thought 'Oh no she sees them half chewed up. Then she laughed, "Oh what a great surprise, look, Teresa, is here." I looked up, and not only were my grandparents standing there without a single bite missing out of their bodies but next to them, wearing a cheerful smile, was one of my mom's closest friends. Teresa was younger than my mom and had been "back East" somewhere going to college, so my mom hadn't seen her for almost a year.

Well, that was "stoooopidd," all that wasted sweat, fear, and nightmares. All these terrors took so much out of me!

In the Early 1970s

In time, after my divorce and counseling, I cleansed my soul. I started going back to church. The Catholic Church I used to go to with my mom, Christ the King, had started what they called Folk Mass. The sermon was in English (they used to be Latin), and there were people playing guitar and lots of singing. My faith helped save me.

But there was still one thing one really big thing that I couldn't wrap my mind around. It was something that had really happened. One of my family members had killed another family member, in the most horrific mind-shredding ways imaginable. I found out the details of it and all the other mysteries when I was seventeen, when I spent a week with my Nono at Big Pink, in a failed attempt to earn money picking grapes. One night after dinner he gave me a book-sized letter from the no-longer-living Curddy. What a revelation!

Chapter 13
The Broken Man

Powder Burns was right. The creature did not return to the Monster Shed. I never saw him again. I was afraid to tell my family about the incident because they might put restrictions on where I could go or what I could do around Big Pink. The fact that I could run wild and free was the only thing that kept me from being bored stiff when I was there.

Powder agreed to keep the whole incident our secret because the creature hadn't actually harmed me, at least not physically. Powder told me he was mad at me because I didn't listen to his warnings. But I could tell that there was another part of him that enjoyed being my hero. He made it much more dramatic than it really was, shooting through the door to the Monster Shed and all.

Powder did talk to the sheriff about seeing the creature in the shed, although he said he was the one who had seen it. Word was rumbling through the Valley like summer thunder about creature sightings. Some folks had seen it run off with vegetables, chickens, pigeons, lambs, and pigs.
Then, a month after I saw the creature, our neighbor Mr. Hacks shot it. It had been hiding out in his water tower. Mr. Hacks wounded it, so the sheriff had to tend to his leg wound. Then they scrubbed him clean, clipped his nails and hair, shaved him, put him in clean clothes and threw him in jail. He was questioned and accused of theft and double murder. He admitted guilt for stealing small livestock and vegetables, but he swore he had never murdered any people or cats.

The St. Helena Star printed an interview done by Sally Sifti, their ace reporter. Powder read it to me and I learned that the creature was really Jess String. He had been a farm worker in and around the Salinas Valley from the time he was eight years old. When he had completed second grade, his parents took him out of school to work with them in the fields. He didn't remember ever living in a house; his family had moved from one field worker's shack to another.

117

These were one-room dwellings some with no electricity or plumbing. They were lit by lanterns and a fireplace, which also gave heat. And there were outhouses and outside showers. It was hard work and harsh living conditions, for sure.

When Jess was sixteen, he jumped on a freight train and never saw his family again. He never worked or had a regular place to live either. Instead, he would jump on a freight train, get off at a small town and hide out in an abandoned house or barn. In warm weather, he just slept in a field or vineyard. Whatever he needed, whether it was food or clothes or anything else, he would steal. When things got too hot as a result of people talking to each other and realizing there was a thief in the area, and he was afraid he was close to getting caught, he would just hop on another freight train and move on to another town.

I saw a few photos of him in the newspaper, but I couldn't see how the man in that photo could have been the creature I saw. Well, except for his eyes. Those spooky eyes were huge and bugged out like two sunny-side-up eggs. With the "creature" in jail, I felt safe, and I got over my fear of the monster shed. It was still creepy, but only in an adventurous way.

The shed had a huge hole in the corner nearest the pigeon coop and there was a beehive in it. Hundreds of busy bees flew in and out every daylight hour and there were wax and honey dripping down the wall. I would throw dirt clods or shoot my BB-gun at it. A few times the bees did fly-bys of my head. There was another hole in the roof where wild pigeons flew in and out. Those I shot with the .22 semi-automatic rifle. I prided myself on being a good shot, but I was too immature to know it was wrong to shoot living creatures just for the fun of it.

I did go into the shed again, just once, about six months after the first time. The Hack's nephew, Bud, came up from L.A to stay with them for a few months. Although at age twelve, he was older than me, sometimes he came over and we would play. One day he noticed the Monster Shed and said, "Let's go in it!" I felt a cold chill run through my body and I was afraid. But I was also embarrassed; I couldn't show fear or Bud would laugh at me and tease. He might never play with me again. So I agreed.

I don't remember very much of what happened that day. I remember it seemed lighter inside and not as creepy as my first visit. I also remember that Bud and I sat on a big mound of damp magazines and he showed me some of the girly magazines that were part of that mound. The next thing I remember, Bud and I were in Nono's vineyard playing cowboys and Indians. That was before it became politically incorrect to do that. Something must have happened between the girly magazines and playing in the vineyard, but I have never been able to recall it.

Resolving the Nightmares

As I followed through on my plan to heal myself, since Dr. Umme was no help, I examined many of my frightening memories like the night the ghost materialized through my closed bedroom door. My fear of the dark, which began when I was two, didn't really get better until I had to convince my own children that there was nothing to be afraid of, that Big Pink was a safe place, just as safe in the total black darkness of the night as it was in bright, happy daylight.

But I had really seen the ghost. It confirmed that there was something strange going on at Big Pink, something supernatural, although I didn't know that word at the time. Those strange goings-on scarred my mind with fear in my early years. But by the time I was twelve, the fear had changed to fascination and I thought it would be cool to see another ghost. Unfortunately, that didn't happen.

And then, there was the shed. It had just seemed to appear one day with its sinister appearance. Like my Nona's Ouija board, it gave off weird vibes that made me tingle with fear. I could imagine it humming with energy, like the noise of cicada; and it gave off strange waves of heat that took shape in my imagination as animals or birds that looked reptilian. I did try to get Powder to look at the eerie creatures I was seeing, but he just commented, "Well.....
Ah....I see... wavering lines. That's it!"

119

But I really had been chased by the creature in the shed. It had given me the heebie-jeebies; no, it was worse than that. It had scared the hell out of me. After I learned the creature was a man, a drifter who was hiding out there, the shed no longer seemed haunted. But it still bothers me that I can't remember what happened to me on my second visit there. And, of course, the most troubling thing of all is that my mom and three Big Pink neighbors are positive: "There never was a building back there." Even after I dug up two photos that showed it in the background, they insisted it was an equipment shed owned by Brusatory. Oh "NO SHED, POSITIVE THERE WAS NO SHED". Then I show them a photo of it and then. "Oh yeah, Brusatory's shed."

As for the Ouija board, I found it again when I was fourteen. My buddy, Woodie, was with me and he said he had used one before, so he showed me how. I tried to contact the spirits of Curddy and my Nona, the board's original owner. I learned later that my Nona was never able to reach the spirit she was trying so hard to contact. The more she tried and failed, the more upset she became until Nono hid it in the garage. When Woodie and I were using it, I thought it was strange the way the pointer moved around, and I accused Woodie of moving it. I knew that I wasn't. But, after a time of wandering aimlessly around the board pointing to letters that didn't spell anything, I got tired of it. Maybe it was spelling words in Italian.

Years later, I bought a new Ouija board, but it didn't feel strange or mystical. I had no fear of it; it was just a toy, nothing like my Nona's which seemed to have mystical powers. When my buddies and I were in high school and drunk, we would take the Ouija board out and contact UFOs, vampires, Godzilla, and other things out of the ordinary. But it only worked when we were drunk.
I once thought it had spelled out the word, "Fire," as a message from my deceased Nona. But now I don't believe that Ouija boards actually contact anyone.

Returning to Big Pink and Curddy

The last time I had seen Curddy, he was on the other side of the screen, watching me sneak a peek at the photo in his closet. Now, we were returning to Big Pink and I was figuring that my first hour wouldn't be spent swimming or fishing at Conn Dam. No. The first hour would be spent washing and waxing the dusty car as my dad's helper. I loved the smell of the wax, but I hated putting the wax on because I could never do it right to please my dad. I was distracted thinking about the upcoming chore and didn't notice my buddy Curddy right away. When I did, I knew something was wrong.

He was sitting in a chair, but not in the sun outside his room where he usually sat. Today, he was sitting at the far end of the porch in the dark of the shade, almost as if he was hiding from the light and didn't want to be seen. He looked shrunken, deflated, somehow much smaller, and ill. What shocked me most, though, was the chair he was sitting in. It wasn't one of our green wooden chairs; instead, it was made of wood and steel and had wheels. It was old and beat up, too.

I don't remember where or when I had seen a wheelchair before that day. It might have been at the Veterans Home in Yountville or one of our many trips there to see the movies for a quarter apiece. But, when I saw Curddy in it, I knew there was a problem; he couldn't walk. My mind tried to puzzle out what had happened to cause this problem. Had a mountain lion gotten to him? Did he get caught on the tracks and have the train run over him? Or maybe he'd gone hunting with Paché and accidentally been shot in the leg because Paché was such a fumbler.

Curddy didn't even look up when Nono yelled to Nona, "Mama, Jimmy is here!" He looked sad, and life seemed to have vanished from his soul. He really did look like he was trying to hide from the world. There he was with his watch open, staring down at the photo. But he was very still, not moving. And I couldn't move either. I was afraid of what he might be like now; he looked like a stranger.

My mom turned around to look at me in the back seat and explained, "Your friend had a stroke.
He can't walk. I didn't tell you before because I didn't want to scare you. I didn't want you to worry and fret and make things in your mind worse than they really are. I thought if you were able to talk to

him, you would know how he really is. I'm sorry. Maybe I should have told you before."

Really? Figure that one out. No, mom, don't prepare me. Just let me be drop-dead shocked, stunned and traumatized. Oh, I'm sure she tried to do what she thought was best for me. And I'm also sure that whatever way she had told me at any time would have hit me hard. It still would have crushed me. What was a stroke anyway? I didn't know. Maybe it meant someone had struck him, hit him so hard with a big stick that they had broken his legs. I didn't know the word "stroke" then, but in a year, when my Nona had one…. well, by then I knew. And I knew what it did to a person. I knew it all too well.

I had a sad feeling that my pal was lost and gone forever, and it felt like a fist had punched me in the stomach and the breath had gone out of me. Of course, my first thoughts were selfish, thinking about what I would miss out on. Then I felt guilty for those thoughts. This was my good friend. He must be miserable, far more than I would be just missing a few walks. Then, I felt a deep sadness. How horrible to be in a wheelchair, I thought. And he must be in pain, lots of it.

I wanted to do something for Curddy, but what? Then, a light bulb in my mind turned on, bright. I knew something that made him happy. Me. I picked my face up off the car floor, put on a fake smile and skipped over to him, spouting gravel behind me. When I got to the porch, I said, "Smile, Curddy! Jimmy's here." And he did.

I wanted to give him a hug, but it was awkward with him in the wheelchair. So, I asked, "My favorite buddy, would it hurt you if I sat on your lap?"

He slowly raised his head and looked into my eyes, seeming surprised to see me. He paused a few moments and then quietly replied, "Jimmy, remember what I told you before? You could never hurt me. You bring joy to my life. Have a seat." He patted a spot by his knee, one of the few clean places on his pants. I sat on his knee, put my skinny, short arms around his neck, pulled his head down and gave him a kiss and hug together as one move. His cheek was like kissing damp, hot, salty sandpaper.

And he hugged me back, strong and reassuring. For those few seconds, it was like everything was okay. I smelled the familiar scent of tobacco, his slight musky body odor and, now, a strong smell of wine. That mix of aromas, along with his large strong hands holding both of my wrists and his comforting voice reassured me that my friend was still there, even though he would never be the same. I realized that our relationship would change. It turned out to be a very big eye opener and contained lessons for me about many things: unconditional love, patience, endurance, determination, purpose, and character.

Curddy told me, sadly, that he would not be able to take me on walks and adventures anymore. I tried to think of something to say, something like, "That's okay. We can still have fun together." But I didn't think it was okay. Not at all. Far from it. My mind raced as I thought of all the things we couldn't do anymore. They were mostly selfish thoughts. I also felt sad and confused. I didn't understand what he could do and what he couldn't. How much of him was the same? I really didn't understand this whole wheelchair bit.

Over the next few days, we spent time together, talking, playing games, with me getting to know the new limited version of Curddy. Things brightened up. We talked a lot. I asked him a question, one of the many that my mind was overflowing with. "Curddy, why don't you own anything? What do you do with all your money?"

He squinted and exhaled through his nose, causing his long nose hairs to vibrate, a little like a wheat field in the wind. He removed a mostly chewed-up stogie from the corner of his mouth and tossed it into the runoff bucket under the pump faucet where it went "pssssst" as the water snuffed out the burning tobacco. Still thinking, he spat out a few pieces of tobacco and then stuck his tongue out to pick a few more pieces off of it. As he began to talk, his voice cracked and he chewed his bottom lip. Then he paused and looked down, opening his watch and looking at the photo of his wife and son that he had told us were dead.

As he snapped the watch shut with his thumb and forefinger, he looked up at me with a big sigh and said, "Let me tell you a story. I've never told it to anyone before. Please, keep it our secret."

"To begin with, my wife and son weren't murdered by gangsters. In fact, they weren't murdered at all. They are still alive. I haven't seen them for over thirty years, and I will never see them again, ever. I send money to them every month and that's why I never have any money. I send it to them through my ex-wife's brother, Sonny. That way, I will never be able to know where they are living. I am told by Sonny that my son wants to be a winemaker. The money I send is more than enough to pay for his schooling. In fact, he must have completed his education by now and be working in some winery in Southern Italy.

"The money that goes to my wife, well, let's call it guilt money. I know you're too young to understand what I did to my wife and son or what guilt is all about, how it can ruin a life, as it has mine. On my trip from Italy, I told a lot of lies. I did it because I wanted to seem like a tough and scary guy so no one would mess with me in the new land. I never murdered anyone. I never even beat anyone up, except in a fair fight once or twice. Well, actually, now that I think of it, I was in a lot of fights. One of those fights was where I got this scar above my eye. I did work on a farm.
That part was true."

I noticed the scar over his eye for the first time. He had so many scars, they had all just blended together.

"What happened to my wife and son was a long time ago. My son is a man by now, no longer that sweet little boy who was so cuddly with long red-blond hair, shiny and clean, that smelled of the orange scent in the shampoo my wife made. He had big brown eyes, and along with his red-blond hair, long eyelashes, and olive complexion, they drew a lot of attention. Always on trips to town, several people would stop to say, 'What a beautiful boy!' After a while, we became bored with all the compliments and responded under our breath, 'Ya, ya. We know he's a beauty."

"Every day when I came home from work, my boy and I would wrestle on the small flowered carpet in our living room. It would usually end with my arms wrapped around him, giving him a big, loving bear hug. And he would say, in a voice pretending he was out of breath, 'I give up, daddy.' And I would say, 'You have to give me two kisses first.' He would usually give me three kisses.

"Being with my wife and son was like living a life in heaven, too good to be true. And just like in the first paradise, Eden, paradise was lost because someone did something they shouldn't have. I did something I shouldn't have and I lost my paradise."

Curddy stopped and said he was tired and had to take a nap. The story would have to continue after his nap.

Curddy wheeled back under the fig trees. I got the green chair from the end of the table on the patio and turned it around to face Curddy in his wheelchair. His nap did him some good; he seemed to have a few sparks of life in him. He patted me on my knee and smiled for the first time this visit, and I noticed that he had lost two teeth sometime between my last visit and this one. I thought, 'He's falling apart. If I didn't know him and saw him on the street rolling toward me, I would run across the street to the other side.' He looked like what my parents would call a hobo.
Now we would use the term 'homeless person.'

But I did know him. I knew his heart, and it spoke louder than his appearance.

He reached deep into the pocket of his filthy brown pants and when his hand came out, I noticed he had a pint bottle of brown booze. I also noticed his hand was shaking and it continued to shake for the rest of the day. He took a good size guzzle and put the bottle back in his pocket. A bit of the booze trickled down his face. Then he cleared his throat and continued.

"It is a long story. Now that we won't be going on any journeys together, let me take you on the journey that was my life. My mind is a little scrambled, so forgive me if I repeat some things I've already told you.

"The story I told your Nono about my life before I met him was made up, a complete lie. I'll tell you everything, just not all of it today. And some of it will have to wait until you are older. The stories won't be in order, but I'll do as much as I can.

"When I first came to America, I got a job at a farm. I was a much younger man; I was strong and tough and could do anything. But I still carried with me a deep sadness, the sadness for the loss of my son and wife.

"I made good friends at the farm, a man, and his wife. Many nights they invited me to eat dinner with them in their cottage instead of at the dining hall with everyone else. Their cottage was small but furnished, clean and comfy. After dinner, we would sit by the fireplace, or in the summer on the sun porch. We would drink cheap, harsh red wine, or even harsher Grappa, and I would smoke strong Italian cigars. The three of us would drink and talk about what we missed from each of our home villages in Italy. Then we would talk about our futures, daydreaming about what we wanted. We talked about someday moving to the Napa Valley, a place called Rutherford.

"As time passed, I lost my sadness. I became excited about life's future possibilities. I grew into a happy, loving person, and I drew people to the new me. Of those people, two were children that I came to love. There were two boys that lived on the ranch. One was a boy, five years of age. His name was Leonardo, Leo. He reminded me so much of my own son. His dad had died from the flu when Leo was three. He needed a dad and I needed a replacement for my son. His mother worked on the ranch doing odd jobs that ranged from doing laundry to grocery shopping and helping the cook.

"There was one other child on the ranch, a boy, Antonio, who was four years old. He was an energetic child and spread joy to all that knew him. He was given the nickname 'Ant.' The Ant was always scurrying around in the dusty yards, followed by clouds of dust, and always nibbling on sweets. His parents owned a market in town. His dad also worked on the ranch and lived in a small cottage by the stables. He took care of all the animals, including Mur-fleas, a shaggy dog that chased after rats in the barn.

"The Ant and Leo were always together, and, when I wasn't working, they were with me. They were my chattering shadows. I loved them and, if they didn't find me, I would seek them out so we could go on adventures. We had a friendship like the one I have with you now."

Somehow I felt jealousy and anger toward those boys. Curddy was supposed to love just me.

He continued. "This part hurts me talk about, so I'm not going into detail, but there was another boy there, Nicco. Above the other children, he was my favorite. One Saturday something happened, something so horrible I don't think I will ever be able to talk about it. My life was never the same after that. My joy was sent packing and, in an instant, I reverted back to the shell I was in when I first came to the ranch, even worse. Soon after that, I left the ranch, and I ended up in Rutherford. I got a job at the Old Oaken Bucket bar as a bartender and I lived in a little shack in the middle of the vineyard.

"When your Nono and Nona bought this place, they came into the bar one day and over drinks, asked me to move into the bunkhouse. Here I had a nice place to live. I didn't have any expenses, so I started sending money to my wife and son. I felt so guilty. You see, the reason my wife and son cast me out of their lives was that my wife had caught me with another lady. My son and wife walked in on me being lovey-dovey with her, something a man should only do with his wife. They ran out of the house and I never saw them again. My wife's brother delivered a note the next day. It was from my wife, saying that I would never see them again. Ever! Her brother's words were stronger and involved threats of what he and his cousins would do to me if I was still around in three days.

"I was ashamed. I was crushed and destroyed. That's when I left for America."

My mind then brought me back to the reason I had felt jealous: those two boys. But then I remembered. He had said there were three boys, not just two.

"Curddy, do you have any photographs from that farm?"

"Jimmy, you have never asked to see any of my photos before. Why now?"

"I never thought you had any photos except the one in your watch. And then I saw the one in your closet. Now, I think you might have more. I want to see what those two boys looked like."
Really I was hoping that one would look like the mystery boy.

"I have a few," Curddy answered. "They are in a cigar box under my mattress. If you want to, you can go and get them."

He had hardly finished his sentence and I was already in his room. I pulled the cigar box out from under the stinky mattress. It wasn't a wooden cigar box. It was one of the kind that 5-cent cigars came in, cheap cardboard with an owl on the lid. My hand was on the lid, wanting to throw it open and see the photos. But the little angel sitting on my shoulder told me that I had been bad to Curddy by sneaking into his room on the last visit. So I ran outside and handed the box to Curddy.

Curddy's hand fumbled, the shaking getting worse, as he tried to open the lid. I took two steps toward him, putting out my hand to help, and then quickly stepped back, waiting for him to open it or ask for help. He finally got it open and stared down into the box. Then he closed it and started to cry. I walked over and hugged him, trying to comfort him with the words my mother used to soothe me, "That's all right. It will be okay. I love you."

He handed me the box and I opened it. There were about a dozen photos, none of them the mystery boy. One of the photos was of the two boys together. One was a boy with a lady. And one was torn in half, the other half missing. Some were not at the farm, but at a park by a creek. Curddy was in two photographs, looking great. Several were of groups of people, mostly men, at a picnic. My Nona was in some of these, but there was something strange. She looked like she was having a lot of fun. In fact, she looked silly. Fun and silly weren't words I ever thought of to describe Nona. In some of the photos, she had a bottle of whiskey tilted up in her mouth like she was guzzling the whole thing. In another, she had a lampshade on her head and was dancing. In yet another, she had Nono's hat along with a cigar, in her mouth. I was amazed. Who was this silly lady? It was certainly not the Nona I knew.

I hadn't noticed that Curddy had stopped crying and was staring at me. I asked, "Is this really my Nona? She looks goofy! I have never seen her so happy!"

Curddy replied, "When she left the ranch where she was working, she was a changed person. Something happened to her that most people would not have been able to live through.

"What?"

Before he could answer, I remembered something about one of the photos. Something about it was familiar. I opened the box and shuffled through the photos again. There. The photo of the one boy alone. The photo edge was torn a little crooked and the boy's right hand was cut off. It had the same background as the photo at the back of Curddy's closet. In it, the mystery boy's hand was holding someone else's hand. This was the other half of that photo.

"Curddy, who is this boy? Where is the other half of the photo?"

He cleared his throat and opened his mouth to speak, and then paused in thought. And I waited and waited some more.

Chapter 14
Death of My Friend

I asked Curddy, my voice a bit shaky with excitement, "Who is this boy, the one in this photo?"

He wouldn't look me in the eye. His head was hanging down and it looked as if he was trying to focus on the two figs that had dropped from the tree and split open moments earlier. While I waited for him to respond, I, too, stared at the figs, trying to figure out what was so fascinating. One fig had plopped on his beat-up right shoe, oozing out overly ripe goo. The other was an inch or two in front of his left shoe.

Seeing them took me on a "fig trip" in my mind. The figs were actually very pretty split open; the distinct shade of the tough purple skin blended nicely with the pink coarseness and speckled yellowish seeds inside. I was reminded of how good they tasted when they were just on the verge of being ripe, not yet squishy or mushy, just a lighter shade of pink. I loved the taste, but I didn't like the texture of the seeds inside, kind of like coarse hair. They reminded me of some kind of disgusting sea life or cow tongue, which Nona served as a special treat. No thank you!

I always chewed the figs fast to prevent the gross textures from lingering on my tongue. Everyone who came to Big Pink ate these figs, so I thought I had to, too. The figs were served along with hard cheese, half stale bread, and red wine, and I joined in to do the same, except that my wine was mixed with 7-Up. Ever since then, when I have figs or fig jam, I enjoy the memories of warm summer nights at the patio table with its tin shaded pool table lamps with very bright glaring bulbs and the "ptik ptik" of the bugs hitting those lights. Every once in awhile a bug dropped to the table, twitching, and flipping, dying, and someone would flick it off the table or smash it dead.

These were nights when I got to stay up late, observing and enjoying every story, joke and song. It was more fun than some of my daytime adventures, and I cherish reliving these memories in the retelling of stories of nights of feasts of all the senses. We all ate and drank and fellowshipped under the shine of the moon and stars that all seemed so much brighter there at Big Pink. It was amusing watching the predictable parts of the evening script unfold as each cast member acted true to their role. But sometimes there were unexpected surprises. It made life at Big Pink wonderful!

In addition to the figs, there were other fruits in tin colanders on the table, some fresh and some dried. My Nono and I dried some of the figs along with apricots on screens behind the slaughterhouse. I helped split the fruit and put it on the screens, and, then, I almost never touched them again. I didn't want to eat them because sometimes when I went to help Nono water the vegetable garden, I would see the birds eating some of the drying fruit. It was disgusting and I certainly couldn't eat anything bird lips had touched. Who knew what they had in their beaks before they ate our fruit?

Now my thoughts turned to the three buzzards that were flying over the vineyard behind the ugly turquoise shack with the rusted tin roof. It was actually someone's very small old house. I thought turquoise was a cool color for a house, but the neighbors up there hated it and said it stuck out like a hippopotamus in a bird bath. They said it didn't belong in the Valley. But Pink was okay?!?!
I had hated buzzards ever since I saw the Red Pony in the movie house in downtown St. Helena. In one scene, the buzzards were shown trying to eat a horse, or maybe even the Red Pony. From then on, it seemed like I saw buzzards everywhere and whenever we saw one, my dad would say something like, "Something must have died." But sometimes he would say, "They're after you!
When is the last time you had a bath?!?"

Now, just as the buzzards were diving to the ground behind the turquoise house, Curddy spoke. "What did you ask me?"

I held the photo in my left hand, stretched my arm out toward him as far as it would go and put my right hand on my wrist to try and steady my shaking hand. As a result, the photo was about four inches from his eyes, nearly touching his nose. I tried to make my voice sound deeper, more grown up, and repeated, "Who is this boy?"

My hand continued to bob around and I had to control my nervousness and excitement. He made a kind of growling throat clearing sound, repeating it twice, but he didn't speak. I waited, waited and waited some more. I didn't want to ask him the question a third time.

Finally, he sat up, looked me in the eye and said, "That boy is Anthony. Remember, I told you about "Ant" and his friends." But I wanted more. I knew for sure that this boy knew the mystery boy. The background of this photo and the one of the mystery boy were the same. So I asked, "Who were his friends?"

"He was good friends with Leo and Nic..... He stopped in mid-sentence. Uh, that's all. Just friends with Leo." But the word had been spoken, and I asked, "Who is Nic... what were you going to say? Yesterday you mentioned a boy named Nicco. Who was Nicco? Do you have any photos of him?"

He absentmindedly shuffled through the photos, shaking his head. "No. No, I don't have one of him."

I didn't give up. "The photo that you have hidden at the back of your closet, the one you got mad at me for looking at? Was that Nicco?"

He answered in a voice that became tearful, "The boy in that photo was someone very special to me. It is private. That is all I want to say."

I tried a different approach. "When did you meet my Nono and Nona? Is that boy someone they knew too?"

He looked at me silently for a few moments, smiled and answered, "One day when I was tending bar up the road at the Old Oaken Bucket, your Nono came in for a few shots of brandy. I met him that day. He asked if anyone wanted room and board in trade for working in the vineyard. I said, 'I'll do it.' As easy as that, I had a better place to live. I moved in a week later and became best friends with your grandparents."

"Wait," I said. "You told me before that you met Nono on the ship coming from Italy. Now you're telling me you met my Nono at the bar."

He began to shake. "Oh, yes. I have told so many lies, I get lost in them. What I am telling you now about life at the ranch is true. Well, except those lies."
"So," I asked, "How did you get those photos of my happy, silly Nona from back then. I am very confused."

He gave a long sad sigh. "Why all these questions? I told you, I came from the middle of Italy and worked my way from New York to California. I got a job working on a farm. I worked on the crops. I made friends there. I spent time with some boys there because I missed my son.
Something bad happened. I moved here, worked in the bar and slept in the back room until I saw your grandparents. Then, I moved here. Then, I became friends with you. That's it. I don't want to answer any more questions about boys in photos, how I got my scars or anything."

He was more upset than I had ever seen him, even angry. I quit asking questions, even though I still had so many. I didn't know what part of what he said was lies. Years later, I found the power of lies. After a while, they get us believing a history that never actually happened.

Now Curddy changed the subject. "I'm sorry we never made our trip over the mountain to meet the sun." We had routinely taken hikes to the mountain behind our house. It was a long walk along the dirt path between our property and our next-door neighbor's vineyard. The path was big enough to drive a truck down and was surrounded on both sides by vineyard. About a quarter of the way back on the left was THE orchard of plums that my family adopted as ours. On our hikes, Curddy and I would pick some plums to eat on our way to the mountain, and, on our way back, we would pick some more to eat on the rest of our hike home.

Sometimes we made it to the foot of the mountain. Sometimes we made it part way up. Curddy always said, "Someday we will walk to the very top of the mountain and, on the other side, we will see where the sun lives." I could see the sun setting, disappearing from the sky and bringing on the night. I figured it had to go somewhere, why not the other side of the mountain? How stupid was I? I was just a little kid, and they didn't teach us about the solar system in Catholic school. At that age, I thought it was really possible to hike all the way to the other side of the mountain. I have no idea how long it would have taken or if my short little legs could have even taken me there.

I didn't respond to his comment. He had reminded me of all those fun times that would be no more and I was lost in thought. He repeated in an even sadder tone, "Jimmy, I am so sorry we never made it to the sun."

"That's okay, " I said. "It would be too hot to meet him anyway. I mean, we couldn't shake hands with him. We would burn up if we did, wouldn't we?"

He gave me a strange look and said, "What?"

I repeated what I had said, but he just looked at me with blankly, like he had swallowed a lizard.

"Okay," I said. "Enough about all that old stuff. Let's play cards." And we moved to the table. I picked up the deck of cards that stayed on the table, held down by a large rock. I tried to shuffle and the cards went everywhere. I gathered them together, noticing how 'seasoned' they were.
These cards had been in countless Pedro games, handled by fingers greasy with salami, olives, pickled pig's feet, sardines and countless other greasy items. They were truly cruddy, but it was a complete deck, the only one at Big Pink until my dad bought the new ones, but no one used them but dad and me.

"Teach me to play Pedro," I asked. This was a card game that all the old Italians played. I had been trying to learn it, but it was very confusing. Curddy had been a good teacher, teaching me the ways of the world. Maybe he could succeed at teaching me Pedro. No such luck. I was still confused and finally gave up. I never did learn Pedro. It was easier to play poker or cribbage.

So we sat across from each other at the patio table listening to the symphony of pigeons 'coo- cooing,' chickens 'bauk bauking' and figs falling, 'platt-splat' on the table and patio. We played poker using wooden matchsticks for chips. After an hour, we were called to dinner and soon after that was an early bedtime which put an end to this distressing, sad day.

I wanted to escape all the memories bouncing around like ping pong balls in my mind, but I couldn't forget them. I couldn't get to sleep. Then, I began thinking about the ghoul from the slaughterhouse. Curddy couldn't protect me from it anymore. He couldn't chase it or fight it. And, as I worried, I was sure I heard footsteps. I was panicked. The ghoul was coming to get me. But he never made it. After a while, I finally wore myself out and fell asleep.

I remember the next morning clearly. I woke up early. The third screech-squawk from the Drunken Rooster did the trick. I dressed quickly in the same clothes from the day before, a dirty t- shirt and levis. Later my mom would make me put on a clean t-shirt because we were stopping at Pometti's Deli to drop off several dozen of my Nona's ravioli and it would be horrible if the Pomettis saw me in a dirty t-shirt.

I tried to walk quietly down the creaky hall, opened the squeaky door and went into the kitchen. I could feel myself smile when I saw my Nona was sitting at the kitchen table in her usual spot on the corner closest to the stove. She had her half-eyeglasses perched on the end of her nose and was reading Nono's outdated Italian newspaper. The fact that she was reading meant that she had finished all of her early morning chores except the coffee. She often waited to put the coffee on until Nono got up; he like his coffee very fresh. After Nono got up, my mom was next, and finally my dad, always in that order. I walked over and gave Nona a lazy, sleepy hug. She gave me a kiss, patted down my Alfalfa-cowlick hair and wished me a fun day. I got my usual bowl of corn flakes, splashed on some milk and several heaping spoonfuls of sugar. "See you later!" I announced. "I'm going down to eat with Curddy." Then I trotted down the stairs to sit on the sea-foam green bench at the table under the fig trees and wait for him

I gazed at the clear blue sky. It was going to be a beautiful day, at least weather-wise. Soon, Curddy came out of his cabin, rolled down the ramp my Nono had built for him and parked at the end of the table close to me. "Hello. Good morning-day, Jimmy." He never got the AM greeting quite right. I replied, "Morning-day," teasing him. But he didn't get it.

I told him some of the stories I had been making up in my mind while I waited for him. I added him into one of them. In it, he was still walking. He came along with me up the mountain and saved me from vicious attacking mountain lions and bears, killing them all with my Nono's shotgun he always brought with us. He had always told me he liked my stories and usually encouraged me to tell more, but this day, he didn't. I said, "Wait! I'll be right back!" I ran upstairs, threw open the door to the mud porch, ran into the kitchen, and smelled the coffee being brewed. I saw that
Nono had his little saucepan of boiling water for his hypodermic needle going on the gas burner so he could give himself his daily shot of insulin. I usually looked away when he did it.

Nono said, "Good morning, Jimmy." He got the greeting right. "Did you want me to make you breakfast?"
"No," I replied. "I already have a bowl of cereal outside. I just wanted to get a cup of coffee for Curddy."

"It's almost done," Nono replied. "I'll bring it down."

I went down to finish my now soggy cereal and told Curddy that coffee was coming. Soon, Nono came down carrying a big wood tray and, on it, three cups, a coffee pot with steam rising from its spout, a short bottle of cream, a sugar bowl and a spoon. He poured me half a cup of coffee, added about a fourth cup of cream and the rest sugar, stuck the spoon in and passed it to me. He gave a cup of black coffee to Curddy and poured another, adding the cream the way he liked his. Nono and Curddy talked like old buddies talk. They had a few laughs at the expense of others like Lena Hyena, her lover Cheezer and her skinny nervous husband, Lew-e-gee, Pig Bristles and the new Witch Hazel, some of the people we would see that weekend. That morning, as we enjoyed our coffee and friendship, none of us knew that it would be the last time the three of us did anything together. I finished my bowl of cereal with extra sugar, and Curddy and Nono drank their cups of coffee with no sugar and each had a refill.

My Nona came down the steps with a big knife in her left hand and a determined, scary expression on her face. She walked across the patio and into the chicken coop. What was about to happen would ruin one chicken's day. It wasn't something I wanted to witness, so I said I had a chore to do.

I got up from the table, walked over to Curddy, patted his shoulder and asked if he wanted to help me. He said yes, so I got behind his wheelchair and started to push him toward the back of the slaughterhouse. In front of the bunkhouses, the driveway gravel was thick and it was hard to push the chair over it, so I asked if he could help by pushing the big wheels with his hands. He did and we got through the hard part. In front of the garage, the gravel was so thin that the wheels made a groove down into the dirt; the pushing was easy there. Where the garden started, the gravel ended. Here the wheels kicked up some dirt to make a misty cloud that dulled the few shiny parts of the wheelchair.

When we got behind the slaughterhouse, I saw my chore waiting. There, hanging from a peg on the outer wall of the slaughterhouse, was a bucket of figs. These were figs that I had picked the day before. I enjoyed doing the picking because I got to use the tool that, as far as I knew, my Nono had invented. It was a Granger tobacco can mounted at the end of a long pole, with a v- notch cut in the lip of the can. When I put the notch under a fig and twisted, the fig would fall, 'kerplop,' into the can. I could even reach the far-up figs, thanks to the long pole. When the Granger can got too heavy, I dumped into a bucket and continued.

Behind the slaughterhouse, there was not only a bucket of figs but also three sawhorses. And on each of these, there were three large mesh screens framed with 2x4s. My job was to split the figs in half and put them on the screen, skin side down. Two of the screens were for figs and one was for apricots that I would pick from the tree right behind the slaughterhouse. While I was working at my chore, Curddy helped me split the figs and apricots and we talked small talk.

Later, Mom called me to come back in and get my stuff because we were leaving for home soon. She added, "Don't go back outside; I don't want to have to hunt you down." About half an hour later, we headed to the car, ready to leave. Curddy was back in his usual spot on the boardwalk in front of his room, sitting in the sunlight. He had a cup of coffee in his shaky hand. As he took a sip, some coffee splashed out of the cup and on to his already soiled shirt. He said, "Say a few prayers for me." Other than that, "Goodbye" was the last word he said to me, ever.

As we drove up the driveway toward Hwy 29, I turned and waved goodbye as he disappeared in the cloud of dust we created. He waved back with a shaky hand. That sight of him in his wheelchair in his favorite spot in the sun was the last I ever saw of him.

A week later, we returned to Big Pink, as usual. This time when we got to the end of the driveway, my dad decided to park under the olive trees. That was the last time he parked there. The next morning, he had to spend a few hours washing the messy olives off his car and waxing it!

My mom opened her car door and pulled the seat forward so I could get out. As I jumped out and began running to the bunkhouse, she yelled, "Jimmy! Come back! I need to talk to you." I took four big strides across the gravel and, then, I saw Curddy's wheelchair at the end of the boardwalk in the sun. But it was empty. Something thudded hard in my chest. I skidded to a stop leaving trenches in the gravel behind my black canvas high top tennis shoes.

I turned to my mom, the question written all over my face. She answered me right there in the driveway, framed by the slaughterhouse behind her. For some reason, I remember everything about those next few moments. I had my hand up over my right eye in what looked like a salute, an attempt to keep the sun out of my squinting eyes. It was bright and hot. I was standing on squished, overly ripe olives and they smelled fermented. I knew they were sticking to the bottom of my shoes and, later, I would have to use a screwdriver to clean them off. I could hear the pond in my Nona's beautiful flower garden. The water was squirting out of the iron lizard's mouth into the top tier of the pond and overflowing to the bottom tier, making splashing sounds. Yes, for some reason, I remember everything about that moment. It's the next few days that are a blank.

My mom looked like she was going to cry. She said, "It's very sad. Three days ago, Curddy didn't come out for his morning coffee or for lunch. Nono went to check on him. Curddy was on his bed, on his side, facing the wall. He had died during the night. He went peacefully, without pain, in his sleep. I'm so sorry. I know what a special friend he was to you."

At that moment, my mind ceased storing things. I don't remember the rest of the day. I don't remember anything about a funeral or right after it. I just don't remember. I do recall two things: the wheelchair was moved to the barn for a couple of weeks. I remember how much I hated the sight of it. To me, at that time, I thought being in a wheelchair meant death was soon to follow. I quit going to the barn to play until my dad took the chair to the Veteran's Home and donated it.

I also remember that I went into his room. Everything was the same. His few belongings were still there. And there, hanging at the back of the closet, was the photo of the mystery boy. I grabbed it, and then I grabbed the cigar box with the other photos. I took the photos out of the box and put the box back. I didn't know if it was a sin if what you took was from a dead person. I hid the photos in a comic book and put them in the bottom drawer of the three-drawer dresser in my bedroom at Big Pink. There they stayed for a while forgotten. All my questions about the photos were still unanswered and forgotten for a long time.

I didn't forget Curddy, though, just the aftermath of his death. I also don't remember anything about my Nona Curtoni's funeral about a year later, or Nona Z's ten years after that, or even my Nono's twenty-some years later. Not one single thing. The first funeral of a family member that I remember is my dad's when I was fifty years old. For some reason I don't understand, my mind has censored out funerals.

So a chapter closed in my life. But I got so much from that chapter. Some things from that friendship were carried with me forever. To me, Curddy was a great man, and, once I learned how he got the scars and what happened to him, I was in total awe of him.

I thought about Curddy over the years and his promise that every secret would be revealed and every question answered "when you become a man and can understand these matters." He told the truth. He just didn't tell me how long it would take or how surprised I would be by the answers and how many lies I had been fed by Curddy and family members.

Chapter 15
A New Friend

Right after Curddy's death, I was sad, mad, and, even though I didn't know the term at the time, looking back I realize, I was depressed.

I had been working hard to solve the mysteries surrounding Curddy. How did he get those scars? What had happened? What changed my Nona's disposition taking away all her joy? Who was the mystery boy in the photos that no one wanted to talk about? And why did my grandparents take Curddy in and let him live at Big Pink for free?

I had felt both excitement and tension when I talked to Curddy about those children where he had worked and then learned what had happened to his wife and son. He had given me some answers and it made me happy. But just when I felt I was close to unraveling all the mysteries, he called a halt to the talk about those old days. Before we could get together, he died.

I felt all the air go out of my balloon. I gave up.

I was desperately in need of fun and distraction, and it came in the form of a new friend and some new revelations about the slaughterhouse and something else I called "The Treasure of the Black Widow Spider."

Three months after Curddy died, my Nono and dad gutted his old room and threw everything into the dump. They removed the wallpaper and curtains and did everything they could to get rid of the stench from years and years of an unwashed drunkard living there. They burned all the wood from the furniture in an outdoor fire pit, the old-fashioned kind with brick on three sides about three feet high. The back side was corrugated tin which slid up and out, so the cold ashes and burned bits of wood could be raked out into the vineyard. It actually took a day to burn everything flammable from his room. After that, they painted and brought in a double-size bed, dresser, night table, lamp and a wardrobe. When my dad and Nono did the remodel of the bedroom, they hired Bachi to convert the other 3 bedrooms of the bunkhouse into a kitchen, dining table, and front room. There was already a bathroom with a shower. So the new renter had everything he needed. They charged $51 a month. Nona had decided she was no longer cooking or doing laundry for the renter. So the room had a hot plate and a small refrigerator.

A month later, a young man moved in and I instantly knew I wanted him as a friend. Yes, I still had Powder Burns and all of my Nono's friends who were always nice and friendly, giving me hugs and kisses in the traditional Italian way, right smack on the lips. But they were old. Really old.
This new man was young, only twenty-two or so. He worked at Charles Krug and looked rich to me. He had a custom 1952 baby-blue Chevy convertible, tuck and roll blue and white leather upholstery and baby moon hubcaps. It had all the identifying hood ornaments removed and it was lowered. It was cool, and so was he. His hair and clothes looked like Elvis's. His name was Roock, not like Rock (star) but pronounced Row-ka. He was a bit on the quiet side and didn't go out of his way to befriend me. But, all my life, if I liked someone and wanted them as a friend, I would just insert myself into their life until they told me to get lost. That rarely happened.

A couple of days after Roock moved in, I found him on the porch, sitting in the sun where Curddy used to sit. He had a bottle of Burgermeister beer even though it was only10 AM. He was smoking a Lucky Strike and had a backup cigarette above his ear. And he was reading a paperback novel, Cannery Row. I learned that he was addicted to reading and, once a week, he walked the railroad tracks to the little market next to BV Winery where he would check out the new books that had arrived and buy five or six to last him the week. He was never without a paperback in his back pocket. When I started chattering with him, he said, "Hold on, Jimbo," and folded the corner of the page and closed the book. Then he squinted one eye. I wasn't sure if that was because the smoke was drifting up from the cigarette hanging off his bottom lip or if the sun was in his eyes. And he asked, "Is it alright if I call you Jimbo? "Bo" for short?

I felt a swelling warm feeling in my chest. A nickname. Wow! He must like me! "Yes. That would be fun."

He asked if I liked to read. He spoke in a quiet tone; smooth, friendly, almost like a professional newscaster on TV. I told him I loved to read, but most of the books in my elementary school library were boring. He showed me the cover of Cannery Row. It showed a group of men, all drinking, dressed in colorful clothing, some torn and tattered. Most of them were drinking out of jugs that looked like what I saw at Big Pink. In fact, the people and the activity looked like a gathering of my grandparents' friends. He even read me a few pages, really funny, about a bunch of drunks going on a frog hunt.

Over the next year, I would hang out with him an hour or so each day. We didn't go on any adventures. Other than going to the market, the only other time we left Big Pink was to go fishing with my dad. But, still, I really liked his cool, calm personality. I liked that he would share his books with me. He would read parts to me, or he would let me read some pages. My fondness for reading was definitely thanks to him.

He could continue to read and converse with me at the same time. One afternoon, I was chattering on endlessly. He would nod or grunt as he plowed through From Here to Eternity or some other war novel. But then, I guess he noted a change in the tone of my voice. He stopped reading and folded the top of the page (he told me this was called a 'dog ear'). He looked at me deep into my eyes. "Say that again? What are you afraid of?"

I had been talking about my fear of the slaughterhouse. He asked, "Do you trust me?"

"Yes," I replied. He wasn't wild, crazy fun like Powder. He didn't take me on long hikes or adventures like Curddy did. I didn't love him. But I trusted and respected him.

He then informed me that on our next visit he would help me get over the fear of the slaughterhouse. "I won't protect you from any beast there. I'm going to prove to you that there aren't any!"

About two weeks later, we arrived at Big Pink and parked in front of the fountain so there were no trees above us. No loquats and no juicy black olives to drop on the car, and no place for a bird to sit and crap on it. I saw Roock polishing his car and noted, "Hey, Dad. Look! Another guy that is crazy about polishing cars!"

"Real funny, wise guy," he replied.

I approached Roock and said, "I do trust you. What is your plan?"

"Let's explore the slaughterhouse piece by piece, and you'll see that is just wood, very old wood, cement, and some rusty metal." He suggested.

The Slaughterhouse

I have told stories about the slaughterhouse and how it scared me. I was sure the Ghoul from the Slaughterhouse was living there. But, what better way to flush out my brain, to dump all the sorrow of losing my friend Curddy? What better way to forget about those photos, about my grandparents' past, than to shock my system? Why not search every bit of space in the slaughterhouse? I knew it was very, very old when my grandparents bought the property in 1925. At the time, it included an old house, later demolished to be replaced with Big Pink, the pink stucco house that stood out from all the others in the Napa Valley. The only explanation for that hideous color was because Nona's name was Rosalia, Rosi, and she liked the pink rose color. In addition, there was a barn, a wood shed, a row of bunkhouses with four separate rooms and a boardwalk porch, and the slaughterhouse, old and rundown, even then. They never did know the exact year it was built, but the best guess is 1880-something.

When my grandparents and mom moved to Rutherford, they tried to determine the history of the place. But the prior owners were gone by the time the Curtoni family of three showed up.
According to my mom, most of the information they did get came from "a really old man that lived somewhere across the vineyard (possibly Manley Lane). He would come over and, if your Nono gave him some wine, cheese, and bread, he would sit and tell stories of the history of the slaughterhouse."

As they sat out under the even-then old fig trees and drink wine, listening to figs plop to the ground and chickens "bauk bauking," they would talk about how it used to be and what went on there.

According to the really old man, the slaughterhouse was built at the end of the 1880s. It operated until about 1920 or so. It was small scale with the owners slaughtering and selling mostly beef, pork, venison, and chickens. The meat would be sold out of a small store attached to the front of the slaughterhouse. There was a livestock pen to the side of the slaughterhouse, at the end of the barn. That was where my Nono put his garden several decades later after he removed the pen. We know that everything grew well there after all those decades of animal manure. The pen really wasn't very big. It probably held about five cows and two pigs. Or maybe it was one-and-a-half pigs and five-and-a-half cows or some variation of that. Anyway, my grandparents kept the pen for twenty-five years or more. They butchered the pigs that went into my Nona's sausage and other menu items my Nona cooked. They also had several sheep; my Nono thought it wasn't Easter unless you had lamb for dinner. Sometimes, he even wanted it for Christmas.

When the slaughterhouse was in business, the pen was where the livestock would wait, eat, get fat, get their suntan and live a (short) stress-free life with no worry about the future. Little did they know. Then one day, they went on their final field trip into the slaughterhouse where they were..... well, the name of the building tells it all.

To give you an idea of what the slaughterhouse looked like, I will try to describe it. But words do not do it justice. It was part of the building, excluding the little store, of about 400 square feet. It was white-washed wood with a tin roof. The roof tilted up from the back to the front. The front half of the slaughterhouse was higher than the back half. Inside, the back lower half was about ten feet, floor to ceiling, and the front half was about twenty feet high. The front half had a foundation that seemed to me to be about a two-foot thick slab of cement, so it was a few steps up to get in the front door.

Here are some of the things that I hated and made it creepy for me. In the front half, when you tried to slide the warped wood sliding door, the rusted steel wheels made a screaming squeal that sounded like a banshee from hell. I had heard one of those on the Inner Sanctum radio show where the scream opened the show and then jumped right into a horrifying episode. But Roock walked me in and out of that noisy door over and over, proving to me that nothing bad was associated with that screech.

Once inside, there was a wooden wheel about six feet in diameter and five feet off the floor mounted on the wall on the left. The wheel had a rope and large steel hooks hanging from it and it was used to hoist up the meat. I was always nervous at the sight of the steel hooks covered in blood. But Roock showed me close up that it wasn't blood on the hooks; it was rust.

I really had no idea of what went on in a place like that until one day my dad took me into a working slaughterhouse where they were killing and butchering cows. It was a horrifying experience and I never understood why my dad took me there. It was, in my childhood vocabulary, "gross." It smelled, and I felt so sad seeing the cows being killed. My memory (and I could be wrong) is that a big guy held a pistol up to the cow's head and pulled the trigger, and that was it.

As we left, everyone could see that I was upset, so to cheer me up, they gave me a cow tail. Looking back on it as an adult, it doesn't make any sense to me that they would think it was a good idea to give part of a dead cow to a kid who was upset by seeing cows being killed and cut up. Stranger yet is that I would find the tail fun, but I did. I used it as a whip the rest of the day, flicking at grapes, tomatoes and a few cats. My mom made me toss out the tail the next day. She said that it was dead, and dead meat starts smelling really bad after a few days.

In the upper room of the slaughterhouse, there was a gutter in the cement for the blood to drain, I guess. When I went there to play, it always creeped me out. My skin would crawl and my hair would stand on end, but still, I was drawn there. I would look around in fascination. It was dark and dusty and had tons of cobwebs and

146

spiders everywhere. I couldn't last in there for very long; I was sure something was going to jump out of the cobwebs or the corner shadows. But, as much as I hated it, it had the power to drag me right back to it.

The lower back half of the building had a thinner cement foundation, only a few inches thick. My mom tells me that there was a huge wine barrel there that went almost to the ceiling. That is where Curtoni's Ruby Red Wine was made.

The Store

Outside, on the right front corner of the slaughterhouse, there was an attached room about ten by twelve feet with a window on the front and one on the side where the livestock pen was. It had two cement steps to a narrow front door. Here they sold the meat and meat products like sausage and salami. There was a heavy wooden door that led from the back of the store into the cooler or refrigerator room where the meat was stored. The refrigerator room was about ten by six feet and its walls were about ten inches thick and filled with sawdust. A trap door about twelve feet up on the side wall went to the outside and that was where blocks of ice were delivered. The ice kept the meat cold since there was no refrigeration. The delivered ice was shoved through the trap-door and slid onto racks that held the ice up above the meat that was stored on the shelves.

Customers walked up the railroad tracks or across the vineyard, and some, I guess, came by horseback or maybe even a few in horseless carriages. They walked up the two steps and into the little store where they placed their order. The owner went into the cooler, got the meat, weighed it and wrapped it in, what else, butcher paper, wrote the price on it and collected the money.

After spending hours with Roock all over the slaughterhouse, investigating every part, it lost its ability to scare me or creep me out. I discovered that there were no ghouls in there, nothing hiding in the dark corners. Roock brought such a happy calm into my life.

After living there about three months, he bought a typewriter, and, each day, I could find him on the patio at the table, typing what he said was going to be his novel.

He would become more important to me in a few months when my Nona died.

Chapter 16
Goodbye to Rosi

No one wanted to be the first one up in cold or rainy weather. It was just not fun. Our weird old rooster could make any abnormal noise he wanted as loudly as he could, even singing God Bless America in Kate Smith's voice, and no one would stir. Finally, out of duty, Nona would bite the bullet and get up around 6 A.M. That's just what an Italian farm wife does. It was time to feed the chickens and pigeons and strangle the rooster. Oh, yes, and to "slop" the one huge hog. Porky was my name for him and I always thought he was sloppy enough without Nona adding to it.

Porky lived temporarily in the shadow of the Slaughterhouse, his final home, before reappearing as sausage on the kitchen table at Big Pink. At that age, I wasn't fond of all of Nona's kitchen creations, sausage being one that was on my "just so-so" list. However, when Porky was served up, I ripped into those sausages like a starved lion devouring a lamb.

You see, I hated Porky. His first pen was located just past the barn and woodshed. It was a smaller version of larger pens that had been around the slaughterhouse when it was active, when blood flowed down the gutters of its cement floor. Porky was about the size of a hippo and had long whiskers (pig bristles) all over his body. He was pink and brown, the brown being mud he seemed to always have splatter on him. He was ugly and mean, but interesting to watch. Sometimes, I would sit on the top rail of his pen and throw food (if you call table scraps 'food') to him: cooked carrot tops, mustard greens, cabbage, leftover dinner and maybe even dessert.
One day, while I was sitting on the top rail of the pen, my right leg dangled a bit too far down into the pen. Porky looked up, snorted and scraped his front hooves back and forth in the mud several times. Then he gave me a look that said, "How dare you?!?" and charged me fast, grabbing my foot. I felt a strong grip and dull pain and squealed like a little piglet. I yanked my right foot up just as Nono pulled me from the fence. We both landed on the ground, me

on top of him. I quickly sat up and looked at my right foot, expecting to see something gross and bloody. There was my foot, halfway out of a slimy, wet, muddy yellow and brown striped sock. I was okay. My right shoe wasn't. But I hated those Buster Browns anyway and, later, threw the left one over the fence too, yelling, "Here. Choke on it!" It was a line I'd heard on a TV movie when a Marine threw a grenade at the Japanese soldiers.

Curddy rushed over to join Nono and comfort me and calm me down, but it wasn't working. Finally, Curddy told my mom, "Why don't you get Jimmy's sandals and I'll take him down to the market to get soda, ice cream, and a few comics. How 'bout that Jimmy?" And on the way to the market, he told me stories about him fighting killer hogs and how Porky would never ever touch me again. He saved my day; I was okay.

That pen was removed a year later and the area became my Nono's much loved, very productive vegetable garden. But every time I walked by where the pen used to be, even up through adulthood, my right leg would involuntarily jerk up. That evening after dinner, I went to see Curddy. I was so grateful to him and gave him another drawing I had just colored. In it, Curddy was tearing apart a pen full of hogs with his bare hands. He looked at me and said, "Oh. So you saw me that day." Then he chuckled. He said he would keep that drawing forever. It was proof of our bond of friendship and his promise to always protect me.

Nona's Mornings

Once Nona finished with feeding the hog, the last of her morning livestock chores, she headed for the cold house, which was as cold as a meat locker. Everyone in there was still sleeping under at least ten blankets with only their noses uncovered so they could breathe. She stopped on the mud porch at the huge wooden chest. This wood bin contained a mix of wood scraps. This fire would make the kitchen warm, toasty and cozy-comfortable in no time.

Next, Nona would turn on the oil burning furnace. This would heat the bedrooms, hall, and bathroom. If she forgot to turn on the oil burner, you could have ice skated on the bath water. I asked her once why she didn't start the fire and turn on the furnace before tending to the livestock. She replied, "That's just silly. No one is awake to warm up."

Goodbye to Rosi

There are so many things from my past that I remember very clearly. But there are others that, no matter how hard I try, I remember nothing. The passing of my Nona Rosi is just bits and pieces.

I have photos of Nono and Nona at the San Francisco airport. Those photos tell me the story of an event: My grandparents were going to fly with another family, the Ciacocas. Their destination was Gerola, the small village in Italy where all four were born and raised. Nona and Nono were dressed up, Nono in a suit with a vest and his tie clipped with a gold tie clip with a gold dollar in the center of it. His gold watch chain looped into his vest pocket where his pocket watch lived, except when he removed it with his right hand, pressed the small tab on the side and flipped open the cover.
He checked the time often, partly, I think, to show off the very old and very valuable watch that had belonged to his Nono.
Nona was wearing a very nice dress with a lace collar and over that, some kind of fur jacket and her pearls. I also was required by my parents to dress up. Fortunately, it was an outfit I was comfortable in, my dark blue, cord pants, pale blue short sleeve dress shirt with a dark blue V neck sweater over it, my usual uniform for Catholic school. My hair was slicked back. I was squeaky clean. In those days you dressed 'to the nines' when you flew on an airplane. In the photo, they were scowling at the camera as if someone told them their pet rooster had been eaten by their hog.

Off they flew. A month later they returned. I had missed them so much and was so so happy to see them back. Nono rambled on about all the relatives he saw, loved ones he hadn't seen for almost four decades. We heard stories of food, friends, family, and drink. it was unfortunate that they did not have a camera, so they couldn't bring back any photos of these relatives. I had heard of some of them because my Nono had read me parts of the letters they sent. These letters came in thin blue paper envelopes with thick red, white, and blue stripes around the sides. I asked my mom why the paper was so thin, almost like tissue paper. She said it was so they would weigh less. Things sent by airmail were charged by weight, hence the tissue envelopes.

It was sad Nono's Papa was already deceased by the time he went back to Italy, but Nono went to visit him at the Catholic cemetery. The family had a crypt with four empty slots, one for each of Nono's brothers and an additional one for Ambrosia, the step-mom who, according to Nono, was still alive at over 100. When Papa had died, he left a bottle of wine to Ambrosia in his will. The brothers, taking their cue from his small bequest, kicked her out of the store and out of their lives.

I was bothered about Nona; she just wasn't the same after they returned. She told no stories about the trip except to complain about how hard it was to get around. The streets were cobblestone and getting to most houses involved climbing steep hills. She was very over-weight and wore shoes with thick soles and big high, but wide heels. Just two weeks after she returned, this stranger in my Nona's body, she had a massive stroke. She did not utter a word or move out of her bed for two weeks. Then she died.

Within a little over a year, I had lost my good buddy Curddy and my Nona who had started my mornings with hugs and weak coffee and the joy of sitting on her lap. I was distraught.

I walked over to see my newest friend Roock. He had never given me a hug or any show of affection and I didn't expect any, but I needed any type of companionship. He was on his porch reading a Hemingway novel, but he put away the book and walked over to greet me. He put a hand on my shoulder and squeezed, then gave me a pat on the back. It was so simple, but I perked up a bit. Then he walked into his room and returned with a large book. On the cover, I saw a shaggy man and the title, Robinson Crusoe. It ended up being the best book I had ever read. It transported me to a land of adventure, far away from my problems. Roock introduced me to a new world of reading actual novels, novels that adults read, not the watered down versions they gave me in school. He and my dad made sure that the novels I was given or bought (for the going price of 35¢ in paperback) were free of sex, profanity or anything inappropriate. From then on I was addicted to reading and made sure I had a pocket-book with me (that's what we called paperbacks then because they fit in the back pocket of my blue jeans).

One day Roock found me on the patio reading a more adult version of Robinson Crusoe, with illustrations and more text than the one he had given me. In his quiet radio announcer voice, he called, "Come over here." Then he walked to the cellar doors and opened both sides, nodding his head toward the cellar, now full of water. He asked me, "Does this fill up every year at this time?"
"Yes," I replied. "When it rains and water sinks into the ground, the water leaches through the half of the cellar that isn't cemented."

"Well then, when you get tired of reading and need something new to do for fun, you can play here. Just don't go in the water. It is full of lots of bad things nature has to offer. But you can float things in here. Go get some old newspapers Salvatore doesn't want."

When I brought them back, he showed me how to make paper boats and paper airplanes. That began an annual tradition of making and sinking paper, as well as tin, boats in the cellar.

I could count on the fact that when it rained at Big Pink the cellar would fill, almost to the top cement step of the patio entrance. I very clearly remember sitting on the edge of the patio and my feet on the first step down, with water just touching my shoes. Each year I would excitedly look forward to the flooding. To my paper and tin creations, I added ones made from scraps of wood from the wood bin that was on the mud porch. I populated them with plastic men, like cowboys and army men. After they were in my boats, I shoved them out to the deep end of the wine cellar and shot at them with my BB gun. WHAT FUN!

After the water drained out, it was another adventure. Armed with my BB gun, a flashlight, and bravery, I would go on a quest to rescue my cowboys, and army men. When I found the tin cans that had been my targets, I would count the B.B. dents and give them a score. Tuna cans were worth 10 points per dent; anchovy cans, being smaller, were 20 points.

Another fun occupation was shooting the ugly swimming larvae that would eventually become even uglier mosquitoes. There were lots of them, tens of thousands. I think I only eliminated about 10. It was hard to hit them because once the BB entered the water, it didn't go straight. Instead, it skewed off to the side, almost like a ricochet. It was still fun, especially after I started using the same method I had seen my dad and buddies use when they lined up a shot of a cue ball. They knew how the pool ball would bounce and where it would end up.

The other memory I have is of all the canned goods that were shelved in a walk-in wood and screen mesh cabinet. These included fruits such as peaches, apples and cherries and vegetables that included artichoke hearts, tomatoes, chard, and beets. There were also jams of every variety, but after Nona died, those got to be fewer and fewer. We actually began to ration those because they were such a gift from Rosi to each of us. When it came to the last three jars, they were pigs feet, and we decided we would never eat them. That way we would always have a reminder of her. Thank God, because I gagged at the thought of eating them.

When it flooded these canned goods were moved to the top shelves of the canning closet in the cellar. Nono would estimate how much wine and canned goods would be needed before the water subsided and guests could easily get what they wanted. The rations we rescued would be brought up and put in the 'cooler' cabinet. In guessing how long it would be before he could enter the cellar, he determined how full the cellar was, how much water had been in there already and how long it had taken to drain out. If he miscalculated, Nono would put on chest-high waders. It was fun watching him slog through all that gross-looking water that had seeped from the dirt and cement into the cellar. Looking back, I wonder if the septic tank was down in that dirt too. ugh.

Yes, there were many distractions to take my mind off missing my Nona. There will never ever again be any meal as fantastically flavorful as Nona's yellow rice, with freshly grated parmesan cheese. It brings tears to my eyes as I write this, thinking how she would make an entire plate covered from edge to edge especially for me. I saw this as a huge offering of her love for me.

Chapter 17
The Treasure of the Black Widow Cave

In contrast to cold winter days, being the first one up when the weather was warm was a special thrill. I would try to sneak down the hall without waking anyone. This was hard to do because every time I took a step, the cold linoleum would crackle and a board would pop. It made me think of someone crushing ostrich eggs while cracking their knuckles.

I would slide across the kitchen floor in my stocking feet, stop at the wood cabinet and remove two one-gallon pickle jars. These contained homemade cookies: rock-hard biscotti, also known as wine cookies because you had to soak them in wine to soften them, so you didn't break your teeth on them, and soft almond cookies. When I unscrewed their metal lids, they broke the silence of the kitchen with their high-pitched screech. It's a wonder these noises didn't wake the whole house.

Once I filled my coffee mug with Stornettas milk, the best milk in the world, but only available in Napa, I would take my 'breakfast' cookies and coffee out to the big patio table under the fig trees. I loved it there so much in the early mornings. It was quiet, peaceful and dreamy. A wispy, ghostly fog meandered through the vines on its way to nowhere, and I watched it until it burned itself out and vanished. By then, the sun was on me, warming my shoulders, and then, in an instant, the rest of my back. It didn't take much in those days to get me excited: a bright blue sky that went up to infinity, going from cerulean blue up to lighter sapphire. Blue has always been my favorite color, and that may have started because of my early mornings gazing at these beautiful shades of blue. Add sun warming my bare skin and an idea for an adventure and I would happily spring out of bed.

Sometimes, an always-welcome gentle wind would coast through the fig trees, and I could smell, or maybe I imagined, the faint scent of the leaves and the aroma of split open figs. Birds often ate the ripe figs, leaving parts of the figs on the tree split open so they could return for their next meal when they wanted fresh figs. There were always dozens of open figs left in the two huge trees. I liked the aroma. It always reminded me of fun times sitting at the big table under those wonderful old trees, eating ripe figs with hard cheese, Nona's homemade salami, and home-cured olives.

Nona and Nona picked the olives themselves from the olive trees.

It was always a good day when I started it with my cookies in the cooling breeze under those fig trees enjoying the breathtaking view all around me as far as I could see. And this day had started out great! I got up before anyone, even the cacophonous "drunken" rooster's wake-up call. I was asleep, but then, in a split second, I was wide awake. I had a mission for the day. I was going to dig up buried treasure, and I needed to do it quickly before anyone else woke up.

Buried Treasure

One day, my Nono was acting kind of sneaky, so I followed him into the cellar. I saw that he was burying a treasure, a Mason jar full of money. It was the most money I had ever seen. He was crouched down, folded over in a tiny crawl space between the outer wall of his house and the inner wall of the wine cellar. There was sand inside that secret compartment, and he dug a hole. Then he put his treasure in it.

I was excited, in a way only a child can be. I had discovered a secret about my Nono, one that no one else knew. In my mind, I began to plan my safari to dig up that treasure. I always liked to imagine new adventures. At this point in my life, I had listened to about seven years worth of radio shows. I loved those old shows like the spooky Inner Sanctum and the mysterious Fat Man. I was fascinated by the way they painted pictures in my mind. I knew what that old Western town had looked like and what Matt Dillon looked like, as plainly as if I were there on that dusty street in front of the Long Branch Saloon. It was all done with words and sound effects, and listening became a mind exercise that developed a strong 'muscle' in my brain; that 'muscle' was imagination. Right then, peeking around the corner, careful that Nono didn't see me, my imagination was racing.

Suddenly, Nono turned to leave the hidey hole. I quickly jerked back so he wouldn't see me. But, even if he didn't see me then, he soon would, because he was heading my way and I didn't have time to escape. I panicked. The only thing in the cellar close to me was a wood rack holding up two wine barrels. Nope, that wouldn't work. I had seconds to hide. Then I realized there were some shelves mounted low on the wall. I lay down on the bottom shelf. Nono left the darkness and walked into the light right past where I was on the shelf along with a stack of his LA Italia newspapers, and a few wheels of cheese right next to my head. He walked up in that big shaft of light and out to the patio.

As soon as his back heel moved off the top step, I bolted. I was able to run up the inside stairs, shove open the door to the mud porch and scoot into the kitchen where I sat down at the king- size table with the linoleum top. I tried to look like I had been there for a while, in case Nono had any hint that I was spying on him. I wanted it to appear that I had been there in the kitchen playing the whole time. So I opened my own personal drawer in the table; this was where I kept all my table toys, crayons, paper, coloring books, colorful rocks, decks of cards, some little plastic cowboys and.........Indians (sorry, that's what we kids called those toy guys with feathers in their hair holding bows and arrows). I also had some real feathers from the pigeon coop floor, that I could put I my hair and pretend I was…uh …a Native American. There were lots of colorful rocks from the middle of the railroad tracks, and four pennies smashed on those tracks by Bluto, my dad's name for the old, big, ugly, smelly, freight train that came by twice a day.

I quickly took out my old drawings, one of my dog Ladybug and me running through the vineyards, and my favorite one of Ladybug swimming across Conn Creek with a stick in her mouth. She was always so cute doing the dog paddle out into the middle of the creek and back. I spread my artwork all over the table and started to color a new picture of Nono and me picking grapes.

I heard the cellar door slam down with a house-shaking thump. I waited and waited, fidgeting nervously. Soon, Nono walked upstairs into the kitchen and sat at the kitchen table next to me. He opened

his drawer and took out one of his little twisted Italian cigars known as Italian Ugly Sticks, the cigar that smelled like a burning bike tire. Then out came a box of Diamond brand stick matches. There was the scratch of the match, and he flamed up his smoke. He then took one of the several clean glasses usually present in the middle of the table, along with a bottle of
table red homebrew, fresh from the barrel on the rack in the cellar. He filled the glass, took a puff, then a swig, smiled at me and gave me his usual slight head nod. The nod was his way of saying, either "Hi!" or "Life is Good!" or "I love you!" or "Happy to see you!" or "I'm okay! I hope you are, too." Or it could be that he meant to say all of them.

I knew then that he didn't realize I had seen him. He didn't give his buried money another thought the rest of the day, but it was all I could think about.

Jimmy's Secret Mission

Now, it was almost sunrise, and I was heading for the wine cellar, under Big Pink. The first half of the cellar was pretty nice, neat and clean. There was a big shaft of sunlight streaming down from the open cellar door. Up high on two of the walls were four short windows that were above ground level. Two of these windows gave a view of the driveway and the feet and ankles of anyone walking past. One pastime I enjoyed was going into the cool cellar on a hot day and trying to guess who the feet walking by belonged to.

The other two windows gave me a nice view of the flower garden and my Nona's pond that had her name, Rosi, spelled out with blue glass, embedded into stones on the front. Pretty flowers in blues, reds and oranges surrounded the pond, flowers I never did know the name of. These short dirty windows also let some more sunlight shine in.

This half of the cellar was nice and familiar to me.
The half my Nono had been in had almost no light. It was dirty, damp, moldy, and cluttered with junk. It was also fragrant with a variety of odors. There was wine and oil, (not olive but heating oil),

but also rotten grapes and a faint essence of a small dead animal. When you walked on the dirt floor, it kicked up some very fine stinky dust that seemed to stick in your nostrils for hours and coated your tongue with something like hot paraffin mixed with dirty flannel.

When I was in that half of the cellar, I always had the feeling that the ceiling was closing down on me, Black Widows, rotting beams and all. Oh yes, I can't forget; it was very creepy, scary and claustrophobic.

Whenever I entered the dark half, the dark side of the cellar, the Cave as I called it, I had a feeling that I was suffocating in an old dirty horse blanket. Or maybe it was more like getting a hug from smelly Olga Delamangura, her flabby, blubbery arms crushing me to her huge bosoms and her four moles or warts or whatever they were. These warts or moles seemed to have a life of their own, reaching out, getting too close to my face. In summer when she wore sleeveless housedresses and it looked like she had a beaver under each armpit. I should say, those beavers excreted a strong B.O. It wasn't pleasant being hugged by her, nor was it a pleasant feeling on the dark side of the cellar. I hated both of those things.

I had planned my adventure out the night before. I just wanted an up-close look at the money; maybe, I would just open the jar. In my mind's eye, I saw it as clearly as if I were right in there. I could feel the soft sand shifting under my knees as I scooted into the secret treasure chamber; I could smell that aromas of wine-soaked cork, mold, and dust that was always hanging around in the far back half of the cellar. I could feel the cold rippled metal lid of the Mason jar, then hear the faint tinny-"screeee * screeee" sound of me unscrewing the jar, and the crisp feel of those hundred dollar bills as I removed them. I even saw myself counting them. But, oh no! The thoughts that came then, due to my good-boy Catholic school training, set off alarms in my brain. I would only look not touch.

I very quietly and slowly opened both doors to the cellar; I knew I would need a lot of light to reach back to that far rear corner, the Cave. I bounced on the balls of my feet at the top step, excited and a

160

little nervous, hesitant to go ahead with my plan. But this was my adventure. It was my chance to be the brave explorer, like Jungle Jim on the corny TV serial. I had to go on.

I stepped down the stairs to the cellar floor. Then I crossed to the Hidey Hole in the back, dark, ugly, half of the cellar. The walls had large dark green blotches of mold with light white fuzz around the edges. Yuck, gross! There was an old wood grape crate overflowing with used corks, half purple from the homemade wine. To make it much worse there were tons of spider webs. I was scared to death of spiders, especially the Black Widows.

I crossed the floor quickly, climbed up on the barrel rack that partially hid the Hidey Hole. I removed the trap door that covered the hole, and then I put my hand into the sand on the other side of the wall, ready to enter into the compartment that concealed the buried treasure. Just then, there was a loud noise. I jumped up almost through the ceiling.

I turned to see that it was just the wind that had blown one of the doors closed. Great! Now I really had to hurry in case someone woke up wondering why the door had been opened. In addition, I only had half the light. As I turned, ready to enter the hole, I felt a something prickly on my hand and looked down to see a huge spider ……. and it was a Black Widow.

What happened next, I can't say for sure. It was a long time ago; I have had dozens of nightmares about it. Fantasy has been mixed in with my hazy memory of what really happened. But, I will give you the little I remember. I went through flat-out stark terror-panic-jumping out of my skin, hair- falling-out fright. As soon as I saw the Black Widow on my hand, I screamed in a loud high pitched "aaaaaaaaaaaaaaaaaaahhhhhhhh".

Now, this is where reality, fantasy, that imagination factor and the nightmares have become mixed. I am just about positive this was the fantasy part: As a result of the high pitch of my scream, rats came out of the walls, running toward the open cellar door; but I was also headed for the door to get out. I was going so fast that I was flying, right over the rats, right onto the patio. Once outside I saw that our dog was chasing its tail round and round snapping as he went; he too was freaked out by the scream. Cats, having heard the squeaking of the running rats started chasing them. Cats from everywhere were running right at me; all sizes and all colors of cats. Because there were so many rats and so many cats, the cats became confused, not knowing which direction to go. There were lots of rats and lots of cats, scrambled all over the patio. In all this chaos, several rats jumped on the back of some of the cats, riding them. I had a quick, almost cartoon- like vision of one of the rats holding on to the cat fur with one paw and riding it, bouncing up and down, like he was on a wild bull. About this time in my dream, I would always wake up.

But back to reality. Here I was, down in the dark, cobwebbed corner of the cellar. I was looking at this messenger of death on eight legs. In a panic, I flicked my hand to the right, away from me, trying to get the Black Widow off my hand. I looked down at my hand and he was still there, and now he looked mad (I couldn't tell you now what a mad spider looks like, but I saw it then). I flicked my hand again, harder this time. As I swung my hand it smashed into the wall, hard; it hurt bad. But at least I knew the spider was smashed and dead.

I was still in a panic; I jumped down to the dirt floor and hit it, running quickly away from spiders, past the ugly mold that now seemed to be reaching out to grab me. I burned rubber going through the cement floor area, the clean, bright, safe half of the cellar. I shot up the stairs, across the patio, and behind the fig tree.

I was shaking, light-headed and my hand hurt like blazes. I was, however, safe and away from spiders and rats and cats, if there were really any there. I remember feeling wetness on my hand, thinking I must be bleeding from smashing my hand into the wall. I turned my hand over, thinking of what to use to wipe the blood off. Just then, two things happened at almost the same time:

I heard my dad's voice from the cellar, yelling something like "Who the hell was in here?!" He would get his answer as soon as he reached the top of the cellar steps. Because right then is when the second thing happened. There was another blood-curdling scream.

The scream was coming from me; the reason for the scream was because, as I went to wipe the blood off my hand, I saw the wetness was not from my blood, it was from the guts of the half-smashed Black Widow, still on my hand, with two legs twitching.

My instincts told me to run to my dad for help.

My dad was coming toward me, and I noticed anger in his eyes. They seemed to be spinning like pinwheels, and smoke was coming from somewhere on his head; on his face he wore a scowl. I thought fast, ran out from behind the tree, holding my hand out in front of me, and started crying, trying out my acting chops as if I was hysterical. Surely my dad wouldn't spank me if I was so upset.

It worked; I got off with a stern scolding from my mom. "Your Nono would never put his money in a jar; he would never hide it in the cellar, and there is no Hidey Hole in the wall. I should know. I have lived here since 1925. So stop making up ridiculous lies."

I know what I say next will seem strange, but it is true. I forgot about the treasure and Hidey Hole for a few decades, and when I did remember, it was under the most unbelievable circumstances.

Chapter 18
Mystery Boy Gets a Name

It had been a while since Curddy died and awhile since my Nona died. I had taken a break from searching for the answers regarding my family's past. I had grown up. Well, a little bit.

It was almost the end of summer. My dad was on strike from his job as a bus driver. I quickly learned what 'strike mode' meant. The good news was that we all had a lot of time together. The bad news was that we had no money coming in. We had to cut expenses. We ate a lot of tuna casserole and pasta. There was no eating out. In truth, we had only ever eaten out at a nice restaurant on one of our birthdays. Other than that, it was once a month at Hokey's 15-cent burgers. But now we couldn't eat out at all or buy anything, not even the TV Guide. That lasted one week, before Dad said. " Well, 15 cents isn't that big of a deal once a week."

My dad couldn't function without the TV Guide as a compass to direct him through the wonderful, new to us, world of television. Each week he would read the guide cover to cover, study it, and decide what to watch each day from the time he got home until his bedtime. Each choice had a red check mark and to be sure he didn't overlook the show, he circled it three times.
So, Dad figured we would spend less money by staying at Big Pink. Plus there were a lot of great things to do up there. I could fish, swim, shoot my BB gun and our .22 semi-automatic rifle with a scope. There were vineyards to romp through, and I could sleep outside on the old metal double bed that eventually became my mom's bed when she was in her 80s. Later, it became my grandson's when he was in his younger 20s and lived with us.

I got up that morning figuring it was going to be a long, hot, boring day. The weekend of my Nono's birthday party was coming. Like all good Italian birthday weekends it would start on Friday and go until about 1.00 A.M. Sunday. Today was Thursday, and I had all day with nothing much to do before the guests began arriving the next day for, what I knew was going to be, a fantastic and rollicking weekend-long party.

I started out by looking through my dresser drawers to decide what to wear. In the top drawer, I found my Davy Crockett T-shirt. When I was looking for pants in the bottom drawer, I discovered my comic book and, in it, the photographs I had retrieved from Curddy's cigar box in his bedroom after he died. I shuffled through the photographs and saw the one of the boy that Curddy had told me was named Anthony or ANT. The other picture I had grabbed was the piece that was originally the other half of that photograph. It was the picture of the boy that I believed was named Nicco. I remembered hearing that name somewhere.

Suddenly, I had an idea. The fog of mystery was starting to swirl. I began remember my side job of being a junior sleuth, getting answers to questions about Curddy, among many other things. Right after he died, I had needed a break. Well actually, it wasn't so much a break as I was just plain fed up with it. It was too much work without ever getting anything. No solutions. No answers.

I couldn't believe it. All it took was the sight of those photos, and I was fired up again. I looked closely at the photo of Ant and thought, "Oh my God!" This might turn out to be an adventure of a day after all. I pocketed both halves of the old photo, ran from my bedroom, down the hall, through the kitchen, and jumped down the cement steps to the patio two at a time. I was off.

I was on an important, secret mission to get some answers to questions about my grandparent's past as well as Curddy's. I didn't know what the truth was; there was so much conflicting information. Did my grandparents first meet Curddy at the Oaken Bucket bar? If Curddy's wife and son were alive, why did he make up the story that they were murdered, then only to tell me they were in Italy? I didn't know if the most recent stories were the most true. Were Curddy and my grandparents trying to purge their souls? Or were the first versions the true ones, but because they thought the true first stories made them look bad, they made up new stories that were lies. "AHHHH"!"

Once Curddy was dead, I couldn't find out anything more from him about those boys in the photos, or the mystery boy. He couldn't tell me how he got his scars or anything else. I knew that I wouldn't get answers from my parents. My mom had threatened me: "If you ask me any more questions about boys in photos or Curddy's scars or about what happened to your Nona in Lodi….I'll…I'll…. well I don't know what I'll do, but you won't like it."

And my Nono had told me several times, "I only want to tell stories of happy, fun times; I won't talk about things that made me sad." So I had given up. Until now.
With all those doors closed, I had to find another one to open, and that was today's secret mission.

But, as usual, there were other things to distract me, including all the preparations for Nono's party.

It was only after dinner that I remembered my plan. I ran down the back steps, across the pink patio, blind to everything around me. Well, almost everything. I suddenly noticed the odor of hot tar, burning weeds and burning rubber all blended together to make a stench that would cause a rat to vomit. That could only mean one thing: Nono was smoking one of his after-dinner cigars. I stopped and turned toward the table. There sat Nono, and in front of him on the table was an empty box of Toscanelli cigars. After I became a teenager I had tried to smoke those "Italian Ugly Sticks." They looked like something fished out of a cat box and left in the sun for a year. Also on the table was the maroon rock with white stripes normally used to hold down a deck of cards. But the cards were not under the rock because Nono was playing solitaire with them

He still used the old cruddy deck, even though my dad had bought three new crisp decks, mostly so when he played Cribbage with me, my mom or the guests that knew how to play, there was a nice deck. The actual Cribbage board was cool. My dad made it out of an end of a wooden grape box and drilled the holes in a big Z pattern. But, tonight, there was Nono using the old sticky, stinky deck of cards.

He always got ticked off when he didn't get the right cards; he would slap down a card, curse in Italian, "Christo, Bastardo @#$$ *&%%" and start a new game. Now, he noticed me and asked: "Where are you galloping off to?"

"I'm going over to play with Paché's cats." Paché had more than a dozen cats, all of them white, except one black one, so that excuse worked. My Nono looked up, gave me a warm smile, nodded his head and said, "Say "hi" to Paché for me."

Paché's Story

It was a short run through our neighbor's vineyard and on to the third house behind the old white and green schoolhouse, which was Paché's house. When I got there, Paché was outside sitting on a chair at a round wood table. He was alone, unless cats count as company. There were two white cats asleep on the table and others scattered around the yard. Paché had a large hunk of cheese and an even bigger hunk of salami in front of him. There was no knife in sight, and it looked like he had been gnawing on both the cheese and the meat with his dentures. Paché had disgusting eating habits like Chest-Arena the Eater. There could have been a contest to determine which of them was the worst.

Seeing how filthy the table was, I thought there had to be cat hair all over the food, not that Paché would care. He was drinking red wine straight out of the bottle, and a constant flow of it dripped onto his bare chest, trickling down to his belly and getting blotted as they reached his pants. It was a revolting sight, but for him, just the usual scene when he was drunk.

Paché had started drinking heavily right after his wife Linda was killed or, rather, died of her own reckless behavior. Theirs was a sad story. Paché and Linda's youngest son was in a car with a bunch of classmates from St. Helena High the summer after their junior year. They had been up at Conn Dam for a day of swimming, barbecuing, eating and clowning around. Eleven of the boys were crammed into a 1950 Ford that comfortably fit six. And, they had been drinking. The boys in the Valley didn't have to scramble to get alcohol. They didn't need to siphon a bit from each bottle of liquor their parents

167

had and add water to the bottle so their parents didn't notice their booze bottle had a lot less in it than the last time they removed the bottle from the liquor cabinet after work to pour a good stiff drink to help the stress, frustration, and depression fade from their mind. No, up in Wine Country, all a lad needed to do was dig out an empty bottle or jar from the wine cellar, take it to one of the large barrels of, usually homemade, wine, turn the spigot and fill it up.

On this summer night, they were the last to leave the lake, right behind a car with six teen girls in it. They had been flirting with these girls most of the day and showing off. Rico was doing front flips off the wood raft in the middle of the small swimming lake. Woody was doing back flips, and Timbo tried to do a double backflip and crashed his head on the raft. The girls acted like they were not impressed. When the girls drove off, the boys left two minutes behind them. The plan was to turn off their lights and sneak up on them. Because there were not enough girls for each of the guys, they started arguing about who should get which girl. Timbo was heated; he was driving, and they were in his car, so he thought he deserved the first choice.

None of them was thinking about how much they'd had to drink.

And, if Timbo hadn't turned to cuss out Rico, they might all have lived.

Of course, if the girls hadn't thought it would be fun to turn off their lights and pull over to the side of the road….. and when the guys came around the big bend they would pull in behind the boys and hit the brights…. Well, then maybe, if not for this, everyone would have lived.

But both of those things did happen. And, the boy's car lights were out and the driver was drunk.

The boys rounded the big bend, known from that point forward as Dead Man's Curve. After he'd cussed out Rico, Timbo turned to look at where he was driving, and saw that he was heading off the road. He jerked the wheel to correct and was on the shoulder of the road as he careened around the bend. He may never have seen the lights-out girls' car. Timbo smashed into the girls' car, pushing it ahead to the left and into a shallow soft dirt ditch. The lucky girls only had broken legs, whiplash, and bruises, plus several other broken bones. The boys, however, went off the road on the right and down the rocky cliff. There were lots of broken bones and four dead bodies. Paché's son Saul had to have a closed casket funeral

The day after the funeral Linda started drinking. At first, it was just wine with Paché. She would drink three times what he did. But that only made things worse. He was drinking to forget. But there they were, staring at each other, two miserable people who couldn't forget.

Then, Linda started going to Don's bar; the locals called it The Don's because of Don's demeanor. Don's was only 300 yards from Paché and Linda's house. As soon as the sun went down, so did her spirits, and, then, she would walk to Don's, rain or shine. Linda usually drank, the old Italian standby, Brandy Manhattans. After a while, for every 3 Manhattans, she would drink an Old Fashion. And she hung out with the regulars, mostly men, drinking and dancing to tunes on the crackly staticky radio, and sometimes playing darts. From time to time, some of the drunks made passes at her and tried to take her home with them, but she always turned them down. She wouldn't even accept a ride home, always walking home by herself.

Then, one night she didn't come home. She was found face down in a ditch with less than 6 inches of water, dead and cold by the time her body was discovered. It looked like an accident, but there was a wound of some kind, like a small bump on top of her head, and her purse was missing.
There was an investigation, but they never found out for sure if she got the bump from a person who stole her purse or if she bumped her own drunken self and someone found her dead and took the purse.

So Paché's son had died because of alcohol, and his wife had died because of alcohol, and in a few years, alcoholism would claim Paché's life. But on this day he was all mine. If I was lucky, he would be friendly and not too drunk. I had always liked him; he was a good friend to my Nono.

There were people in the Valley that were his friends, and a few even loved him, so he had not given up on his life. After all, his oldest son was still alive.

Paché had some unique qualities, perhaps because of all the alcohol, or maybe because of his permanent sadness. His skin color was olive, but he could be black or white as his appearance changed from good to bad. He would go from being a nice-looking, pleasant, elder Italian resident of the Napa Valley, to looking like a Skid Row bum. When he was cleaned up, bathed, dressed nicely and shaved, with his big batch of unruly gray hair combed, he was not bad looking. But that only happened when he was sober, and that was usually on major holidays, or Sundays when he would put on a suit and tie to go to church. When he was drinking, he wore torn and tattered pants held up by frayed suspenders, and a tee shirt with straps. If he was home and didn't have company and the weather was warm, he would often be shirtless, as he was on this day.

Paché without a shirt was a sight best reserved for the blind. If you were going to sit close to him you might pray for a temporary cessation of your sense of smell. His breath was atrocious; on top of that, he belched a lot. When he belched, the odor that came out was so offensive that even he couldn't stand it, he would wave his hand back and forth in front of his mouth, and this succeeded in sending the foul odor wafting up the nostrils of anyone within 12 feet of him. If people had an adverse reaction, like wrinkling up their noses or gagging, it sent him into fits of laughter.

He had a huge smile that reminded me of the crow, Heckle, the buddy of Jeckle in the cartoons named after them. Along with that, he had a little high pitched laugh that was like the cackle of a witch. He laughed or cackled often and loudly. His personality was best described as rascally. He found much humor in life, and he liked pulling practical jokes. He would laugh at things no one else thought funny, but because of his cackle others hearing him would laugh at him.

Paché was the star of some of my favorite stories, including "The $1000 Fishing Pole." But this is not the time for those stories. You only need to know he was a real character.

Today, he was sharing his salami with a few of the cats. Since he didn't have a knife, he was biting off chunks and spitting them at the cats. If they happened to be sleeping, they woke up when one of his spit salami bombs hit their heads. It was gross. The cats were all around the yard, but since the majority of them were deaf, they didn't move when I ran up into the yard. The black one heard me approaching and ran off.

I ran up to Paché, patted his hairy shoulder and half out of breath, greeted him. "Hi, Paché!"
"Hi, my little Jimmy!"

I didn't waste a second. I put a photo of Ant, on the table in front of him. Paché bent over to look at it and spilled wine on it. I picked it up, wiped it off and held it up in front of him. He bobbed back and forth from the photo, trying to focus. I had noticed earlier that the boy in this photo from thirty-five or so years ago, had half of his front tooth was broken off. Paché's son Mario had half a front tooth missing. And I knew that Paché was a long-time friend with my Nono, maybe as far back as Lodi. So maybe the idea I had percolating in my brain was on the right track.

"Paché, is this Mario when he was a little boy?"

"Yes that is Mario when he was a boy, but back then, we called him by his middle name Anthony, or Ant."

I quickly asked, "Is this photo from Lodi?" "Yes, that was Lodi"
I looked at him, not moving, thinking, for almost a minute. He belched, fanned the foul smelling gas away from his face, then wiped off his mouth, guzzled some more wine, and chewed a hunk off the cheese.

I asked, "Was Ant friends with a boy called Nicco?"

He looked at me with blurry eyes, silent. Finally, he opened his mouth and in a somewhat wheezing voice, blowing out very dead breath, and said, "Yes he was friends with Nicco."

I asked, "Who is or was Nicco? Is this him?" I shoved the second photo in his face. It was the photo from the back of Curddy's closet.

Paché answered quickly, I sure without thinking what he was saying because a few sentences later his brain must have censored him and slammed on the power brakes. He started out "Nicco was very cute. You don't know him, how could you not know who he was? Hezzz your
………..your… I…I…I."

Then he slammed on his mental brakes. He shut up. He started rubbing his ruddy face, making a "scrrr scrcho" sound as his rough callused hands rubbed against his four-day-old whiskers. A few minutes later he said, "I just don't remember who he was, just a friend of Ant's. Ask your Nono."

I started jumping up and down with excitement. I whined, "Please, please Paché tell me."

He shook his head so fast it looked like he was trying to shake his head off of his body. Now that would have been one way to stop him from drinking; headless people don't usually eat or drink, I thought.

He objected, "No, no, no it's not my place to tell you that story. What happened at LODI is in part responsible for your Nona losing the part of her that was fun, silly, and always a happy person. Basta, enough! I've said too much. I am drunk, don't listen to my rubbish. My wife Linda told me that when I had too much to drink, I babbled on and on; that I just need to shut up."

At the mention of his deceased wife, Linda, I became fearful and wanted to get away from him, fast. I knew that he was moments from becoming a sobbing, drooling idiot. If anyone, even Paché himself mentioned Linda he would go to pieces, especially if he had had too much to drink.

"Goodbye Paché," I replied. "See you around."

I trotted home, pretending I was Rattler, the horse from the State Game Farm. I would ride Rattler when we went to the house of our friends Roy and Alma; they lived at the Game Farm. The horse was so named because he once stomped a rattlesnake to death. He also rattled me when he jumped a little creek and dumped me face first into a muddy bank. Yeah, that hurt and was embarrassing, but mostly it hurt. I learned why riding bareback could be a dangerous undertaking.

So, I galloped all the way to Big Pink. I approached my Nono, still at the patio table, only now he was smoking his pipe.

I rocked back and forth on the balls of my feet, humming "It's Howdy Doody Time" while I worked up the nerve to ask THE BIG QUESTION. I was chickening out. I turned, took a few steps toward the house, stopped, turned, walked up to Nono, and patted him on the shoulder, as I did earlier with Paché. Then I asked in a quiet voice, "Who is Nicco?"

The pipe dropped from Nono's mouth, spilling burning tobacco on the table. I ran to the little pump house and grabbed the old, dirty, dented tin measuring cup. After several attempts at the tight faucet, I finally got the water on and filled the cup. I left the faucet running, as I hurried to the table and dumped it on the embers that were burning through the linoleum tabletop. That worked to put the fire out, but the water and ash ran off the table onto my Nono's lap, he didn't even flinch.

I apologized pathetically, "Sorry Nono."

He didn't respond, so I walked over and turned the water off. From behind me, I heard Nono say, "Did Paché tell you that name? What else did he say?"

Now I was starting to get really nervous, almost panicky. I wished so much that I hadn't asked the question. But now I needed to answer his question. I nodded yes.

173

"Was he drunk?" Nono asked. "Never mind. I know he was. When he gets drunk, he talks crazy talk." Then he chided me. "You ask too many questions. You don't have to know about everything that has happened."

I was stunned and embarrassed. Nono had never spoken to me in that tone of voice before.

I mumbled "Sorry," and walked quickly away into the house. I told my mom "I'm not feeling good. I'm going to bed." Of course, she gave me a look like I just gave birth to flying blue pigs; going to bed early was something I never did.

After I got in bed, I pulled the covers over my head and prayed hard that Nono wasn't mad at me. I was not afraid of The Ghoul from the Slaughterhouse that night; I had other things on my mind. I soon escaped from my scrambled thoughts into a more pleasant dream world.

I slept in late the next morning. When I finally got dressed and went into the kitchen Nono came over to give me a hug and kiss. "It is nice to see you this late morning." All seemed forgiven and forgotten. That day would bring early guests for Nono's birthday party.

But, all the energy had gone out of my search for information about the Mystery Boy. I never wanted Nono to speak to me in that tone again. And, after his birthday celebration, we went home.

Our new home in Pleasant Hill had so many things to distract me. I had many friends, and we had fields to explore, a creek right behind our house, and hills where we found fossils. We had bikes to ride and baseball fields for endless games of ball. Now, when my family went to Big Pink on the weekends, I would bring a friend or two along. We ran wild up there, shooting our 22s at targets and birds, and playing hide and seek in the spooky slaughterhouse. All the puzzling questions about my grandparents' past got locked away in a back room of my brain, replaced by fun, fun and more fun.

The next time I revisited those mysteries was in 1963 when I was seventeen. I was in the kitchen at Big Pink when Nono came up to me and said, "Come with me. I have something to show you; something mysterious, something special, something just for you."

And that was how my Nono took the first steps on the road to full disclosure, the truth and answers to questions that I had pondered for years, even if they had been on the back burner of my mind for the most recent years. I had made so many efforts to gather the puzzle pieces and get them to fall into place. Finally, the picture would begin to emerge.

Chapter 19
Rediscovering the Valley

When I was eight-years-old, a family friend took my family to my first play. It was at an amphitheater somewhere in the Oakland hills. The play covered one year, and each season was a separate act. At the end of the first season, they dimmed the lights and changed the set from snowy and cold to warmer and prettier. I was awestruck at how each act used a completely different set.

The beauty of the Napa Valley is just like that. Each season presents a new backdrop for the next dramatic act.
ACT ONE

I still remember harvest time. It was as if the whole year was leading up to this, curtain time. The curtain rises, and the cast takes center stage. Men, women and, for most of the first three-quarters of the 1900s, even children, came out early in the morning and started weaving through the lush ripe rows of grape vines. They moved quickly, all with many years experience, completely stripping all the bunches of grapes from one grapevine before moving on to the next. Sometimes there was a low, thick fog early in the morning. I remember looking down from our kitchen window, and all I could see were hats or heads floating through the mist; then, as they bent down to pick the grapes they disappeared from view. Soon the rising sun would chase away the fog. Then you could clearly see the workers.

Families living in the valley would look out and see a sunny day and get excited thinking about the fun they would have at Conn Dam swimming, and barbecuing lunch on the pits made of rocks and rebar. But the pickers would be cursing the sun as it pounded down on them with its searing heat. The work back then was much harder than it is now with the modern systems and methods. The term 'back-breaking' would have been honestly earned then. The vines of my grandfather's vineyards were entirely different than what you see now along the scenic Highway 29. When bare of any fruit or leaves, you could see that the grapevines had thick trunks and twisted branches covered with gnarly, ash-grey flakey bark. When they were all full and grown in with leaves, and grapes you could see these tiny offshoots that reached out to grip on to whatever was near. These were like very skinny greenish-yellow octopus arms, tendrils that grabbed on to something and twisted around and around it. As all grape vines did this, soon they were woven together, the foliage so thick that it became a solid mass. In the evening when everything was fully grown, and the sun dipped down behind the mountain, the grape leaves no longer looked like a green quilt.

Instead, they first looked grayish and then they began to look like an ocean and the breeze would create rolling waves.

Because of the dense foliage, the grapes were not always all visible, instead, hidden in the massive amounts of leaves. That was why it was easy for workers to cut themselves. In the 1940s, it was discovered that the pressure for the pickers to work faster and faster resulted in more and more cutting injuries and tests found that the juice from these grapes contained 1% of blood. That would be unbelievable. And it is…. But it was quite a joke at the time. The workers usually wore long sleeve work shirts which protected their skin from getting scratched by the hard, rough branches and vines. The long sleeves also protected them from the sun, as did the straw hats. There was not a lot of concern or awareness about skin cancer in those days and thus my grandfather and some of his friends developed skin cancer and or lip cancer. The smoking of pipes and Italian cigars didn't help.

The wicked sun, along with the hard work, could cause a rookie to pass out if he did not cover up and drink lots of water. I would say only a brainless fool would go out in that sun without a hat or water. But, then I was a rookie and a brainless fool at seventeen. I went to work in the vineyard dressed as I would for school. I even wore my twist boots. These were boots that zipped up tight over my ankles so when I was twisting the night away I wouldn't sprain an ankle. I may need to point out the twist was a dance. Years later, when the Beatles became popular in the U.S.A., young people wanted to dress like them, and I became known in my circle of friends as the first guy to have Beatle boots when, really, they were just my old twist boots. By then, they were embellished with a few drops of blood from my

177

grape picking days. Or maybe it was just grape juice. Not only did I not dress properly, I didn't even bring water and also, wore no hat. The field workers had not only big hats but also water, even the children. Some of them used large jars, some with the labels still partially on, torn and dirty, but still readable, Best Foods Mayonnaise was the most popular with the smaller French's Mustard jars for the children.

After one hour of picking, I was in pain. It was my first job other than mowing lawns. I had no experience with hard work or manual labor. I was sweating, and the sun wasn't even on us yet. My knees were wobbly from crouching down, my box wasn't full, and I had completed only three or four grape vines. The other workers had completed a whole row, filling several wood crates and stacking them in individual stacks with their names neatly printed on each end. It was important that the names were readable because they were paid by the box. When the workers completed the row assigned to them, they reached into their jeans or a pocket on their usually filthy, greasy Ben Davis overalls, and pulled out some sort of notebook to scribble on with pencil stubs they had sharpened with a pocket knife. Their jeans were often stained with grape juice or even blood, the result of carelessness and cutting without actually seeing what they were cutting. Grape picking was often a guessing game. You would grab a bunch of grapes in one hand and cut with the other, making a guess where the stem that held that bunch really was. The knives they used had blades not much bigger than a tablespoon, curved like a small scythe and razor sharp. Each had a wooden bulb-like handle with a looped cord attached. The worker would put his hand through the loop so if he dropped the knife, he wouldn't lose it.

The crates for the picked grapes were heavy rough wood, split and splintery, and once filled, each one took a Sumo wrestler to pick it up. These crates were old, the wood stained by decades of grape juice (and not-to-be-forgotten blood stains). The worker would place the crate under the grapevine, squat down and with one hand search among the leaves, find a bunch of grapes and use the small knife with the curved blade to cut the grapes loose and drop them in the crate. This process was repeated until the crate was full. Then it was lugged to the end of the row and marked with a name. The worker would then grab an empty crate and return to the grapevine where he left off and repeat the process. For this hard work, the pickers earned somewhere around 25 cents a box, sore, creaky knees, and a pain in the back that aspirin, the only painkiller available to them in those ancient days, only slightly helped.

Some of the field workers were pickers only, and when the grape harvest was over, they moved on to the next crop of whatever was ripe and needed picking elsewhere. Others stayed on to do pruning, grafting or all the other things I saw my Nono do in his own vineyard. There were little cottages where the year-round field workers lived. These cottages or shacks were on the property of the wineries they worked for. Inglenook housing would be better-described as a 'shack' or 'rat trap,' There was a bed, just a thin mattress on the floor, a wood-burning stove to cook on and heat the place, and one bare bulb light hanging from the ceiling, often with dangerously frayed electric wires. There was also some type of small table, about big enough for two plates the size of 45 rpm records, with no room left over for a salt shaker. There were usually two chairs, some that rocked, even though they weren't rocking chairs. It was a joke that someone from Beaulieu-BV had come over and sawed one leg of the chair shorter. There was no indoor plumbing. The outhouses (there were two, so no waiting) had candles on a plate by the toilet hole and a rolled St. Helena Star newspaper to kill the black widow spiders and at least stun the rats. Then there were more old newspapers that would never pass the Charmin test.

Only one person died in a rattlesnake-related death. That person, Ivan, who had just up from Mexico two days earlier, did not get bit. He went out to the Crapper (so named for Thomas Jonathan Crapper, thus the nickname Crapper or the John. Honest, no joke) and found the box of matches right inside the door with the half moon cut out of it. When he went to strike the match, he forgot to close the box. A spark went into the box and ignited all the other matches. As they flared up, the bright light revealed a huge rattlesnake in the corner of the crapper. The snake didn't like the light, so it rattled. Ivan jumped back and his butt hit the wall, which knocked him forward where his knees hit the 'toilet seat.' He fell forward into the hole, hitting his head on the way down, knocking himself out and Well, he drowned in the muck

Those were the Inglenook worker shacks.

B.V. had bathrooms located in the center of the cottages. There was a toilet for every six cottages and a shower for every 12 cottages. There were also large sinks between each of the cottages that could be used to wash ''Rutherford dirt" out of their clothes. Most workers didn't need or really desire to do that daily or even weekly. The inside of B.V.'s cottages was nice. They had comfortable beds with box springs and a table with four chairs. The light actually had a glass shade although it usually attracted about 100 dead bugs. The cottages at B.V. also had indoor plumbing for a sink. They made three washing machines available and clothes lines with clothes-pins. These washing machines were like big steel buckets with a lid on top and above that two large rollers to squeeze the clothes and 'wring' most of the water out before hanging on the line. Fewer than 50% of people alive today even know what these looked like. So B.V.'s accommodations were nicer, they paid three cents less a crate than Inglenook. Both wineries gave all their employees a 50% discount on wine purchases. None of the vineyard workers would pay the overblown markup prices. They would buy wine by the gallon jug from the owners of the small acre vineyards who made their 'Home wine.' Not only was it cheaper, it was better.

ACT 2

After the grapes were picked, they were processed through several steps, cutting them off the stem, removing leaves and crushing them into juice in a barrel. That juice then aged for two years, a long act indeed. The scenery in Act 2 changed and became interesting, if not beautiful. The leaves started turning colors, shades of brown, orange and gold and fell off the vines. Soon, all you could see were bare brown branch-like vines. You could view them as artistic sculptures or, with some imagination, huge spiders with dozens of extra legs reaching up to crawl up and out of that vineyard. Perhaps they would creepy crawly their way over to the Inglenook workers' shacks and break through the paper-thin walls.

ACT 3

Revitalized the vineyard with the joyful yellow of the mustard plants. They grew in thick, covering most of the soil surrounding the brown spider vines, preventing the spiders from escaping. The combination of these bright yellow flowers and green leaves of the mustard plants intermingling with the spindly brown vines created an astonishingly beautiful composition for the photographers' art. Even a child could take a photo so dynamic that it could be framed and placed on the living room wall.

ACT 4

Brought back the green of the leaf buds, soon to be an even brighter green and growing to the size of leaves worn by those statues of the long-ago Roman art era. Soon you could see the little nubs in clusters that would eventually grow until they developed into grapes ready to be cut loose and dropped into a crate. The drama would begin again. Fired From Grape Picking
Now it was my turn to be part of the cast. I had marveled at the workers who picked grapes in all kinds of weather conditions and never had a permanent home, instead, living in the ramshackle housing provided by the vineyard owners. Some of them even slept in their pickup trucks which they loaded sky high with all their belongings, somewhat like the truck in the movie, Grapes of Wrath. Even in these hard conditions, they were happy and often sang songs in Spanish. I often wondered if the words of these songs were translated into English, would we discover the lyrics were about how selfish and inconsiderate the big bosses were? Not only were these people happy, they were kind and considerate to me.

My grandparents' friends looked down on these people, referring to them as "those Mexicans," usually said with lips curled like the words tasted rancid as they came out. I just figured that all the New Americans had been discriminated against when they first came to America before they moved to their new "empire," and now they had someone else to discriminate against.

My parents had brought me up to Rutherford three days earlier on a Friday, afternoon. Nono had them take us to the Food Mart in St. Helena. He pushed a cart as I loaded it with junk I would want to get me through the week, beer, coke, cookies, candy bars, four packs of Pall Mall, t.v. Dinners, tuna, bread PB&J etc. Nono was so happy I would be staying to keep him company that he paid for everything.

FIRST DAY ON MY FIRST REAL JOB, PICKING GRAPES

It was a hot, hot day. By noon, I was sweating, dirty and in a world of hurt. To add insult to injury, I was so slow and inept at picking grapes, I was fired by lunchtime. I gave the bag lunch I had brought with me to Sean Garcia, the kind man who had helped me to fill some of my wooden grape crates and I limped home to Big Pink.

I had been hobbling along between the train tracks, stepping on each of the wood ties. By the time I reached the spot where the dirt road from Hwy. 29 crossed the railroad tracks and made the right turn, my bad right leg was dragging like a wooden peg-leg leaving a rut all the way behind me. When I was fourteen-years-old, I had discovered a golf-ball-sized tumor behind my left knee. It was then I learned that I had a neurological disorder, Neurofibromatosis. It causes tumors to grow on the nerves and crush them. After I turned fifty-five, I needed to use a wheelchair. But, on this day, as I slowly made my way to Big Pink, I still saw a bright future, just not as a grape picker.

When I got to the patio behind Big Pink I crashed onto the closest seating. Sadly, it was the most uncomfortable piece of furniture on the property. It could have actually been used as a torture device.... who ever thought a chair made of grapevines could be comfortable?!?! Maybe they had run out of rose branches. I was too beat up to move. I smoked a Pall Mall and before I finished it, Nono came trotting down the back steps. He had a 2-gallon copper pot that, when she was alive, my Nona had used to cook polenta in. On this day, Nono used it to caddy sardines, cheese, the always present always hard-stale bread, several 'rare expensive' Italian cold cuts, figs, a beer, a bottle of premixed also ever-present Italian classic,

Brandy Manhattans, and some empty jelly jars which we used for wine, cocktails, beer, and soda, almost everything except coffee. He had a smile on his mouth, in his eyes and his voice as he said "Jeemee how are you? I heard from Paché that you had a hard day."

That God-damn Paché, the Valley gossip! No one could figure out how he found out every bit of dirt that went on from Oakville to St. Helena. Well, I guess he found out some of it by buying drinks at the Old Oaken Bucket, the sleazy bar in Rutherford. My dad used to say, "The Old Oaken Bucket is what the field workers use for a urinal.." I knew that wasn't true because several times when I walked with my Nono to the market or post office that used to sit where the Rutherford Grill is now, he would go into the bar that was across the corner from the market. I would sit on a log that was at the base of the outer market wall. This entire wall was painted with an advertisement for Coke. It showed a frosty cold glass Coke bottle so big that it could fill a tanker truck. There was an elf-like guy with Coke bottle top for a hat. On a hot day, I would almost drool looking at it. So I would blackmail my Nono by saying, "If I have to wait under this sign while you go in the bar, I need a bottle of Coke for my thirst and a Scrooge McDuck comic book, so I don't get bored." On these days, while I was waiting, I saw that the guys didn't use the Old Oaken Bucket that hung from the sign for a urinal, they used the outside wall of the bar.

Now, thanks to Paché I couldn't ease my way into telling Nono I had been fired. It actually worked out well, because Nono, knowing I had had a "day from Hell," had brought me a 'Care Package' He delivered it to the large table under the fig trees. I shuffled over and sat on the bench that had a back on it; an added bonus was that it faced the beauty of Morrisoli's vineyard and the mountain range beyond it.

By the time the sun was setting behind this mountain, sending glowing reds and oranges out to us, we had downed enough Brandy Manhattans for me to tune into the green and rust-colored leaves on the grapevines and the deep purple grapes that in two years would be pleasing people as they savored the deep purple of the wine they produced. Above the vines, the mountains had a dreamy pale shade

183

to them, making them seem like a mirage with parts fading in and out of focus. Then the sun's rays shone above the mountain. Curddy, my old buddy from my young childhood had always said, "Jeemee, one day we will walk to the top of that mountain and see where the sun goes to sleep at the end of the day." Unfortunately, we had never made it. But on this day there was a light yellow fan of light sitting on top of the mountain, and above it, fat spears of magenta, rose and yellow shot out toward us, each vying for our attention. For me, the magenta won; for Nono, he liked the rose. I had never thought that as a young, almost-a-man (or so I thought), I would be talking to my old world Italian Nono about how beautiful the magenta and roses were.

Chapter 20
Solving the Mystery Begins

Curddy had always told me, "When you are older and know more about life and understand about people, then you will get your answers." I thought I understood life long before I was seventeen. And yet my questions remained unanswered.

QUESTIONS LIKE: What was it that had made Curddy sullen and a loner? Had something broken him? Was that something embodied in the scars on his arms, chest, and neck. Had whatever wounded him physically also scarred his soul? Curddy seemed lost in some long ago life, haunted by something that had taken away his joy in life, and I knew it had to be something more than losing his wife and son.

And why didn't my Nona sing and dance when company came over like I had heard she did before they moved to Rutherford? What had happened to that "happy-go-lucky Rosi" who joyously danced with half a dozen men?

I knew my mom hated being an only child, and I knew how desperately my grandparents wanted a son. So why didn't they have more children?

Why was my mom afraid of having candles burning in the house? I knew that had come from her mom, my Nona. But where did that fear come from?

And why, oh why did I get the strange sermon from Nono about forgiveness whenever I was upset with someone? What was the horrible, unforgivable event he was talking about?

Now that I had graduated from high school, I was drawn back to the Valley and a job picking grapes at Inglenook. I stayed with Nono at Big Pink and figured on working for several weeks, but I only lasted half a day. Picking grapes was hard work. My legs couldn't take all the bending down and I was too slow. The other pickers completed a whole row in the time it took me to pick two vines. So instead of working, while spending time at Big Pink. It was during that week after I got fired from picking grapes, that I started bonding on an adult level with Nono. We spent many evening hours after dinner talking while we smoked pipes or Toscanelli cigars.

It always surprised me that the tobacco was fresh in that can forever, and I really mean forever. When I found a half full can of Nono's Granger 40 years later, it still smelled fresh. When he peeled off that dark blue plastic lid, a sweet, rich tobacco aroma would escape from the can it had been imprisoned in. One can lasted him for months. I smoked a cherry-flavored tobacco that came in a pouch, and every time I opened it, this incredible earthy cherry scent drifted out but smoking it was even better. Those odors had a comforting, feel-good effect. After that time, whenever I smoked a pipe or smelled the smoke from one, it reminded me of those good times at Big Pink.

At the time, there was no TV at Big Pink, so our evenings were spent talking or playing cards. The dialogue was different each night, but the cast was usually familiar, just the two of us. It was on my last night there that my Nono spoke those inviting words: "Come with me I have something to show you, something mysterious, something special, something just for you."

He got up from the table and started walking toward his bedroom. I quickly got up to follow him. This sounded exciting, but I had no idea just how exciting it would actually be. We didn't have far to go, just a little over a dozen feet, through the kitchen door, into the always-dark hall, over the grate on the floor that covered the oil-burning heater, and then a few more feet along the crackling linoleum floor and through the doorway into Nono's bedroom. As I followed him, I noticed that even at 78, Nono had a steady gait and strong upright posture. I remember walking behind him that day thinking that he didn't look or act like an old man.

I had been in his bedroom less than a dozen times. A couple of times I had snuck in there to snoop around, once even opening a drawer. I had found a lot of silver dollars and a roll of 20s big enough to choke a moose. Seeing all that money made me nervous and, feeling guilty, I ran out to the yard. For a reason I can't explain, there was something almost sacred about this room, maybe because it was supposed to be off-limits for me unless I was sent in to get something for one of my grandparents. A few times when I was still a little kid, I was sent into the bedroom to fetch Nono from his afternoon nap. He napped with his shoes off, clothes on and the bedspread over him up to his neck.

The two bedroom windows always had the shades pulled down, so when the sun was on them, it cast a pleasant, calming golden glow on the room, the color of butterscotch LifeSavers. Sometimes when I went in to wake Nono and the sun was in the 2 o'clock position, the glow cast its light on the mirror over the dresser, and it reflected on Nono from behind his head. It looked like he had a halo. Oh, yes, I knew halos, oh, so well from three years at Catholic school, where all the statues had halos. Nono always looked peaceful and kind as he slept and he always had a smile on his face as if he was reliving some great moments of this life. I used to imagine that he was dreaming of his times with Nona when she was still alive, of them working together in the garden or walking with me, each of them holding one of my hands. I know the thought of those walks brought a smile to my face.

Now, Nono walked over to his dresser with me behind him. I could see his reflection in the mirror, his big smile, and happy eyes, and he was nodding his head as if he were thinking 'Yes, yes, finally.' He opened the top middle drawer, took out his comb, sleeve garters, and money clip with the Italian flag on it, a leather cigar case, a belt buckle with an Italian flag, and one cufflink with the flag on it, too. Then he paused. Now, the drawer was empty. He took out his pocket knife, opened it and pried the false wood bottom out of the drawer. He removed several hundred-dollar bills, a large thick envelope, and a photo. He handed me the unframed photo. It was an old photo, one I hadn't seen in years… the Mystery Boy.

I was stunned, almost speechless. After a few croaking attempts, I said, "Who is this? This is Nicco in this photo? Who is he? Where is he?"

Nono looked me straight in the eyes and said with a quiver in his voice, "My son." Then he said in a more controlled voice, "My son."

I was stunned. It was obvious that everything I had been told about the boy in the photo was a lie. My grandparents had always wanted a son but never had one. It was a lie. My mother an only child. Another lie. I had to pause before I said anything because if I translated my thoughts into words, I was sure I would have regrets.

I finally asked, "He is my uncle? Where is he?"

He pointed to the thick envelope: "This is for you from Curddy. It is to fulfill his promise to tell you everything when you became an adult, including what happened in Lodi." I was puzzled. Let's read the story in this envelope together, and I will fill in the blanks. No more lies"

I had a photo of the boy I thought was Nicco in my right hand, staring down at it, oblivious to everything else in the world and the universe. I noticed the photo was shaking because my hand was shaking; actually, my whole body was trembling. Was I nervous or was it fear that had me quaking? Or was it excitement? It was a little bit of all three. There was fear because I was afraid to ask the Big Question. When I was a young child, I had asked about the photo of this little boy in the strange clothes numerous times. That photo used to be above the fireplace, the fireplace that was not used because my Nona was terrified of fire. But when I asked, I was greeted with anger or a dismissive, curt attitude from my mom and Nona. In the past when I had asked my Nono, he had looked sad and just didn't say anything. I didn't know what response I would get if I asked again after all these years. I was nervous because I knew I had to ask, but I didn't want to upset Nono. But I had to ask, I just had to, but I shouldn't. But, then again, Nono did give me the photo. How to ask, what to ask, when? I was squirming. If I don't ask the right way, I might blow it. How, what, when? I was excited because I couldn't believe that after all those years of no answers, now I would get some. How exciting! It was the mystery that had plagued my childhood, lost in the past, all but forgotten. Now maybe I had a chance to get answers. In a few minutes, this whole thing could be solved. Of course, I was shaking, from fear, from nerves, and excitement.

I looked up; I noticed that my Nono had placed the thick envelope he had just removed from the secret compartment at the bottom of the drawer, under his left elbow. He was looking down at the floor; I wanted him to look up at me. When he did, I would ask him. He fidgeted. He moved the envelope up some, almost placing it under his armpit as if he was afraid to drop it. But then, he moved it and moved it again, all this time looking down at the floor. I thought he was nervous too.

Then Nono looked up. He smiled at me, winked, and gave me a nod. I knew this wink and nod. It was kind of like our secret code. At times when my mom was ragging on me about who knows what, he would give me that wink and nod, and then intervene, saying something like, "Jimmy, come with me; I need your help."

When my parents would go out to a movie or dinner, they would leave me with my Nono and Nona, saying, "Put him to bed at 8:30; he doesn't need to stay up late with all your friends." Nono would give me that wink and nod, and I would end up partying until our car's headlights hit the barn door as they were driving down the driveway. I would then fly up the steps, run through the house and swan dive into bed. The wink and nod always meant it all would be OK; he was there for me; in today's terms 'he had my back.' I was always happy to see his wink and nod; it warmed me; it was a shelter from the storm.

He winked, nodded and added a smile. That was my signal.

"The boy in this photo, this is Nicco, THE boy Paché told me about when I was a child. Nono looked at me right in my eyes; I saw in his eyes compassion. He responded, "As I said, that is my son, Nicco Curtoni. My son." he said with pride.

Now there was a tornado in my mind, spinning wild and out of control, tossing my thoughts all over and scrambling my brain. What I thought I knew about my family was wrong. There was a family member I didn't know about. Where was Nicco? Why did my grandparents say they always wanted a son if they already had one? Why all the secrets and lies? How or why is it okay to lie to a child?

It felt like the ceiling was smashing down on me, and the walls squeezing in. I felt a crushing weight on my head and shoulders. It seemed like I was shrinking. And the tornado went out of control. It was as if my mind was vaporizing and escaping like steam out my ears. Answers, questions, mixed-up confusion. Maybe Nicco was born 'defective.' My Uncle and his wife gave birth to a child that was, as my parents told me, 'severely retarded.' My uncle and aunt put the child in some kind of home, never to be seen again. Maybe that is where Nicco had been, alone, growing up with no family, no one to love him. I couldn't imagine my grandparents doing that. So where is he? I stood there like a fool, with my mouth open; my eyes had a glassy million-mile stare. I was lost in a maze of mystery.

My Nono must have sensed that I was stupefied, turning catatonic. He said, "I know what your next question is: where has he been, why have you never seen him or ever heard anything about him? It can be answered in several words, but then you would have many more questions. Let's go sit in the kitchen; I will get the bottle of brandy and as we drain it, you will get all your answers. All of them." His actual words, quotes, were not in such clear English but I have captured the essence of what he had to say through this story.

He took the fat envelope from under his armpit, extended his right arm toward me and said, "First read this then we can talk." I grabbed it fiercely as if it would get away from me. I stared at it; everything else in the room was out of focus, and my eyes focused on the envelope. It was very thick; the envelope paper was old, turning yellow, and there were two words written with a fountain pen. The handwriting looked like the hand that wrote it was shaky. Was the author of these two words nervous, scared, old, or defective? Who wrote those two words, 'For Jimmy'? I turned the envelope over; there was nothing on the back except a purple splotch that looked like it was wine. The other thing I noticed was that the glue had given up its grip and the envelope was no longer sealed.

I broke out of my trance at the sound of footsteps. I looked up to see my Nono's back as he walked out the bedroom door. I followed him to the kitchen, walking fast as if he would vanish if he were out of my sight. When we entered the kitchen, and he said, "Get two glasses, and if you want to mix anything with your brandy, get it too."

Now my brain was starting to unscramble; the tornado, losing its power, was returning my thoughts to me, but not necessarily back to where they belonged. I felt like I needed to pound on my head so things would fall back into place. I did, but it didn't help. My next remedy was to drink a lot, fast. I needed straight booze, but I couldn't drink it that way. I was not 'Man enough,' as my buddy Woody would say. I still had about four years until I turned 21.

I will say that Woody and I had been drinking alcohol since we were 14 years old. At my grandparents, I had been drinking diluted wine with the Italians since I was seven, and beer at 13, with my German grandmother. But Woody and I were drinking to get drunk. We drank beer or pilfered booze from our parents mixed with coke, 7-Up or orange juice. We had a bottle of Vat 69 Scotch that we ripped off to try and prove we were tough, but we never were able to drink more than one sip a week. I didn't learn to appreciate good scotch, bourbon or tequila for over a decade after this

I opened the cabinet that was above the refrigerator and grabbed two jelly jars. Then I opened the refrigerator, got a 7-Up, and went to the freezer to fill my glass with ice. Then I sleep-walked to the table, pulled the chair out and sat in my usual spot at the left corner of the table. Nono sat across from me. He put the bottle of brandy down between us. He nudged the bottle over to me, and I slid a glass over to him. I poured half brandy, half 7-up, drained it, and then downed a second one. I shuffled to the refrigerator got another 7-Up, made a third drink and said, "OK, tell me some stories.

Nono said, "Do you mind if I have something to drink first ?" In my rush to get toasted, I forgot to slide the bottle to him. He got up and went to the cooler cabinet. When he opened it I caught a whiff of what we kept in there. I had a desire to grab some cheese, salami, and fruit from the cabinet; everything would be nice and cool. Nono grabbed the bottle of sweet vermouth. On his walk back to the table, he stuck the bottle up to his mouth, grabbed the cork with his teeth twisted the bottle and pulled the cork out. This must have been an

Italian thing. I recalled my Nona, Zia, and Cheezer doing it that way, as well as Guidi who owned the St Helena Olive Oil place where we bought cheese, salami, pasta of every shape and sizes, anchovies, sardines, capers, and just about everything except olive oil. My Nono, mom, dad and I went there on average twice a month. Every time we went in, Guidi got out a bottle of brandy and removed the cork with his teeth, because he didn't have a spare hand. He had the bottle in one hand and four glasses in the other, a dirty finger in each one. He would distribute glasses to my family and pour everyone about 'two dirty fingers' of brandy. He would make a toast, something to do with family, health or prosperity, clink glasses and drink. After he did this, he always thought to look at me, shrug his shoulders, hand me the bottle and then grab it back, shaking his head. So on this night, watching Nono and enjoying the aroma rising from the cooler, I thought of Guidi's. Nono poured half a glass of brandy, and mixed it with sweet vermouth and took several big, long gulps. He wiped his mouth with his shirt sleeve.

Then he said, "Read the letter. When you are finished, I will fill in the blanks. I will answer any questions you still have. I don't know what the letter says. I never read it. I just know it is a confession, a clearing of all the feelings of guilt, regret, sorrow and distress the author suffered. Drink up and read."

I looked at him; I mean really focused in on his eyes and mouth, analyzing him for a twitch of his mouth, a flicker of his eyes, something to tell me he wasn't being honest with me. I saw only sincerity and love. I was deep in thought as I continued to look at his face, frozen in thought for several minutes.

Then I said, "Before I read the letter I want you to answer two questions." He nodded.

"Who is the writer of the letter?"

He answered in a calm, strong voice, "Miss Crabsi, the school teacher, wrote it for him, for Curddy. He was the author of everything the letter says."

I let that sink in. The heavy envelope I was holding supposedly contained Curddy's tell-all explanation of how he got his scars and why that accident cast a cloud of gloom over him for the rest of his life. I remembered Curddy saying something like "When you are older you will get all the answers." This letter from Curddy contained answers about Curddy. But Nono said after I read the letter he would fill in the blanks. Hopefully, the explanation would include why my newly- discovered uncle was not now part of his and Nona's life. It should answer those big questions and many others. That excited me, but I was still a mess of mixed emotions.

I continued to deal with my nervousness, my mouth so dry I could hardly talk. So I drank some more. I wanted to rip open the envelope and speed-read the letter. But another part of me dreaded what I would find out, causing me to hesitate. I kept waiting for Nono to glance up at me as a sign I should proceed, but he kept his eyes lowered.

My distress made me irritable: the room became too hot, the wooden chair too hard on my butt, the drink too strong, and the air too stagnant. I needed a cigarette; at least it would change the air quality. I pulled out a pack of Pall Malls, stuck one in my mouth, and pulled out my Zippo; when I opened it, the distinctive "click" seemed extra loud. At that "click," Nono looked up and his eyes focused on the source of the noise, and then said, "Let me have a light, I need to relight my cigar." I handed him the lighter; he used it to light his cigar and handed it back to me. Both of us were using tobacco as a crutch to be able to hobble through this journey into the past, an unpleasant past. I gave a flick of the flint wheel; it produced a spark that produced a flame, a flame-thrower-sized fire. Carefully, so I wouldn't singe off my eyebrows, I brought the flame to the tip of the cigarette. Ahh, that first drag was the best part of a cigarette.

I took a few deep drags, instant gratification; each drag seemed to give me more courage. As I spewed smoke up toward the ceiling I noticed, the white smoke from my cigarette was mingling with the bluish smoke from Nono's cigar, creating a big grayish cloud hanging above us. I had an amusing thought that this was symbolic of the cloud that had been over this whole story of Curddy. I was procrastinating.

Did I really want to know this story that my family and friend had tried so hard to keep from me? It was the old "You can't un-ring a bell." Once I learned what happened, I had the feeling it would be rattling around in my head forever.

Now, with a dry mouth, I croaked out "Next question. Where is Nicco?"

Nono looked me and said in a wavering voice, "Nicco is no more. He is dead. He was killed in a most horrible way."

Nono's answer brought the tornado back in my mind; only this time it was bigger. I croaked out, "How… when……, how was he killed?"

I stopped. Now I felt a bit woozy and nauseated. Was it the polenta we had for dinner? Nono's polenta wasn't anywhere near as good as Nona's, but it had never made me sick before. Or maybe it was the rabbit stew served over it; at least I thought it was rabbit. Then again, it could have been the three drinks of brandy and 7-up. On top of all that, I now had an uncle I didn't know, but he was dead and "killed in a most horrible way." Now, I had another question: "Where, where was he killed?"

Nono answered, "Lodi. Everything started at Lodi and most of it ended at Lodi."

The story of Lodi and its tragedies unfolded over the next few days. That was a long night's journey into daybreak.

Chapter 21
It All Began in Italy Gerola,Italy

There was a small group of friends that gathered on Sunday evenings at Salvatore Curtoni's parents' house. It was a warm and welcoming home, in every sense of the word; during winter, there would be a big roaring fire in the stone fireplace. In the summer, they would open the many windows and a refreshing cool breeze came in from the Swiss border just north of them. There was a great view from any window. To the east, you could see the church with what must have been the tallest steeple in all of Italy. To the north were the beautiful mountains. On the west was a pond with a variety of fish that supplied a dinner to those fishermen that were patient. The pond also provided fresh fish for the family market. South was, well, to the south there was just the Castle Brizoni and the walled-in yards that kept everyone out and, as legend told, kept the crazy Hazetini Brizoni in. On top of all that, the Curtoni parents welcomed everyone as they arrived, handing them a big glass of wine made by their oldest son.

It wasn't the view that the group came for, or to see the ghost of Hazetini running around with a hatchet, chopping heads off her family, or the harsh crude red wine complete with sediment. They were explorers; they had a purpose, and they came to plan. They could have had their meetings anywhere, but everyone liked to meet at Curtoni's house because it was above Curtoni's Market, the family's very profitable business. The friends never were in need of wine, food or deli items because everything was just about 10 feet below them. Salvatore's dad, Papa was a good host; however, he would make Salvatore work it off if the group consumed too much, which they did often. Even though most of them were still in their teens, there was no problem giving them alcohol.

This group called themselves the New Americans. It may have been more to the point to call themselves the America Hopefuls because their vision was one of them becoming prosperous citizens of America. They knew about America mostly from Joseph, Joe. He was the leader of the group; Joe always gravitated to being the leader of any group he was in. As an adult what loss he had from being short, he made up for with muscles and thick arms, covered with lots of thick dark curly hair. He was what was referred to then as barrel-chested. He had thick dark wavy hair that he usually covered with a cap that was too small for even a ten-year-old. His pale brown eyes always sparkled like they were reflecting something, like someone waving sparklers. His nose could be described as hook-like. But all these features combined to be a better total than each of its parts deserved. Girls found him attractive.

Even as a child, he was a good leader and he was a good explorer. He was fearless. He welcomed dares; it was his chance to show off how brave he was. He would make some small change by betting other kids that he could do some incredible feat or another. One of his better bets was that he could jump from his rooftop to the Mangeli's roof next door, then on to the next roof and on until he had jumped the gap between six rooftops. He won every time. That is, every time he tried this trick in Italy; he wasn't as lucky when he tried it in San Francisco. He walked with a limp for the rest of his life.

In addition to Joe being a natural leader, brave and daring, he knew the most about the desired destination that the group had chosen, California. Joe subscribed to a newspaper from San Francisco. By the time he received it, it was about one month late. Instead of being 'news' it could have been called 'olds'. But it didn't matter that it was old news; what Joe was looking for were stories that told about successful people, jobs or land prospects. He wanted to know what was available in different parts of California and where was the best place to start a new life in America. From the newspapers and a few books he read, Joe was the expert on what it would be like to move to California. There was never a second of doubt in the group that Joe was the one to lead them on their quest. The group was young; Joe was the oldest member at 22, while the others were between 16 and 20 years old.

When the 'New Americans' gathered it was fun, interesting and exciting. Most of the group looked forward to this meeting as the high point of their week. They liked to talk about what their lives would be like in California. These evenings were spent planning, dreaming, and sharing ideas of what they wanted to do for jobs once they got out to The West. They had a goal, a vision of a life offering more than the future that was ahead for them in Italy. Much of what Joe told them about California was romanticized and embellished. That was okay; it gave them hope, something to look forward to. Joe had a gift for making people feel good about who they were and what they were; everyone loved Joe.

After all of Joe's research, he came up with a destination, a least a starting place, Lodi, California, in the United States of America. It wasn't beautiful; it looked nothing like their hometowns or surrounding countryside. But none of that mattered because it would just be a temporary home. Some of the New Americans knew they wanted to go to the famous city of San Francisco. There were a lot of Italians there; they would not be strangers in a strange land. They probably wouldn't even have to learn English; how wrong they were.

Joe thought Lodi would be perfect for what the New Americans wanted. It was a new and growing area; there were cattle ranches and farms that had large fruit and vegetable crops. By 1905, there were more than two-and-a-half-million grape vines in Lodi. There were two ranches that had cattle, vegetables, fruit, and vineyards. It was at one of these farms that Joe had a job if he made it there.

Even though San Francisco and the Napa Valley were more desirable locations, Joe hadn't been able to find any job prospects there. Everything cost more in San Francisco. So, Lodi would be the group's starting place. As the group talked and planned, it was decided that Joe would go first, be the scout. He would get a job and see what opportunities there were for the others. Then he would send for the others as he was able to find them jobs. The others would go as soon as they had enough money. They would travel in pairs and they would settle in the same area, starting their own little colony. That way they would get jobs and support and help each other until they earned and saved enough money. Then they could venture out to more desirable homes. Those were their plans; but not all the New Americans reached their goals.

As planned, Joe was the first to go to America.

Lodi was indeed an area that showed great prospects for the future. In addition to the farmland, there was a thriving city that had its first automobile in 1900 owned by Doctor Barret. It was no longer the wild, wild west. The town even had an opera house. The city became incorporated in 1906; at that time, the population was 2000+ people. Central California Traction Company had completed construction in 1908 for an electric passenger rail line linking Lodi to Stockton and Sacramento.

At the start of 1910, the City of Lodi purchased Lodi Water, Gas and Electric from Cary Bros. Company. They also opened the first library and, most important, their first municipal sewer system. The city had mostly people of German descent, as did a lot of the farms there. However, there was one cattle ranch that also grew crops and had a large vineyard. It was owned by an Italian, the cousin of an uncle of a friend, or something like that. It was there that Joe had a job and where he wanted the others to follow. He hoped he could get all of them jobs at Rancho Mario with him.

But, after Joe left for America, the group lost its heart. There was no one to fire them up, no one to paint that burning vision in their minds. Sadly, the meetings grew less frequent and fewer attended. The next person to make the trip was Salvatore Curtoni. Since no one else was ready to make the trip, he went alone. After he left, his girlfriend Rosealia Aquistapacé (Rosi), made an effort to lead the group and get them fired up again. It worked and birthed in her was a new talent. For lack of a better word, she became boss,. but she got things done. This came in handy for her first job in America, tending to the needs of dozens of farm hands.

Salvatore met Rosi in the family store. After Salvatore's mom passed away, Rosi became the pasta maker. The deli part of the family market made a large profit, so it was important to have a good pasta maker. Papa had dinner at Raymond Tonelli's house a few months after Sunny's rosary and service. Raymond's daughter Rosi had made the ravioli served with zucchini in a thick butter sauce heavy on the garlic with mushrooms and rock hard bread cheese on the side. The ravioli was the best he ever tasted. He hired her to make about a dozen pasta dishes because Ambrosia, his step mother, said she was tired of doing it. From her first day, Salvatore was love-struck. It took about a month for her heart to be stirred by him.

The group had not set specific dates of departure. Joe couldn't possibly know how long it would take him to establish himself and be able to hire his friends. No one really knew how long it would take to save the money they would need to pay for traveling expenses and the $25 cash they had to have when they arrived at Ellis Island. The plan had been Joe first, then Salvatore and Fiscalenia, known as Fisk. As it turned out, Rosi would be third to arrive. Many of the others never left Gerola.

An Italian-American Reunion

In 1997 there was a reunion held in Petaluma ,California for the families of those who had come to Northern California from Gerola in the early 1900s. Only three family lines other than the Curtoni and Acquistapacé line were from the "New Americans" who had met above Curtoni's market. The others had met each other during their first decade in California. There were about 100 adults and a sprinkling of children, at the reunion.

The event was organized by a priest from Gerola who came to bless the event and brought 25 people with him. Folks who attended met relatives, some they didn't even know they had. They ate and drank lots of wine, had a church service and took lots of photos, and talked and talked. Only three people who had come from Italy spoke fluent English; most of the others spoke only Italian. These three were busy translating. But conversations continued with only a few words, extreme facial expressions and lots of hand gestures, something Italians are legendary for. They all talked until the sun set, plunging the picnic area which had no lights into darkness.

Everyone had fun that day and promises were made to write or even visit Italy and tour. Addresses were exchanged and some emails, too. But for those in Gerola, there was only one email address. The only way they could get or send email was when Leo drove out of the hills down to the next village that had what we would call an Internet Café.

One American, Raymond, had actually been back to his Nono's birthplace. He described the only bar. The bar itself was an old door with peeling red paint on white-washed saw horses. On it were unlabeled bottles of wine, white and red. There was also brandy, rot-gut whiskey, sweet vermouth, oily gin and dry vermouth. The toilet in that bar was just a hole in the floor. If you remember the village in The Godfather movie where Michael Corleone meets his first wife, that's what Gerola looks like today. There were very few indications in Gerola that it was not still the early 1900s when the New Americans were there.

Leaving for America

But now it was 1910 and Salvatore was ready to start a new life.

Before he boarded the ship that would take him to his destiny, he just stood on the dock staring at it. He noticed that above the waterline, it was painted deep blue halfway up and had a red stripe about three feet wide with white above that. There were two smokestacks, also royal blue, with small puffs of smoke slowly rising from them. It looked very royal.

Beside him, his family was also stunned and speechless. To him, the ship was something dream- like, almost unreal. He had never seen a ship before, other than in a book his buddy Rocky had. It was actually only a drawing of the Mayflower. The book was a gift from Rocky's Nona and was titled First Trip to America. His Nona had written in Italian, "To my little traveler: One day, you will land on these shores."

Salvatore had never been on water in any vessel other than a two-person rowboat he and Rocky had used to go out to the middle of the pond by his house. It was the place where they fished. Each of them had fishing gear consisting of a bamboo pole with a piece of dark cord tied to the end and several rusty hooks crusted with dried worms from other trips. For bait, they used worms to catch trout, bluegill, and crappie, but to catch black bass they used night crawlers, huge worms. These they would dig out of the pomace pile next to Doyin's home winery. This was a huge purplish pile of the remains, the pulp of the grapes after they went through the device that removed the stems and seeds from the fresh-picked grapes and

the crusher. You could shove your hand in the pile and draw out about half a dozen fat worms. While they fished, the boys drank Grappa even though they were just in their teens. Grappa was a strong brandy drink that was distilled from pomace. If they got drunk enough, they would dive into the cool mossy water.
Sometimes they came out slimed and feeling itchy, but if they were drunk enough it didn't bother them much.

Since this was Salvatore's only experience being on water, the huge ship took him aback. He didn't know how to swim, but he could dog-paddle. He understood everyone aboard the ship would have life jackets, so he wasn't worried about drowning. It was a couple of years before the fate of the Titanic would strike fear into most ocean travelers.

As he stood on the dock being jostled by passengers rushing to get on the ship, he thought of the little rowboat compared to this behemoth. His memories of those blissful outings helped diminish his fears and he determined that his outing on this ship would be just as pleasant. He would just have to think of the ship as a huge rowboat. He didn't have a fishing pole, but he did have Grappa. Now he just needed to get on the ship and find a friend.
As he met people, he introduced himself as Salvatore Curtoni and told them he came from a little village in northern Italy, Gerola. He would describe it as being close to the Swiss border, and tell them they would see some of the Swiss influence in clothing and houses and various other characteristics of the village. There are still many differences between the Italy of the north and Italy of the south. There are blondes in Gerola; it would be hard to find many down at the tip of the boot. There are different dialects, and, skin tones get darker and darker the farther south you go. The food is different, too ask for pizza in some locations and the response might be "Pee what?"

If someone asked, "What town is Gerola close to, a place I would know?" his response would be, "It's near Lake Como, a most beautiful area." Gerola was and still is, a little village with steep cobblestone streets.

The question fellow Italian travelers asked on the ship was, "Why did you leave your homeland?" Salvatore's answer was quite different from most, and sad too. There simply weren't very many opportunities for a career in Gerola, except for the market. Salvatore worked with his three brothers in the family store. His Papa was the boss man of the store; well not really.

Hazel/Ambrosia was the boss-woman-man. Ambrosia was a mean monster of a woman, who, unfortunately, was Salvatore's step-mom. She married Salvatore's dad after Salvatore's mom died. Ambrosia was strict and liked to slap her stepsons in the face if she got mad about something they did, which was almost anything they did. Of course, this only happened a few times before the brothers did something about it. They slapped her back. When she ran to Papa, he shook his head and smiled, "They're doing what I taught them; if someone hits you, you hit them back." She stopped the slapping.

She was never happy and liked to control everybody and everything. Papa seemed to be happy with the way she ran everything. Salvatore didn't know if that was because Papa loved her (how could any person love someone like her?) or maybe because it had been too hard for Papa to run the store and raise the four boys after his first wife died.

Salvatore loved his brothers and Papa and knew he would miss them greatly, but he had to go. He had to get away from that woman. Plus there was something luring him to California. He wanted to go to the place his friend, Joe Pitzini, was sending him letters from, Lodi, California, where Joe worked on a cattle ranch. To Joe's friends in Gerola, he was a cowboy. There was a job waiting for Salvatore there; there was a future there, a new life, an escape from Ambrosia. America was calling him; he set a goal to leave his little village for the wide-open spaces of America when the new year started. But he wasn't able to get away in January, it wasn't until June 1 that he was able to get away. Then he was at the rail of the ship waving goodbye to his brothers, Papa, and his girlfriend and wife-to-be Rosealia Aquistapacé. After he left, he and his brothers exchanged letters. At first it was a letter a week then it became once a month; it would be 41 years before he saw them again. He and his father wrote to each other once a month, but he never saw his Papa again after the boat pulled away from the dock and Papa very sadly waved what would be his final goodbye.

It was in 1927, the Friday before Easter, that Salvatore left his house in Rutherford and walked between the railroad tracks to the post office to get his mail. He was happy to see a blue airmail envelope, knowing it would be from one of his brothers, but he didn't open it until he was home, sitting at the kitchen table, with a glass wine and his pipe spewing fragrant smoke. He opened the envelope with a big smile and a spirit of anticipation, expecting joyous news of a new baby or family wedding. But the first paragraph hit like a freight train; his Papa was dead from a heart attack. He never again would see his father. A deep sadness hit and tears flowed onto the letter, into the wine glass, and on his hand holding the smoldering pipe.

But on that June day, as he waved goodbye, he fully thought he would be seeing his family in a few years. The fact that none of his family came to live or even visit was a mystery never to be solved.

There were a few other people from Gerola on the ship; Salvatore knew some of them, but they were old, in their thirties, and all they did was complain about 'the old country'. He didn't want to clutter his mind with negative thoughts. He wanted to find someone that was excited and enthusiastic about what the future held, so he set out to make new friends. The more friends he could make, the more entertained he would be. It was easy for Salvatore to make friends; he loved people, had a great personality and a positive outlook on life. What better way to meet people than a hot game of cards!

Making a New Friend

Several days into the cruise, he got into a game of Pedro. About an hour into the game, several things became obvious; two of the men were drunk and headed for trouble, and the tough guy, with the tattoo of a heart with the names Maria and Jamie on his forearm, was ready to blow if they made any more rude remarks about the Northern White Italians. The drunks were from southern Italy and there was, with some, prejudice between northern Italians and southern Italians. The tough guy wore a black shirt unbuttoned half way, showing a muscular chest and a gold St.

Christopher medal hanging from a chain. He had his sleeves rolled up to show his bulging biceps. When asked his name, he said, "None of your business." He hadn't smiled or talked much the whole game and he appeared to be looking for a fight.

As the first drunk from the south slammed his cards down and said, "Take that you northern scum," Tough Guy jumped across the table and grabbed both the drunks by the throat, two hands, two throats. In seconds, both drunks had bloody faces, missing teeth and, possibly, broken noses. When the fight started, the card players jumped back out of the way so they wouldn't get hit, and so they had a better view of the fight taking place; actually, it was more of a beating. Both of the southerners were just about unconscious when Tough Guy pulled a knife out of his pocket. He opened the knife revealing an exceptionally long curved blade, a very unique knife. Salvatore had seen enough; he put his hand on Tough Guy's wrist and said "Basta," enough. Salvatore was strong after years of hoisting crates of olive oil or any other items that stocked the shelves of the family store, but he was not as tough as Tough Guy. Nevertheless, he had a look in his eyes that said, 'Trust me, I am your friend.' Then, Salvatore said, "Come with me; I have some Brandy Manhattans in a skin and Grappa with your name on them." Tough Guy glared at Salvatore, shook his hand off his wrist, then said, "Let's go I'm thirsty."

Salvatore told Tough Guy to wait by the front of the ship. The air was better there; at the rear, you had all the body odor, fish smell and the essence of garbage that the wind carried to the back of the ship. When he returned, he was holding a bottle in his left hand and in his right hand, nothing, no glasses, zero. He said, "No glasses; we will just have to drink out of the bottle, like pizans. We will start with Grappa." That was fine with Tough Guy.
They drank and talked. Well, mostly Salvatore talked for the first half of the bottle; Tough Guy was mum. Salvatore knew the grappa was strong enough to "put hair on your chest, curl your tongue, cross your eyes and pucker your lips." Finally, Salvatore asked, "What's your name?" The reply, "Curddy." "Where are you from?" Curddy's response: "North." Salvatore asking, jokingly, "Russia?" "No. In the

north of Italy. Not all the way up; just a bit above Roma in Lombardy region.

When the bottle was empty, Salvatore smoked his pipe and Curddy rolled a cigarette to smoke. Then, over three pipes of tobacco and five handmade cigarettes, Curddy told his story. In those days he wasn't much on talking and even worse on telling stories. He started, "Where would you like me to start, with when I killed the guys that murdered my wife and son, or should I start with how I learned how to kill a person with my bare hands?"

Chapter 22
Curddy's Story

"Let me roll another cigarette and I will tell you my story." Curddy said, in a tone that sounded like he wasn't sure he wanted to proceed. When it was rolled, Salvatore struck a match on his belt buckle, engraved with a big SC. Once it had burned off the sulfur smell, he held it toward his new friend. Curddy took the offered flaming match, cupped it in his hand, held it up to his cigarette, and gave a few shallow puffs. Then he took a deep drag, as if he needed the nicotine fortification to get through his story. He blew the smoke straight up and watched as it drifted toward the back of the ship; it disappeared after traveling just a few feet. Salvatore waited through a few more puffs, then said, "I shared my bottle with you; how about sharing your story."

Curddy looked at Salvatore, smiled and said, "Sure, why not; I could use a friend. I can't remember the last time I had one, or if I ever had one, other than my brother. Will you want to be my friend after I tell you all the bad things I have done?"

Salvatore responded, "I have always been a good judge of people. I can tell when someone has a good heart or when they are wicked. I tried to tell my dad that Ambrosia, my stepmother, had an evil soul, but he didn't believe a boy could possibly know such things and went ahead and married her anyway. I know that you may have done bad things, but you are a good man at heart. I can see it when I look at your eyes and ignore the tough guy exterior"

Curddy laughed. "Don't bet your life savings on that." Salvatore waited, and then said, "I have my life savings in a money belt around my stomach, but I'm not a betting man." (That would only be true for about another 6 months.) "If I was a betting man I would put my money on you."

Curddy replied, "Well, I'll give you my short version starting when I was in my teens. My dad was a farmer. My brother Jako, and I worked with him each day on the farm, taking care of the farm animals, which included ten cats and four pigs, as well as the usual livestock, cows, goats, sheep and one nasty llama. The work was hard, but life was good. Dad was loving and kind. Even though there was always work to be done, he made time to take us fishing, hunting or just on hikes. He was everything I could ever want in a father, he taught us the importance of family, to be honest and trustworthy, and he taught us how to become good men. I loved him so much; he always seemed to know what I needed from him."

Curddy seemed a bit choked up. "Our life was great right up until the time Dad drowned trying to rescue my brother from a rushing river. Thanks to help from two fishermen in the area, my brother made it out of the water alive; my dad didn't. I was helpless as I witnessed it from the riverbank. I froze, something that I will forever feel guilt over, even though I know I could not have saved him. I didn't know how to swim; neither did my brother or my dad. We had lived by a pond that we fished in, but it was too scummy for us to go into."

He paused, blew out his breath. Then he continued. "After my dad died, we lost the farm. My brother, Mamma and I moved to the city. I tried to get a job, but the only thing I had experience doing was working on a farm and there weren't any farms in town, so finding a job was hard." Curddy went on to tell about his mamma getting a job as a cook for a rich man and his family. She loved her job, but the pay was not great. Her sons had only been able to pick up odd jobs here and there, until one day, when Curddy walked with his mamma to her job and met her boss, Domingo. Domingo looked Curddy up and down, and then said, "You look like a strong young man. How would you like to work for me?" Without asking any sensible questions, like 'Doing what?' Or 'What's the pay?" He said yes.

For the first weeks, he did deliveries of some mysterious packages with Pietro, Domingo's nephew. Three weeks in, Pietro took Curddy out of town up into the hills. They were there a week. It was training, Pietro said. Curddy didn't ask any sensible questions like, 'Why do I need to learn how to shoot a pistol, shotgun and rifle?' Or 'Why do I need to learn how to throw a knife?" He just trained and learned.

207

A week later, he discovered why when he accompanied Pietro to the house of Wine Stain Salivio. Wine Stain was so named because of the red mark that covered his left cheek down his neck to below his collar. Few knew that the stain, known as a port wine stain, spread wider across his chest. Even fewer knew if this was a birthmark or a scar. Wine Stain owed Domingo money, lots of money, from a weekend-long card game. Wine Stain refused to pay; he thought he was a tough guy. Domingo was tougher.

When they got to Wine Stains door, Pietro took his short barrel shotgun off his shoulder and handed it to Curddy, saying, "If shooting starts, fire off both barrels." Pietro kicked in the door and ran into the house. Wine Stain ran out of the kitchen firing a pistol. Bullets hit the wall on each side of Curddys head, sending chips of plaster into Curddy's cheek, causing a bleeding wound. Before the first drop of blood from his cheek hit the floor, Curddy fired the shotgun, both barrels, shredding Wine Stains wine-stained face; he was dead before his head hit the floor; that is, what was left of his head.

After that first killing, Curddy got a big raise. With more money came more killing. Domingo had a lot of enemies; some owed money just because Domingo said they did. Some were Domingo's competition in one or another of his businesses, and he didn't like competition. He was not Black Hand; he was not Mafia. He was just a very bad man who hired a lot of men that needed money more than morals. It became so easy for Curddy to forget how to be the man his dad taught him to be. His dad had taught him that if you had a job, you give it your all, but his dad never had a job in mind like killing. The years went by, day in, day out; on and on went life, or what Curddy knew as life. He learned many ways to kill a man, even without using weapons, only his bare hands. He never liked doing it; it was just a job; just business, nothing personal. He also reminded himself that these were all bad people he was killing. They were people who had hurt or even killed others.

Then one day at a family picnic, Curddy met Domingo's youngest daughter, Maria. Actually, they had met once before, three years earlier, when she was sixteen. But, that warm day at the summer

208

picnic, they fell into a dream state, drunk in their infatuation with each other. Soon, infatuation turned to love; love turned to marriage and marriage turned to family when Maria gave birth to Jamie.

Life was great. One thing Curddy hadn't forgotten was how to be a good father. He remembered all the good things his dad did with him, how to be loving, kind, and patient. He wanted to be a dad just like his father was to him. He loved Jamie more than he had loved anyone. Jamie and Maria brought out the best in him. Maria soothed the beast that Curddy had become. The work part of him never came home; only the husband and dad Curddy came home.

Anyone who gambles knows that no matter how much you win, the day will come when you lose. Domingo had been responsible for a lot of other people losing, losing their families, their lives.
The time had come for Domingo to lose, lose his family and his life.

The Coyote was seeking revenge for his only son's death, someone that Domingo had ordered murdered. Curddy was the person who had carried out the order. The Coyote's order to murder Domingo and each and every member of his family was given to Two Ton Tony. Two Ton Tony was a skinny weasel of about 110 pounds, and his name was not even Tony, it was really Raymond. Two Ton's specialty was a pocket knife with a long curved double-sided blade, all the better to slice you with. With this knife, Two Ton slit the throats of Domingo, his wife, his oldest daughter and granddaughter, and also Maria and sweet little Jamie. Pietro was thrown in for free.

When the slaughter happened, Curddy was away in the next town, sent there by Domingo to purchase some of the latest pistols made by the master gunsmith, Aldo Chenini, who made unique 8-shot revolvers. It was those pistols, one in each hand, that Curddy emptied into The Coyote.
But for Two Ton Tony, he used something more personal, his bare hands. He started by breaking both of Two Ton's arms, and slowly went on to break more and more bones. As Two Ton was screaming in intense pain, Curddy started strangling him; the screaming became gasps for air, followed by death. Once Two Ton was dead, Curddy took the large knife with the long curved blade out Tony's pocket

and started cutting him, to pieces. None of the pieces was ever found.

Nor was Curddy found by the avengers looking for him.

Curddy couldn't be found because he had moved to a small fishing village where he lived a quiet contemplative year, licking his wounds and trying to discover the real him. His wife's gentleness and the memory of the good person he was when he was with her made him desire that person of the past. He started thinking about what Maria would want for his life. She would have wanted him to live a good life, to be a good person, to help others, and be the kind of person that he was to Jamie and her.

After a year in the peaceful little village, he seemed reborn. Curddy vowed he would change his life; he would be a person that Marie and Jamie would have been proud of. He would put Italy behind him; he would put his old life behind him. It had not been easy trying to subdue his darker side.

As he wrapped up his story, he used the example of the evening's card game fight to illustrate that he still had a lot of taming to do. "So I am off to a new world for a new start on a new life. Now tell me your life story."

Salvatore was a friend of many. One of the reasons almost everyone that met him liked him was simple: he knew how to listen. He knew that in listening closely, you could hear the story under the story; you could see the real person, and in seeing that, know what that person needed from another person. Salvatore suspected that part of Currdy's story was possibly made up, fiction, and perhaps most of it was a tall tale. But why would someone make up a story so violent? What could he be covering up that would be worse than killing people? Why did he feel the need to act so tough? Those questions, like many in Salvatore's own life, would not be answered for years.

Salvatore was tempted to embellish his life story too. But he knew people liked honesty from their friends, so he told his short history. For the rest of the trip, they filled in the blanks on their life stories.

By the time they reached the shore of America, they were good friends and would remain so while they were both alive.

Salvatore convinced Curddy to travel with him to Lodi in California . It wasn't a very hard sell; Curddy had no specific place he was going, just a place he was getting away from. Furthermore, Salvatore told him that with his experience on a farm he should be able to get hired on with him at the ranch. Then Salvatore said, "Before we step on land, on the soil of America, I want you to put a final end to the old you. Let's agree that neither one of us will ever tell anyone about your past.
That 'you' doesn't exist anymore. Why not change your name too?"
But Curddy replied, "The old me is gone forever, but my name was given to me by my father and I am keeping it."

"Yes." Salvatore replied. "I suppose you should. But, if I'm right, that pocket knife with the long curved blade is the one you took off Two Ton Tony and used to cut him up. Drop it over the rail into the ocean, lost and gone forever." Curddy said "Not yet." Then he held out his hand.
Salvatore shook it and Curddy said, "Thank you, my new best friend."

Chapter 23
Coming to America, Sal's Story

People came to America from many different countries for many different reasons. They believed there were opportunities in this New World, a chance to prosper, more freedom and, yes, paradise. They came with expectations. Depending on their country of origin and where they settled, they might or might not be accepted; they might even be despised. Some learned a new word, a never- before- experienced human trait for them, prejudice. It was a hatred, not because of anything they did, but simply because of the color of their skin, their religion or where they were born. Many became disillusioned and disappointed and, after a year, some had had enough of America. They wanted to go home where they were accepted and understood the language, to the families they had left behind. A few made it back home, many didn't.

Others became successful and happy. Salvatore was one those. His initial goal was reached the minute he stepped on the ship heading to America, leaving his homeland and family behind. His destination was the United States of America, but his goal was also to get away from his stepmother. There were times after his father married her that Salvatore wished he could put a hex on her. Mrs. Mangani was rumored to be able to do that causing the cursed person to go blind or never be able to speak again. Though he couldn't do that, he cursed her silently under his breath.
So, now, he was going to get out of her world, the Curtoni Market and household where she had proclaimed herself Queen and, for that matter, King, too. She didn't deserve the title, nor was she qualified for it. She was, in her heart and soul, a cruel dictator.

Salvatore's family had been a close and loving one. His dad, Nicolas, was a kind and loving man, a mentor to his three sons. He was a large, strong man respected by everyone that knew him, and many knew him because they were regular customers in his Curtoni Family Market. Family, friends, and customers all called him Papa, a nickname given to him by Horse-Face Chiloni. Chiloni suffered through life with this insulting nickname given to him by his stepfather. Of course, everyone had nicknames, but none so cruel and unflattering.

The Curtoni Family Market was the only one in Gerola that carried everything. They had a complete delicatessen with all kinds of homemade pastas, prepared by Salvatore's mom, a nice woman everyone called Sunny because it described her personality perfectly. Sunny loved to sing and dance around her spacious kitchen as she stirred pots of different sauces; she danced on to her table where she created many varieties of pastas. By the time the market opened in the morning there was a smorgasbord of freshly-made foods in addition to some of her canned goods.

Sunny was a happy, youthful lady. She enjoyed each day as if God had made it just for her. All she wanted out of life was to be with her husband and children and enjoy what they shared as a family. But, as a bonus, she was able to use her gift of cooking and preparing food to share with her village, a talent that brought her praise and fame in her small world of Gerola. Sunny knew almost all the store's customers by name and their preference of foods. If you came into Curtoni's market, you would often be called over to the counter to get a sample of one of Sunny's specialties.

Newcomers to the market were usually drawn by recommendations about Sunny's specialties. They would ask for her by name, misspoken though it might be. Once someone asked for "Sue- me;" but the family always knew they wanted to meet Sunny. Some were surprised to meet a small, short lady with lots of dark, curly hair and no makeup, unless you counted the fine dusting of flour in her hair or tomato paste smeared on her face. They fully expected this well-known cook to be big and round. Sunny would smile up at them through her thick eyeglasses, wipe her
hands on her apron and shake hands with them with her right hand while pushing her glasses back on her nose with her left. Everyone got a smile and a warm welcome.

The oldest son, Knuckles (so named because he spent part of the day punching balls of dough with his knuckles) was the baker. He ran the best bakery in town, or so he told everyone. He was big like his dad and was the protector of his younger brothers at school. A lot of students were afraid of Knuckles. This was not because he was such a good fighter; it was because of a misunderstanding about the origin of his nickname. A guy named Knuckles must be a good fighter! Knuckles liked to do things with his brothers, like playing cards or reading to them. He was the definition of a good big brother. After all the Curtoni kids were adults, the siblings remained close friends.

Salvatore was nicknamed Saint or Saint Sal because of his nice personality, mild temperament, honesty, sense of honor and his ability to get along with everyone. He was also a peacemaker when that was needed, dealing with irate customers or even with some of his friends who got into fist fights after having too much to drink. There were a lot of fist fights in their small village because there simply wasn't a lot else to do, especially if you didn't have a lady friend. Eat, drink, sing, play cards, watch paint dry….. fight!
Saint Sal's responsibility was growing the produce for the market. He kept the vegetable gardens and the small orchard with a variety of fruit trees in a very tranquil, peaceful setting by the pond. The pond also was home to a variety of fish that, once caught, would be sold in the market.
Seafood was Sunny's favorite and she made a fantastic fish stew. The ingredients changed based on what shellfish she could get, and the rest was whatever was caught in the pond.

Salvatore loved working in the gardens and developed a talent that in the future would be referred to as a green thumb. He cared for his garden in the same way someone would care for a beloved family pet. This gift would be an asset throughout his life and assist in his future success.

The final offering at the Curtoni Family Market was provided by the family butcher, Chopper. Chopper was actually Saint Sal's uncle, the brother of Papa. He had managed to chop two fingers off his left hand and was also missing two fingers off his right hand, but not as the result of his job. Drinking and betting resulted in the loss of those! He did have both thumbs which he kept on placing surreptitiously on the scale so the customer ended up paying for more than they actually got. This "extra" money was his drinking and betting money. When Papa caught Chopper cheating the customers, he got mad and Chopper would promise not to do it again. But from time to time he still took advantage of the customers. No, Chopper wasn't anything like his brother, but he was family and would always have a job at the market.

Sal's younger brothers also helped in all the areas of the market. The family enjoyed each others company and did many things together, including work. They had love for each other; they had fun, and they were almost rich. They had everything they needed and more. It was a great life. Life was good.

Then it ended. Sunny died.

She was in her kitchen making gravy (sauce) for the raviolis when she had a heart attack. Her youngest son, Capi, was with her, singing to her as she cooked. Suddenly she groaned, put her hand to her chest and fell to the floor. Capi yelled, "Papa, come fast! PAPA!!!"

Papa was downstairs in the market, and he knew in an instant something terrible had just happened. He had never heard such fear in his young son's voice. By the time Papa reached Sunny, she was dead. A deep sadness that seemed endless followed. So great was the pain and sorrow that Salvatore felt like a knife was piercing his heart. In many ways, the family never recovered from Sunny's death.

Everything changed after the instant she took her last breath. Sunny had been the light and life of the family, the heart and soul. A bit of every family member died that day in the kitchen. Papa became sad and depressed. He lost interest in the Market and didn't even come down for the first few months. Knuckles had to take over as the temporary store manager. Because Sunny was no longer there to run the delicatessen and make pastas, Knuckles hired Hazel. She was the friend of a friend of Chopper's and was rumored to be a good cook. As it turned out, she was good at making pastas, but she was an ogre with people. Salvatore would never forgive his uncle for bringing Hazel into their lives.

It was absolutely astonishing that Papa was drawn to her shortly after he returned to the store. That attraction, in the absence of the one he loved, made him vulnerable and he fell in love, or maybe it was just need. In any case, things turned ugly at that point. Against the pleading of his sons and brother, Papa married Hazel, the one they called Witch Hazel. And then she changed her name to Ambrosia.

So Hazel, now Ambrosia, was running the market. Her management style was to treat her new stepsons and step-daughter like slaves. She was a mean, grouchy tyrant. Because of the stress and constant pressure of her oppressive personality, even the brothers began lashing out at each other. They quit doing things together. The family began to crumble.

That happy, fun-loving time became a dim memory, one that Salvatore knew was gone for good. He became depressed and felt deep despair. He and his siblings were shocked at the change in their father and how he could tolerate this horrible woman. One of them suggested that when their mom died, Papa did not know how to function without her. He was the head of the household and he managed the market, but, as the saying goes, "Behind every great man is a great woman." Sunny was that woman. Papa didn't know how to do any household tasks. He couldn't cook, do laundry, iron or clean. He wasn't good at math or business. Sunny had really done all that; she was the real head of the household, and without her, Papa was lost.

So, Papa needed a woman's help to run things. And that was what Hazel did best: run things. She had grown up with nine brothers and one sister. Her mom had died giving birth to her sister, so Hazel had handled all the motherly and household duties. She ran a tight ship. She had to. And with her in the family, Papa could function again. But it was at a very high price: the happiness of his children.

Then one day, Joe Pizini walked into the store, asked for Saint Sal and said that he had something for him. They had been friends since childhood and Joe knew that Sal was unhappy and looking for a way out of this hell. Joe knew the way out, all the way to the far side of

216

the earth: California. Joe invited Saint Sal to the next meeting of the New Americans club, his newly formed group.

When Sal said yes, he would be there, Joe asked if the meetings could be held there at Sal's house, upstairs above the market. And from then on, that's where the New Americans met.

Two great things happened as a result of those meetings. Saint Sal discovered the road to America. And, at the first meeting, he met Rosealia Aquistapacé, the woman who would become his wife. Rosi had come to the meetings only because a friend had talked her into going with her. But once she had met Saint Sal, the two became inseparable.

Once Joe departed for America, Saint Sal knew he had to follow. His main goal was to get away from Witch Hazel and never see her again. He knew he would miss his dad and brothers, but they were no longer the same people they were before Witch Hazel became the dictator of the family.

Saint Sal promised to write to Papa and his brothers each month and he kept that promise as long as he lived. He also promised Rosi that he would get her to America within a year after he got there and they would get married. It was another of many promises he kept.

But once he was on the boat, no one ever called him Saint Sal again. He would be Salvatore from then on.

And in 1953, he returned to Gerola, along with his wife Rosi, and saw his two brothers who were still living.

Chapter 24
Arriving in America

Ellis Island and a Stagecoach Ride

After the long ocean crossing, the ship arrived at the lower bay of New York Harbor and anchored before it got to Ellis Island. The ship had to wait in the harbor because it had docked after 5 PM and health screenings, which were required of every immigrant, were only available from 7 AM-5 PM. Some ship lines did the health inspections on shore at Ellis Island, but some, including Salvatore and Curddy's ship, had their inspections on board.

The next morning was cool and overcast, with dark rumbling clouds that looked like big gray boulders low enough to touch. The passengers got up early and were eager to go through the screening because it meant they were one step closer to being set free to explore America. This first examination was very stressful for most of the passengers. Only the few Americans on board did not have to be screened, and those who traveled in first class were pretty much assured of passing. But others began expressing their worried thoughts in verbal fretting: "What if we don't pass? Will we have to go all the way back on this wretched ship?" One of the medical inspectors, picking up on this stressful worry, reassured them: "If you do not pass the health inspection, you will go to Ellis Island and be put into quarantine there until you are healthy. We will not send any of you back to where you came from. We want to welcome you to the United States of America." Sometimes an immigrant would be delayed by weeks, each day being torturous for those chomping at the bit to see this famously fantastic nation. It was even worse if they had to be separated from family. And, sadly, there were those, especially ill children, who died before they tasted of the "Land of the Free."

Once medical inspectors completed the shipboard examinations, they would leave the ship, and it would be allowed to proceed slowly around the tip of Manhattan. As the Statue of Liberty came into view, everybody cheered. It happened on every ship that ever entered the harbor; Lady Liberty represented a new life, unlike anything they were familiar with. Especially for some from very oppressed nations, this freedom was something they had only heard of or read about, something most of them had dreamt about every night of the cruise.

Once anchored, barges would come to transport the cleared passengers to land. After the health inspectors, the next Americans that the passengers met were on land. These were interpreters who met with passengers in groups of 30. Most interpreters spoke six languages or more, so they were able to help passengers understand where they needed to go and the procedures for completing other requirements, including money exchange. Finally, the passengers were released to go meet America

They made it to America! Now Curddy and Salvatore had to travel from the East Coast to California, specifically Lodi, California. They did this partly by train. It was a long, hot trip and the train cars very quickly became sweaty and smelly. After all, there were no bathtubs on the train, and there hadn't been any on the ship either. These travelers got to smelling really, really bad, and being in such close quarters made it almost unbearable.

On the second day, Salvatore met an Englishman whose name was Greg. Greg had an Italian wife, so he was able to speak both English and Italian. After being introduced to Curddy, Greg instructed them in a new card game, Poker. Playing cards on the train was a little bit difficult. If you weren't able to get a table in one of the food or bar cars, players had to play on the floor or balance a suitcase on their knees sitting across from each other. That wasn't too bad. But, later, when they were on the stagecoach, even the suitcase on the knees didn't work so well. When they hit one of the million bumps in the road or holes big enough for a rhino to fall into, the cards, along with the suitcase, would go flying. Then they would have to try and remember what cards belonged to what player and honestly retrieve them. Eventually, Salvatore taught Greg how to play the famous Italian card game Pedro.

Having a new friend to talk with helped with the boredom. Greg was a funny little guy. He was about the size of a 12-year-old boy but had a handsome man's face. He wore thick-soled shoes with a big, high heel to boost his height. He had an unusual trick or as he called it 'a special talent.' He claimed he could identify a person's nationality by their 'scent'. Since most of them reeked to high heaven, he said it would be a bit more difficult.

Because he was short, people didn't notice when Greg casually walked over and stood next to them, especially at train station rest stops, in crowded rooms. He would cough a few times and then act like he was taking a few deep breaths. He was really sniffing. Then he would look at his friends and reveal what his nose had detected they were. It was a bit dicey, because he used the common slang for the different groups, "Mick, Spic, Wop, Kraut, etc." Today, he might be arrested, but in those days, people weren't so hypersensitive. Nevertheless, one time, he called out "Spic" a little louder than he intended. The man he was trying to identify turned around and punched him in the jaw knocking him onto the filthy floor of the train station. The man bent over and said proudly in broken English, "I'm na Italiano, stupid Limey idiots." Then he spat on him. Greg got up from the floor and dusted himself off, missing some of the cigar butts and a red sucker that stuck to him. Salvatore made sure that was the last of that game. Besides, he could never prove he was correct with his guesses; it wasn't like either Salvatore or Curddy were going to ask a person if they could look at their passports.

One morning, Greg asked, "What do you chaps think of my beard. I have been growing it for two weeks now." Salvatore and Curddy looked at each other and laughed out loud, bending over with tears in their eyes. Curddy noted, "I have seen better beards on a tomato. It actually looks like dried spinach." And that's how Greg got his nickname: Spinach Chin.

During stopovers at train stations, there was time to get out and walk around and find a nice, or at least adequate, restaurant. They could go to the market and buy food for the next leg of the journey. Spinach Chin liked to get into a poker game to win some money. He was good at 5-card draw which was pretty much the only game they played. If he won big, he would treat his two new Italian friends to dinner, drinks, and wine.

As the travel continued, Salvatore had to suffer through Curddy's tall tales or outright lies about what happened to his wife and son. Some of the stories he told Spinach Chin were completely different from what he had told Salvatore on the ship. But Salvatore didn't mind. Curddy was a good storyteller, using different voices and facial expressions, jumping around and putting his whole body into delivering a dramatic rendition of what supposedly happened.

Spinach Chin told a story about a two-day poker game he was in with four other players. It ended in a fist fight. One player was Charles Whitford, a famous stage actor who had lost 600 pounds over the two-day game (money not weight). Charles quit two hours before the game ended.

Spinach won over a thousand dollars, but he had to pick up the pot of the last hand off the floor. The Russian he had won it from called him a cheat and took a swing at him, tipping the table over in the process. Spinach sensed a punch heading his way and ducked. When he brought his head up, it was right to the underside of Ruskie's chin, knocking him out cold, which was a good thing because the Russian could have used Spinach Chin as a toothpick. Actually, in the end, it wasn't a fist fight at all, but more of a headbutt.

The men swapped stories every day, never seeming to run out. Curddy's stories were mostly outrageous and fierce. Spinach Chin's stories were usually about his ability to outsmart someone or out-muscle others, with him ending up victorious. The stories about out-muscling someone had to be total B.S. because Spinach Chin had muscles the size of a Hummingbird's. Salvatore told true stories about his wonderful childhood, which had included trips to Switzerland to go skiing or mountain climbing. There were many stories about his brothers, his Papa and his much-missed mom who had passed away years earlier. And then, there were the horror stories about the evil, mean, sadistic witch that had become his stepmother. He reminded them and himself, that if it weren't for her, he would not have been driven out of his home, and he would never have come to America. How that would have changed the lives of future generations.

221

It was the early part of the Twentieth Century, the dawn of a new world, one of science technology and machinery. In 1910, new and exciting things were happening around the world. The impossible was becoming possible, especially in America, the land of opportunity. The automobile was making appearances in cities all across the country. Inventors were on the threshold of developing a "flying machine" so that people could fly like birds, only faster and without feathers. There were many fascinating new inventions to make life easier and give people more leisure time and consequently more enjoyment and fun in life. The stagecoach that the men had to switch to in Tucson, Arizona, was one of those things that would be replaced in the coming technological era.

As they got off the train, Curddy said goodbye to Spinach Chin, but Spinach replied, "Not goodbye, my dear friend. I am going to the same city as you. Lodi, right?" Spinach had told his new friends all about the fabulous restaurant his brother owned, noting that it served "Cowboy food and British food, and the best selection of tea this side of London." Salvatore had figured that a fine eating establishment like that must be in the famous city of San Francisco. Surprisingly, it was in Lodi, a smallish but growing town. By now, folks in Lodi even had telephones. The relatives who were separated by thousands of miles or even a vast ocean had previously resigned themselves to the fact that they might never see or talk to those family members again. But the day was coming when they would be able to call long distance, although it would be very expensive.

The name of the restaurant in Lodi was supposed to be KING AND QUEEN'S PALACE. However, the sign maker had misspelled it, and it became KING AND QUEEN'S PLACE. That sign maker was in the habit of making mistakes on other signs in town and was hounded to fix them or give a refund. Eventually, he skipped town, leaving people to do the best they could to change their signs. That usually resulted in a mess, which is why Spinach Chin's brother had left his sign alone. It would be "King and Queen's Place."

If any of the six passengers crammed shoulder to shoulder in the stagecoach had been on the wildest roller coaster on Coney Island in June of 1884 when it appeared as fantastical new ride, or thereafter, they would have said, by comparison, that the stagecoach ride was wilder and scarier with more twists and turns. There were times when the driver had the horses going so fast that a wheel hitting one of those Rhinoceros-sized holes would send all six behinds off the seat and into the air. Then there were the twists and turns and diving and soaring. It was not only terrifying, but it was also physically punishing. When the passengers got out at a rest stop, they walked around like they were drunk. It had taken a long time for them to regain their land legs after being on the ship for so long; the same was true of getting rid of "stagecoach legs."

When they arrived at the end of the line, they had someone waiting for them. Greg's brother greeted him and drove him to his new home on one of the two horses his brother had brought. Curddy thought that Spinach Chin likely did not have much experience riding horses because Spinach had told conflicting stories about his horsemanship. One the horses awaiting him kept prancing and looked a bit wild. It would be quite a joke to give the wild one to the Britisher. Curddy thought of his own interaction with horses and shuddered.

Joe came from Rancho Mario to greet Salvatore and brought a wagon with two horsepower (no automobile there, yet). After Joe and Salvatore greeted each other warmly, Curddy was introduced to Joe. He promptly asked Joe for a job. Joe laughed in his usual, unusual high-pitched laugh which sounded a bit like a crow being baked alive. Curddy, thinking he was joking around, mimicked Joe's laugh. There were several awkward moments of silence. Salvatore thought, 'Well, that just lost him the job.'

But Joe broke the silence. "Do you have experience with horses?" Curddy answered, "A barn full, or should I say stable full of experience." And Salvatore thought, 'I bet that is a lie.' So, they got on the wagon and had a surprisingly smooth ride to the ranch thanks to the 'lightly' paved roads.
There were now automobiles around in an increasing number, and thanks to them, the city budget had money set aside to keep roads nice and somewhat smooth.

When Curddy and Salvatore arrived at Rancho Mario, they were greeted by Mario himself. Salvatore introduced his new friend Curddy and Mario promptly, officially hired both of them. Curddy thought, 'That was easy, I like this America already.'

Joe had been on the ranch long enough to learn broken English. He had been promoted to vineyard manager and made some friends. He introduced to Curddy and Salvatore to some of the ranch hands that were in and around the bunkhouse. Joe showed them where their bunks and small unfinished wood dressers were. Then he said "Look under your bunk, and you will see the most important thing. Curddy pulled out something that looked like a large white ceramic bowl. He asked, "Are we supposed to bring this to dinner for our soup." Everyone around broke out in gut-busting laughter.

When Joe stopped laughing, he responded, "No, it's a bedpan; you pee or poo in it."

Thanks to Joe, Salvatore and Curddy quickly settled in. But every night they had soup or stew, guys would yell out, "Curddy go get your bedpan to serve your soup in."

Mario and his wife, Candy were both Italians. At first, Mario and Joe interpreted for Salvatore, Curddy and a few other Italians working at Rancho Mario-R.M. It wasn't easy because there were many dialects in their different home regions. It was once said that there were 'a thousand different dialects' in Italy. Some thought, mistakenly, that these different dialects were just bad Italian. But that isn't true. Dialects in Italy were and still are real languages that originated from Latin before 1861 when Italy was born. This Latinization took place before the Roman Empire times. In Northern Italy, the dialect was derived from German; other dialects had influences from Slovenia, Greece, and Croatia. Eventually, in the 1870s, politicians decided that a unified country needed a common unique language. The modern world "lingua Italiana" came from Florence, mostly because it was it was the cradle of Italian Literature, and the "official" Italian would be that of Florence.

But now, Salvatore and Curddy would learn American English. It was just part of living in this new country!

Chapter 25
First Year in America

Curddy's First Year

Curddy's first year in America was a good one. Slowly the pain and depression of the last year began to lift. He started putting all the heartbreak and sorrow over losing his wife and child behind him. He would go through more changes over the next year than he had in all of his life prior to Lodi. America, or the small part of it that he saw his first year, was very different from what he had expected. The ranch was huge, much bigger than the farms he was used to in Italy. The city was a real city with real bars, not just a table with four or five bottles on it in a cellar and, adding to the ambiance, nettings of cobwebs in every corner. Downtown bustled with many motorcars and had nice restaurants where you could get new foods Curddy had never even heard of. There were always lots of people walking around town, and something was always going on.

It was a real treat to get paid and go into town with some of his new friends for dinner and drinks. He fit in with all the ranch hands and was learning English, picking up bits of it while he was working. He enjoyed the work, but of all the tasks, the one he liked the most was working with the livestock.

He spent a lot of his day on horseback. At first, he had a tough time learning how to ride, having never been on a horse. Cows and horses were the biggest animals he had ever seen, and he saw them both, close up, for the first time, on his first day at the ranch. He was awed by the beauty and majesty of the horse he was given to ride. The horse's name was Bucky, a scary name for a horse to a guy who never ridden a horse before. Curddy renamed his horse Cal, for California.

For weeks, every part of Curddy's body suffered pain from falling off the horse and landing on his butt, his back, his head and just about every body part that could make contact with the ground. The problem was that he didn't know how to get the saddle on the right way, so he tried to ride bareback. He was sliding and slipping off the horse; he tried holding on to the mane, but then he felt eerie sitting on this huge living breathing creature. He swore he could feel the horse's heartbeat vibrating against his legs. He only felt that way for a few seconds, though, before the vibrating moved to his head slammed against the ground as the horse jumped over a creek. Curddy ended up with his face in the mud.

Curddy learned how to put the saddle on properly, but then he didn't know how to mount the horse. Or he would forget to put his feet in the stirrups once he was on the horse, or forget to hold on. But contrary to his name Bucky, renamed Cal, never bucked him off; Curddy was the one that needed to be tamed and trained.
Curddy became a big fan of stories about the Old West and gunslingers. He had never even seen a storybook about the Old West. It wouldn't have been of any use to him anyway. Even if someone had given him an armful of Old Westerns or any kind of book, he couldn't read English. It was enough effort even to understand spoken English. When he spoke, it was very broken English, with a lot of signs and gestures and a few Italian words thrown in.

The way Curddy learned about gunslingers was from the Chicken Kid. He was given this nickname because he took care of the chickens, feeding, watering, collecting eggs and cleaning out the pens and coops. The 'Kid' part arose from the fact he was only about 17 or 18 years old. He really hated being called Chicken, but he liked the Kid part because it made him think of Billy the Kid in the books he read. Those books had been left behind in the bunkhouse by someone long gone.
There were about a dozen torn and tattered paperback books about the Old West, gunslingers, whiskey, gunfights, bank and stagecoach robberies and all that fun stuff. The Kid read them each several times and would tell Curddy these stories at night in the bunkhouse. Ten other men in the bunks listened in, too. It all sounded fascinating to Curddy. Through these stories, he started to reinvent himself. He bought a revolver, holster, and cowboy hat and convinced Joe he needed the gun because of coyotes, and a 'damn' mountain lion.

When Curddy went to town, he wore all black and a fancy cowboy hat, and he walked with a swagger, his boot heels pounding loudly on the wooden walkways. He saw himself as a bad hombré and acted the role. But it was all acting, and the role did not suit him. There weren't too many 'gunslingers' in the bars in Lodi. Curddy's 'costume' earned him lots of laughs and teasing. He was fit and tough, though, with bulging muscles and, after about half a dozen bare-knuckle fights, word got around: "Don't mess with the cowboy in black with the tattoo on his forearm." Curddy's 'gunslinger', bad guy act lasted about one year. Then someone motivated him to change.

That someone wasn't big and bad, but rather someone small and feminine, the third of the New Americans to arrive at Rancho Mario. When she got there, everybody and everything changed. She taught him that you don't have to act like a tough guy to get people to like and respect you. She saw the real Curddy, a kind, gentle, caring young man; she coaxed it out of him. He discovered his soul. In his first year, he had learned how to ride and care for a horse, how to tend to cattle and goats; he became a real cowboy, a fake gunslinger and a good fist fighter. Later, he gave away his gunfighter gear to the Kid, a move that would eventually end in tragedy.

Curddy continued learning English. He made friends. He had fun; he really enjoyed his life. He felt he owed Salvatore for all the good things now in his life, so he insisted on buying him the first drink every time they went to a bar. He liked to drink, but he no longer had to get plastered to endure his life. He had a purpose. He had a good job; he had friends. In short, he had a life, a good life.

Salvatore's First Year

In the meantime, Salvatore's first year at the ranch passed quickly. He had a job he loved; he impressed his boss with his ability to raise healthy productive crops. Even though Salvatore had become good friends with Curddy and made other new friends, he missed his brothers and dad. It was the first time in his life he had been separated from any of them. He would patiently wait for letters from family and Rosi. Unfortunately, the only option for hearing from them all was the incredibly slow mail. It was all 'snail mail' in those days.

Finally, the day came for Salvatore to write that letter to Rosi. His letter had the promise of a job, in fact, a choice of several jobs. She chose two of them, one of which ended up being a good choice. Unfortunately, the other ended in tragedy. But at that time, their life looked filled with joy and promise of a good life.

With all the new inventions Americans were enjoying, there were new jobs available. Some smart thinkers saw opportunities for servicing the now-common automobiles. Wagons had been very simple to repair, but automobiles required some training to be able to work on the motors. With the advent of the airplane, there were opportunities for men (at that time, only men) to become pilots. This career was viewed as dashing and daring. And the telephone opened new jobs mostly for women as telephone operators. And, of course, all of these time- and work-saving inventions gave everyone more leisure time; life now included fun, formerly quite rare for American pioneers.

Not everybody loved this new land, though. There were some disappointments; they were unhappy, and after a year, some immigrants had had enough of America. There were those that wanted to leave and return to their home countries and the families they left behind. The comforts of home, a place where they were accepted, and they understood the language called to them. A few made it back; many didn't. But many more became successful and happy.

Rosi Comes to America

Back in Italy, Rosi was continuing to work at the Curtoni Family Market. She had been raised in a close, loving family. Her dad, Nicolas, was a kind, loving man, a mentor to his three daughters and son. Her mom was tall and a bit heavy. Her hair had turned white when she was only 24-years- old, and because she wore rimless eyeglasses that slipped down to the tip of her nose, she always looked grandmotherly. Nicolas was a large, strong man, respected by everyone that knew him.

Many were regular customers in his gun shop. Rosi's brother Rocco was shot in a hunting accident when a hunter saw movement through the trees and mistook it for an animal. It was opening day of deer hunting season. The irony didn't escape Nicolas that the instruments of his trade had caused the death of his only son.

By now, Rosi clearly understood why Salvatore had fled to America. The "wicked stepmother" Ambrosia was still controlling everything and everyone around the market. The arrival of Salvatore's letter couldn't come too soon. Rosi set off for the New World with her sister Antoinette with whom she was very close.

It was a very rough trip for Rosi from Ellis Island to Lodi. The train was uncomfortable and Rosi never did well with discomfort. On top of that, something happened on the trip that separated the two sisters. Whatever it was, the two never spoke again, although Salvatore made every effort to bring them back together.

Antoinette was known as Toni in America. She and her husband Jacamo arrived in San Francisco they bought an acre of land. Soon their property on Nob Hill was surrounded by the homes of very wealthy people, and Antoinette was babysitting for their children who called her Mama Toni.

Jacamo owned the tobacco store down the hill. Because he was always sampling his wares, he constantly had a drool of tobacco juice dripping from his chin, unless he was spitting the disgusting brown juice into a brass spittoon.

Rosi and Antoinette's family never knew what caused this death of their sisterhood, their friendship. Every Christmas from the 1940s through the '50s and into 1960s, Salvatore would leave their home in Rutherford to celebrate with family at Mama Toni's, leaving Rosi behind.

Salvatore and Rosi's daughter Gemma would join him. Since she had no siblings, she loved her cousin Jim, Toni and Jacomo's son, as if he were a brother. When Gemma and Jim became adults, their spouses and children came together for Mama Toni's legendary

Christmas dinner feast. But it all happened without Rosi. When Mama Toni, Jacamo and Jim went to Rutherford, Rosi would go two vineyards away to stay with Mary Villa, a friend from Gerola.

Rosi arrived in Lodi, dirty, sore and road weary on September 15, 1911, a bit over a year after Salvatore had arrived. Salvatore had been bragging to all the ranch hands about his wife-to-be, about how beautiful and fun she was, to say nothing about her cooking skills and her experience as a seamstress. All of them were imagining her beauty, not to mention feasts and repaired torn shirts and pants. Salvatore could hardly wait to show her off; he would be so proud.

What a shock when everyone got their first look at this supposedly gorgeous, magnificent, stunning lady they had heard so much about! No one saw any of that woman when Rosi got out of the coach and stepped onto the dusty ground. She looked like she had been in a tornado and then rolled down a hill; her hair was a mess and had something in it like feathers or straw or both, almost as if she had worn a chicken nest on her head for a hat.

The smiles melted off the faces of all the ranch hands who were waiting to meet her; was this what Salvatore thought was beautiful? Good grief, what did an unattractive lady from Gerola look like? Her clothes looked and smelled like she had traveled across the United States in them, without ever changing, not even once. That was almost true, probably because she had been in them for the whole trip; her luggage had been lost, and her sister's clothes were too small for her. Several evenings, depending on where they stopped, she would wash out her over-clothes and sleep in her undergarments. The next time, she would sleep in her over-clothes and wash her undergarments, but nothing ever really got clean, and they smelled to high heaven.

A few days after her arrival, Salvatore went to town for some gardening supplies and stopped into the bar for a drink. Bob, the bartender, was laughing as he related a version of Rosi's arrival he had heard the night before from Chico, one of Salvatore's crew. The following briefly describes the wince-eliciting sight the ranch hands saw, as according to Chico:

"A woman that looked like she had a huge skinned tomato for a head, stomped out of the coach; she somewhat resembled a charging bull. I think I even saw steam shooting from her nostrils. On her bloated body, she wore cheap rags that looked like they had been stewed in a cauldron of mud. An odor wafted off her body and assaulted the nostrils of every breathing being on the ranch; a few horses started running around their corral making a noise that could best be described as screaming. A bird dropped dead out of the sky; the dogs started growling, and then barked, and started biting the fence posts. The stuff on top of her head that must have been hair was sweat-plastered so it looked like a dark leather cap. She had black shoes that looked like they could stomp Grizzly Bears to death; her ankles were about three times bigger than her shoe size so they bulged over the sides of her shoes. I think Salvatore was shocked and stunned. He probably wanted to run away from the ranch, away from California, away from this stranger and worlds away from marriage. But being the kind soul he was, he gulped, put his arms out for a hug and walked toward her. She stopped him with a stern look and a few harsh words in Italian. Then she followed Mario's wife to get cleaned up. It looked like that would take about a month. She didn't even give her husband-to-be a hug or kiss, not that he would have wanted one."

As Bob retold Chico's story, the five other guys in the bar burst out laughing. Salvatore was not amused and told everyone so. "That is a very funny story; it's just not true." But the truth was not too far off from Chico's version. Surprisingly, he had left out her stepping in a fresh steaming pile of horse shit.

And so, the first year ended. Salvatore was one of the immigrants that became happy. In time he would become successful in achieving the goals he had set in coming to America. Some goals took longer, years even; there were unforeseen disasters and tragedy that postponed full happiness. But through them all, Salvatore would remain strong. He would not be deterred from his goals that included having a house and a vineyard, making his own wine, and getting married and having children. He would not give in or give up; he would never allow events, misfortunes or disasters to toss him off track, like his father did, collapsing and giving up. His father could never undo the harm he caused Salvatore and his brothers. Salvatore vowed to live his life so that he would not need to undo anything harmful he had done to his family or friends. If you don't do something bad, dreadful or shameful, then you don't have to undo it. Those were words he lived by.

Chapter 26
The Birth of a Son

If we were to ask ourselves, "What is the greatest single event in my life, so far?" there would be a wide range of answers. The greatest single event, up to that point, in the lives of the Curtonis was the day their son was born, and each day got better after that. They became the picture and definition of the perfect happy family of three, or four if you add in Curddy. The Curtonis took in this wounded soul and treated him like a part of their family. He had lost his family in Italy, and he suffered from guilt knowing it was entirely his fault. But he had now gained a new family in California and would be forever grateful and loyal to the Curtonis. It is good to belong, to be with other people; to be included, to have a family. Rosi was responsible for many of the improvements in Curddy's personality; she even developed in him a sense of humor. This was something foreign to him; he was amazed at how much more enjoyable life became when you could view things looking for laughs. It was especially good if you could laugh at yourself rather being depressed over something stupid you did.

The Curtonis had both been praying for a son. The first thing Rosi would do when she entered the church was to light a candle and kneel in front of the flickering light; then she would pray for a baby boy. Salvatore didn't go to Mass every week, so he would do his praying on his knees in their bedroom, under the framed Jesus drawing that had the blessed palm frond on its corner. He was a strong believer in the power of Jesus Christ, but he believed a prayer is a prayer, no matter where you say it. Prayers work, even without melting wax.

Their son was born in their cottage, on a cold, rainy night in December. On that evening, there were a lot of people in their tiny home, some to help, some just waiting to see the newborn when it arrived. Some had bets on if it would be a boy or a girl. Everyone in the cottage had entered with muddy feet and wet clothes, some of them even smelling like a wet dog. The waiting people took turns rotating in and out of the area radiating heat from the wood burning stove fueled by old grape vines and trunks which emitted a pleasant aroma. There was a path of mud from the front door to the dinner table and back around the stove; soon the floor looked more like the bare wet earth outside than a wood floor.

There were two helpers in the bedroom, assisting with the delivery. The others were just waiting for a report of the baby's gender, waiting to collect or pay out wager money. Mario's wife acted as midwife with the help of Letty, the assistant cook. The birth was quick and easy. Rosi was a strong, tough, sturdy woman and that helped make it go well.

When the first cry of the only-seconds-old newborn echoed around the inside of the tiny cottage, everyone ended up in the bedroom, crowding around the bed to see the youngest resident of Rancho Mario. As Salvatore and Rosi looked at their pink-faced, crying son, they knew their prayers had been answered. He was the proverbial 'bundle of joy'. He was cute, cuddly, and had an angel's face topped with plenty of dark hair.

They named their beautiful son Nicolas after Rosi's cousin, a kind gentleman, respected and admired. Salvatore started calling Nicolas, Nicco. Rosi thought it was a shortened version of Nicolas, but in fact, the name came from somewhere else. In town, Salvatore had seen a clothing store called Nicco's. They had very nice, expensive clothes, the kind Salvatore swore someday he would wear, but not now with the job he had. He would eventually get nice suits and dress shirts with huge stiff French cuffs and mother of pearl cufflinks the size of a silver dollar, just like the ones displayed in the window of Nicco's. He would dress up, right down to the 3-button vest, gold watch fob, and Borsalino hat with the duck feather in its band. He would also get a nice leather belt with a mother of pearl buckle, in the center was a big "SC" in rhinestones. He wore the hat with the front corner pulled down, slightly dipped down over his left eye, something he saw in a magazine ad. There were only two words on the ad:

"BORSALINO = CLASS"

He liked the name of that store; it would always make him think of class and style, like the clothes in that store. So, the child became Nicco, although sometimes Salvatore also called him Sonny, because his cheerful personality reminded him of his own mom, Sunny.

Time went by fast, and soon Nicco was looking ahead on a countdown to his fifth birthday. Those years were the happiest Rosi or Salvatore had ever experienced. Nicco was a gift from God, an angel. He was such a happy, sweet child; he simply inspired joy and hugs from everyone. Even the gruffest of the cowboys couldn't resist giving him a pat on the head or picking him up to give him a hug or a ride on their horses. His spirit spread joy and light over the whole ranch.

All the ranch hands loved Nicco, too, and the whole ranch was his playground. His parents trusted him there and thought that the ranch was safe for him to explore; there was so much to discover and experience. And it was safe for everyone, right up until Friday, Sept 15, 1916, at 11.30 AM.

Nicco's godfather was Curddy, his favorite grown-up friend. Curddy felt honored to be Nicco's godfather. It was an important role, especially to the 'old country' Italians. He took his role as a 'backup parent' seriously. Curddy was always doing something special for Nicco. He made him a rope swing; he bought a wagon and would put Nicco, Leo, and Ant in it pull them all around the ranch. He carved things out of wood, a dog, a horse and other toys and gave them to his buddy Nicco. He also carved a cross that he gave to Rosi because she loved Jesus and went to church every Sunday and sometimes on Tuesday, too. Once he carved a play gun out of wood and gave it to Nicco. Then he cut up an old inner tube to make thick rubber bands, and Nicco became the only boy around with a rubber band gun. Everywhere he went, Nicco had the butt of the gun sticking out of his pants pocket and the rubber bands, ammunition, around his wrists. He would shoot bottles, birds, lizards or anything the size of or smaller than, a cat, which meant cats were often fair game. His mom always got upset when he shot birds, even though they were not really hurt; a few times she even cried, so he felt bad and stopped shooting birds. He was a sweet soul, loving and kind even at his young age.

Nicco was also a talker, a chatterbox. He talked about everything, all the time, to anybody. He had an inquisitive mind, always asking questions like 'Where do the stars go in the daytime; are they still up there or do they follow the moon? How do you put new shoes on a horse? How do you get milk out of a cow? Can you teach me how to tell time on your watch and on the sundial in Candy's garden?' He would listen to the answers intently and file the information away in a safe place in his mind, a place that was easily accessible; then he would put it to use. He had an incredible mind for his age.

Sometimes he would milk the cow to get milk for his breakfast. He impressed his buddies by telling time on the sundial or Curddy's pocket watch. Curddy would let Nicco have his watch from Friday evening until Sunday night, his days off since he didn't have any schedule to follow from Friday eve until Monday morning. The watch was old: there was a crack in the glass face, scratches all over the back, and it had a piece of rope for a fob; the rope looked like one of the ties used in the vineyard because it was.

Nicco loved to help, so even though he wasn't allowed to put horseshoes on a horse; he could pass them to Hoss as he put them on. Because it was hard for him to pronounce some of the names like Guido, Napoleons, Sebastian, etc., Nicco had given nicknames to a lot of the ranch hands. The names were logical so that he could remember them easily; the names related to their jobs, Hoss, Blackie, Garden Man or Gardener, etc. And there was the already-named Chicken Kid.

Salvatore and Rosi spoke mostly Italian when they were in their home. Rosi only knew a few words of English and, at first, it had taken a lot of hand gestures for her to understand what the ranch hands or her helper, Letty, were saying, and they, her. Salvatore spoke English and understood it enough to be able to translate sometimes, as would Mario and his wife. Eventually, Rosi learned enough to be able to communicate adequately, without too many hand gestures.

The ranch hands' vocabularies were mixed, some Spanish, German, and a few Chinese. Each spoke a mix of both their native tongue and English with an accent left over from their homeland. So it was not hard to understand why Nicco spoke a unique version of English, with an undefined accent. For that reason, some of the names Nicco used were a little garbled, like "Callby" for cowboy, " "Blouseman"- for bossman, and so on.

Nicco's vocabulary improved mostly because Mario and his wife worked with him to teach him English. He had a larger vocabulary than Ant or Leo. Two evenings a week, he would get a lantern and make the short walk to Mario and Candy's house. He would sit at a table in a room they called the library. He was fascinated with this room. There were many books on shelves completely covering one wall. Another wall had maps on it, one of California, one of the U.S.A., and one of the world. His favorite was the one of his neighborhood, Lodi, because the places on that map were ones he knew or knew of.

Nicco would sit at the round table with Candy and Mario, and they would talk. Sometimes they would take a book from the shelf, blow off the dust, open it and read several paragraphs to Nicco, then have him repeat the words. Some of the books had drawings; they would ask Nicco to tell them what he saw. The goal was to have him use words, correcting him as needed. He would get treats for success; he loved his lessons.

Nicco told his parents just about everything on his mind, his thoughts of what he liked, his few areas of worry, or his dislikes. He had one hate, he told Mama and Papa: "I hate that bastard Roy Ass; I would like to chop his arms off, and then he couldn't pinch me ever again, and chop off his legs so he could never hurt another animal. Besides, what kind of stupid name is Roy Ass, and that's not a nickname? He said that is the name of his family."

Papa said, "You can tell us when you are mad and tell us when you feel like you want to do something that you think is bad. That way we can talk about it and think about a good way to deal with a problem. I plan to do something about Roy Ass myself. I am tired of listening to him be mean to the Mexicans, the few Chinese and the Portuguese. He is especially mean to Rain, the one Indian we have here, calling him Sitting Bull@#$%. And don't repeat that word. I hate to see bullies in action, and I have made a vow to myself. That vow is that if I see a bully bothering someone or an animal, I will step in, even if I could get beat up; that way, I will never again feel guilty for allowing an injustice to a person or animal."

That vow made Nicco very happy. Several times he saw Roy Ass kick his own dog repeatedly, and the dog was yelping in pain. One time he couldn't stand it anymore; he ran over with tears streaming down his cheeks, gave the dog a protective hug and told the dog, "Nice dog, nice dog." He looked up at Roy's ugly face and begged, "Please, please, don't kick him again. Please don't hurt him." Nicco's heart had a terrible pain. Nothing else mattered to him at that moment. He wouldn't let go of the dog, and he couldn't stop crying. He had never experienced a feeling like this; he was almost out of his wits and didn't know what to do. Roy reached down and pinched the skin between Nicco's neck and shoulder. The pain was intense, and Nicco collapsed; his arms and legs gave out. Roy reached down, picked his dog up by the scruff of his neck and walked off, dragging the dog beside him. He looked back and said, "If you tell your dad, he will get mad and come after me. If he does, I will kick him around worse than I do my dog, so shut the hell up and stay out of my business; you had that hurt coming for touching my dog."

Nicco didn't tell his Papa about this Roy Ass incident, but he made sure never to go where Roy would be with his dog, ever. He couldn't stand to see that cruelty again. However, one time, he could hear him cussing and the dog yelping in pain. Nicco ran to Mario, the ranch owner and begged him to make Roy stop, but Mario said, "It is his dog; he is trying to train it, and it is up to him how he does it."

Yes, Nicco was happy to hear that Papa was going to do something about Roy, so he proceeded to tell his Papa all about that incident. Papa was silent, unmoving at first. Then he gave Nicco a hug and said, "You should have told me. I am not afraid of Roy. Don't ever let someone try to scare you or threaten you; if it is a big person, you tell me; if it is another child, stand up to them. One more thing, you can talk to us about anything, but do not swear, even if someone is a bastard."

Overall, the ranch was a great place to raise a boy, so many people contributed to his life's experiences. The Kid, or Chicken Kid, taught him how to ride a horse, in a way. Nicco could sit on the saddle and hold on, but the Kid would ride alongside on his horse and control Nicco's horse. He loved it. If the Kid rode faster, Nicco would giggle and say "Faster, Kid, faster." The two of them would play cowboys and Indians. Nicco was always the cowboy because he had the rubber band gun; Kid would be the Indian. For some reason, they didn't stop to think how the one real Indian on the ranch, Rain, would feel about this game that cast his people as the bad guys. Kid even made a bow out of a twig and string; it didn't have arrows, just invisible, pretend ones. Some of the ranch hands would tease the Kid saying things like, "Nicco has another playmate his age."

Another ranch hand, Chuckie, taught Nicco how to catch fish, even though Chuckie couldn't catch fish himself. Whenever he went fishing, his Mama would say, "Nicco, catch us dinner." Every time she said it, every single time, he answered, "Three big fish, one for each of us." Sometimes when Papa was there, he would add, "I better go to the fish market if we are going to eat dinner."

Each day was a new adventure.

Chapter 27
A Morning to Enjoy 6:00 A.M SEPT 15 1916

Having been brutally awakened by his alarm, Salvatore swung his feet off the bed on to the bare floor. He noticed the floor was warm on his bare feet and the wood rough; more than once he had gotten slivers in his feet from this coarse wood floor. During the summer, and up until October, the cottage was hot during the day and retained some of the heat during the night. He hated it in winter, going from the bed to the bathroom with bare feet; it was like walking on ice. Without thinking about it, before he stood up, he rubbed his feet back and forth on the floor to warm them, as if it were winter. That's how he got the slivers in his feet, but after awhile he would forget and do it again.

To save on those cold walks, he wanted to use a bedpan like he did when he was in the bunkhouse so he didn't have to get out of bed. But his wife had said, "You have a choice. Either the bedpan or I will be in the bedroom, not both; you choose." He didn't mind giving in to her requests. She was organized, smart, and strong. She liked managing all aspects of their lives, but in a kind, loving way, not bossy or pushy. She had a way of putting things that reminded him of his Mama. His Mama, while she was alive, ran everything at home and in the store. Papa did what he did best; he was everyone's friend. He shared wine, words, food, and wisdom. The relationship had worked well for Salvatore's parents. Like father, like son, Salvatore thought; it worked for his relationship with Rosi, too.

He made a mental note to get a carpet on the bedroom floor before the cold weather came. It was either that or get better tweezers to remove the slivers. He would get a thick carpet that would be soft, but thick enough so that the cold wouldn't rise up through the cracks in the floor. He had made this mental note every year in the five years since he moved into the little cottage, but still no carpet.

Salvatore usually took a few minutes each morning sitting on the edge of his bed, thinking of past pleasant times. On this day, for some reason, his mind had been swept away to more memories than usual. Maybe it was because their wedding anniversary was in a few weeks and he had been thinking of how great the past five years had been, thanks to Rosi.

He thought back to that day when he moved from the bunkhouse into the cottage. It was two weeks after he got married and three weeks after his bride to be, ROSEALIA ALGETA AQUISTAPACHÉ, had arrived at the Rancho Mario. Salvatore had been bragging to all the ranch hands about his wife-to-be, about how beautiful and fun she was. He could hardly wait to show her off; he would be so proud. What a shock when everyone got their first look at this supposed gorgeous, magnificent, stunning lady, they had heard so much about! No one saw anything of the woman that Salvatore described when Rosi got out of the motor coach and stepped onto the dusty ground. She looked like she had been in a tornado. Salvatore was surprised at what he saw when she arrived. He stood there with his mouth hanging open. He had prayed a lot that night; he thought it might take a miracle to bring back his lovely Rosi.

God had answered Salvatore's prayers that night. Rosi spent the night in a room in the main house. Mario's wife Candy was very happy to have another woman around. After she helped Rosi clean up and 'air out' her troubled mind, they sat down to eat, drink wine and talk. A woman who looked almost like the old Rosi exited Mario's cottage almost 24 hours after her arrival. By the evening of her second day at the ranch, she had recovered enough to enjoy and appreciate the party they had put together to welcome her. That night, there was a cook-out to welcome Rosi and have everyone meet her. It was the real Rosi who shone like a gem that night. She sang, she danced, she played a concertina, and she drank with all the 'guys'.

Because she and Salvatore were not yet married, he still slept in the bunkhouse. She had moved into the cook's cottage; after all, she was the new head cook. That night, all the men were giving Salvatore pats on the back and congratulating him on finding such a great woman. Chico had apologized for the hundredth time for his storytelling in the bar.

The wedding was held in the small white wood Catholic Church in town. They went to San Francisco for two weeks on their honeymoon. When they had returned, Salvatore moved into the cottage with his new bride.

A year after the wedding, Rosi gave birth to a son, Nicco. Salvatore had reached his fourth goal. First, he had escaped from his stepmother's clutches. Secondly, he had found a job that he loved in America. Now he was married and had a son.

All those memories ran through Salvatore's mind as he sat there on the bedside trying to wake up. He sat on the edge of his bed reviewing his life and thinking of celebrating the anniversary of his wedding to Rosi. The celebration was early because the harvest was coming about the same time of their anniversary. He was filled with joy about his married years; he was a fortunate man.

Now he had another goal, to buy his own house and vineyard in Napa. He knew right where he wanted it, next to Joe. Joe had been responsible for paving the way from Gerola, Italy to California, for Salvatore and a few others. Joe, his buddy, had gotten him the job at Rancho Mario. A year later, Joe had moved to Rutherford and kept writing to Salvatore to join him. Rosi and Salvatore had set a date for their move that they would have to change twice. The new date was one year off; only 12 months more and then he could be his own boss. He would be a husband, a father, a landowner and a winemaker. He knew that in a year they could save the money needed.

'Well,' he thought, 'enough daydreaming.' Time to get up and go do the job he was being paid to do. He got dressed and walked into the kitchen.

He saw Rosi, but Nicco was not there. Nicco was usually up before him. He liked getting up when his Mama did so he could help her in the chow hall, putting out the simple breakfast for the ranch hands. Where was he now?

He sat down thinking about that damned alarm; he hated it. It caused him to start each day grouchy, but it did the job and his grouchiness always ended after his first cup of strong coffee. He usually didn't say anything until his spirit got the best of the grouchiness and overtook it, replacing it with friendship and warmth. He would never allow any anger to be taken out on Nicco or Rosi. Nor was he ever angry in public; he had a reputation to uphold, being cool, calm and collected.

6:30 A.M.

Finally, Nicco came in, sat on his dad's lap and waited for breakfast. Salvatore told him that he was taking Mama into town for the night to celebrate their anniversary. Nicco asked to go too but was happy when he heard that he would be spending the night at Mario and Candy's house.

With Nicco taken care of for the evening, a reservation at Deluca's, the nicest restaurant in town, flowers to be delivered table side, and a musician to play the accordion and sing Rosi's favorite songs in Italian, everything was set to make this their best anniversary yet. Salvatore loved his family, his job and all the great friends at the ranch.

He had a great life.

Rosi's morning

Rosi had been up since 5:15AM. She liked getting up early. The day was so peaceful and quiet at this time. She opened the hatch of the 4-burner Wedgewood stove to put the wood in and get it burning, so it could heat the room and prepare her first cup of coffee. She would have a stove just like it when she lived in Rutherford. It was the only place in the house at Rutherford where she allowed a fire, except for a stick match when Salvatore was lighting his pipe or an ugly-stick Italian cigar. After she left Lodi she would be deathly afraid of fire, something she passed on to her daughter, Gemma. This fear stayed with Gemma for the rest of her life.

This morning, as every morning, she put on her rimless reading-glasses and began to read one of the Italian newspapers, even though it was already 6 weeks to two months old. Then she had her second cup of coffee, strong, dark, and black. She went to the window seat where she could see the sun rising, as well as the ranch hands starting their day. She said her Rosary, as usual, and didn't move on until she had prayed every last bead. A third cup of strong, hot coffee was her reward. She never started a day without her Rosary and coffee. In a way, it was a kind of superstition. Would God honestly cause harm to her if she didn't say a prayer for every single bead? But today would be the last time she did this, other than at Mass. Even then, she wouldn't return to church for ten years after this date.

When she had finished the last prayer bead, she returned the Rosary to hang around her neck along with the St. Christopher medallion on a silver chain. Nicco and Salvatore had matching St. Christopher's. Rosi said, "St. Christopher will protect you from harm as long as you wear his medal." For added back up, she had all the medallions blessed by Monsignor Bertoluci, when he visited the Catholic Church in town. Some forty years later, she would come home from Italy with a very expensive gold medallion of the Virgin Mary she said had been blessed by the Pope. Less than a month later, she had a massive stroke and died. We often wondered if the Pope had really blessed it or if his powers were a lot less than advertised.

As if the Rosary, the prayers, and the medallion weren't enough insurance, Rosi insisted on kissing everyone's medallion before they left the house in the morning. And while she was doing her kissing she would say a short prayer in Italian.
After she hung the Rosary on her neck, she got her last cup of coffee. This one she sweetened with cream and two spoons of sugar, stirring it with whatever was close by, a knife, carrot, a finger, or, sometimes, even a spoon. After her coffees, Rosi started on the morning chores. She went to the chow hall to prepare and set out breakfast for the ranch hands. It was usually corn flakes, milk, hard-boiled eggs, and fruit, if any was ripe, and oatmeal. There were two 4-sided toast racks that could be put on the stove flame if someone wanted any toast. Then her assistant, Letty, came in and took over.

That done, she went back to her own kitchen to get the day's breakfast ready for Salvatore and Nicco. She gave them more variety than the ranch got; one day, eggs and ham, then pancakes, oatmeal, cornflakes with fresh fruit on top. And, as always, fresh milk.

At 6:20 A.M. the bedroom door opened and Salvatore came into the kitchen, whistling. He seemed to already be in a good mood, even before his coffee. Rosi said, "Morning to you. I will get you your first cup of coffee and start your breakfast." As she brought him the coffee, she leaned over and gave him a sweet tasting kiss. "You taste like blueberries," he observed. Rosi answered with a blue lipped chuckle. Now the coffee pot was drained, so she put on a fresh pot so Salvatore could have refills.

As Nicco came into the kitchen, he gave his mom a kiss, and then sat on his father's lap and gave him a kiss. Some mornings, he would eat his breakfast while on his father's lap. And so, on this day he asked, "Mother, may I eat breakfast on Papa's lap?" She was already walking to the table and answered by placing his breakfast in front of him and Papa.

Salvatore sat with one arm around Nicco, giving him half a hug. His other hand held a heavy, empty, white coffee mug. "Mama, would you kindly refill my coffee mug, please," he asked. She responded, "Sure, do you want sugar to sweeten it or should I just give you another kiss?"

Nicco and Papa laughed at this question. It was something she asked from time to time when she was feeling happy and everything was right in her world. Papa said to Nicco, "Mama and I are going into town tonight to celebrate our anniversary. Mario and Candy are going to take care of you.
You will sleep in their big house tonight." 8:00 A.M.
Salvatore said goodbye to Rosi, giving her a kiss, and said, "I will be home early today to get cleaned up and dressed for our big night. Can you make sure my suit is ready?" She gave him a kiss back, pulled out his St. Christopher medallion, kissing it and praying. Then she answered, "Your suit is ready, but your nice dress shirt has a spot on it. Don't worry. I am doing laundry today; if it doesn't come

246

out in the wash, I was going to use a spot cleaner on it. I will take Nicco over to Candy's at around 4:00, so he won't be under foot when we are trying to get ready."

Nicco objected: "Hey! I don't get under your feet; just look on the bottom of your shoes. Do you see any of me under there? No, you don't." They both laughed. Salvatore walked over and ruffled his hair and then patted it back down.

Rosi turned to Nicco and said, "Tell me what you have planned for this nice day?" Nicco replied, "Wow! I'm going to. play in the sandbox."

Salvatore hated to leave his pleasantly warm kitchen with the aroma of fresh brewed coffee and Rosi's faint scent of perfume. "You are a great wife and mother. I love you."
As happens so often in life, people don't think about enjoying each moment. They don't consider that it might be the last one they get with a special person. We don't ever think that this might be the last time we have all our physical abilities. Death can come in one second. It is cruel and quick and leaves many wounded souls.

One moment all is good; the next, we wish we could back up, just to have things as they were, even for a few moments. We wonder if we will ever be that happy again. We think we won't but, in fact, we will. Life is a series of sad and happy moments, mostly happy. We want the happy moments to last forever, but we are told nothing lasts forever. There is much more good in our lives than bad; sometimes it is there and we just can't always see it clearly. The lesson to be learned is NOT that there will always be bad things that happen. The lesson is: enjoy each moment.

Salvatore and Rosi had enjoyed their usual morning routine and banter without thinking about any of these things. No matter what era we are in, we are the same from generation to generation. We don't consider that 'this may be the last of...... whatever it is.' Their minds, as ours, were overflowing, busy sorting the priorities for the day. If they had only known in advance the change that was coming, the trauma that would rob them of the love, the joy so important to them, they might have savored their morning even more.

For Salvatore, this would be the last time he would be so happy in many years. And, for Rosi, it would be the end of happiness.

Chapter 28
That Friday Remembered

6:30 AM FRIDAY SEPTEMBER 15 1916

Nicco

There was some kind of bird outside Nicco's window; it kept chirping and tweeting, and those sounds crept, or rather flew, into his dreams. He imagined that there were birds attacking him. He ran and ran. They chased him and he jumped in the water trough and was saved. The past week, he had had several dreams of being chased by someone or something; they always ended with him being saved by jumping in the horse trough. He was thrashing about, tossing and turning in bed as he fought off the attacking birds. Finally, Nicco woke up, thanks to that feathered alarm clock of a bird outside his window, that had inspired the bad dream, and had finally frightened him into jolting wakefulness.

There wasn't much in the real world as he knew it that frightened him. But bad dreams about things he didn't think up or make up gave him the shakes. When he asked Mama about why he was having those dreams, she had given him two possible answers. One made sense, but the other scared him and caused shivers down his spine like icy cold water. The part that made sense was that his new sandbox was close to the water trough and he used it to get a lot of buckets of water to put on the sand; wet sand was better to build with. So the trough was a place Nicco liked and went to when he needed something. The attacking birds in the dreams could have been because of the fear of the mountain lion everyone was talking about at the ranch because it was attacking in the area.
But then, Rosi told Nicco another possible reason for the nightmares: "My mama was known in her village as a type of 'Dream Teller.' People would tell her their troubled dreams, and she would tell them what they meant. She often said the nightmares were a warning of something bad that was going to happen."

Nicco asked, "Do you think something bad is going to happen to me?" Rosi didn't answer; she was deep in thought. She didn't tell Nicco that she also had the ability to interpret some dreams, although she didn't have a vision of what Nicco's nightmare meant. She just felt fear, a deep blackness that overtook her thoughts, she shivered and felt the icy fear run down her spine.

Curddy

Curddy awoke reflecting on the wonderful changes in his life. He thanked God for bringing Salvatore Curtoni into his life. He wasn't expecting a favor or blessing from the Lord; he thought he was not worthy. If anything, he deserved to be cursed and punished for all the wrong he did and all the pain he caused those closest to him, his wife and son. Then, there was the embarrassment and disgrace he left for his parents to wear. He had had no choice; he had to disappear, leave Italy. He chose to flee to America because it was said to be the land of opportunity. That had proven to be true.

In a way, the new friendship with Salvatore had saved his life. Salvatore: "the Savior"; yes, he was. When he got on the ship that would take him away from Italy and deliver him to America, Curddy was at a low point in his life, in fact, the lowest. Back in Italy, he had destroyed everything of value in his life; he felt like an empty shell, worthless. Leaving Italy and all its bad memories behind was something he was pleased to do. He was also trying to close out many good memories. Those good times simply weren't obtainable anymore, and remembering them caused a sharp pain in his heart, a pain that intensified the more he remembered; so it was best to forget about everything he had left behind him. Everything, good and bad; forget it all. Ahead of him was a new life; behind him was disaster, and along the way was salvation, in the form of his new friend.

It had seemed like a chance meeting at that card game on the ship, but maybe it was fate, not just chance. Was it, in fact, God's plan that they met, or did both of them just happen to be at the same place at exactly the same point in time? Either way, that moment they met was the first flap of the butterfly's wings.

Early in the journey, Curddy learned a new definition of a friend and realized, before meeting Salvatore, he never had any real friends; only acquaintances. There was something different about Salvatore ; he was special, and that was obvious.

By the time they disembarked at Ellis Island, Curddy had a growing enthusiasm about the job opportunities for him in Lodi, California. He replayed in his mind the turning point when Salvatore said, "My friend Joe is a foreman at a big ranch; he will hire you, and we will work together. It will be great. Someday I will have my own vineyard and you could work for me." Whenever he felt down or bogged down in memories. he would recall this conversation and its promise for his future.

Next, he remembered when he was given a tour of the ranch. He had seen all the things he was now so familiar with, the stables, the pond and creek; vineyards, orchards, and vegetable gardens, the cow pastures, the barn, bunkhouse and chow hall. He was introduced to the ranch hands as he toured. When he finally had to admit that he had lied to Joe when he said he had worked with horses, he wasn't fired. He was asked if he would like to work with cattle or in the vineyard. He decided on cattle, with an option to trade and work in the vineyard at harvest time if he hated cows. It was quickly apparent that he loved the animals.

He had been trained to do his new job by a crusty old cowpoke with the name of Dusty Quick. He was tall and skinny, but he looked and talked tough; his skin was a dark walnut brown. In fact, he looked like a piece of buffalo hide in faded, dirty, worn-out clothes. He had so many wrinkles on his face that it seemed as though if his facial skin were stretched out it would have covered an elephant. And he was always squinting, even at night in the dark. To complete the look, he had a big fat, thick Fu Manchu style mustache, usually peppered with dried food.

On the first day of work, Curddy called him Dusty. That didn't sit well. He said in a gravelly, angry voice, "My name is Dusty Quick. My nickname is Gun, Gun Quick." He talked slowly and with a heavy southern drawl. Curddy then asked, "Where are you from?"

251

Dusty said, "England. You mean you couldn't hear my British accent?" That was a crock. But, strangely, as fate would have it, about 30 years in the future, Curddy would meet another strange character, in a place known as Rutherford, and that guy would go by the equally absurd name of Powder Burns. They talked the same, walked the same and looked like their skin was cut from the same hunk of rawhide.

Dusty was a good teacher, but he was also quite a character. He was a teller of tall tales, and he was a joker. He soon became a very close friend to Curddy, and he finally admitted that his real name was Sam Jones, born in Canada. Once he was in California, he worked hard to develop his tough southern cowpoke persona. He lied about his job experience working on ranches and the amount of time he'd been in California. He had found it easier to get jobs and fit in with most of the work crews if he sounded like he was from the southwest and looked seasoned. After a while working with and being around men that spoke with accents like he pretended to have, he always spoke that way. Then again maybe that was a lie too, you just never knew with Dusty.

Curddy had a lot to learn, and it was hard physical work. He learned how to ride a horse without falling off or being thrown off. Just thinking about it brought back those pains. By the time early evenings came, he was snoring away in his bunk, the pain eased some with brandy. Time passed quickly at the ranch and before Curddy knew it, he was an 'old cowhand;' he settled into the job and into life at the ranch with his new friends. He enjoyed being one of the 'cowboys.' In his first year, he learned how to ride and care for a horse, how to tend to cattle and goats, and he had become a real cowboy and a fake gunslinger. He was a good fist fighter, although the only fights he was in were mostly the ones he started. Currdy remembered how everybody and everything started to change when Rosi got to Rancho Mario. It changed for the good. Rosi took an immediate liking to Salvatore's friend. She had seen the real Curddy or at least the potential for him to be a kind, gentle, caring young man, rather than the tortured person he was, fighting demons from his past. She and Salvatore included him in many of their activities. Rosi tried to slowly coax the "good Curddy" out of him. She helped him discover his soul. He had been taught that you don't have to be or act like a tough guy to get people to like and respect you.

Yes, he thought, he still drank a lot for a while. He still had a lot of sorrows he wanted to or needed to, drown. Regrets, regrets, regrets; drinking helped. But time heals most wounds or at least lessens them. He was away from all his life's problems, not only by geography, but also mentally and emotionally; the past was becoming a faded picture. He became a part of a loving family. While he still liked to drink, he no longer had to get plastered to endure his life. He had a purpose; he had a good job; he had friends; in short, he had a life, a good life.

As Curddy considered the years that had passed, he remembered when Nicco was born and how, with that, he himself had been reborn. As Nicco had grown, Curddy's love of the boy had grown too, and he had found purpose. In a way, he regained his own son who had been lost to him years earlier. He had a son substitute He almost quit drinking and all the ghosts that had lurked in the corners of his mind vanished. His mood became sunny; his mind was sunny and free of shadows. He had a godson; he was important. He was always doing something for or with Nicco. In a way, he lived for the boy, Nicco.

Nicco had two friends that Curddy liked. One was Ant; he was a very smart boy. The other was Leo, who was shy and unsure of himself. Ant was a natural leader; when he played with the other boys, he always set himself up as the boss, the sheriff, the foreman. Sometimes he would mimic what he overheard Joe or Mario saying when giving orders to the ranch hands.

Leo lived with his mom; no one knew or talked about where his dad was. Curddy thought part of the reason Leo was so shy and insecure was that he didn't have a dad. So he tried to spend some special time with Leo too, doing things a dad would do. Leo loved Curddy and was always excited on days they were together, going fishing, hiking or just talking, and usually, Nicco was with them. Curddy had to be careful not to make Nicco jealous; that could backfire and cause harm to Leo.

Some people reinvent themselves, once, twice or more. Curddy had reinvented himself when he went through his 'imaginary' gunslinger phase. Then he dropped that when Rosi again helped reinvent him. Sadly, life and events would reinvent him again into a downward spiral; no one and nothing would help him out of it for over 30 years.

But at Lodi, he had arrived at a place where he accepted the idea that nothing could change the harm he had done and he could not undo the past. He learned that he could control what he did in the present and the future and how he treated people. He vowed that he would do as many acts of kindness as he saw possible. Whenever someone needed something, he would be there. There were many opportunities to help someone that presented themselves to Curddy every day; he helped as many as he could. He became a very unselfish, very giving man; it became the new him.
At 6:30 AM, Curddy dressed quickly; he was anxious to get out to the cattle. Maybe the mountain lion would come around and he could shoot it. Ranchers from all around would be buying him drink and thanking him. He didn't know it, but he would have a chance to be a hero today, only it wouldn't involve a wild animal.

Leo, Nicco's Friend

He had often wondered what it would be like to have a dad, a father, and husband for his mom, so she wouldn't be lonely or sad. His buddies, Nicco and Ant, had dads. He saw how their dads hugged them, sat them on their laps to tell them stories, ruffled their hair, kissed them, wrestled and played with them.

Sometimes at night, when Leo was helping his mom clean up the chow hall after dinner, they would walk to their cabin and pass Nicco's house. He would look in the window of Nicco's kitchen and inside he would see Nicco, his Mama, Miss Rosi, and his Papa, Salvatore, sitting at their table. They would be playing cards, reading, or just talking. Nicco always looked so happy, laughing or at least smiling; everyone was happy. It all just looked so nice, cozy, and comfy; it was something his heart cried out for.

From the Curtoni's window, a rectangle of light projected onto the dusty gray earth. In this projection, there were the shadow forms of the three Curtonis; but because they were only ghost images with no facial features, they could be anyone, so Leo imagined them to be him with his mom and his dad. He dwelled in the land of make-believe a lot. During the day, if he wasn't with Ant and Nicco, he would sit on the creek bank under the shade of the willow tree. While sitting on the stump of a long-ago-removed tree, he would write in his mind the screenplay of his perfect life. In this life, not only did he have a dad; he gave his dad the face of Jesus Christ, just like the drawing in Nicco's parents' bedroom. He gave his dad the name Jesse, the name of a ranch hand who, from time to time, would give him a ride on his horse.

Both Anthony-Ant's and Nicco's dads were very nice to Leo. They called him names like Buddy, Champ, Ace, Big Guy, or, his favorite, Partner. At first, he didn't understand why they called him those names. He asked his mom, and she said, "Those are terms of endearment, just like when I call you Honey or Sweetie. It's nice that they are so friendly to you. Remember to always thank them when they give you something or do something for you."

Leo loved his mom; she was, as Mister Mario said, "Durable." When he asked Mario what he meant by that word, the answer he gave was, "She traveled from New York all by herself; well, she had you, but you were an infant. She traveled with a group of strangers, but there was no one who helped her. It was very hard, and there were a lot of dangers along the way, but she arrived here unharmed and not distressed or bothered. When I say 'durable,' I mean she is tough, strong; she doesn't get upset. I have only met one other woman stronger than her, and that's Rosi. You are lucky to have such a mother; I know she loves you so very much. You are lucky." Chicken Kid had been spending a lot of time with Leo's mom and he was always nice to Leo, too. But Kid didn't seem like a dad; he seemed more like a kid, a friend. He asked his mom, "Are you going to marry The Kid?" She shook her head and said, "No he is too much like a child, not grown up yet."

Sometimes he would lie on his back on the ground in front of his cabin and look up at the clouds and daydream about what it would be as if The Kid were his dad. In these daydreams, he thought of Kid taking him fishing. The Kid would be lying on the ground with his knees up. Leo was in front of him; he had a bamboo stick with a string tied on the end, and on the other end of the string was a big fat squirming worm on a hook. Leo would be leaning back against The Kid's raised knees. The Kid was talking to him, telling him how much he loved him. But Leo's dreams of The Kid being an affectionate, warm, wise, mature grown-up were usually interrupted with ones where The Kid was just being a kid.

Leo was called shy by his mom, and he actually was very shy. He was nervous around groups; he was insecure, afraid of strangers. It took him quite a while to be at ease with Curddy, the Kid, Ant's parents and Nicco's parents. It was different with Nicco and Ant because he grew up with them; it was big people, adults that he was afraid of. He was very afraid of Roy S, but he was gone now.

Leo was happy that Ant and Nicco were his pals; they were nice to him, and they were fun to play with. They were the only kid friends on the ranch; in fact, they were the only kids he knew in his whole short life because, other than short trips to town, Leo had never been off the ranch. In a while there would be other children on the ranch. He knew little about the outside world; he had never been to school, knew no other professions other than ranch hand or storekeeper. He had never been to church, and although he had heard Nicco talk about God, he had never met Him; he didn't know where God lived. All he knew was that Rosi went to a place called church on Sunday to visit God.

If someone had asked Leo if he was happy, he would have answered "Yes, but I want a daddy." He did have so much and a lot of what he didn't have, he didn't even know existed. He was lucky; he heard that a lot, he was lucky. He was to have two very unlucky days.

8:05 AM

Leo heard Nicco in his sleep, calling him to wake him up. His eyes opened; he looked at his window, and there was Nicco, with a big smile. He said, "Let's go; we have a lot to do today."

Leo quickly got dressed and ate some cereal. He told his mom that he was going to play in Nicco's sandbox. Unlike Nicco's parents who saw the whole ranch as Nicco's playground, he always had to tell his mom where he was going so she could be confident that he would be safe. She said, "Alright, have fun."
With that, he ran over to Nicco's house. Today was going to be a special one for him. Ant was gone, so he had Nicco all to himself. They were going to play in the new sandbox that Curddy had built for Nicco; then, at noon they were going to Candy's garden for a picnic. What a great day it is going to be!

11:20 A.M.

Leo said, "I am going to take the bucket over to the trough and get water. Then we can make a little pond in the sand."

Nicco replied, "Good idea." Nicco pulled out his rubber band gun, removed a rubber band from his wrist, put it on the gun and said, "I will keep you safe from bandits."

Chapter 29
Disaster Strikes

As Salvatore finished his coffee, his mind was absently listening to Nicco, but at the forefront of his thoughts was fear about a disease hitting the grapevines. Fortunately, the disease never came. His real priority for that moment should have been to pay attention to what his son was telling him and respond in a focused way. And now, his mind had moved away from the diseased vineyard on to another problem, one he had already solved, but kept reliving. He had fired Roy, and everyone on the ranch was glad.

A week after Roy was fired, Salvatore had to deal with another problem, involving prejudice, abuse to animals, and just plain being a jerk: Chalk. The work day had been almost over, and he was headed to his cottage when he heard angry cursing. As he walked in that direction, he saw Chalk standing over The Indian, as he had first been named. Later he was called Stone or Stoney and now was called Rain. Rain was all dusty and lying in the dirt on his back.

Salvatore decided his way of dealing with Roy had worked well, so he did the same in this situation. He walked up to Chalk and did a sideways kick to Chalk's legs, dropping him to the ground. Then Salvatore ordered Chalk, "Get up and grab your stuff from the bunkhouse on your way to the gate. You are fired for being a bastardo to everyone. I have warned you about being abusive toward Rain, and after I found out that you called Nicco "a weasel-faced bastard" I should have taken my straight razor to your ears. So get up, shut up and be gone."
Chalk jumped up, red-faced with rage, and when he spoke he was spitting out each word: "I ought to beat the hell out of you for knocking me down. No one gets away with doing that crap to me."

This made Salvatore uneasy, especially since he was not a fighter; he was always the peacekeeper. But he called Chalk's bluff: "I would love to see you take a swing at me or use that," nodding to Rain's knife, now in Chalk's hand. While Chalk thought about it, Salvatore bent down and grabbed a small log off the nearby woodpile; he brought it down as hard as he could on Chalk's knife holding hand. Chalk screamed like a stuck pig. Salvatore found Moe in the crowd that had gathered and asked him to help Chalk get his stuff together and give him a buggy ride to town.

Salvatore's last words to Chalk were, "If you come back here, I will get Curddy's rifle and shoot you. We will all say it was self-defense; everyone here hates you."

Why was this scene replaying in his mind, today of all days? To him, it seemed strange that his mind was dwelling on Chalk and his parting promise to get revenge. Was it a sign, something he should watch out for? He didn't even hear what Nicco was telling him, and, without really hearing, just continued responding with "Yes. Good. I see." Finally, his thoughts returned to life in his kitchen. Later, he would relive those moments, but in the replay, he was always totally focused on Nicco and Rosi.

Aow it was time to earn his pay. As usual, that meant saying goodbye to his little family and hello to Chico, Giuseppe, and Charlie, his work crew. They would put on their leather 'aprons' that had in their pouches sections of hemp rope, pruning shears, curved knives, long knives and other tools of the trade. Once geared up, they would head out to the orchard, vineyard or the fields for a day's work in the sun.

That morning Salvatore was whistling as he walked out to the vineyard. He pulled the leather strap that held his pocket watch and looking at it, saw it was 8:05 AM, less than four hours until lunch. He put his watch back in his pocket, started to whistle again and went to work. He said 'good morning' all around to his crew; they were good men. His work crew had high respect for him. The Butterfly Effect

It would be hard to pinpoint the exact second when a situation goes from good to bad; when a nice day becomes a nightmare. Can you predict the results of each and every action before it happens? Logic tells you the likely result of an action. If you jumped off a 20-story building, you could expect to die. But, if you go to the roof of a 20-story building to get a better view of the Bay, you would never expect to be hit by a low flying airplane; but it could happen. Is that fate, that you were destined to die at that moment? But, what if you decided to walk the four blocks to get a better view of the Bay? Then, you live; no airplane hits you.

The Butterfly Effect says that every simple action starts a chain of events that result in an unpredictable consequence. An example: a butterfly on a leaf in a tree flaps his wings; the air waves from his flapping wings hit a leaf, and the leaf drops to the water below the tree. The leaf floats downstream and soon drifts to the bank of the stream. A scorpion creeps to the leaf and gets on it, causing the leaf to dislodge from the shore and drift downstream for miles. The leaf bumps against a man wading in the stream, the scorpion crawls off the leaf onto the man who just got in the water and stings him, and the man dies. He dies all because of that butterfly. Even in this example, observe how many, tiny, things had to happen to bring about the death of the man.

It was a chain of events started by the butterfly. What if the butterfly had landed on a different leaf? What if the man got in the stream two minutes later? The leaf would have continued downstream; the man would not die at that moment.

What was the butterfly that caused the chain of events that brought death and destruction to Rancho Mario? How many more people might have been born; how many lives helped, if that one life had not been lost that day? If only they could go back in time and change just one little thing. Is that too much to ask? Only we all know it is not possible. Not only were there many events that occurred, but also that at least five people participated in the series of events that brought them in contact at the exact time together.

The exact moment that shattered the world for this small group of people in Lodi was 11:30 AM on Friday, September 15, 1906. There was nothing that morning that gave a warning of the hellacious disaster that would visit the world of those good, innocent people at Rancho Mario. No one did any specific thing wrong. These were nice people. Bad things do happen to good people.

This bad thing was so bad that people later asked, "Where was God at that moment? How could something so unimaginably nightmarish happen?"

11:30 AM

Chico

Chico was walking from the vineyard heading to the chow hall. It was too early for lunch, but it had been a hot day, and he wanted to wash up and get something cold to drink. Just before he turned the corner of Salvatore's cottage, he heard a loud, strange noise and froze. It was a shriek like he had never heard in his life. He heard that sound echoing in his brain every day until he died at 84 years of age. It sounded like an animal screaming and roaring in pain. His first thought was "The mountain lion!" He panicked; he wanted to run, away from what sounded like a demon from hell. Then he heard another sound; it was like a child crying out for help.

His next thought was to run to the bunkhouse to get the rifle. No time; he pulled out his knife and ran around the corner. There he stopped dead in his tracks at what he saw. Just then, Curddy ran by Chico and bumped into him causing him to fall to his knees. He started crying. The next thing he was aware of was Mario shaking him and yelling in his face, "Take Bullet and ride as fast as you can to town. Get the doctor and tell the sheriff. Go now!"

Chico came back with the doctor; it was too late for one but not the other two.

When the doctor finished all that he could do, he said to Mario, "God was blessing one family. There was nothing I could do for the other. I have never seen anything this horrible in my thirty years as a doctor, a tragedy beyond comprehension."
He felt a hand squeeze his right shoulder in a comforting way. He turned to see that the hand belonged to Matt, the sheriff. Matt said, "I agree with you on that one. In my twenty-five years as sheriff, I have never seen or heard of anyone being killed like that. I couldn't even imagine it in a nightmare. Doc, there are going to be a few people that I don't think even you can heal. I have seen people commit suicide over less; you should keep an eye on them."

Doc replied, "I will be back to check up on Leo in a week. I will see how the others are then." But when he came back a week later, it was too late. The "others" were gone, away from the ranch and the horrors that lingered in every corner.

The damage that had hit the Rancho was as devastating if a tornado had bulldozed its way through the middle of it and done a u-turn for a second round of devastation. Sadly, in this case, the damage was scraps of lives left, not rubble from buildings

Was there a single action that could have prevented the end result? Examine this instance: If a person didn't put a bullet in a gun, the gun couldn't shoot anyone or anything. The single action this day was not dangerous in the way a loaded gun could kill someone, but the end result was the same. However, a single action alone would not have caused any harm if dozens of other events hadn't brought everything together. If any one thing had not happened at the instant that it did, the outcome would have been better, possibly even okay.

Beyond the death of one person, there was the death of happiness at the ranch for a long time to come. Wounds like that do not heal quickly, if ever. The closer the relationship with the harmed person, the longer the healing process. The aftershocks from this one accident caused strong, deep tremors in lives of three people, much more than the others.

Three people who suffered physically due to this 'accident;' one only suffered briefly before, mercifully, death took him. Another was in the hospital for months and then continued to be in physical and emotional pain and suffering for the rest of his life. The third person hurt was Leo, a young boy. The Doc came out weekly for the first month, then once a month. But his services were no longer required after March; he healed in half a year. A year after the accident, Leo died, too, but not from this day's injuries.

Of the people emotionally and mentally beaten up, one person, Salvatore, brought those tremors under control in a relatively short period of time and was comforting to the other two people who felt aftershocks for the rest of their lives.

The exact moment that the butterfly flapped its wings that day could have been 5:30 AM, the moment Rosi Curtoni entered her laundry room.

Five people, who rose at different times on that September 15th and left to four different destinations, all ended up at the same place at the same time: 11:30 a.m.
Rosi Curtoni got up at 5:15 A.M. Salvatore got up at 6:00 A.M. Nicco got up at 6:30 AM, and at 8:00 he went to his friend's bedroom window and knocked. He woke Leo and told him to get dressed and come over to play in the new sandbox.
Leo got up at 8:05. Curddy got up at 6:30 AM.

Salvatore

Salvatore started walking from the vineyard up toward his cottage. His plan was to drop in and say hi to Rosi on his way to the chow hall for lunch. He also wanted to see how Nicco was enjoying playing in the new sandbox. He smiled when he thought how nice it was to have so many people who loved Nicco and were always doing something for him, the gift of the sandbox just the latest offering.

He looked up at the clear blue sky, so blue and deep that he thought he could see all the way to heaven. The sun was warm as it shone down on his upturned face. Wow, what a day! He thanked God for all the blessings He had given to his little family, and then he smiled, walked faster and started whistling. He often thanked God for things; he also asked God for things. He didn't say the rosary the way Rosi did; he didn't light candles in church. He didn't think that he had to say' formal' prayers like Our Father or Hail Mary, but he prayed daily. He would go to a quiet place and talk to God, sometimes asking for something for his family, friends or himself. Sometimes, he would tell God his fears. Then he would wait and watch to see how God was going to answer his prayers. Sometimes, what he asked for came to be; other times, God responded by not giving him what he asked for, but rather what would be good for him. The local priest told him that God answered prayers in three ways. One is YES; He gives us what we ask for. The second is NO; He gives not what we ask for, but what is best for us. And, third is WAIT; He can see what will happen in the future and answers our prayers when the season is right.

On this beautiful day, as he walked along, he didn't ask for anything, he just gave praise to God. He had no clue that, in moments, his whole world would change, and he would be begging God for many things. Those would be the most important requests of his life and God would be there to help and comfort Salvatore and Rosi.

He walked past the barn, kicking up hot dust that assaulted his nostrils. Chico was ahead of him walking to the chow hall. He was almost to Rosi's laundry room, where Salvatore knew she would be doing the laundry at this time of day. Then he heard it, a sound that cut to his soul, a sound that would ring in his ears for decades. It was a terrible shrieking wail of something in agony or immense pain. He stopped in his tracks. Ahead of him, he saw Chico stop too.

Then Chico turned as if he was going to run away or maybe go to the bunkhouse. Instead, he turned, pulled his knife out of its belt holster, and rounded the corner and looked toward Salvatore's cottage. Then, the awful scream came again. Salvatore froze. Just then, Curddy came racing up on his horse and jumped from the saddle. He hit the ground running; he ran past Chico hitting him and knocking him to the ground.
Then Salvatore heard a different scream of pain. He thought, 'Chalk came back for revenge, and was acting it out on Rosi or Nicco.' He reached into his apron for a weapon, but all he had was a curved vine knife. He ran toward his cottage, and then what he saw caused him to recoil in horror.

Currdy

Curddy had been riding his horse, out around the cows, checking to see if all was good. He took a last drag off his hand-rolled cigarette. He then licked his thumb and forefinger and pinched the fire out of the butt; he wanted to ensure it was dead before he tossed it to the ground. There was always the possibility of fire at this time of the year. He remembered there had been a fire on Mister Cowell's

Cowell Towne Ranch, nicknamed the COW TOWN RANCH, in 1912, and it had taken out the ranch house, barn and half of the bunkhouses. Due to quick actions of cowboys and family members, no people or animals were harmed, but it had caused huge expenses to rebuild or replace the buildings that had been destroyed.

He pulled his rifle from the saddle cocked it and put it back. He was ready for action. He liked his rifle, but sometimes he missed his revolver. He had given it to someone on the ranch, an action he would later regret, as his action signed the death warrant of a young member of the ranch family. But that wouldn't happen for almost two more years. After today's events, he would drink a lot; but in two years, he would drink even more because of his guilt for giving the gun to someone responsible for the shooting death of a child. He gave the revolver to The Chicken Kid, who gave it to Letty. But Letty's son, Leo, found the gun by accident, it shot a bullet into his own chest. Leo died on the bare wood floor in his kitchen. He was saved from the events of this disastrous day to die in such a sad way, less than two years later.

Curddy's job for the day was to ride around and track a mountain lion that was rumored to be around the cattle the night before. He could find no tracks. Curddy was a bit fearful when he thought about the possibility that a mountain lion could attack him. If, of course, it was even true that there was one around. The talk around the bunkhouse was that the whole thing was a hoax. No one he knew had actually seen someone who had been attacked; there were just rumors. He did see a man at the town bar with scars all over his body. The guy told everyone he had been ripped up by a mountain lion. It turned out this was true, but it had happened hundreds of miles to the north.

11:20 AM

Curddy slowly started riding back toward the ranch house. On Friday, everyone liked to get to lunch early; it was roast beef day. As his horse trotted along, Curddy glanced over the herd; all looked good. As he got closer, he could hear Nicco laughing and talking to someone. It made him think back to last night and the fun time he had at Salvatore and Rosi's cottage for dinner and brandy. He always felt such joy and love there. Even on the coldest of winter nights, his heart felt warmth. Nicco was so cute as he sat on his lap and told him a story about catching a fish in the nearby creek. Curddy was Nicco's godfather and he loved the boy as much as if he was his own son. Curddy's life was great; he was a part of the Curtoni family, and he had a substitute for his missing son.

He trotted along, lost in his happy thoughts. Suddenly, he heard screams and shrieks, then more screams, and yelling. He thought 'The lion.' Was that the sound of a wild animal, or a person screaming in pain? NICCO! He rode faster than his horse Willy Boy had ever galloped. He rounded the barn; then, he looked in the direction of the sound and saw something horrifying.

Nicco 8:00 AM
Nicco answered his Mama's question: "I am going to get Leo, and we are then going to come back to play in the sandbox. Then we are going to have a Picnic at Candy's garden."

She gave him a kiss, then kissed his St. Christopher medal and said, "Have fun; be safe." 11:20-11:30 AM
Nicco watched as Leo got the bucket of water, brought it back and dumped it on the sand. Nicco laughed as Leo spilled some of the water on his head. In the heat, it dried in minutes.

It was moments later, as they were building a fort out of sand, Nicco suddenly saw a very bright light, blinding, followed, in a split second, by pain, the worst pain he had ever experienced. Then there was nothing; he left the pain and life behind as he passed into the here-after.

Leo

He was having such a fun time playing with Nicco, just the two of them, without Ant to torment him.

Suddenly, he saw a blinding light coming from where Nicco was. Then he, too, was covered in brightness and then pain. Leo screamed, shrieked; the pain didn't stop. It got worse by the second.

Then someone picked him up and ran with him and dumped him in water. That was the last thing he remembered about that day.

Curddy

As he was racing toward the sounds of pain and panic, he came into view of the source. In the sand box that he had helped to make were two children engulfed in fire. As he got close to the sandbox, he jumped off his horse while it was still at full gallop. He hit the ground running and, seconds later, he picked up the first boy, ran to the water trough and threw the boy in the water. Then he ran back. His shirt was in flames, but he picked up the second boy and ran with him.

Curddy felt immense pain; his skin felt like it was melting off him as the flames covered his chest, stomach, arms, and neck. He made it to the trough a second time and dumped the second boy in and then passed out into the water.

Salvatore

He saw Curddy run with a burning bundle, a boy; he dumped him into the water and ran back toward the house. Salvatore made it to his backyard in time to almost collide with Curddy. He had another boy on fire in his arm; Curddy himself was in flames and bellowing in pain. Salvatore felt a blazing heat as Curddy ran past him.

'Oh God, whose two boys were those?' Then he remembered. Ant was gone. 'Oh, God! Nicco was one of the boys. Oh no, please no! What happened? How did something like this happen?'

Then he collapsed; his legs just gave out. He felt faint, weak, and helpless. The next thing he knew, Mario was kneeling in front of him talking to him in comforting tones. He didn't know how much time passed, but it had to have been quite a while. He noticed there were men all over the yard now; many of them were crying. 'What was Mario saying to him?' Then he understood the words, "Leo was badly burned on his right arm. But I am sorry to say, very deeply saddened to say, Nicco was burned to death, in this tragic accident."

Salvatore then said, "Rosi. Where is my wife?" Rosi

267

Rosi had just finished ironing and getting Salvatore's suit ready for their big night on the town. She thought about those first few days in Lodi, how much she had hated America and the ranch. Now she loved it; they had a nice home and they were surrounded by good friends.

She stuck her head out the window, looked down, and saw Nicco and Leo playing nicely in the sandbox. She said, "I have some old serving spoons and pie plates I will give you to play with in the sand. I'll get them as soon as I finish ironing."

She had to clean that spot off Salvatore's dress shirt and another off his suit coat; then it would be lunch time. On the ironing board, she had a pan of cleaning solvent. She dipped a rag into the cleaning fluid and rubbed the spot. Suddenly the cleaning fluid caught fire, flames burning high out of the pot. When she thought back on it, she was never able to understand how the fluid caught fire. Seeing the flames coming out of the pot, she panicked. She grabbed the handle of the pot, ran to the window and threw the flaming liquid out to the yard. She had forgotten that there was now a sandbox beneath the window, a sandbox that Nicco and Leo were playing in. The flaming fluid landed right on top of Nicco and some splashed on Leo's arm.

She heard the screams, looked down, and realized what she had done and passed out.

Chapter 30
The end of Nono's story

After the accident, events that took place over the following weeks and months were a heavy haze in the minds of those close to the injured parties and with the injured, even more so. As happens in times like these, the mind mercifully blocks out a lot. People don't want to talk about the horrors; they want to forget and move on. The sheriff came that day; he determined it to be an accident.

The Doc came and got Curddy to the hospital after he tended to Leo. Miraculously, Leo wasn't too bad off, and it was determined that, in time, he would be healed except for some scars on his arm. Curddy was severely burned, and his condition was touch and go for the first ten days. Then he started healing, a slow physical healing. He would spend the rest of his life trying to gain emotional healing. He blamed himself for not saving Nicco, even though he was most likely dead by the time Curddy got to him. Once he was released from the hospital, Curddy moved around, eventually ending up in Rutherford. He lived in the back of a bar for a while; also, he lived with Joe, his former boss at Rancho Mario, a newcomer to the Valley.

When Joe had saved enough money, he had bought a small house with vineyards surrounding it. He only had eight grapevines on his small piece of the Napa Valley. It cost too much to buy vineyard acreage, too. But he could afford this small property. Joe didn't want to continue working for someone else, he wanted his own vineyard, without the responsibility for overseeing all the employees, keeping everything working like clockwork. His new home had three bedrooms, a kitchen with a dinner table squeezed into it, a living room with a fireplace and an enclosed sun porch. Joe went to work at the B.V winery doing a bit of everything.

Joe had discovered this heavenly valley thanks to Mario. Mario had gathered his staff leaders and treated them to a weekend at a spa in Calistoga at the Hot Springs Hotel which had been opened by a Mr. Brennan in 1862. Most of the clients were wealthy residents of San Francisco. The secrets of the hot springs had been discovered over

500 years before by the Native Americans but, of course, they hadn't been wealthy at all. Mario and Candy, along with Joe and four others, had spent three nights there. On their second day, someone they met while swimming told them, "You need to go back to Rutherford and visit the BV Winery. Ask for a tour and see how they make and bottle their wine. Afterward, they will give you their wines to taste."

Mario and his crew did just that. They loved the tour, especially the tasting part. When they finished, they felt a bit tipsy and decided they should eat before driving back. They were told there were no restaurants nearby and they would need to go to St. Helena. They responded, "No, we feel drunk and need to eat, and coffee would be nice too." They were sent three vineyards away where they discovered a whitewashed slaughterhouse. There was also a little store there where they could get salami and other cold cuts, cheeses, and bread. They bought some olives that had come from the two olive trees that framed the slaughterhouse. Joe thought this property could be what he would like to buy, where he would like to raise his family.

But, as it turned out when Joe was ready to move, that property was not available. The owners weren't ready to sell, and it would have been too expensive for him anyway. Instead, he bought his little place two properties away, just behind the old green and white two-room schoolhouse that said 1888 under its bell tower. Coincidentally, the property with the slaughterhouse would later be bought by Salvatore and Rosi.

When Curddy arrived in the valley, Joe got Curddy a job as a night watchman at BV, but after a month, Curddy was fired for being drunk at work numerous times. After that, Curddy got hired at the OLD OAKEN BUCKET bar where he drank a lot.

Curddy's upper body, arms, and neck were covered by deep scars, and he was a horrid sight to see. The time passed slowly for him. He slept on Joe's sun porch rather than in a bedroom because he often got up in the middle of the night. He drank at work, after all, it was a bar; he drank at home, played solitaire and smoked and slept a lot.

He escaped from the world. Most of the time, he just sat outside facing the sun on days that it was shining; or he would look out at the vineyards and mountain, staring into oblivion, thinking, regretting. He again thought of how he had ruined his relationship with his wife and son; he thought about sweet little Nicco who had been like another son to him. Nicco was dead because he wasn't fast enough. It would be years before he would start to enjoy life again and then it was due to another child, a boy. Sometimes he would stare at an old photo of his wife and son, or the one of Nicco, all the time sad.

He missed Rosi and Sal, too.

The Curtonis had to rebuild their lives; they needed a massive healing to survive. Right after the accident, Rosi and Salvatore almost immediately ran away from Lodi. Nicco's funeral service was in a Catholic Church, and he was buried in the Catholic cemetery in San Francisco. They moved to San Francisco to live with Mary, a friend from Gerola, Italy. She took them in immediately and cared for them. For months they just vegetated, slept, and ate sparingly, even though Mary was a good cook. They read a lot, Rosi, the Bible, and Salvatore the two Italian newspapers Mary received from Italy delivered to her door. And they walked around this city which was, to them, incredible.

After what Mary thought was enough time (actually far too much time, but she was too kind and compassionate to force the issue), she told them she needed their help. It was costing her more each month for the food and all with them being there, she needed rent money. They both got jobs in the soap factory and began to make new friends who soon became like family. Their Little Italy of friends gave them love and the feeling of safety and warmth. These people became friends for life. Many of them spent lots and lots of weeks at what would become the home of Salvatore, Rosi and their daughter Gemma. It was eventually named Big Pink because of its paint job. It was always easy to direct newcomers to their home. They said. "Just past the Oakville Market, on the left, you will see a pink palace; that's us.

Salvatore and Rosi also helped each other to heal. Salvatore never once blamed Rosi for the accident, never, even if he was drunk, mad or in an argument with her. He again earned his old nickname, Saint Sal. Decades later, Salvatore would share his wisdom about forgiveness with his friends and family, and it greatly helped some of them in times of need. Many people marveled at how Salvatore was able to move on.

Rosi had a harder time. She was never again the same fun, carefree person. How does someone get over the guilt and horror of an accident like that? No one knew what went through her mind or her soul. She never talked about it. She was strong and went on with life. She did have a fear of fire and never allowed candles inside at Big Pink. The fireplace in the front room was never used when she was in the room.

After they moved to Rutherford, they started a new life. The past was in the past. It was time to move on. They brought with them a child, their daughter, Gemma who was 5-years-old. Gemma had been born at Mary's House in San Francisco.

Sometime after moving onto the property, Sal and Rosi demolished the old house; it had gaps in the walls where the winds blew in. It creaked and groaned as if it was asking to be put out of its misery. Gemma begged them to rebuild; the house noises haunted her at night. When they rebuilt, they kept the old slaughterhouse and made their wine there. The bunkhouse was fixed up a bit and brought them some money when they took in boarders. The barn was good as it was. The pen that kept livestock waiting to be slaughtered was kept for a while. They added a chicken yard and chicken house The new home was a big stucco house it stood out like a toad in a sugar bowl. Their new life became one with lots of friends, parties, homemade wine, good food; it was a joyful life. All that had happened in Lodi began retreating into the past.

Curddy's rebirth started as a result of Salvatore and Rosi moving to Rutherford and taking him in again. They let him live in one of the bunk beds out of the eight that were on the property. They soon rented out the other seven beds, but Curddy stayed there for free. It was one of many things they did for him to try to repay him for all the pain and disfigurement he endured for trying to save Nicco. He had a family again, but now it was a family that had shared a horrible accident together. The three adults continued their healing process together, assisted greatly by the new scenery and friends around them.

1963, In the kitchen at Big Pink

It had been a long exhausting night. Between Curddy's letter and my Nono's stories, I now had my answers. The mysteries had all been solved. The mystery boy in the old photographs, both the big framed one and a smaller one, was Nicco Curtoni, son of Rosi and Salvatore. Had he lived he would have been my uncle. My grandparents didn't want to answer their grandson's, my question, "Who is that little boy?" It would have drained them emotionally to talk about it, and it would terrify me. How could they say he had been killed at Rancho Mario when his mom, my Nona Rosi accidentally threw a flaming pot of cleaning solvent on him, burning him to death. When questioned, they would put the photos away. After a while, they would bring the pictures out again until I harassed them again.

What had happened to Nicco explained why the Rosi of old was gone; that fun Rosi went up in those same flames. The new Rosi ate and drank a bit more than normal; she gained a lot of weight; she wore cheap homemade 'house dresses' and didn't fix herself up. Her hair had turned white at an early age. But life went on. Salvatore supported her, and when families bond together, they can conquer almost any problems or crises.

Another mystery that was solved was related to Curddy's son and wife. They had not been murdered, as he had told everyone. He had been caught cheating, and his wife banished him from their lives. And now I knew that his terrible scars had come from the fire that injured Leo and killed Nicco. That is how he had been so horribly disfigured and also why he was so shattered.

Much later, when I was older, I went into Ray's Bar on Main Street in St. Helena. The bartender kept looking at me until he finally asked, "Didn't you used to be that kid that was following Monty around?" I shook my head: "I have never known anyone named Monty." He pursued it, "Yes, you are Curtoni's grandson, Jimmy, Jim, right?"

I nodded my head and replied "Yes." He thought for a few moments, and snapped his fingers and smiled. "Curddy. Everyone called him Curddy. I knew his son, Jamie Monty. Monty was Curddy 's real last name."

I almost swallowed my tongue. "What? Where did you meet Curddy's son?"

His answer surprised me. "I worked with him at a winery in Santa Rosa. He and his mom moved to America when Jamie was 19 years old."

I couldn't understand "You mean Curddy's son was close by all this time, and he didn't know it?"

"Oh, he knew it. I think he was afraid to face his son after disgracing his mother." All this time his son was living on the other side of the mountain.

Twenty years after Rosi and Salvatore moved to Rutherford, I was born to Gemma. They now had what they had been missing for decades, a young male child. Because of this, I was the recipient of more love than the average grandson.

My adventures at Big Pink not only spanned my childhood and teen years but also my adult years. I brought my wife, young son, and daughter up there many times, every Easter for eight years until my Nono got cancer and could no longer take care of the vineyards and had to move in with my parents. I have many photos of Nono with my son Mike or holding my infant daughter, my little girl Dani, with joy and pride radiating off him.

It was in 1974 that we had to sell the place. It was a sad, sad goodbye when we walked out of the big house for the last time.

Chapter 31
Remembering Nono

I will always remember Nono. I was very close to him. After Curddy died, my Nono added "being Jimmy's buddy" to his 'job description' by taking me on adventures and spending one-on-one time with me. He tried to fill the role Curddy had played in my life. Even today, I still dream of him, still alive and me being with him. In my memory, his image never changes. To me, he looked the same at the time he passed away as he did in my earliest memories of him. Perhaps the only difference was his teeth. He eventually got dentures that gave him a completely different look. I had to get used to that!

In the image I have in my mind, Nono resembles Anthony Hopkins, the way Sir Anthony looked about 1990, except that Nono had very large hands. I'm not sure about Sir Anthony. Nono's hands told stories. The backs of his hands were dark, the only tan part of his body. Nono's usual uniform had consisted of grey work pants and a matching grey shirt, with cuffs buttoned, and on his head a large brim straw hat to protect his head and face from the sun. Only his hands were left bare. Sometimes he didn't wear the hat, and some damage had already been done to his face by the time he was 50. His hands especially spoke of all those days in the sun working in his vineyard and the vineyards of his neighbors. They were scarred from the branches that scraped them.
There were lots of brown spots and some red ones. They were the ones that might have been the infants that grew up to become the cancer that killed him some 14 years later. Although the backs of his hands were rough, his palms were smooth and gentle, comforting to hold when we went on walks or when I ventured with him into the haunted slaughterhouse, so he could retrieve something like the big wheel of cheese he kept in the old meat cooler. I always thought if there was bomb coming our way on a Russian missile, we would be safe in that cooler room; it had walls 8 to 10 inches thick.

When I was going through the hell, depression, and despair of divorce, Nono had me stay with him for a while. We went hunting and hiking and talked and ate together, drinking plenty of red wine. He had a lot of wisdom to impart; it helped get me back among the living. When my car was ripped off, he helped me buy a new one; when an uninsured driver smashed into me head on and totaled that car, he helped me again.

Big Pink's 2.4 acres were sold for either $64,000 as my mom remembers or $74,000 as I remember. Nono had a master bedroom and bath built and moved into my parent's house. I came often to visit and enjoyed many meals and afternoons with him. He was, and in my heart, still is a great human being. He loved life; he loved people and people loved him. I can remember only two times in my whole life that he was unhappy with me, and I deserved it. He a was kind and gentle man, easy going and not upset much. I think he enjoyed every day, at least after he moved to Rutherford.
It was a crushing sorrow for him to have to sell Big Pink. Five decades of his life were spent there with his wife Rosi and all his friends, and so many wonderful events took place there. He saw his only child, my mom, grow up there. He saw his only grandson, me, grow up there. He played bocce ball there under the huge fig trees. He buried his money in the cellar under Big Pink. Yes, the best times of his life happened there.

He missed his beloved gardens and seeing vineyards all around him. He missed working in his own vineyard, picking, pruning, and primping. He missed making his own wine in the slaughterhouse. He missed using his .22 to go hunting for rabbit that would go in his stew along with vegetables from his own garden. He missed taking table scraps from dinner, putting them in a pot and taking this gourmet feast down to the barn. As he trotted down the back steps toward the barn, he would start yelling "Gat, gato gato gato." Then he would smile when almost a dozen mangy, skinny, ratty-looking feral cats came running out of nowhere for their dinner.

Nono ventured into the cellar several times a day to fill a jug full of wine from one of the barrels of his homemade red. But there was another reason he liked coming down to the cellar. Under the stairs that went from the cellar up to the mud porch, there was a little room with a screen front that let cool air in. This was the canning room, where my Nona put everything she canned or pickled; the shelves were usually full. For years after she passed away, we were still enjoying the delicious items she had preserved in Mason jars. Nono liked to come down to get something to eat with dinner or the next day's lunch. He never did eat everything that was in there. I guess he went down to see and handle the things she had prepared so he could remember Nona and feel close to her. I think he replayed the memories of the two of them working together to prepare those food items and the joy they had knowing that many friends would enjoy them. He missed his cellar.

The wall above the workbench was covered with hundreds of items he had scrounged from everywhere. All of it was old; so many spider webs they looked like gauze covering everything. He had old spurs and cowbells from Lodi, some horns from various animals and a few horns of the "ah-ooo-gah" kind, too. There was gear for horses, old tools that were unusable, and anything he found in the vineyard hung on that wall. It was nothing but 100% junk, garbage, but he wouldn't part with it. In fact, I have some of that old stuff and junk hanging on the fence in my backyard in Pleasant Hill even now.

Nono missed his annual trip to Petaluma to get baby chicks, and later enjoying the eggs or chicken for dinner. As I remember it, that trip was usually taken on 120-degree day in a car with no air conditioning. He missed the wide open, beautiful sky. Now, he lived in a place cluttered by power wires, polluted with smog, and the non-stop procession of loud airplanes flying low overhead on the way to and from the little Concord airport. Those planes were a poor substitute for his pigeons that had flown overhead on their way back to their coop after a day of sightseeing all over the Valley.
Most of all, Nono missed hosting the unending stream of people that had come to stay at Big Pink for a night or a week. He had an unselfish spirit, always wanting to share all he had with friends. He liked sharing the beauty of the surrounding valley by welcoming people to come and stay. He was known and respected in the Valley from Oakville to Calistoga. Any and all were welcome at his home, Big Pink, and many came. And he was also welcome in their houses.

At his new residence, he couldn't walk over to the surrounding houses and enjoy time with friends. In Pleasant Hill, he had no friends, only my parents and me. He had moved into one large bedroom with a backyard patio. It was a poor substitute for the big house, with its bunk houses, wine cellar, slaughterhouse, barn, chicken coops, pigeon coops, and pond with very old Koi. There was no longer a large vegetable garden or trees where he could get olives, fresh figs, peaches, apricots, and loquats. The kitchen wasn't warmed by a wood burning stove but a wall heater, just not quite as cozy.

Sadly, I think the reason he died only a year-and-a-half after he left Big Pink was a broken heart. His heart longed to return to the place and the life he would never, could never, have again. He left his heart in Rutherford.

Chapter 32
The $1,000 Fishing Pole

Sometimes, I look back on my youth and wonder if it was real. There were so many crazy adventures with my older Italian friends that I have a hard time picking out which one was my favorite. But I think one that rises to the top was the fishing trip I took when I was 15-years-old. It featured an all-star cast that included my dad and Piétro, a friend of my Nono's. Piétro was close to seventy-years-old and quite large. He was funny, although that was rarely his intent; he was just kind of a bumbler. My dad, in one of his mischievous moods, had nicknamed him Pistol Pete, or PP for short.

I had brought my friend Andy along, too. He was one of my classmates and a funny person without trying. But unlike Pistol Pete, Andy wasn't a bumbler. He was just really casual and laid back, so much so that I nicknamed him Wasted. His eyelids were usually half-closed, and he had a low energy persona, moving very slowly and lazily, almost as if he had consumed a pint of whiskey. He was a really nice guy, always in a good mood, too, but he never told his face that. Andy also made hilarious observations about people and events that unfolded around us. My parents liked him; my mom because he was an altar boy and my dad because of Andy's dry sense of humor and the fact that Andy could hold his own as a fisherman. On a previous outing, a couple of my friends had joined us for fishing when a storm came up. The other two ended up puking their guts out. But not Andy. He ate two tuna sandwiches and clearly held his own.

On this day, we were going out on Lake Berryessa. I was set for an epic trip; in addition to all my fishing gear, I had a lunch that included salami, cheese, bread with garlic spread, anchovies and hot peppers. I also brought along my transistor radio. This was in the days before boomboxes that were nearly as large as refrigerators. My transistor was about the size of a pack of cigarettes. Oh, I had some of those, too. My Lucky Strikes were rolled up in my tee shirt sleeve, and the Zippo lighter was in my Levi's coin pocket.

Finally, as part of my gear, I had my army surplus WWII canteen. The problem was that when I clipped it on my belt, it shared its wetness with my pants. My dad, of course, laughingly teased me, "Do we need to bring an empty coffee can for you? You know. A pee can?" When I looked where his eyes were gazing, I had seen a slowly growing wet spot right in my crotch area. So this time, the canteen was full minus its canvas cover. And I had filled it with something I thought would "make my day." The night before, I had gone down into my Nono's wine cellar with my canteen and a funnel and drained red wine into my canteen, filling it to the brim.

We started our day very early, as all good fishermen do: 5 AM. Piétro was our navigator since he had been to this top-secret fishing hole many times. He had told us it was a quick and easy drive with only one bad curve. After the twentieth bad curve, my dad commented, "I thought you said there was one bad curve!" Piétro grinned and noted, "I meant to say one bad curve after another." Then he laughed with his high-pitched 'eeeehaaaww, eeeehaaaww' that sounded exactly like a donkey. We didn't think it was funny at all, but shortly, the laugh would be on him.

While we were navigating our twisting-turning ride, sometimes meeting ourselves along the way, Piétro told us a long story about his rare 50-year-old, handmade, one-of-a-kind split bamboo fishing pole. He talked about it the way a newlywed might talk about his wife or a dad about his firstborn child. On and on, he went: "I've been offered $1000 for it!" he bragged. "It's perfectly balanced, a masterpiece. I could land a marlin with it. I rub it down weekly with a suede cloth made from a rare white buffalo. And I never take it out of the case unless the weather is warm and perfect." On and on, he went. By the time we arrived at his secret, sure-to-catch-your-limit fishing hole, he was ready to tell us the Pope had blessed his rare, sacred fishing pole.

There were already ten people at the fishing hole when we arrived. To whom was it secret?!?!

We all gratefully escaped the story and the car, a 1950 Chevy two-door. My dad and I opened the trunk to get our gear out. Piètro had the passenger door open and was getting his pole out of the back seat. It couldn't go in the trunk, something about keeping it at body temperature. His pole case looked like it had been made to house a very expensive pool cue. As he slowly opened the case, one of the hinges gave out a "screeeeecccch." He stopped, reached into his shirt pocket and removed a little tube of graphite powder. He shot a cloud of dust at the offending hinge. Then he continued opening the now-silent case. The inside was a beautiful emerald green velvet.

Inside the case were four pieces which Piétro put together to make one fine-looking, deluxe, one- of-a-kind bamboo fishing pole. Once together, he made several pretend casts, whipping the pole back and forth over his right shoulder. He asked, "Did I tell you they had a photo and a short article about this fishing pole in Field & Stream Magazine?" He shook his head 'no,' answering his own question.

"Did I tell you how I got it?' I ignored his question hoping he would shut up. But he continued, "When Clark Gable was here with his honey, Carole Lombard, making a movie around 1940, they stayed at the Bond house, off the Silverado Trail. I was a groundskeeper there. One night, Clark and Carole got into an argument, and she left to go to Ray's bar in St. Helena. I was close by because I had been standing under their window so I could hear every word of their argument, and Clark called out to me. He asked me if I would go to the Rutherford market and get him a bottle of whiskey. The problem was, he didn't have any money. So, in his movie star voice, he promised, "If you come back with at least a pint of any brand of whiskey, I will give you something worth more money at once than you ever had. It is even said to have mystical powers. You see, I was in Africa making a movie and had dinner with some kind of tribal prince. He gave me this item and told me it was crafted by a Medicine Man and it was always lucky." Then, Clark opened a drawer and removed this case and when he opened it, it was this rare fishing pole."

Wasted responded and in a loud, excited voice said "Oh my God! "A magical fishing pole!!!'

Piétro nodded his head twice, like a punctuation. On his way to the trunk to get his reel, he leaned his pole up against the car. But he had placed it in the doorway of the car. Along came a gust of wind that SLAMMED the car door shut, right on his fishing pole. The sounds we heard were definitive. "Slam-bang...snap...snap....." And then from Piétro, "OH GOD! NO NO! AGHHHHH!"

I was at that stage of life where I found humor in other people's accidents or misfortunes. I busted out laughing, almost hysterical, weeping, red-faced, rolling on the ground laughing.

Piétro opened the door and we heard three more sounds, "plop, plop, plop" as each of the three broken pieces of his now-worthless pole hit the dirt. Piétro was in tears, only not from laughter. "Oh, Madré, bastardo porta!" he cried. This just caused me to shift my laughter to an even higher gear. I couldn't have stopped if my life depended on it.

It was quite a scene, PP hugging the three pieces of his ruined pole to his chest, rubbing his face and hair, and moaning and crying, and me, rolling on the road with laughter, oblivious to the danger as four more cars headed our way toward this amazing, secret fishing hole. My dad was trying to look concerned for PP and mad at me for laughing, but I could see the upward curve and quiver of his lips as he quenched his own laughter.
Then Wasted took matters into his own hands. He walked over to PP, patted him on the shoulder and feigned concern. "This is terrible," he said, compassionately. "But we can use some Elmer's glue on it when we get back home." He gave two more comforting pats and turned to me, saying, "Well, we only have normal old store-bought fishing poles. They're not blessed, but they're also not broken. Let's go fishing!"

With that, we climbed a few hills and hacked through the brush, after ten minutes arriving at the premium fishing spot on the lake. We sat on a big rock overlooking the lake where the water was deep and clear. From there, you could see to the bottom and could often see the fish swimming around. In fact, part of the fun was being able to see when a fish was ready to hit someone's line. Sometimes, I would point at someone and yell out, "Hey, don't move! Big Buford is ready to hit your line."

Now, there wasn't really any Big Buford. It was just a name I gave to a fish that didn't exist. The real Big Buford was the name given to a hamburger at Rally's fast food in Kentucky. I had never been to Kentucky. At that point in my life, I had never even been out of California. How often or how much I yelled out about the make-believe fish mostly had to do with how much wine I had downed from my canteen.

That day, we had a good view of the whole lake. It turned out to be unfortunate for us that everyone on the lake could also see us, especially one specific person, the game warden. This was a problem because neither Wasted nor I had a fishing license. But at that moment, we weren't worried.

When fishing on the rock, you had to be careful. The top surface was dirt and gravel, and the rock itself was only about 5 feet by 5 feet. When I went back later, I saw a kid on top of the rock cast with so much force that he cast himself right off the rock into the cold water below. "Kersplash."

When standing to cast, you had to remember that right behind you there were bushes and trees that were hungry for your fishing lures. I had snagged at least half a dozen Super Doopers and Peter Pipe Gigs back there. Once, I unknowingly snagged a treble hook in the trunk of a tree behind me; when I whipped the pole forward to cast out, I snapped the tip of the pole off. That earned me a few laughs from the old timers fishing close by. I didn't think it was so funny,

Because of the rock's visibility from most of the lake, if you were on the rock it was like you were on stage. Only experienced fishermen should fish on the rock. Note that I said 'should,' because every once in awhile, a rookie would go out on the rock. When this happened, all the veteran fishermen would pass on a little whistling tone which would be the signal that some novice was about to make a greenhorn move that would result in some kind of accident, triggering hysterical laughter in the audience.

We had been on rock for about 20 minutes with no fish in sight, so I changed the lure. When I stood up to cast I carefully looked around me to make sure I was clear of the trees and not too close to the edge. As I glanced to my left, I saw the game warden's car, working its way along the winding lake road, and he was headed straight toward us. I cried out, "Oh, shyist! Let's go... game warden." We stood up and started to evacuate the rock. When I turned around, Wasted wasn't behind me. 'What the hell…?' I looked up, and there he was scrambling up the cliff on his way to the top of the hill. As he turned to look at me, he had an unusual panicked look on his face. The dirt was loose, and the faster he tried to scramble up the hill, the more he was slipped backward. That was weird; I had never seen him nervous or unnerved about anything. He abandoned his new, bright yellow plastic tackle box; it slipped off the top of the rock and"kersplash." It floated for everyone to see. In an instant, there was chatter and laughter all around us. Then he did something even stranger; he threw his fishing pole into the lake.

I was heading for our car, fast; my plan was to toss my fishing gear in the car before the game warden saw it. With my head down I tore off, beating feet to our old Chevy. My heart sank with a 'klunk' when I looked up and saw a guy in a dark green and brown uniform between me and the car. It was none other than the game warden. He was looking straight at me, and he looked official in a scary way. He said "Let me see your license. Now!" I stuttered and stammered, finally bleated out, "I wasn't driving." He glared at me: "Do I look like the mother-flicking Highway Patrol? See what it says on my hat?! State Game Warden. Where is your ripping fishing license?"

I replied in a slow, steady voice, "I am sorry sir. I wasn't fishing. He replied, "That fishing pole in your hand has a feather lure on it that's still wet. I saw you and some other doofus out on that rock, fishing. Ever heard of binoculars? I could even read the Lucky Strike logo on your cigarette."

He lifted the binoculars hanging on his neck, then nodded at the rock. He kept his gaze in that direction, almost as if he stared long enough he would have déjà vu and see us there again. I waited. His head slowly swiveled back at me, his gaze telling me that he was waiting and, additionally, that he was getting to the brink of being mad. I gulped. "Okay, I'm sorry. Yes, I was fishing and I don't have a license. Sorry. I'm sorry, really......I...ahh."

He stepped close to me and yelled right in my face, "Save it. I have heard every excuse in the book and some not even written. So can it, Buddy-boyoh." As I was wiping his spit off my face, I thought 'Buddy-boyoh? What kind of backwoods, inbred country hick was this moron?!?' As he started to write me a ticket. I turned to see where Wasted had gone. I noticed his yellow tackle box still floating below the rock where we had been illegally fishing. I figured his rod and reel were under the water in the same area. 'What an idiot!'

Then I heard a noise like a little trickle of rocks; I looked in the direction of the sound and saw what was, by then, a waterfall of rocks. I looked up to see what was causing this avalanche. There was Wasted about fifteen feet above us on the top of the hill close to where I had just come down.

I had come down the sloped dirt part, though. He was trying to come down the shale side of the hill, and he was slipping and sliding; then, he was on his back, and then airborne for the last 6 feet. Finally, he landed on his knees and hands with a loud "Smack" right on the road. He got up, casually acting like he didn't hear the dozen or more men around the lake laughing their guts out.

Now, this is my favorite part of the story because it shows the way Wasted's mind worked, or rather, didn't work. As he walked toward us, I saw that he had about a dozen assorted wildflowers, including poppies and lupines in his hands. They were now somewhat crushed, torn and tattered after his roll down the hill. His pants were ripped out and his knees bleeding, and he had a bleeding scratch across his cheek; he was filthy.

The game warden, without an ounce of compassion, said, " License, Buddy-boyoh." Wasted replied, "Oh no. I don't drive yet." Mr. Game Warden let fly in a boiling hot verbal assault. "You two wise ass punks %$ and you can *&8% . Now I want to see your FISHING license!" Wasted in his half asleep, slow motion, almost-back-to-his-normal-semi-comatose manner said (drum roll please)… "No, I wasn't fishing. See no fishing pole, no fishing gear. I was picking flowers." With that, he shoved his fistful of flowers right under the nose of Mr. Warden and said ,"Here smell."

I thought, 'He didn't really just say, "I was picking flowers." He is about to get us thrown in game warden prison, probably in cages with wild dogs and feral cats.'

Then the Game Warden replied, "There is a $10 fine for fishing without a license; there is a $100 fine for picking wildflowers. Now tell me again what were you doing?" Without blinking, Wasted tossed the flowers down to the lake and said "I was fishing sir."

Later, as we walked off with our pink $10 fine tickets in our hands, I stopped, looked at him and said "PICKING WILD FLOWERS?!!!" He looked at me and said something even weirder than the wildflower thing. He just replied, "Fishing is better in Ohio. My aunt has a pond on her property; we don't need a license." I shook my head expecting to hear a rattling sound; something had to be loose in there because I couldn't make any sense of what he was saying. I said, "What the hell does that have to do with anything?" He said "I am going there this summer, why don't you come back and stay with me for a while."

I smiled and responded, "Are you a good diver? Because you are going to need fishing gear to fish in Ohio, and yours is at the bottom of the lake." In typical Wasted style, he replied, "Nah, I could care less. I'll buy new stuff."

When we joined my dad, I noticed Piétro had found some kind of black tape and pieced together his shattered rod, now just a $1 fishing pole. It was more black tape than pole. This caused more uncontrollable laughter, and even my dad joined in. PP swore at us in Italian.

On the drive home I was belatedly embarrassed and hung my head in silence, as did Wasted. But then, he could have just been asleep.

Chapter 33
Big Left Turn

I was E-X-C-I-T-E-D, like a little kid on his first trip to Disneyland or a teenager anticipating a date to the drive-in with a popular girl that is extra friendly; maybe even as excited as an adult getting married..well, then again, maybe not quite that excited.

But I was also afraid. I was seconds away from something I had wanted to do for 30 long years. It was something I dreamed about while sleeping. And it was something that I dreamed of when I was awake every time I drove by our old property in Rutherford in the Napa Valley. I felt like this next hour or so was going to be a dream come true; I really did. I was positive because just seeing the inside of the house and nothing else, that alone would thrill me. I didn't know how many of my childhood experiences would come back to me. I wondered if some would be memories to shock me. By this time in my life, I had forgotten most of the events and crazy characters that always seemed to be hanging around at this place. Here we were, on the property that my Italian grandparents used to own.

Getting here

This dream of going on a tour of the former Big Pink was being fulfilled because of my wife and a gift she had given me months earlier. We had stayed at the picturesque little town of Yountville. It was two weeks before Christmas, and the town had Christmas decorations everywhere. There were little lights in all the trees and strung on all the ancient-looking light posts. Some of the lights were bright white, some pale blue, but there were no other colors; some blinked, some didn't.

We stayed at an inn where the rooms were converted cabooses. They were very quaint and fun. Right next door was a huge brick warehouse that had been converted into 40+ shops, including a frozen yogurt shop and three restaurants. Close to the warehouse was the world-famous French Laundry, referred to by most food critics as "One of the best restaurants in America." We did not eat there; a meal or two with wine was rumored to run around $400.

We ate at a Mexican restaurant and sat on the patio that was warmed by huge heaters, so it was cozy. There was a fog drifting through the little town, and the lights gave a special glow everywhere. It created an almost heavenly mood, hypnotic in its beauty. By sitting outside, we not only had a good view of this Christmas cheer, but we were also surrounded by it. It almost made us feel like getting married again, right there in the fog glowing all around us.

The next morning we were on our way toward St Helena to VSattui Winery. I could see ahead of us to the left of Hwy. 29, my grandparents' old place. We had been coming up to the Valley about four times a year to eat fantastic food and taste lots of wine. You could spend all day tasting wine for free. Over the years of driving past the old place, I had noticed many changes. The biggest change occurred when the then-current owners covered the pink stucco with a grayish wooden shell and created a new entryway into the front room. Later the hundred-plus-year-old slaughterhouse had been torn down. It was replaced by a stone structure that looked like it had the same footprint and silhouette as the old slaughterhouse. What could it be??? I had questions every time we drove by, like, "I wonder if my old bedroom is the same? Do they still have chickens?" And on and on.

On this day, though, my wife had made what I later named, "The Big Left Turn." She said, "All those questions you have; today we will get answers." Then, she turned and drove down the gravel driveway. At first, I panicked. All the people that lived along Hwy. 29 hated tourists. Well, maybe the word hate is too strong. But the Valley residents are not happy about the bumper to bumper stream of cars that makes it hard for them to get out of their driveways. What they really do hate is people driving down their driveways looking for wine tasting. That is why they have signs that say, DO NOT ENTER -PRIVATE DRIVEWAY or NOT A WINERY--WE HAVE MEAN DOGS or KEEP OUT! I

HAVE A SHOTGUN. My personal favorite shows a snarling, rabid bulldog chewing on a shotgun...that one didn't need words. Because of these life-threatening signs, I was more than a bit panicked.

For the first time in decades, I was in a car driving down this once-familiar driveway. Deb got out of the car and walked toward the front door. I ducked, down trying to become invisible in the front seat. She knocked on the door of the house, and when a man opened the door, he was on the phone. 'Oh great,' I thought.

He paused his call, and she said, "My husband's grandparents built this house, and we would like to get a tour of it some day." The man perked up, got off the phone and replied, "We have been wanting to find out all about the family that was the first to live here. There seems to be a kind of "romance" and spirit of love and fun when we're in our dining room or when my wife is working in the garden or sitting on the back patio under the two big fig trees." I got out of the car and joined the conversation:
"That's because those were the places where all the good times constantly generated those emotions. By the way, under that nice wood shell, the house is bright pink stucco." I knew these were not the people that had bought it from us and put the shell on. I wasn't sure if he knew what was under there; he didn't. "Pink. Really? No, I didn't know. My wife is going to be excited about this. Let me call her."

"Margo, come here; there is someone I want you to meet."

In a minute, a woman came from the garden area where my Nono's vegetable garden was. She had a casual looking, but perfect gardening denim shirt on. It said Slaughterhouse Cellars above the left pocket, and atop her blond hair was a hat that also said Slaughterhouse Cellars. The woman was nicely tanned. She brushed the dirt off her hands, smiling.
The man spoke again. "Oh, I forgot to introduce myself. I am David Slabby, and this is my wife, Margo. Margo this is….." He looked at us.

"Jim and Deb. I think you can figure who is who. Margo, my Italian grandparents built this house."

She gave a big smile, and her blue eyes sparkled with joy. "We have been trying to find the true story about the people who were the longtime residents here. We heard rumors about Old Man Curtoni and big Rosi. We heard that Mr. Curtoni had built that fountain-fishpond for his wife's birthday." The pond she was referring to was a two-tiered cement and rock fountain with the cobalt blue glass spelling out ROSI 1936. I thought I remembered the blue glass was from a Milk of Magnesia bottle.

She put her hand out to shake ours and noticed the dirt on her hands. "Sorry about the dirt, she said. "I was just planting some tomato plants."

"I don't mind," I replied. "I had that same dirt on my hands when I worked in that very earth."

They invited us in to see the old place. As anxious as I was to see it again, we felt we had disturbed their day and insisted that we come back another time. We set a date in January for lunch.

The Visit

One month after our drive-by, we were driving down that driveway again. I didn't know that, on this day, a whole new life experience would be born. There would be times in the future that would be so fantastic that they would seem dream-like, even euphoric.

This place was where I had grown up; it was filled with memories and feelings of warmth, love, fun, adventure, sadness, and fright. And to cap it off, there was the memory of the time I saw a real live/dead ghost. Deep in the heart of my life that began in this valley were mysteries, ones that I had forgotten. These memories, lost in the past, came back to me as I got out of the car.

Oh, yes. There was a badly scarred man and a mystery photo that would disappear for a while if I asked about it. There were mysteries: mysteries that, once solved, had been shocking and devastating to me at the time. When those mysteries had been revealed, I was only seventeen. I couldn't even imagine the horror my family had been through. I didn't think I could have recovered from it, but somehow one family member did. He was an amazing person, my Nono.

At the end of the driveway were buildings that housed memories of some of the best times of my life. From 1925 to 1974 this property was owned by my grandparents. My dad was away in the Navy fighting WWII, so we pretty much had to live there. My mom was working at the BV winery in the bottling room. After I was born, her job was caring for me.

At the end of the driveway, there were five people, standing and looking at us as we were looking at them. At first, I didn't recognize any of them, but my wife knew who four of them were. The two people looking relaxed and happy were the owners of the former Big Pink. Living in a peaceful, quiet valley and owning a vineyard surely brought a happy and smiling, relaxed countenance. Two others were Bachi and Eda. My mom had been born in San Francisco in Eda's mom's house when Salvatore and Rosi had lived there. Eda and her family moved to Rutherford after the Curtonis did and lived in a house next to Joe. When she was 17-years-old, she had met Bachi in the Curtoni's kitchen. Six months later they were married. Eda would remain my mom's best friend for the rest of her life. The other lady was a neighbor, Bev.

We first went through the new stone building that had replaced the slaughterhouse. It was a two- story guest house. The wainscoting was varnished wood from the outside of the old slaughterhouse. The 10-inch thick door from the living room into the winery came from the doorway to the cooler room in the slaughterhouse. The old barn had been replaced with a garage. But the bunkhouses were exactly the same. The pigeon coop, chicken coop and chicken hut were gone. In their place were grapevines, a much more practical use of the land.

The back patio was exactly the same. The fig trees were still there, but cut back smaller. The side of the kitchen below the windows was also the same, with the Wedgewood stove and tile counters. And the front room and dining room were almost exactly the same. The bedrooms, however, were completely different. I had such a glowing feeling of being back in that loved but lost home.

We had lunch out on the deck which was new. It was a beautiful day. Two winemakers dropped by while we were there and we enjoyed listening to them talk about the art of winemaking. We drank Margo and David's Slaughterhouse Cellars Cabernet, and it was excellent. That was the beginning of fantastic friendships, not only with Margo and David but with their neighbor Bev, too. In July, we would attend their bottling party and make another dozen or more good friends, including a rocket scientist. And Slaughterhouse Cellars became our favorite cab, starting with their 2002 which was bottled in 2004. It sold for $75 a bottle or, for friends and family, a discounted rate of $44. Sadly, the cabernet is no longer made.

This incredible day out proved that you actually can go home again. Kind of.

Chapter 34
The Bottling Party

That Friday night I had hardly slept, I was too excited about what I had recently experienced and the anticipation of what would be coming in mere hours. It was now Saturday morning around 9.45 AM. Deb and I were in our car driving the short distance to where Slaughterhouse Cellars was going to bottle the 2002 Proprietors Reserve Cabernet.

We knew we were about ten minutes early, but I was super pumped up. Four guests were already there. Deb parked and assembled my scooter, and I was off.

One of the advantages of being disabled is getting to zoom around on a power chair or scooter. Even though I can get around on crutches in some situations, it is safer and more enjoyable to use one of the powered vehicles. It's an experience that everyone should try; it is fun, and it gives you an interesting perspective on the world and people as you silently cruise by them and drift through groups, sometimes unnoticed.

I drove my scooter over to the group of people gathered around two tables under the two very old olive trees. There were donuts, champagne, the makings for Bloody Marys and coffee.

I gave a "Good morning" to all and proceeded to introduce myself to the person that I hadn't met the night before, their neighbor Mike. Mike lived in the house where Powder Burns used to live in my childhood. I told him my history with the house he now owned. There was the married couple that lived in the other half of the house at the time and they had a teenage daughter named Janice; she was about six years older than me. Because she didn't have friends her age close by, she would play games with me, or we would walk down to one of the two little markets on the corner where the Rutherford Grill now sits. I would read comic books, and she would read the movie magazines. She would buy me an ice cream, soda or candy bar, my choice.

I remember how those two stores looked like twins, from the outside. They were little old country stores that were the places for Valley residents and vineyard workers to buy groceries or other needs without having to go to St. Helena. Most of the vineyard workers did not have cars, and it was a long walk to St. Helena. The big wineries imported workers from around the world, from China, Mexico, and even Jamaica. The first sightings of Jamaicans in the stores were greeted with stares and caused a lot of finger pointing and whispering. The Jamaicans could walk to the stores, but the workers at Beringer were transported on the back of a flatbed truck. Flat was also the condition of the springs, and the passengers had to link arms to keep from being bounced off the truck like ping pong balls. Many suspected that the driver purposely hit every bump and pothole so he could make jokes about his "Mexican Jumping beans." It was not unusual to hear racial slurs directed to the "foreigners." The driver of the Beringer truck was a stressed-out mess by the time he delivered his passengers back to their junky mini shacks. All the way to the store they loudly sang songs in Spanish, the same two songs over and over. Then when they got to the store, it took them fooooor-everrrrr to make their purchases, their revenge for the bouncy ride. After doing that for a year, the driver committed suicide. No joke. It is doubtful that he shot out his brains because of the Hispanic shoppers, but that's the rumor that echoed around the valley for decades.

When I started to tell Mike the tales of Powder Burns, he stopped me. "Wait you are joking; you're making this up, right?" I replied, "No. I know that his real name was Robert Burns and he was from a Wild West Show. I know that when he was talking with adults, he didn't talk as much like a cowboy. But he was fun for me to hang out with. I have such good memories of your place."

Mike was the son of Bev, the lady we had met the day we had lunch with the Slabbys and Bachi and Eda. Mike's family owned all the vineyard behind Margo and David's, that beautiful vineyard extending all the way back to the mountain with the beautiful Long View of Heaven. There were about a dozen other new people that were not at dinner Friday night. It was, again, a great group of people. Many of them asked a variation of, " Are you the grandson

294

of the Curtonis that built this house?" I would reply, yes, and tell a story or two about growing up there. One person who didn't know who I was said, "You have to see the scrapbook Margo has. It was made by the grandson of the people that built this house. It has photos showing the history of this place."

At about 10.30 AM, the bottling process began. There were two barrels to be bottled, one of Slaughterhouse Cellars and one of Et La. Et La was a term that had something to do with sword fighting which was how the two winemakers, Steve from New York and Rocket Scientist Max, had met.

It was another perfect Valley day with a clear, deep-blue sky and just warm enough. Where the breakfast table was set up, under the old olive trees, the air was a slightly scented with the fermentation of decades of old olives crushed underfoot. There was an atmosphere of excitement, not just on my part, but from everyone, even the fireman's frolicking beer-drinking dog. If I could sing, I would have belted out "Oh, What a Beautiful Morning!", from the musical, Oklahoma.

The bottling process was fairly basic. The people doing the first few steps were experienced, having done this half a dozen times or more.

The Sucker

Because I could not get my scooter up into the winery, I had to be told what happened, so I might be a little off on this step. Someone has to be the "sucker," the person who sucks on the tube that comes out of the wine barrel to start the flow of the wine. The barrel has an attachment with three spouts inserted into it.

Once the Sucker gets the wine flowing…..

The Filler takes over.

This person shoves, crams, or places the empty bottles on the spouts, fills the bottle and passes off the filled bottles to…..

The Topper

This person has a measuring cup of wine and tops off the bottle so that every bottle has the exact same level of wine.

Now the bottle goes to….. The Corker
He or she puts a cork in the mouth of the full bottle of wine, places it under the 'cork press,' and pushes the lever down. This shoves the cork all the way in. Next is….

The Crimper...

who shoves the top of the bottle into a little machine that seals the top and neck of the bottle with foil. Years ago, before they discovered that it was bad for your health, they used lead for this.

That all takes place in the winery. The bottles are then packed twelve to a box.
The final step involves….. The Labeler(s).
There was a long table under the olive trees. On top of the table were six wooden racks with slots on each that fit three bottles of wine snugly. There were blue tape marks on the top and bottom on each side where the bottles sat. These lined up where the self-adhesive labels were to go. The front label came from a painting of the Slaughterhouse with an olive tree by each corner.

The back label was a note from Margo and David telling about the grape crop that went into that year's Cab, then thanking the people who had helped with the harvest and the process of removing seeds and stems by name. The apparatus that did this removal looked like a huge corkscrew over a stainless steel trough. The grapes on the property were professionally picked and then made into wine by David with help from his winemaker friend Jason. They used the facilities of the winery where Jason was the winemaker. David kept fifteen rows of grapes that were picked by family and friends in September at the Harvest Party. It was from these grapes the one barrel of wine was made.

The one barrel of Slaughterhouse wine yielded 24 cases of 12 per case, plus four large (magnum) cases with six bottles per case. The

Et La produced just a little less. Each person that helped got a bottle of each wine.

Lunch was served when all the wine had been bottled. Decanters of both wines were at each table. Lunch Break
After lunch, there was a four-hour break. People could take a nap on the lawn or on one of the beds in the old bunkhouse. These were not the same beds that were there from 1930 until when the place sold in 1974. They were nice new beds, but instead of eight, there were only two.
Everyone was free to walk through the vineyard, check out the winery, or just walk around the property on a self-guided tour. Some people went back to their hotel rooms for naps, and some went wine tasting at nearby wineries as if they hadn't already had enough wine by then.

I was having a blast. By now, I had met over two dozen friends of Margo and David. What a unique group of people! There were winemakers at lunch from two of the better-known wineries; it was fascinating talking to them about winemaking. There was a lady who had authored a book about her experiences working with animals and using acupuncture to heal them. And there were neighbors, some that were old friends of my Nono and Nona and my mom.

Of all the comments and questions I got from people the one I found amusing was, "Are you old man Curtoni's grandson?" They called him "old man" because they didn't know his first name. I had three people refer to my Nono as 'old man Curtoni.' He would not have been happy with what, to him, would have been disrespectful. old man Curtoni rather than the name he always insisted on, Salvatore.

I would say "Yes, I am. To me, he was Nono; to friends, he was Salvatore."

Some of the people had heard some of my stories, passed on from the night before. A few had several stories mixed up.

For example, on Friday night I told the following story:

When I was five-years-old, I had a really cool play rifle. It had a grip below the barrel which was used to cock the gun. Once it was cocked, I dropped a ping-pong ball down the barrel. Then I was set to go hunting. I shot chickens, but the fired ping pong ball was so weak that the hens didn't even flinch. When I was finally able to hit a fly, it would be a little dizzy, staggering for a while and then fly off, looking like a drunk, weaving through the air. Then one day, I forgot my rifle out in the vineyard. When I went back to get it, I couldn't ever find it. I told another story about hunting there with my dad's .22 rifle.

Early Saturday morning, just minutes before the bottling started, a car came speeding down the driveway. It parked by the table under the olive trees. A man came rushing out of the car with the six wood racks that would be used for bottle labeling. He set them up on the empty table where six people would soon be working. Then, he walked over to me and squatted down, so we were at eye level. This is something I appreciate; otherwise, I have to crank my neck up to see whoever I am trying to talk with. Worse still, if they are standing above me, then I am level with their butt. I don't like talking to butts.

This new friend said his name "Grif." He told me a story of finding a 22-rifle in the vineyard; it was old and covered with dirt and had a name on it but all he could read was a " J." I shook my head and said, "Good try. Whoever retold the story from last night at dinner messed it up. Mine was a toy gun, and it never had my name on it." But this ended up being the beginning of a great friendship. For the next year, we referred to each other as "My best new friend." Sadly, Grif passed away in July of 2017; for me, it was a sad loss of a one-of-a-kind friend.

After lunch, I walked around the backyard. Every place that I passed had memories. My 14-year- old ghost was carving JIM into the fig tree. Then, I could see the ghost of a very angry Nono, as mad as he ever was at me because he thought I might kill or harm the tree. That would be like a toothpick killing an elephant. I looked on the back of the tree to see if I could still see my carving, but couldn't find it.

Grif said, "If you did that almost 40 years ago, the tree has grown a lot, so your carving would be up higher." I paused and thought to myself 'Is that true? Maybe he is messing with me.' I looked up 2 feet, 4 feet, then 6 feet. Maybe way up there, or, no, that might just be a flaw in the bark. I gave up.

As I walked by the cellar, I remembered the Hidey Hole.

Down those three steps and a left turn, 30 feet, look up. There would be the long forgotten hidey hole, a place that once hid hundreds or thousands of dollars, cash. When my wife came to me and put her hand on my shoulder, I realized that I had been standing there for about 5 minutes, seeing a young boy with a black widow on his hand and my Nono hiding money in the sand in the hidey hole.

I snapped out of it, turned and kissed my wife and said. "Want to go on an adventure?"

I put my right foot on the first step, on my way down to what could be a short exploration that might end all those dreams of trying to dig in that hole in the wall, to find the treasures, that my childhood self had seen being put there. But in addition to the treasure, I wanted to see those back steep stairs that would take me up to the mud porch, and into the light, bright, cozy kitchen.
Those stairs used to be loaded with wine and all kinds of junk. I hoped to find one of those old Italia newspapers left behind, forgotten. Just anything I could touch and see, any item, could be a time machine to take me back to all the adventures that I had acted out as a kid in this dark, creepy cavern.

I suppose some of it was a bit of a fantasy, being in a deep cave looking for the mole people, like in the grade D horror movie I saw on TV when I was nine-years-old. Once, I saw a mole up close and personal when Nono caught one in a trap with big spikes. They were ugly monsters even at their small size.

This afternoon, I could see the waterline from the top of the stairs, where the water had stained the walls from 70+ winters of flooding. Maybe I could find one of the boats that I used to sail on the lake in the cellar when it flooded. Or perhaps, in some remote corner, I could find one with B.B. holes, one of many that I would sink over the years.

Now it was time to take my first step; I lost my balance and fell forward. For the next few seconds, I anticipated my head hitting the cement, hearing the sound that it would make, like a hammer smashing a coconut nut, and feeling the pain that would follow, like the world's worst headache, and then blood, lots of it. I imagined the dizzy-fog stupor. I knew all this because I had taken a bad fall only a few months before.

My next thoughts pondered how I could stop this. The only thing I could come up with required four legs to pull it off. I could do nothing. So I braced myself mentally.

Just as my other foot was starting to come off the ground, there was salvation. A guest, Ted, saved me. He put both hands on me and grabbed my shirt by the collar, and the back of my pants. He then pulled me back to a position with both feet on the ground. He was someone I never again saw at any function after, but it was a good thing he was there.

After a moment, I restarted my trip down to the cellar. Deb took over holding the back of my pants and Ted held my shirt. As soon as I had both feet on the cellar floor, I could see the hidey hole. Almost six months earlier, David had insisted, "There is no hole in the wall, no trap door. That's just a fantasy of your childhood." But he was wrong. It was right there, semi-hidden behind two wine barrels. The door was off and the hole open. Talk about excitement!

There it was, after all these years, actually forgotten for a long time. Right there, only feet away.

There was only one problem. To get to it, someone would need to climb up and over a rack holding the two wine barrels, a wooden rack that was about 4-feet-high and 4-feet-deep. It would require someone who could climb. I couldn't do it; Deb couldn't do it. But

Ted said, "I'll do it; let me get a flashlight." I had one in my back pocket and gladly handed it over.

Flashlight in hand, Ted climbed up to the barrel holder/rack. Once he was up there, he used the flashlight to clear out about 30 years of cobwebs. Some were thin and wispy, but some were the thickness of yarn, except a much uglier color than any yarn ever made. I really hoped we would not see the huge spiders that had made a web that big. I have this running joke routine with my friend at Slaughterhouse, Margo, and I tell her all these 'scary' stories of my experiences with black widows. The truth is, I have seen more black widows in Pleasant Hill than in Rutherford.

I confess that I thought of yelling at Ted, "LOOK OUT YOU HAVE A BLACK WIDOW ON YOUR SHOULDER." I could imagine him jumping about three feet, and landing on his back between the boards with spider webs wrapped around his head. Now that you have that image in your head, erase it. I didn't say that.
I had enough sense to respect what Ted was already doing to get into the 3-foot by 4-foot hidey hole. Ted was in. After all this time, another mystery would be solved. Did my Nono leave any money in the Mason jar under the sand, or anything else? I remembered seeing a Mason jar containing a watch, a ring and one cuff link on the kitchen table. Later in the day it had disappeared. And before that, there was the time I saw him hide that jar full of folding money. I also knew that when my Nono sold his house, he left many things behind. He was so very sad to be leaving his garden, wine cellar, vineyard, party patio, and house. He wanted to just grab some items and get out of there. So it is possible that there still could be treasures, under the sand in the hidey hole.

"Are you sure this is it?" Ted asked. I replied, "Is there sand in there?" "Yes."
"Dig down," I instructed.

But then he said, "The sand is filled with cat crap; sorry, I'm out of here." So another disappointment I could not believe it. I was so close............
After Lunch. At Slaughterhouse Cellars bottling party 2004

After the failed attempt at digging in the sand to try to uncover Mason Jars filled with folding money and jewelry, we took a drive to La Luna store. This very unusual store is owned by a Mexican family. You could buy everything here from diapers to wedding dresses and even caskets. Birth to death and everything between. Switchblade knives? They've got them. Best tacos in the Valley? Yep. Spanish language comics and paperback books. Little statues of skeletons, masks of wolverines for Halloween. Something for everyone.

I just went there to get a few cigars for the evening and a pint of whiskey. Not finding any familiar brands, I had to settle on Burrito Bandito Whiskey. The label had a drawing of a grizzled bandit with bandoliers holding something in his hand that looked like a dead rat or weasel. Did they have weasels in Mexico? I wondered. The whiskey was 103 proof. Then, for a bottle of red wine; I had to settle for a brand I had never seen before, something like Viva Zapata. When we checked out, the clerk, who looked like her age might have matched the proof of my whiskey, asked. "Do you want firecrackers, salsa, bullets?" "No thanks." She didn't give up. "What about a flask for your Bandito?" I got the flask.

Then we went back to our hotel to rest up and regain our strength for the rest of the day. When I got up, I poured the whiskey into the flask and accidentally spilled some on the room's desk. I grabbed a towel and wiped it up. I then noticed a bit of the varnish and stain had come off the desk. Yikes! I covered the bare wood with the ice bucket. Deb laughed, "You aren't really going to drink that turpentine?!?!"

I froze. I clearly saw the image of a flaming pan of turpentine flying out of a window, landing on top of a beautiful, mop-topped, innocent boy. I responded by shaking my head no and threw the empty bottle and the full flask in the wastebasket. Deb gave me a concerned look with questions marks all over her face, along with some shoulder shrugs. I decided I wasn't going to tell her about the image and the real reason I tossed it out, so I came up with an excuse: "I do listen to your warnings about what can harm me."

"Don't you want to save the flask?" She then bent down and fished the flask out of the trash and handed it to me. I took it and the flask leaked on my hand. She asked, "Why don't you take it back to the store to get your money back?"

"No that old lady is probably in one of the caskets displayed in that last aisle. She looked like she was about 10 minutes from knocking on death's door. Besides, whoever is there at the register, might try to sell me hand grenades or pickled chicken heads. Forget it."

A Perfect Ending to the Day

It was about 4.30 when we returned to Slaughterhouse. We got there a bit early and seated ourselves on the back patio. The caterers had set up a bar and some out-of-this-world appetizers with Napa Valley original creations. The bar was set up on the table that had been Margo and David's dining room table.

My Nono had made that table and another that was its twin from scraps left over from the building of the house. They were seven feet long and three-and-a-half feet wide, with linoleum glued to the top. The legs and side had been painted seafoam green, as were the chairs and benches.
Margo removed the linoleum, sanded it down and then varnished it. That table brought the memories back more than anything there.

The emotions flooded me. Everything had happened at that table. Nona would sit me on her lap there in the mornings. She gave me my first coffee and wine at that table. It was where I helped her roll gnocchi and separate her ravioli. We had eaten hundreds of meals there, all of them filled with excited conversation, laughter, and love. And it was there that Nono had told me about Nicco's death.

I broke the emotional fog I was in and ordered a white wine for Deb and a Manhattan for me.

Grif's car rolled up and, after he got out, he said, "Follow me, you two." I had been on crutches since I got out of the car at 4:30, but because of the thick gravel, my knees were getting wobbly and hurting, so I got on my scooter, and we followed Grif to the table he chose for us. He showed us four plates, each with a label like those on the Slaughterhouse wine bottles, with our names scrawled on the blank side: ~ Deb. ~ Jim. ~Grif. ~Cyri. He patted me on the back and asked, "Do you need my help transferring from the scooter? I wanted to sit with you folks if that's okay."

There were six tables of eight people; one table had four seats. The tables had blindingly white table cloths with burgundy cloth napkins. The centerpiece included a big green candle in a hurricane lamp with a glass chimney. There were a bunch of grapes, not yet ripe, but pretty, surrounded by some leaves and vines. There were festive light bulbs shaped like little green grape bunches strung all around the yard in the trees. With the grape lights and table candles as the only light, it was all very romantic and blissful.

We sat. For the rest of the night with Grif, we had everything I could have wanted, drinks, food, cannoli, and lots of wine. We compared the just-bottled 2004 with some 2003; the Et La and a bottle the size of a torpedo were circulated. It was from Peju winery right across from Slaughterhouse. We were to pour some in our glass and sign the bottle with a sparkling gold pen. The food included pastas, prime rib cut to order, twice-baked potatoes, zucchini and green beans from Margo's garden and Caesar salad with lots of anchovies. There was a jazz group with a bass, guitar and a saxophone player. They were hot and really cool.

That evening, two of the guests had known my Nono and shared fond memories of his, once legendary, hospitality. None of them remembered my Nona who had been gone almost 50 years at that point. Everyone buzzed with excitement and joy. It was exactly as it had always been at Big Pink.

Chapter 35
An Italian Christmas

1954 Christmas - A month after my 9th birthday, the day before
Christmas Eve

I was sound asleep when I heard the noise. It sounded like someone
was shoving cats into a cement mixer. I could hear their bones being
smashed and ground up, mixed with the cats' screaming and
screeching racket. But it wasn't cats or any kind of machinery. It was
my Nono's rooster. His name was Mario he was named after Mario
Lanza, the greatest Italian singer of that time. I heard that the rooster
had once eaten chicken feed soaked with whiskey and maybe that's
why his morning call was so alarming.

The fowl alarm clock did the trick. I jolted out of bed and dressed
quickly. I had a job to do on this cold, early morning. I ran down the
back steps, across the gravel driveway, jumped up on the porch and
banged on the screen door to Curddy's room. My buddy was going to
help me hunt for a Christmas goose. I didn't know at the time that the
chances of us finding a goose rummaging through the grapevines of
the Napa Valley were slim to none, especially since there weren't
any ripe, shiny purple grapes to entice them. Nonetheless, Curddy
had said he would help me make my Nono's yearly wish for a
Christmas goose like the one he had in Italy come true. Of course, in
Italy, Nono didn't hunt down a goose for Christmas dinner. His
family owned a market with a full deli and butcher counter, and
that's where their goose came from. Each year when Nono expressed
his wish, Nona responded, "Ahh na, not in my house. No goosing
and no goose at Christmas "

Curddy answered the door wearing a furry coat that made him look
like a bear and an orange cap with pull down flaps that covered his
ears. I asked why he was wearing an orange cap and he responded,
"Because it's cold out and my ears freeze."

"But why orange?" I countered.

"So other hunters will see me and know I'm not an animal," he replied. I got it.

"Wow! Yeah, they could think you were a really fat bear!" I was too young to know that was rude.

Curddy strapped his shotgun over his shoulder, and off we went, tromping down the dirt "road" that separated our property and grapevines from the Stack's. He never took the rifle off his shoulder though, because we didn't come across a flock of geese. We didn't see a single goose or even a bird of any feather. On our way back to my grandparents' place, I was dragging my feet through the gravel looking sad. But Curddy, in an unusually happy voice for him, cheered me: "No worries, my small buddy. I have a backup plan. Go up and tell mama we are going somewhere with Joe."

We walked across two families' vineyards and up to Joe's. As we approached his house, I spied him on the screened porch drinking coffee. When he saw us, he raised his cup as if he were toasting us, and then rushed out to greet us. I was puzzled. "What are we doing here?" I asked.

"Joe's going to help us hunt for a Christmas goose." Curddy replied. We got in Joe's truck and drove to the market in St. Helena. Once inside, Curddy told me, "Now we are going to hunt in here for a goose."

I groaned. "That won't be much of a hunt. I've been here with Nona when she bought one once. Follow me." That is how my Nono got his Christmas goose.

My Nona didn't change her stance on not cooking a Christmas goose. Sadly, by this Christmas, she had passed away and Christmas dinner was being cooked by my Zia, my great aunt, in San Francisco. Zia had never cooked one before or ever again, but she did this one to honor my Nono's wishes.

The first seven years of my life, my Nona would make the raviolis and gravy for Christmas Eve. It was a special treat for me to help my Nona with the making of these little square pillows of pasta stuffed with her "secret mix." I still have the special rolling pin that shapes them and the little cutting wheel to cut them apart.

After Nona Rosi died, the Christmas Eve family gathering moved to our house. Each year from 1952-2000, the menu would be the same. My mom would make the sauce, or as the Italians called it, gravy, to go over the ravioli that she would get from Momma Molina's, a legendary pasta maker. She would also roast two chickens that she bought at the local PX. My other grandmother (I called her Nona, too, even though she was German) would sometimes join us. In 2000, Debbie took over hosting the family meal. She changed the chicken to lobster, and the ravioli come from a deli and tasted great.

In recent years, Christmas Day has been pretty low key and sometimes it is just Debbie with me. I miss all the family that is no longer alive. It is a bit sad thinking of those departed loved ones. And, I miss the traditional Christmas day that I grew up with.

This is the story I retell each Christmas, a story of the traditional Italian Christmas in my family, the ones I miss so much.

Christmas at Zia's

When I think of those holidays, descriptive words like loud, warm and foggy come to mind, followed by fun and lots of love and lots of special foods and wines. It was family and tradition.

Until I was in my late 20's, we spent Christmas days at my Zia's on Twin Peaks in San Francisco. The same family members were always there: my mom and dad; Zia and her husband, my Zio; their son Jim, my mother's cousin, and his wife Mickey; and their children Jim Jr. and Janet. Zia would greet us at her front door: "Maah--deee Cruss--miss, aah Zemma, Boobb, ah bambino leetel Jimmie." Even after I was married with children of my own, I was still "leetel Jimmie" to her. "Blessa, blessa." She was usually munching on something and her lips were covered with olive oil instead of lipstick. You knew it was Christmas if you received a slippery, oily kiss on the lips.

Once we entered her doorway, we were in her hands. She could have said, "I will be your tour guide for the day. Sit back, relax. I will take care of your food and drink desires. I will tend to your every need to make this a very MERRY CHRISTMAS." She could have said that because it was so true. She directed our day's adventures until we exited that same front doorway.

As we walked down the hallway on the path to the living/dining room, we drifted through several sensory zones. There were the warmth and the pleasant smell of a wood fire in the fireplace; in the kitchen, it was the aroma of a turkey roasting. A pet bird chirped a greeting, and, finally, for me, there was the joy of seeing my Nono's hat and coat hanging on a coat hook in the hallway, reassuring me that he was there.

As we got closer to the living room, there was a whiff of strong coffee percolating in the old dented pot on the front hot plate covering the wood burning part of the old Wedgewood stove. JUST LIKE AT RUTHERFORD; in my mind's eye, I could remember the coffee bubbling up into the little glass top of the pot and how I watched it as a young child as it grew darker and darker. I knew what shade of the liquid my Nono liked, and when it came up, I would yell, "Nono, your coffee's ready!"

As we entered the living room, there was the joy of seeing my Nono, Zia, Zio and other relatives, the ones we saw only at Christmas. There was the pleasure of hearing my Nono and Zio talking in Italian. In this room, there was also the unique scent of the old cheese that I knew had been carved off the huge wheel that was in the cooler cabinet where it sat beside hard sticks of salami, other cheeses, and French bread. There were hugs from family, affirming our special bond of love. And there was the faint sound of the old Philco radio that sat on the fireplace mantel, its tubes casting a yellowish light on the wall behind it. The volume was always so low that you might think you were just imagining those Dean Martin and Al Martino classics.

By now, my senses of sight, smell, sound and touch were in overdrive. But one was missing and soon to be experienced. TASTE.

Zia and Zio

Zia was my Nona Curtoni's sister and their personalities were almost identical, except for the quiet sadness that sometimes overtook my Nona. Zia was always in a mood that bubbled with gusto.
She embraced life and shared her zeal with everyone around her. I suppose she was the female Italian equivalent of Zorba the Greek. I never saw her down, and I bet she was never defeated. Yes, Zia was a very commanding presence, a force to be reckoned with, in a good way. She was tall, a very sturdy and strong woman. Well, I guess she and Nona really weren't all that identical, but these sisters were tough, cut from the same cloth (or perhaps asbestos). If there had been enough sisters to field a football team, they would have been unbeatable.

As we entered Zia's home, we would each get a big crushing, wrap-around hug and a wet kiss on the cheek. Roses were her favorite flower, and she always had a light scent of roses about her. I always felt safe and secure when I was with her.

As far back as I can remember, she always wore a cotton housedress that had a faded floral print of some kind. The only time I saw her in something different was at my first wedding when she wore a light blue dress and, over it, a pretty dark blue coat with a fur collar. On any other day, she wore her house dress with a full length apron with a front pouch pocket; there was always a dish towel hanging from that front pocket. That towel worked as a hot pad when she pulled the turkey roasting pan out of the oven. The clean end was used to polish up the little jelly jars she would bang down in front of each of us at the dinner table for us to drink wine from.

Next, she came out of the kitchen with a label-less green bottle of amber wine. She pulled the cork out by putting it in the corner of her mouth, biting down on it, twisting and popping it out. Then she would pour wine into every glass. Kids, parents, grandparents, everyone drank a Christmas toast, clinking glasses all around the table and then sipping the cold, sweet wine. It was funny how Zia would keep the cork in the corner of her mouth as she talked and poured the wine. It kind of looked like she was smoking a stogie.

Zia wore no makeup. Her hair was steel grey and white and was always gathered in a hair net. It stayed the same length and style, year after year, decade after decade. And she always looked the same and never seemed to age. To me, she looked to be about 70 years old until she passed away at the age of 99.

There were other sisters, three more still in Italy, in addition to my Nona in Rutherford. Their last name was Aquistapaches, pronounced "A-KWEE-sta-pa-chee." Nona and Zia had come to the U.S. together, arriving at Ellis Island in the early 1900s. My Nona told me later of the horrors of being seasick on the entire trip across the sea. Their future husbands had arrived a year before at the same port. Antoinette, my Zia, came to marry and become a Ruffoni; Rosilia became a Curtoni.

Both women were fabulous cooks. To them, serving a huge delicious meal to friends and family was a mission statement. Everything was homemade, pasta, ravioli, gnocchi, salami, sausage, olives, polenta and on and on. They provided a delirious overindulgence of an eating excursion at every meal. Neither of them ever went by a written recipe or measured anything. Food was their expression of love, and we all loved to be loved in this way.

My Nona didn't come to Christmas dinner at Zia's house, ever. After they traveled to California together, they never spoke to each other again. It must have been one hell of a rough trip. But two days before Christmas, in the early morning, my Nono would walk out to the end of his dirt driveway in front of Big Pink and stand out on Hwy 29 where he would flag down the Greyhound bus and take it to San Francisco. He would then take a cab from the bus depot to Zia's where he would spend the next few days sitting at the big table in her front room talking to her and my Zio.

Nono and Zio would drink wine, eat and smoke cigars that looked like something a dog left on the lawn and tasted about the same. Zio chewed some brand of tobacco and smoked Toscanellis.
Nono never "chawed," thank God. There are not many things grosser to a child than kissing someone that smells like a dirty spittoon

The two old men would tell endless tales of the "Old Country" and reminisce about what and who they missed. Nono would talk about working in the BV Winery and, of even more interest, tell stories about his job as the gardener at the BV mansion and the gossip about the owners, the De Latours, their parties and the misadventures of their adult children and famous friends.

Zio would talk about working at Royal Tallow, where I think he made soap. I figured that was why he always smelled and looked so clean. A lot of the regulars at Big Pink worked at Royal Tallow and had met through Zio.

My times with my Zio ended the Fall that I turned seven when he passed away, but my memory of Zio never dimmed. He always dressed nicely, wearing good-looking gray wool slacks and a crisp white collarless shirt with a nice brown sweater over it. Strangely, he always had a few days' stubble on his cheeks, enough to scratch my face every time he gave me a kiss. The "Italian traditional" kiss was always right smack on the lips. He spit the tobacco he chewed into a copper- colored spittoon. It was always on the floor by his chair, surrounded by a splash zone. Zio's breath always had a scent of brandy and wine mixed with the slight hint of tobacco. He was a soft- spoken, kind and friendly gentleman and he was a man that everyone loved and respected.

Yes, everything was exactly the same at Zia's each year. We knew exactly what to expect, and we were never disappointed.

Christmas Day

My family's agenda for the day was carved in marble. We went to the 10:45 AM Mass at Christ the King Catholic Church. When we walked out of the church, we shook hands with the priest and exchanged "Bless you" and "Merry Christmas." Then, we got in the 1949 Chevy (in later years it was a 1961 Renault) and made the hour-long drive to San Francisco. We parked across the street from Zia's along the curb right in front of an empty lot. When we got out of the car, we always took time to look out over the empty lot to see the beautiful city of San Francisco. It had to be one of the best views of the Bay and the City. After checking out the beautiful scene, we crossed the street and started the stairway climb up to Zia's house.

Zia's house was atop the hill, so from the sidewalk it was a steep climb up cement steps that twisted left and right around the beds of Zia's beloved roses on each side of the stairway. At the top of the stairway, two wooden steps took us up to her porch. Once on the porch, we had two choices. The door on the right would take us up to the second story house; the door to the left took us to the first story house, my Zia's home.

There was a large key-like crank on the door. Three turns of the key produced a ringing sound similar to the little bells on tricycle handlebars. You remember the ones; you pushed a little lever with your thumb and it made the sound of an old phone ringing. That bell brought Zia to the door and we were warmly welcomed into her home for the feast that followed.

After we passed through the living room with its large round table that seated at least twelve people, we came to the kitchen. It had a cement floor that slanted down toward a bathroom where there was a floor drain. I guess the idea was that after a fast and furious day of cooking you could just hose the floor off. The kitchen had two ovens, a refrigerator and a large work table that was covered with carrots, zucchini, celery, potatoes, parsley, onion, garlic and whatever else was going into Zia's soup.

Back in the living room, warm hugs and kisses were being passed around among all those who were there. Some non-family members were regulars for at least five of our celebrations. Mr. and Mrs. Russo came by for a few drinks before they were off to several San Francisco "high society" parties they attended each year. I was sure they were the life of the party wherever they went.
They certainly added a sparkle to our gathering with their stories of living in Paris and its artist's society that they used to be a part of. We would also hear about their California escapades, such as dinners with the Governor and other famous people.

The Russos were born in France in 1910, so they had seen a lot of history take place all around them before they moved to San Francisco after World War II in 1946. They were snappy dressers. He wore flashy tuxedos, some silk, and others, velvet. She wore a rainbow of bright colors. It almost looked as if she had started with a white dress and then went into her studio and painted it with a dab of color from every paint tube she owned. He wore a beret; she had very fancy hairstyles, different each year. On top of her elaborate hairdo, she wore hats that looked like a few birds may have given their lives to adorn them. Yes, the Russos looked like the stereotypical French couple. To a kid like me, they seemed like movie stars. Mrs. R wore a lot of makeup; her cheeks were very red, as were the rubies on her jewelry. I thought that was where their last name came from since the Italian for red is "rosso." To me, she was beautiful, and I would always get a big smack of a kiss on the chin from her. Her bright red lips would leave a stunning lipstick tattoo on me which was my very special Christmas present. Yes, I kind of had a crush on her, as any child entering adolescence might for a pretty woman who kisses him on the chin.

The Russos rented the second-story house above Zia's, which she owned. They were my Zia's best friends and were kind and caring people. They were there to help any time Zia and Zio needed anything. Because Zia and Zio didn't drive, it was a problem for them when special events like Christmas came along. Zia needed to go to at least six different places to get what she needed for the Christmas feast. There was North Beach for the ingredients for her special sauce, and then, Fisherman's Wharf for the famous San Francisco sourdough French bread. And she had to go somewhere else to get the items for her antipasto plate. She was very precise about what she wanted to serve her guests, and Mr. Russo patiently drove her all around town. And he listened to the non-stop chatter in her gravelly voice about how the butcher tried to overcharge her or the crab was not fresh. These stories always indicated that if anyone tried to pull any crap on her, she would make them very, very sorry.

While waiting for the start of dinner, Dad and I played cribbage. We didn't have a lot of choices of things to entertain ourselves with. There was no TV at Zia's, and it was a little hard to join the conversation when they were all talking Italian, so my dad and I were kind of out of it. We could have sung along with the radio, I suppose if we could have heard it. So, instead we brought our own deck of BEE playing cards and a cribbage board Dad had made out of the end of an old grape crate, and we played for a nickel a point. I still have that board. When you turn it over, it still has the Inglenook Winery name and logo painted on it. I can remember the rainy day he made that board in the barn at Big Pink.

About this time, Zia would come out of her kitchen and ask, "What can I get you to drink? Wine, and maybe Birley's orange soda for the bambino?" When she wasn't calling me Jimmy, I was the Bambino. Now, Baby Ruth may have loved the nickname Bambino, but as a 14- or 15-year-old, I was embarrassed and turned red every time she called me that. I thanked God that none of my buddies ever heard that. My nickname would have been Bambino or 'Bino instead of Vince. Even though I still had some of the first glass of wine to finish, I would take the orange soda. Orange would have been number six on the list of sodas I liked, but it was my only drink choice at Zia's other than wine or brandy Manhattans mixed with too much sweet vermouth and without the best part, a cherry. So I drank the soda and soon had orange lips and a craving for a Coke.

When finally Jim Ruffoni and his family arrived, the festivities could begin. They brought gifts and new life, a younger perspective. I could talk to my cousins about movies, and whatever was happening in the world of teens.

And, now the serious eating and drinking could begin. The Meal
A ray of sunlight filtered through the lace curtains onto the shiny copper birdcage giving the little canary a glowing appearance. I used to think that the sun heated its vocal cords, because the warmer the sun, the louder he sang. It always amazed me how such a tiny bird could sing so loud. His beautiful voice always cheered up the room and boosted the spirits of everyone that heard this sweet feathered angel's songs.

The large dining table was covered with a very "seasoned" plastic tablecloth with a faded pattern of grapes and grapevines. There were two things on the table. One was a Mason jar containing about a dozen breadsticks, which were usually hard and stale. Those had been on the table for as long as I could remember. In fact, some of them might have been the very ones from when I was five-years-old.

The second thing on the table was an ashtray. It was a small metal sculpture of a snake twisting around a pole and atop that pole was the small plate that worked as the ashtray. One of the men who lived at the bunkhouse at Big Pink had made it and traded it for a week of room and board, a value then of about $7.50. My Nono had collected it and given it to Zio for a birthday gift ages earlier. Speaking of room and board, the reason they gave me for Nona not coming to these dinners was that she said she had an obligation to cook Christmas dinner for the eight boarders who were living in the bunkhouse. After all, they paid $30 a month for a bed and three hot meals a day. But, I knew, even as a kid, that she didn't want to be in the same room as her sister.

By mid-afternoon, most of us would be in a seated state, having had too many drinks. Nono and Zio would be talking in loud voices so they could be heard over us yelling, "Fifteen two, fifteen four," playing our cribbage game. My mom would usually stand in the doorway between the living-dining area and the kitchen so she could talk to everyone. After all, Zia spent almost all of Christmas day in the kitchen.

We knew the meal was ready when Zia brought out the clean little jelly jars that would be our wine glasses, with four in each hand. Next was the bottle of wine for our second traditional holiday toast. Zia usually gave it, and it was something like this: "God blessa all our families and those old relatives in Italy and Happy New Year to our young ones. Please let my cooking taste good to everyone that eats it. Also, Happy Birthday to you, Lord." Then, with tears brimming in both eyes, she would lift her glass above her head, bring it down, kiss the outside of the glass and then drink it down in one lo-o-ong sip.

Next, Zia brought out a big green glass plate with sections that contained peppers, black and green olives with their pits, marinated mushrooms and artichoke hearts, caper berries, slices of raw zucchini, celery, carrots, figs, pear and apple slices, orange and tangerine wedges and more. Then, came a huge pink oval-shaped dish brimming with sliced meats, salami, mortadella, pancetta, ham and every cold cut you had ever seen and some I never saw except there at Zia's on Christmas Day.

Every year my mom and her cousin would tell my Zia, "This prosciutto (or whatever) is too expensive. You don't need to buy that for us. You can't afford it." I always thought that was an insulting and rude thing to say, like "Hey, you're poor. You can't afford the good stuff." But after these same comments every year, Zia would respond, "All year I look forward to giving this feast to my family, my loved ones. You just nevera no minda bout my money." Then she would put one hand on my mom's shoulder and one on Jim's shoulder and yell out, "Now, mangia!"

Then, out would come the strange square blue glass plate, and it would have thin slices of about six different cheeses. With it, came a basket of different breads and rolls. Another bottle of wine followed with Zia tapping the neck of the bottle on the lip of every glass and refilling each one.
After about thirty minutes of appetizer munching, Zia and my mom would grab everything that was left on the table and take it into the kitchen to be put away after dinner. Then came dinner.

Dinner was usually turkey, stuffing, green salad with oil and vinegar dressing (our only choice), Swiss chard, gnocchi with pesto sauce, and homemade cranberry sauce, extra-lumpy style. Oh, and my very favorite yellow (saffron) rice. I loved it and could eat it every day of the year. Usually, I got it once during the year from my Zia and twice a year from my mom. While she was still alive, my Nona spoiled me and cooked yellow rice for me often. There would be ravioli with tomato sauce, too.

The bread basket and antipasto trays were still left on the table, so we really had an overabundance of food. Dinner usually ran about an hour with lots of conversations going on at once. I chattered with my cousins about "Texas Chainsaw Massacre" or the latest movie we liked, or we discussed the top 40 songs that we liked to dance to. We discussed the latest dance sweeping the nation like the Twist, Mashed Potatoes, the Monkey or others.

My mom chatted with Jim Sr. about some of the old Italian friends they grew up with. Jim saw many of them often because he bought his foods and wines at the same places they shopped. Others he saw when he stopped in at Pumantelli's to get his early morning coffee.

My dad and Mickey, Mrs. R, liked to discuss current events like what was up with the mayor of S.F., the Governor, the President, etc. No matter what my dad really believed, he would always take the opposite stance of Mickey because it was his way. He loved stirring it up with people. He always got a kick out of getting people fired up and then when they started yelling in anger, he would start laughing. Through it all, if anyone wanted something passed to them, they would have to shout it out. We kids often had to stand and shout to be heard.

After the meal was finished, the ladies would go to the kitchen and start the coffee. They put away all the food and did the kitchen clean up in record time. Of course, there was no dishwasher, only human hands.

Now, the coffee pot was put in the center of the table on a trivet that was shaped like a donkey. I guess that was maybe because if you bought a pound of ham, they gave you a free Jackass. Jim Jr. brought out clean glasses and a one-quart glass bottle of fresh milk that was delivered to Zia's front porch hours earlier, and it was time for dessert.

There were several musts for Italian Christmas dessert, at least with the Curtoni and Ruffoni families. One was Panettoni, a sweet bread-cake with raisins and candied fruit. There would also be some very hard wine cookies or biscotti. Another very special treat I've not had in over a decade was Torrone, a nougat candy with almond slices in it. It came in beautiful little gold- trimmed boxes that looked like scenes from the art in a chapel. When you removed it from the box, the candy had a tissue-thin piece of rice paper on the top and bottom of it. I would remove the rice paper and place it on my tongue where it would dissolve, a bit like a communion wafer was supposed to dissolve. But, per the nun's instructions, "When the wafer is placed on your tongue, do not chew it; let it dissolve; do not chew it. It may get stuck to the roof of your mouth, but don't stick your finger in your mouth and try to flick it out. Just leave it." So this sweet candy brought the additional pleasure of flicking it out of my mouth if I wanted to.

By this time in the day, the sun had set and fog had surrounded the neighborhood. All the porch lights were on, giving off a yellow glow that mixed well with the few red and green lights people had on their houses or in their windows. Each year as we left, I would take a look around to enjoy the Christmas beauty of the lights and fog that I knew I would not see for another year. I remember one year seeing those pretty lights peeking out through the fog and having a moment of déjà vu…. have I seen this same scene elsewhere?

So, with goodbye kisses for Zia and Zio and many thanks for the fantastic meal, we would pile into our car, and my Nono would leave with us. Every Christmas he came to our house to visit and I would have a roommate for a week. But as full and fun as the day had been, the best part of my day was still coming. As we walked to our car, Jim would say, "You guys come by our place for a drink, okay."

Jim and his family lived in a "modern apartment," really a house with cool furniture, a hi-fi that played the current hits and Coke to drink. For me, this was a high point of Christmas Day every year. Their place just always looked so great. As we were sitting in their front room visiting, I sipped Coke while looking at their pretty Christmas tree, there was my déjà vu. They had cotton under their Christmas tree and underneath the cotton were different colored Christmas lights glowing through it, looking just like the lights glowing through the fog by my Zia's place on Twin Peaks.

It completed my Christmas.

Chapter 36
Memory

I am asked from time to time "How do you remember all these stories?"

John Irving wrote: "Memory is not static, like a photo or video. Instead, memories constantly change shape and rearrange themselves until the actual truth of what happened is indistinguishable." (The World According to Garp)

We could rephrase this: "All memories are lies."

My interpretation: "Memories are works of fiction we write in our mind, editing as time passes."
Both of these are overstatements, but both are true in some small degrees.

As I think back to the stories I have told, people who know me will say that I tend to retell, at least in part, some of these visits to my past. I think our memories are made up of what actually happened, mingled with how we wanted things to go, sometimes with things better than they were, or with us becoming the hero. If we are in a melancholy mood, there is a tendency to make the memory of events more negative than they really were.

To confuse matters even more, there are large gaps in our memories. Sometimes there can be a bit of confusion about whether the event we remember happened at seven-years-old, nine, ten or whenever. It is strange what a small percentage of events we remember. That's life. We don't have total recall or accurate recall, and in telling these tales, I call them as I think I saw them happen, as I remember them.

Some of my stories are memories of memories, things that happened, for example, at Christmas when I was young and at every Christmas as I remember it. I am not just recalling one or two Christmases, but back over forty years, as memory builds upon memory.

My stories begin when I was about 5-years-old, and are based on memories, emotions, and stories told to me in later years by family and old family friends. I have a huge box of old black and white photographs, and these photos tell many stories. The longer you gaze at them, the more you remember. In most instances, I can remember what was going on when the shutter clicked, and I saved that exact second. It often brings back memories of the events leading up to the photo and what followed.

I used to have my Nono tell me stories in the evenings about his old days, and after a healthy consumption of wine, he would become more animated. He would use different voices, and he had a thick Italian accent when he did speak English. Sometimes he used Italian words because he either didn't know the English words or thought these words were best expressed in Italian. This was about 10% of his vocabulary. He would laugh and laugh until all of us were laughing too, and his arms would be swinging, and his hand motions would triple what normal Italian or English words could express. He not only told those stories, but he also lived them again.

When my mom was still alive, I could occasionally get her to tell me stories of growing up at Big Pink. But, to get her to tell me these stories, I had to ease her into the memories of past events. If I asked her about something from her past, she would say the same thing I heard from her over and over. Every time I asked about Nono or Nona or about their past life experiences, my mom would say, "What! Are you writing a book? Leave them alone." If I answered, "Yes, I am." She would counter with, "Well, leave this damn chapter out, for God's sake!" I never could understand why it was 'for God's sake'. Why wouldn't God want me to tell these stories?

One thing that has been a big factor in my stories and brings back some of these memories is my senses. Sensory experiences are reccurring themes in my stories because the Napa Valley was and is a feast for the senses. I learned that at a young age, and I remember many events in terms of what my senses experienced.

As an example, grapes and grape juice take me back to a day when I was about ten years old. I am by my Nono's vegetable garden, where there is a trellis standing over the path between the vegetable garden and the slaughterhouse. I am under the trellis looking up at the almost ping- pong-ball-sized Muscat grapes. It's a hot day, but it is cooler under the shade of the pretty green and yellow grape leaves, and the ripe grapes glow golden from the sunlight beaming through them. The grape bunches hang down through the wire overhead. If I jump up, I can grab a few grapes at a time. Some squish and leave a sticky juice on my hands, and I can smell the sweet perfume of the juice. When I bite into the grapes, my mouth fills with the sweetest grape juice I ever tasted, right up until years later when I tasted Muscat wine. I feel the pulp on my tongue, separating it from the skin that felt rougher. My tongue works the skin to its tip and then, "Pittoie," I spit it out at a target I drew on the slaughterhouse wall.

Whenever and wherever I stop at a railroad crossing and hear the train rumbling in front of my car, I am taken back to the old loud train that came by Big Pink twice a day, spewing stinky smoke and noise. It was rusty and dirty and sounded like it had hundreds of clanking chains hanging from it; the noise seemed to come from tons of metal parts grinding together, screeching like a Banshee on a Highway to Hell. It was a freight train; it had only two people on it, both in the engine car. If I was at the end of our dirt driveway when it came by (easy to do since I could hear it five minutes before it got there), the two men who looked older than the train and just as rusty would wave to me through the always-open window of the engine car. Their faces looked grayish, like ashes. I imagined them opening the fire-pit door to add wood, and getting blasted in the face with smoke, heat, and ash, and baking their skin to the point that it looked like beef jerky. I remember putting coins on the tracks and, after the train passed over them, I would run out to find the flat pieces that no longer looked like pennies or nickels but now looked like copper or silver potato chips.

The railroad tracks also offered a challenge; I would try to make it all the way to the store walking just on the rail. I never made it. Whenever I brought a friend with me to Rutherford, we would have races on the rails. They often ended with my knee bashing down on the rail or ties. On hot days, there was a chemical smell of the tar-like substance on the wooden railroad ties. In addition, there was a scent of baking steel, shiny from the sun reflecting off the top of the silver-colored tracks, clean and slick from the train wheels buffing them up twice a day. The spikes and side of the tracks where the train wheels didn't touch were orange with rust. I would get a rusty stain and scent on my hands when I tried to pull out an old spike that was sticking up a bit. Thanks to my dad's help, after years of trying, we collected about six corroded spikes which I hid in my secret spots in holes of tree trunks. Those old olive trees are still there, and the railroad spikes are most likely still hidden deep in the large natural holes in both trees.

That freight train came long before the Wine Train that now carries many more than two people. If you are by the tracks when the Wine Train goes by, there will always be someone on the train who will wave at anyone standing by the tracks.

Thanks to Margo and David of Slaughterhouse Cellars, not only have I been able to see my grandparents' old place, but we have attended annual Bottling Parties that begin with Friday night dinner for a small group of their friends who have become our friends. This is followed by the Saturday Bloody Mary breakfast followed by the bottling of a barrel of Slaughterhouse Cab, but also another barrel that friends of theirs made. Lunch follows, then cocktails and a catered dinner. And then, there's Sunday breakfast. This event is a high point of every year.

When the grapes are ripe and ready to pick there is a Harvest Party. This is another 3-day event with the same game plan as the Bottling Party, only we pick grapes. A dozen or so rows of vines are set aside for friends and family to pick. The rest of the vineyard is professionally picked and then processed using a local winerys equipment.

The harvest is a fun and interesting process. Each 'picker' has a very sharp curved knife and a plastic bin. The grapes are cut loose and dropped into the bin. Once the bin is full, someone in an ATV picks it up and dumps it in a large bin approximately 4 feet by 4 feet. There is an empty duplicate bin with a large stainless steel V-shaped trough on top. A big snow shovel is used to transfer the grapes from the full bin into the trough. There is a big corkscrew blade mechanism in the trough. This removes the stems and seeds, dumps them out the side into a garbage can and drains the pulp and juice into the bin. Sometimes the grandchildren actually get in and stomp the grapes. There are still small pieces of stems that have to be removed. The pulp remains in the bin, covered with a tarp, for ten days and then goes into the crusher. Someone comes to the bin several times a day to 'punch down' and mix it up.

The new wine sits in a barrel for two years, after which it is bottled.

My memories are like that. As they have sat in my memory bank, they have aged like fine wine. One thing is clear. I had a great childhood. How special it was growing up in Napa Valley in those earlier days of the wine business! I had experiences that none of my friends had, except those friends I brought up to Big Pink with me on many weekends from the time I was seven-years-old until I was eighteen. After that, I brought my wife and young son Mike, and soon after, my daughter Dannielle. Oh, it made my Nono so happy to hold Mike or Dani on his lap and tell them stories. He loved to have them help dig in his garden or come from the garden with a hand holding a bunch of carrots or lettuce. Some of my favorite photos are of him holding their hands and taking them on a walking tour of his vineyard.

In one haunting memory, I drive up to Big Pink with a friend, something I often did after my divorce. I was single; my ex-wife had moved to Seattle with our two children, so on days off I had a lot of free time. My Nono would be such a comfort to me, along with the beauty and peace of the valley.

As I tell and retell these stories, I am filled with joy, like I am living it again. I was able to see and experience a Napa Valley that is gone and will never again be duplicated or encountered. It is much more than anyone has yet been able to capture in movies or books. But, I can try.

24000570R10197

Made in the USA
San Bernardino, CA
01 February 2019